T0265915

DEMON'S BLUFF

BY KIM HARRISON

BOOKS OF THE HOLLOWS

DEAD WITCH WALKING

THE GOOD, THE BAD, AND THE UNDEAD

EVERY WHICH WAY BUT DEAD

A FISTFUL OF CHARMS

FOR A FEW DEMONS MORE

THE OUTLAW DEMON WAILS

WHITE WITCH, BLACK CURSE

BLACK MAGIC SANCTION

PALE DEMON

A PERFECT BLOOD

EVER AFTER

THE UNDEAD POOL

THE WITCH WITH NO NAME

THE TURN

AMERICAN DEMON

MILLION DOLLAR DEMON

TROUBLE WITH THE CURSED

DEMONS OF GOOD AND EVIL

DEMON'S BLUFF

THE SHADOW AGE

THREE KINDS OF LUCKY

ECLIPSED EVOLUTION

FIRST CONTACT

TOTALITY

EMERGENCE

DEMON'S BLUFF

KIM HARRISON

ACE
NEW YORK

ACE
Published by Berkley
An imprint of Penguin Random House LLC
penguinrandomhouse.com

Copyright © 2024 by Kim Harrison
Penguin Random House values and supports copyright. Copyright fuels creativity, encourages
diverse voices, promotes free speech, and creates a vibrant culture. Thank you for buying
an authorized edition of this book and for complying with copyright laws by not reproducing,
scanning, or distributing any part of it in any form without permission. You are supporting
writers and allowing Penguin Random House to continue to publish books for every reader.
Please note that no part of this book may be used or reproduced in any manner for the purpose
of training artificial intelligence technologies or systems.

ACE is a registered trademark and the A colophon is a trademark of
Penguin Random House LLC.

Book design by Kristin del Rosario

Library of Congress Cataloging-in-Publication Data

Names: Harrison, Kim, 1966– author.
Title: Demon's bluff / Kim Harrison.
Description: New York: Ace, 2024. | Series: Hollows
Identifiers: LCCN 2024010897 (print) | LCCN 2024010898 (ebook) |
ISBN 9780593639986 (hardcover) | ISBN 9780593640005 (ebook)
Subjects: LCGFT: Fantasy fiction. | Novels.
Classification: LCC PS3608.A78355 D455 2024 (print) |
LCC PS3608.A78355 (ebook) | DDC 813/.6—dc23/eng/20240318
LC record available at https://lccn.loc.gov/2024010897
LC ebook record available at https://lccn.loc.gov/2024010898

Printed in the United States of America
1st Printing

For Tim

DEMON'S BLUFF

CHAPTER

1

"THE AUTHORITIES CLEARED ME OF INTENTIONAL DEATH," THE woman said, Brice's dramatic come-hither lilt and low-cut blouse making my eye twitch as she indolently lounged on the couch across the low coffee table from me. She'd arrived first and was being careful, moving with an exaggerated slowness to hide her vampire-quick reflexes and threatening fangs, but it was that very wariness that had me on edge.

"I assumed I was asked to come to extend my apology in person," she finished mockingly, and the mousy man at the head of the table bristled.

"You can take your apology and cram it up your filthy, decaying hole of a—"

"Whoa, whoa, whoa!" I interrupted, lifting a hand before it got out of control. *Again,* I thought, stretching my arm to rub out the dull throb gained while separating them the first time. "Victor, the I.S. doesn't have the last word. Sit. Everyone take a breath. Have a drink."

Lip rising to show a spit-shiny fang, the onetime professor at Cincy's university pushed back into his chair, a glass of orange juice in his tight, undead grip. As the city's subrosa, mediating the minor power struggles of Cincy's vamps was occasionally part of my job—especially between the dead ones. Pike had wanted to bring them together with the hope of finding restitution, and when two vampires disagreed, it was best to bring the biggest guns you had. That would be me.

I eased deeper into the indulgent leather chair, eyeing them both in a wary annoyance as my old vampire scar began to tingle, the virus-laced bite responding to the pheromones both undead vampires were kicking out. Victor and Brice went silent, the former in frustration, the latter in calculation. If I was feeling it, the living vampires downstairs were, too, and I glanced across the room at Pike. Nodding, the living vampire unfolded his length to go turn the air exchanger to high. Below us, the rhythmic thump of a too-enthusiastic live band drifted up the wide, open stairway along with the intoxicating scent of pizza and too many vampires.

Piscary's on a Friday night, I thought as I glanced over the large room. By rights, the band should be up here with the more exuberant crowd to leave the sedate members to enjoy the calm, sipping on wine and the subliminal boost from the party, but Pike had recently begun to use the second floor as a semi-public space to mediate arguments. Kisten had done the same thing with a pool table and dance floor instead of a wet bar and a ring of chairs and couches around a low table. That Kisten's pool table was now in my sanctuary serving as a secondary spelling space would probably please him—even if the felt was burned and the slate cracked.

"Sasha's death was not accidental," Victor muttered, his eyes a dark pupil black, and I checked my phone for the time. Ivy was bringing in Constance, and they were late. "Brice lured Sasha into a situation where she had no control, and then she killed her knowing full well I didn't have a second scion who possessed enough stamina to sustain my needs."

It was a problem, and whereas an accidental death was not a punishable offense in the unwritten law of the undead, an outright culling of another's support system was. "That is what we are here to determine," I said, sneaking a glance at my phone again.

"Let me call down for another round of drinks," Pike said, and I winced. *Yeah, let's add more alcohol to the mix,* I thought, even as I acknowledged the logic behind it. Alcohol wouldn't slow them down or mellow them out, but it would remind them of what it was like to be living, and *that* might shift them into a more amenable frame of mind.

He really does know what he's doing, I mused as the heavily scarred man in his early thirties moved gracefully to the stairway to beckon a bartender halfway up. His black hair was wavy and short about his ears, and his summer tan was already beginning to fade. No beard, but a midnight stubble gave him an attractive, bad-boy cast. He was officially Constance's scion now that the undead vampire was no longer a mouse. I knew the arrangement was tasteless to both of them, for though the undead could survive on any living blood, they craved that of their living kin, and if it was taken from someone who loved them, it was almost enough to fill the hole the lack of a soul left. Hence the tradition of cultivating living vampiric scions to support their undead brethren.

And whereas it was obvious that Pike didn't love Constance, he did enjoy the boost of power that sipping on undead vampire left in his veins. Though powerful in their own right, living vampires had only a portion of their undead kin's strength and pull. After almost a month of sharing blood with the undead, Pike had again regained the sexual lure and charisma he'd had when I'd first met him.

I stifled a shudder, enjoying watching Pike move about the room as Victor prattled on.

Living vampires were my Achilles' heel. All the benefits of the undead, and only half the risk. Pike was clearly off-limits, not because he was out of my league but because I knew better. And yet as my gaze drifted back to him, I smiled, pleased to be able to call him my friend.

His slacks were black, and his matching lightweight shirt was classy and sharp. Soft-soled shoes made his steps silent and his limp hardly noticeable. The scars about his neck and arms, though, were mottled and obvious. They weren't the bedroom-fun kind, rather the kill-you variety, and he took no pains to hide them. In short, Pike had had a very hard life evading his older brothers' lethal intentions. Which made the fact that one of them, the worst, was currently sitting in a beanbag chair in the corner all the more incredible, the older man focused on a handheld game with the intensity of a ten-year-old. But then again, Brad was down to about a ten-year-old's level of intellect, despite the man's temples beginning to gray and the first lines showing about his eyes.

My smile faltered at the flash of guilt. I needed an Atlantean mirror to break the curse I'd put on him. That I'd thought it was a white curse at the time was the only thing keeping me out of Alcatraz's high-security wing. Now even that excuse was running thin, and the coven of moral and ethical standards was on my case. Again.

"Orange juice and a Bloody Mary," Pike said as he set the two drinks down, a soft shudder making his hands shake when he breathed in their mix of anger and smug satisfaction.

"That bitch of a woman stalked and lured my scion away." The rim of brown around Victor's pupils narrowed further as his eyes went entirely black. "I demand restitution. As the city master, Constance has a responsibility to see that I get restitution."

Pike eased to halt behind my chair, not in protection but to watch the open stairway.

"You poor, deluded excuse of an undead," Brice mocked. "I didn't lure Sasha away from you. She came to me. You are a disgrace. No wonder you can't maintain a family."

"Don't you dare talk about my family!" Victor held his orange juice with a white-knuckled grip.

Brice shook her head, but it was exactly her seemingly reasonable attitude that rubbed me wrong. Still, I smiled at her, stifling my unease at her too-long canines and her unreal grace. She was faster than me, too. "Poor Sasha," the undead woman said. "Victor had been neglecting her. She wanted more aggressive bedroom play and he couldn't provide."

"That's not true!" Victor's face went bloodless, tension pulling him to a dangerous stiffness. "I loved Sasha. Her virus levels weren't sufficient for what she wanted to give me. We were slowly increasing them. She knew that. I didn't want to hurt her. I loved her." Eyes narrowed, he focused on Brice stretching languorously in the chair like a lioness. "And you killed her twice. Before her time."

"Easy," I said, glancing at my phone again. *Where the Turn are you, Ivy?* Victor had undoubtably loved his scion—before he had died. Now all he remembered was having loved her. The undead clung to that memory as if it was their last vestige of humanity—which it was. Victor was right

4

to be upset. It usually took half a lifetime to gain the skill to convince someone that they were loved, luring a new victim into risking death as their scion to keep an undead in their semi-alive state. With Sasha gone, Victor would likely perish before he figured it out. It was the undead's tricky forty-year ceiling come early. Most didn't survive it. Those who did were truly manipulative.

Like Brice, I thought when the woman set her Bloody Mary down and leaned forward to show her scar-decorated cleavage as Victor continued his derisive tirade. Brice had died in the sixties during the Turn, and now that Constance was again out in the open demonstrating her ineffectiveness, it seemed likely that Brice's slow plotting to make a bid for the city had shifted into overdrive.

Put simply, Constance wasn't a good city master vampire—even as a front. It was why the DC vamps had sent her here in the hope I'd off her in a fit of annoyance. It would have landed me in jail and out of their hair—and Constance in a permanent grave. I'd promised to protect the outclassed undead vampire from her kin if she'd be the front to my control of Cincinnati, but the diminutive Black vampire was erratic at the best of times.

Which was why Ivy and Pike were handling her enforcement duties. As much as Victor was in trouble, I was starting to suspect that *we* were the ones in danger. Brice obviously had her eye on taking over the city. Perhaps the DC vampires had put her up to it. They'd love to see me gone. I was doing a better job of overseeing their people than they could, probably because Ivy, Pike, and I didn't put the capricious demands on a vampire population that a master vampire did.

"Where is Constance?" Brice said, her curt voice cutting into Victor's latest accusation, and my attention snapped to her. "This needs to be settled."

"She's on her way." I forced my fist to ease even as I tensed. This entire fiasco was Brice's plan to get her and Constance in the same room. Maybe breaking the spell that had turned her into a mouse had been a mistake. The hidden threat was always more convincing than the visible one.

I gathered myself to rise and find a quiet corner to call Ivy . . . and then I blinked as Brice exhaled and every last thought I had seemed to melt.

Pike's knees buckled. He caught himself against my chair, his breath going shallow as he fought off the undead woman's sudden pull. All my exposed skin was tingling with a delicious sizzing sensation, and I froze as the memory of teeth sliding cleanly into me surfaced, a pang of desire going right to my groin. I forced my hand from my neck, embarrassed that I had put it there, one lone finger tracing a delicious path to my clavicle as if I was a vampire junky. Jenks would laugh his wings off if he were here.

"See?" Victor pointed at Brice as the undead woman stared, her gaze black in a hungry passion. "She's doing it again! What scion can resist that? I swear I'm going to pull your fangs out and give them to my niece for her sweet sixteen."

"I'm going downstairs," Brad said suddenly, his eyes pupil black as he tossed his handheld game aside and stood. The pheromones were hitting him hard. He was getting randy. The restaurant, too, was getting loud. Between Brice and Victor, there were too many vamp pheromones in here. The air system could not keep up.

My hands trembled, and I didn't dare take anything more than a shallow breath until I forced the memory of Ivy, and Kisten, and every undead vampire I'd ever run into from my thoughts. Pike, too, had gotten control of himself, and I felt a small flicker of victory even as Brad started for the stairs. Brice was good, but I'd fought better. She couldn't maintain her pheromone level, and the air was clearing already.

"You good here?" Pike said stiffly as he went after Brad. Having him up here hadn't been the best idea; leaving him downstairs was a worse one. The living vampire had no restraint, no memory—because of me.

I have to fix this, I thought, using my guilt to pull me out from the edge of Brice's ecstasy. "Nice try, Brice. Maybe in another fifty years," I said as I dropped my gaze to my phone, and the undead woman's expression became livid.

"Where are you?" I texted Ivy, one hand on my phone, the other touching the butt of my cherry-red splat gun. It fired spells, not bullets: a witch's ancient weapon made modern. Brice was clearly upset that she'd given me her best shot and that both Pike and I had brushed it away like the annoyance it was.

"She made me put on jewelry," came back immediately. "Be there soon."

Thank the Turn, I thought in relief as I set my phone on the table with a little click. Constance equated jewelry with being civilized. The vampire wore enough to bring down a camel. Quantity, not quality, was her motto.

But Pike had used Brad as an excuse to get behind Brice, and the woman's eyes narrowed as she drummed her fingers once in a tight, bloodred-nail staccato.

"Relax." I set my weapon beside my phone in an unspoken threat. "Both of you. I will not tolerate Constance walking in here with you at each other's throats." Because a blood exchange between two undead vampires would kill them both, as the two slightly different viruses that animated them battled with each other. It was how I had lost Kisten, and a flicker of heartache took me. *Damn you, Elyse, for dangling the spell before me to bring him back.* It was a lie. It had to be a coven trick. Even Al didn't know the magic to recover the undead, even as a ghost.

"Constance is a puppet." Brice's expression held a mocking sureness. "Any justice you get from her will be at a witch's grace, Victor. How sad. Going to a witch for justice?"

Behind her, Pike tried to coax Brad into sitting down again, but the older man was having none of it, wanting to fulfill the promise the undead pheromones had instilled in him.

"Constance will give me restitution," Victor said, his pupils shrinking as his fear took over. "And if she doesn't, you'll wake up with a stake in your heart."

Brice laughed, throwing her head back to show her long, scarred neck.

"Hey!" I shouted, and even Brad stopped arguing with Pike. "Bring it down a notch." I reached a thought out to the nearest ley line, laying a sliver of my awareness in the ancient energy source and making me part of its loop. Power flowed through me, waiting for direction. It lifted through my curly hair, snarling it even through the straightener charm.

Victor seemed to rally as Brice settled deeper into her chair, my show of power giving her pause. "I don't have anyone to take Sasha's place," the slim man protested. "That mid-century whore has sent me into a downward spiral I can't escape."

I sighed, knowing how that felt: frustrated, angry, out of control.

Brice mockingly sipped her drink. "If you can't survive, you don't deserve to."

Victor's eyes flashed to black.

"Pike!" I called as the mousy undead man lunged at Brice.

Brice had been expecting it, and she flung an arm out, beating Victor's reaching grasp away. The man ran right into her raised knee, and his breath—which he didn't really need—rushed from him in a whoosh.

I stood, splat gun pointed. I didn't shoot since Brad had launched himself at Victor, the memory-challenged vampire oblivious to the danger as he grabbed the undead vampire's arm and flung him away from Brice, the greater threat.

"You dare attack me!" Brice shrilled, rising to meet Victor if he should manage to get out from behind Brad and Pike—who had worked him into a corner. The music had gotten louder, thumps vibrating the floor as I stood before Brice, gun pointed and confidently shaking my head.

I knew she'd dodge the charm—she was an undead after all—but having the spell pistol in my hand gave me a feeling of strength. If she touched me, I would fry her with a jolt of ley line energy.

"Sit your ass down!" I demanded when Brice turned to the stairway, a flicker of fear marring her certainty. Constance was here. I could hear the calls downstairs welcoming her.

"I will not be governed by a witch." Brice's lip rose to show a glint of fang.

That was all the warning I got.

She lunged for me. I fired three shots off before she grabbed my wrist and squeezed.

Pain lanced through me. Images of Ivy flickered through my brain, and then I yanked on the ley line, funneling enough raw energy through Brice to fry an entire henhouse of chickens.

Brice shrieked and let go. A fisted hand swung, liquidly fast. I hardly saw it before it smashed into the side of my head and sent me reeling.

"Brad, help Rachel!" Pike shouted, and then Brice swore as Brad rammed into her, headfirst. The two of them hit the chair and flipped it over, arms and legs askew. I couldn't see straight yet, and I got to my feet.

"A witch can't rule a city!" Brice snarled, and with a quick lunge, she grabbed Brad and dragged him to her mouth.

"Pike!" I shouted as Brad went slack, utterly overwhelmed. The monster of a woman had him, mouth fixed to his neck as she dragged him to a corner.

Brice couldn't hold him and fend us off at the same time, and as Pike abandoned Victor to help his brother, I imagined a circle around the mousy undead vampire to pin him down. No one liked being downed by witch magic. Too bad.

Rhombus!" I shouted, more to tell Pike what I was doing than to trigger the spell. Energy flowed, and a smut-tinted, gold and red barrier of pure energy rose up, encircling Victor. The circle wasn't drawn, so it wasn't foolproof, but it would be enough.

Pike exhaled, a thankful slant to his brow as he ran for his older brother. I was right behind. A single bite from a master vampire had the potential to bind the victim, turn him or her into their shadow—a brainwashed-and-abused blood whore as opposed to a lovingly maintained scion. But I'd seen a flicker of fear in her. Brice didn't have the chops to be a master vampire. If we could get her off Brad in time, he'd be okay. That is, if she didn't just snap his neck.

Please let him be okay, I thought, remembering the ecstasy of a vampire bite, the pain, the need for it to continue. I had taken away Brad's ability to protect himself. If I couldn't keep him safe until I could return it, then I had failed. Twice.

Hunched and ugly, Brice took her bloody mouth from Brad. "Stay back," she practically hissed. "I will drain his last blood from him, and then I will take both of yours," she added, dragging the slack man in her grip to the stairs. "I will not be ruled over by a witch and an incompetent, chip-fanged half-bite who was sent to die at your hands. I will not!"

"Let Brad go," I said as Pike inched closer, eyes on his brother. I had the power to stop this, but he had the best chance of matching Brice's supernaturally fast reactions. I'd wanted to see how Constance was going to handle this. Too bad the erratic woman was late.

"Fine," I muttered.

Pike glanced at me at the single word. I might as well have said "go."

Silent, Pike lashed out a fist at the woman's head.

Brice predictably jerked away. I was already moving, going in low since I'd probably end up on the floor anyway. Dropping, I swung my foot to knock her feet right out from under her. Brice blocked Pike's first punch, but his follow-up hit the same instant as my leg swipe and together we knocked the woman down. She shrieked as she fell, arms swinging.

Pike was right there, pulling his brother from the undead vampire's grip. A smile found me when the woman landed hard. Her mouth was red from Brad's blood, and her eyes were black from anger and an old hate—hate that I was living and she was not.

"You will both die for that," she intoned.

My hip hurt where I had hit the old floorboards. We were both down, and I shook my head, uncowed. Oh, she was as scary as all shit and had the power to enforce her words. But I wasn't a witch. I was a witch-born demon. And I had had enough. "*Stabils*," I said as I drew a small wisp of energy from my chi and harnessed it with a curse.

Her pupils shrank in fear as I flicked the gold-and-red-hazed walnut-size curse at her.

It hit her square on the chest and she collapsed, unable to move but for her mouth and the smallest movements to keep herself alive. Or dead. Or undead. Whatever.

"You dare!" Brice shrieked as the spell soaked in and even her tremors stopped. "You dare use your magic on me?!"

I glanced at Pike gently tending his brother. "Yeah, I dare."

"I will kill you," she raved, and I got to my feet, slowly as everything began to hurt. *When did I hit my elbow?* I thought, flexing it. The *stabils* curse was not infallible, but there was no chance in two realities that Brice would figure it out. Until I broke it, she wouldn't be able to move apart from her mouth. I'd gotten the joke curse from Al, and the demon apparently liked to hear his victims beg for mercy. "You won't last the week!" she predicted.

"It's possible," I agreed, my gaze going to Ivy and Constance now making their dramatically slow saunter up the stairs. Ivy was svelte and competent in her working leathers, her long, enviably straight black hair pulled into a swaying ponytail. Her brow was furrowed in annoyance, and her very red lips pressed together. She moved like a dancer and looked like a model—and she was my friend. It wasn't an easy thing when she was a living vampire: most of the cravings, none of the drawbacks, all of the hang-ups.

Beside her, Constance's petite frame seemed almost childlike, her brown skin and chemically eased hair styled to the fashion of another century. A red scarf drew the eye to her neck, vampire-junky style, contrasting with her stark white business dress. She'd cut down on the jewelry, and only three strands of gold and one string of pearls draped around her neck, the latter a twin to the one that Ivy now sported. More gold hung from her ears like shimmering waterfalls, and every finger had at least one ring. Her grace was undeniable, her confidence beginning to appear real, not contrived and holding a hidden fear as when we had first met.

Constance was a long undead, and I still hadn't figured out how she had survived without the pretense of love most of them cultivated to convince people to sustain them. She loved no one, and no one alive loved her. That we had found a way to work together instead of killing each other had really put a crimp in the DC vamps' day.

My largest concern was that unlike Brice raving on the floor, Constance had more than enough ruthlessness to rule a city on her own, and the night she decided she didn't need me might be my last. Jenks maintained that she already had, but that she was lazy and liked me doing her dirty work.

And as I felt the coming bruise on my hip, I prayed he was right.

"You are a puppet!" Brice raved, her black eyes shifting until they found Constance's tiny white shoes. They had rhinestones on them, gauche and glittery. "You let a witch dictate what you can and can't have? You are a disgrace!"

"Mmmm." Constance used her toe to flip the woman over, frowning at the sheen of blood left behind on her small shoe.

Ivy edged close, her dark gaze placid. "You okay? I got here as fast as we could." Her lip twitched as Constance bent low to coo over Brice's earrings even as the downed vamp ranted.

"We managed." I stretched my arm to ease the pain in my elbow. "Pike, how much saliva did Brad take? He going to be all right?"

"Think so." Pike carefully probed his brother's torn skin, dabbing at it with a napkin. It was clotting already. "She doesn't look like a heavy hitter," he added when Brad shuddered, feeling it even out cold as he was. "Unfortunately he doesn't have the coping skills anymore. It's like seducing a twelve-year-old."

"I'm sorry," I said, and Pike's concern vanished.

"He knew what he was doing. It's not your fault."

But it was. I had to fix this. Trouble was, I wasn't sure how anymore.

"Brad." Pike gave his unresponsive brother a shake. "Brad? Snap out of it, man. How hard did she sting you?"

The man's eyes opened, and he blinked, surprised when his reaching hand found the napkin at his neck. "What happened?" His gaze went to Brice, her teeth stained red as she snarled at Constance. "Did I have fun?"

Pike grinned as he hauled his older brother up. "Yeah. You had fun. You need a shower, old man," he said, and Brad smiled, his worry that he had done something wrong vanishing.

"You finish here. I've got him," Ivy said, her annoyance at Constance shifting to one of fond, benevolent concern as she cuddled Brad close and took him to sit in one of the chairs.

"You good?" I asked Pike, and he touched his nose, twisted and lumpy from having been broken one too many times. He was fine, and together we turned to Constance and Brice. Victor was sullen and angry behind my circle, forgotten. It was probably the story of his life—which was why Brice had targeted him. I broke the spell with a small twist of thought, and the protection circle dropped.

Constance glanced at Victor in dismissal. "You were supposed to wait for me," she said to me, her high voice petulant.

"I didn't do anything permanent," I said. "You want me to let her go, too?"

Constance shrugged, then slammed her foot into Brice's gut. "Shut up!" she shouted as the woman grunted, meeting Brice's black stare with her own. "I see what you are doing," Constance added, her tone shifting to a hard knowing. "This isn't about you killing Victor's scion. This is about you. And me. And my city."

My eyebrows rose, impressed with Constance's assessment.

"Morgan was right to turn you into a mouse," Brice rasped from the floor. "You are weak and ineffectual. A witch? You let a witch do your killing?"

Constance's lips pulled from her teeth in an ugly smile. "Truly?" she said, and a chill dropped through me as the small, undead woman bent low, a tiny hand gathering Brice's blouse and lifting the woman up. Constance was so short that Brice hung with her knees touching the floor. But she didn't stay there long, and I gasped, shocked when the short vampire tossed Brice into the air with one hand . . . and cut her throat with a concealed knife on the way down.

"Constance . . ." I complained as Brice hit the floor, her life's blood pouring from her in a short gush. Shock registered in the vampire's black eyes, and then they silvered. She was dead, fully dead. "Damn it back to the Turn. I didn't ask you here to kill her."

Victor had gone still, properly cowed as he retreated to a corner, and I moved to stand between him and Constance.

"No?" The small woman took the napkin that Pike silently handed her and wiped Brice's blood from her skin, frowning when she realized her suit was spotted as well. "Why did you call me, then?"

Brice's muscle tone was going slack fast. She'd been dead for a long time, and she'd begin to decompose soon. Ten minutes, tops. The older they were, the faster it happened. "Seriously?" I said as I wondered if Ivy still kept the body bags tucked behind the big pasta pot downstairs. "I'm not taking the rap for this."

Constance tossed the bloody napkin onto the dead woman. "You must kill to control," she said, telling me exactly how she had survived this long with no one to love her. "The sooner you learn that, the sooner you won't have to do it anymore."

Have I underestimated her? I thought in worry as Constance's gaze rose to take in the rest of the room. Victor bowed his head, and Pike had moved to stand beside Ivy and Brad, wary and tense, that fallen chair between her and them.

"Is Brad injured?" Constance cooed suddenly. "Pike, I don't like the disregard you have for your brother's safety. He shouldn't have been here."

I inched closer to Ivy. "There are other ways of dealing with problems besides killing one of the feuding parties. You just orphaned an entire family and Victor is no better off."

"I'm fine," the frightened undead whispered, but it only made me angrier.

"You see so little, Rachel," Constance said, sounding like a poor version of my demon teacher, Al. "It's not your fault. You've lived only a fraction of years and all of them alive." Motions holding a sultry satisfaction, she went to sit in the largest chair, making it into a throne. Immediately Ivy stood. Brad alone remained seated before her, the childlike vampire getting away with it as he scratched his neck to stimulate his bite.

"Relax, Victor. You will not be killed by me," Constance said, and the undead vampire exhaled in relief. "Though Brice was right. If you can't handle a little competition, you won't survive."

"A little competition?" Victor barked, then bowed his head. "I was not in competition with Brice," he muttered. "She used me to get to you. But the result is the same. I have nothing."

There was a new, petulant lilt to Victor's voice. It was manipulative, and it worked.

"See, Rachel?" Constance played with her strand of pearls as Pike stood the fallen chair upright. "The ability to see into the future can be obtained even though one is young." She beamed a close-lipped smile. "Victor, because of your vision, I gift you with Brice's scion to take as your own. The blood will be tasteless, but it will sustain you. Treat him well, and perhaps you will learn how to convince another you love them and, in turn, prosper."

"Thank you, Constance," he said, clearly annoyed. "I would like the rest of her—"

"The rest of her children, I will take for myself because you didn't bring Brice's true intentions to my awareness," Constance said, her eyebrows high in a questioning threat. "Everyone is happy," she added, making it a demand, not an observation.

Or dead, I thought, trying not to breathe. Brice was beginning to smell like a dead chipmunk. I had to get her corpse out of here before she reached the dead-cat stage.

"It's a win-win!" the vampire said, relishing the chance to use the new-to-her phrase. "Victor won't starve. I get an influx of much-needed children." Constance stood and went to Brice. "And *this* won't become strong enough to irritate me," she added as she lifted Brice up by her neck. "You should have seen this and taken care of it yourself, Rachel. Learn to kill your own snakes. I'm not your mother."

I began to protest, words failing me when Constance threw Brice's body down the stairs. The sudden, horrified silence followed by the expected uproar made Pike wince, and he pinched the bridge of his nose at the obvious rush to the door. One of the serving staff looked up the stairs, then vanished to hopefully find a body bag. If not for her clothes, Brice would have left bits of herself behind on each step. She was decaying fast.

"Yeah, well, easy always seems to turn and bite me on my ass," I said.

Pike's gaze flicked from Brad to me. "I should probably take care of that," he said, drawing Brad to his feet.

This was not how I had expected my night to go. The issue was settled, though. Victor wouldn't starve and the word would go out that Constance was doing her job. Such as she saw it.

"Go, all of you," Constance said even as she smiled at Victor and patted the chair beside her. "Victor and I need to chat."

"Ah," I said as Victor's eyes went a frightened pupil black.

Pike skidded to a halt, Brad's elbow in his grip. "I'll stay," he offered, reminding me of Kisten—always trying to protect me from his more savage kin. "The morgue staff will need to be sweet-talked, and you're better at that than me."

"It's going to take two," Ivy said, her smile forced. "And a pizza would help. Hey, Brad? Let's get you downstairs. You want a pizza?"

"No," the petulant vampire said, but Ivy cooed and coddled him, drawing the resisting man downstairs with the promise of a drink. The body at the foot of the stairs shocked him—he had forgotten it already—and Ivy made light of it, asking him if he wanted to help wrap Brice up in a piece of plastic.

"You sure?" I asked Pike.

Pike nodded. "I'll tend to Brad with Irene. She's good with him." His brow furrowed with guilt. "I shouldn't have brought him tonight. He's getting worse."

I winced, head down. "I'm working on it."

"I know."

Constance pointedly cleared her throat, earning a dark look from me before I slid my phone off the table and headed downstairs, being careful where I stepped to avoid the ugly smears. Someone had already wrapped Brice, and the scent of decay was quickly being overpowered by the smell of pizza. Most everyone had fled the restaurant, leaving only a few knots of customers gathered around the now-silent band to gossip. Brad was already at a table with a small pizza someone had abandoned, holding a handheld game that he had played a hundred times but was still brand-new to him.

Pike was right. Last week, Brad would have been able to hold his own, react fast enough to keep Brice's teeth off him. He was declining, and I'd had no luck finding an Atlantean mirror. It was the only way to break the curse—the one that the coven was harassing me about.

"You brought your car, right?" Ivy asked as she easily hoisted the plastic-and-duct-tape-wrapped body over her shoulder.

"That is not going in my car," I protested, but her superhuman strength aside, three were not going to fit on her motorcycle.

Ivy grinned. "Why not? You've got a two-body trunk, easy. Besides, I can't manage a pizza, a body, and you on my bike."

Sighing, I filed in behind her as I took the extra-large with everything in hand and dug my keys out of my pocket. Perhaps me trying to do the job of a master vampire was not a good idea. It was still better than letting Constance have free rein. It had only been a few weeks since I had turned Constance back from a mouse, and the woman was already settling in, not into old patterns but entirely new ones that were likely going to keep me dragging her collateral damage to the morgue.

Kisten, I thought as I followed Ivy out the rear door, pausing to take a deep breath of air smelling of gas and oil as I looked across the river to Cincinnati glinting in the dark. Even Kisten would have made a better undead than her, and he was only a few years older than me when he had died twice. Using Piscary's as a place to mediate and air issues before they became problems had been his idea. Too bad Kisten was nothing more than ashes in Ivy's closet now.

And still the coven's offer to give me a way to bring him back burned. Even if he would only be a ghost, they would ask for too much in return. Like a demon.

CHAPTER

2

IT BEING AFTER MIDNIGHT DIDN'T MEAN THAT THE CITY'S SERVICES weren't busy. Even so, Ivy and I got only a few cursory looks as we walked through one of the rear entrances at the building that housed the city morgue, a six-pack of Topo Chicos and a pizza in my grip and a black-plastic-wrapped body over Ivy's shoulder.

Her smooth pace screamed confidence as Ivy strode past the lobby desk, giving the man there a curious gesture: a two-fingered peace sign that turned into a single upraised index finger with a twist of her wrist, sort of a two-into-one sign. The man started, then reached for the phone.

"We, ah, don't need to check in?" I asked, my hip complaining as I hustled to keep up.

"I just did." Ivy's scuffed black boots thumped a steady cadence on the tile floor. "We are on city business," she said, a soft smirk brightening her usual stoic expression. "They don't want a paper record of us being here."

The guy had called someone, though, and a flicker of worry lit through me despite her cool certainty. "City business," she had said. As in Constance's business. The woman wasn't entirely above the law, but her actions and words would rarely be questioned. Piscary had been like that, and an ugly feeling trickled through me. I was taking care of Constance's bodies. This was not what I had signed up for, and that a pizza and a couple of Topo Chicos would buy Brice a no-questions-asked drawer in the morgue didn't sit well.

Ivy's lips pressed and her pupils widened as she sensed my unease. That gesture at the back lobby desk said she'd clearly done this before. I hadn't, and I didn't like where this might be heading. I was supposed to be holding Constance's reins, not the other way around.

"Hey, I like the necklace," I said to distract her, and Ivy reached to touch it.

"Thank you," she said, seeming to be embarrassed as she fingered it. "Constance wouldn't leave until I put something on. Said I would be civilized if I was to represent her."

Represent her. There it was again.

"It was this or an antique hair pin," Ivy added, oblivious to my thoughts. "I haven't worn a hair pin since I was twelve." Her pace slowed, focus distant. "Piscary gave it to me."

I grimaced, wondering if I could smell decay through the plastic— even over the scent of the extra-large with everything. I took a breath to ask her how Constance's city management classes were going, my words unsaid as my phone hummed from a back pocket.

Shoulders rising, I awkwardly wrangled my phone out. "It's Trent," I said in surprise. He was supposed to be hiding in the ever-after from the FIB, and that he was calling meant he had risked coming to reality. Not a big thing when a ley line runs through your estate, but if the Federal Inderland Bureau caught him, he'd be dealing with more than charges of creating illegal genetic medicines—he'd be in prison for it. "Hey, hi," I said when I answered, and Ivy *almost* stifled a grimace. "What are you doing this side of the ley lines?"

"I'm not." Trent's smooth, melodious voice hit me as if I'd been sipping tequila all afternoon, and I found I could smile. The sound of crickets was soft behind him, and I figured he was probably in his manicured garden, standing in the ley line, not really here, or there, but enough of both that he could reach a cell tower. "Everything okay?"

I glanced at Ivy. "We made the news?" I asked, and he chuckled.

"Piscary's did," he said. "I knew you were there tonight." He hesitated. "Ah, everyone okay? Will you be needing bail?"

A trill of delight tripped down my spine. He was on the run himself, and he had asked if I needed bail—and I loved him for it. "Not yet," I said. "Maybe later. Constance is practicing tough love with Cincinnati and I'm cleaning up after her."

As soon as the words left my mouth, my expression froze. I was cleaning up after her. As if I was her lackey.

"Mmmm." Trent's soft utterance deepened my frown. "You up for a late dinner? I can get Al to watch the girls."

Al would love to watch his girls; the demon would drop everything at the chance. "Sounds good. You're at home, right? I'll bring it. What are you in the mood for?"

Ivy scuffed to a halt before the elevators. "You won't need bail," the living vampire said sourly, and I lifted my foot in a slow sidekick to hit the down button before she could reach for it.

"Something with vegetables," Trent said sourly. "All Quen cooks is potatoes and meat."

"Will do." My voice had gotten soft, but I couldn't help it. "Bye. Love you."

"Love you, too," he said. "Desperately."

My smile was soft as I disconnected and tucked the phone away. "Trent says hi," I said as I hit the down button again, this time with my knuckle.

Ivy stared at the silver doors as if they were magic mirrors. "He did not."

Her tone was a flat nothing, and I eyed her, trying to figure out which one of her hang-ups I'd just walked over. She had a lot, and most of them weren't her fault, which was why I forgave her for them. "You want to join us?" I asked as the doors opened.

She walked in, motions stiff. "No," she said shortly. Propping Brice up in a corner, she took her phone in hand and began surfing.

"You're welcome to." I set the drinks down and hit the button for the basement. "Trent won't mind." The elevator began to descend. The faint smell of decay was becoming obvious. Bringing bodies in through the back door wasn't SOP, and the air system couldn't handle it.

Ivy didn't look up from her phone as she absently yanked Brice up. "All the way out to his estate? No thanks. I've got plans."

"Okay." I lifted the pizza box higher and breathed at a seam.

"Okay," Ivy echoed, a familiar tightness to her voice. She was testy, probably because Constance hadn't cooperated and she'd gotten to the party late, putting me in a danger that existed only in her mind. I hadn't been in any danger.

"Ah, you do know I could have dropped her at any time," I said, trying to work this out. "I was only waiting to give Constance a chance to handle it."

"That's not it." She squinted over her phone at me. I made a questioning face, and her brow scrunched. "Trent is good for you. You know that, right?"

My lips parted in surprise. "Ah . . ."

Ivy yanked Brice's corpse up straight again. "What I mean is, you think before you act now, and you're not trusting to chance as much. Steady." She slumped where she stood. "Your life expectancy is longer with him than with me, and I hate it."

"Ivy," I whispered, and she shrugged as I touched her shoulder, my eyes glistening. She and I had a past, and I knew we had a future. It wasn't the one that Ivy had wanted. Planned on. Plotted for.

"I'm not complaining," she said as she ran the back of her hand under her nose. "Just pointing it out so you don't screw it up. I don't have to like it," she finished softly. "Vampires bring out the worst parts of you, and elves bring out the best."

"And demons?" I said as the doors opened and a cool chill eddied in around our ankles. I picked up the six-pack and followed her into the low-ceilinged, tile-floored hallway. "Because demons are so steady."

Ivy shot me an amused look over her shoulder. "Al would sooner set himself on fire than hurt you," she said as she walked, and a feeling of guilt flickered. "Don't mind me. I'm happy. Happy for you, happy for me."

I had to move fast to keep up with her, following the big blue arrows on the wall to one of Cincy's oldest morgues, buried at the base of a city building.

Unfortunately Al wasn't the only demon in existence, and my boots scuffed the dirty tile as I wondered if Ivy's mood might be stemming from the fact that the last time we'd been to the morgue together had been to identify Kisten. We had gotten here too late. Someone at the I.S. had pushed his cremation up by two days to eliminate any possible evidence of wrongdoing. It was very much like what we were doing here. The I.S. worked hard to keep the city's master vampire happy. That I was now doing the same bothered me.

"Gurney," I said when we turned a corner, and Ivy unceremoniously dropped the wrapped body onto it and pushed the wheel-rattling cart through the next set of double doors.

"Hey, Jack!" I heard her exclaim faintly as I lingered in the hall, eyebrows rising at the sign over the door. CINCINNATI MORGUE, AN EQUAL OPPORTUNITY SERVICE SINCE 1966.

Nineteen sixty-six. That was the year the Turn began, when all but the elves came out of the paranormal closet to save what was left of humanity and prevent society from complete collapse. Roughly forty years later, humanity was still a minority, tough justice seeing as the plague was probably their fault, as it had been traced to a bioweapon that had gotten loose and spontaneously fixed itself into the genome of a genetically modified tomato. The now-extinct, fuzzy black tomato that could handle drought and cold temps had been distributed across the globe. It was going to save the world. Instead, it destroyed it.

"Tamwood, no," a masculine voice said, and I pushed through the double doors. "Not tonight."

It wasn't Iceman behind the desk, but Jack, and I set the six-pack on an empty gurney just inside the door as Ivy wheeled Brice's corpse deeper into the large rectangular room. File cabinets lined one wall. An ancient, ugly desk that should have been thrown away in the seventies sat across from them. This was the admittance room. The morgue itself was beyond a second pair of swinging doors. There were no necropsies or autopsies performed here. It was strictly storage, either for one of Cincy's mortuaries or, in the case of living vamps crossing into their undead stage, for self-repair. Intervention was not allowed. If the vampire virus couldn't mend

22

their body in three days, they would starve and die their second death—from a lack not of blood but of aura.

It wasn't common knowledge outside of vampiric circles that it wasn't actually blood that the undead needed but the aura the blood carried. The soft energy given off by the soul bathed the body, convincing the mind that a soul was present and that they were alive. Lose that, and the mind shuts down to bring the mind, body, and soul back in line. It was the vampire virus that tricked the mind into believing that borrowed auras were from its own soul, and if an undead wasn't able to take in blood for any reason, as soon as the residual aura was gone, the mind realized the body was dead, and it followed suit.

"Where's Iceman?" I asked, and Jack's gaze shot to me.

"Night off." Clearly nervous, Jack stood up from his thick textbooks and tugged his scrubs straight. "Ivy, I can't."

Ivy locked the gurney's wheels. "Come on, Jack," she wheedled. "I brought you dinner. It's you or the river. I'm only thinking of the river otters. You like river otters, right?"

The young man's gaze lingered on my developing bruises and the obvious floor burn. "I saw the news. That's Brice Witherspoon. She's got to be at least forty years dead. There will be questions. You can't tell me no one saw you bring her down here."

I set the pizza beside the Topo Chicos on the empty gurney and lifted the lid. Ivy had her foot on the desk, pretending to tie her boot to show off her physique. The guy was a student, though, and I knew where his true desire lay. Smirking, I took a sliver of pizza, eyes closing as I angled it into my mouth.

The "mmmm" that escaped me was one hundred percent real. Tart and tangy. Piscary might be twice dead, but his legacy lived on in his pizza, and I practically groaned as the cheese lifted and pulled. *Pizza has vegetables on it.*

I wasn't sure why Jack was being so reticent despite it being as irregular as all hell. The I.S., or Inderland Security, was who policed the paranormals. They didn't like *me*, but Constance technically owned *them*, which was why Ivy had brought Brice's body here instead of the no-questions-asked safe-haven box at Spring Grove Cemetery.

"Of course people saw me bring her down," Ivy said, a flicker of annoyance crossing her face when she realized he was watching me instead of her. Mood closed, she took her boot off the desk. "You don't think *I* did this, do you? It was Constance. Brice made a play. Lost. End of story."

Jack waved a hand at the hall, pointing. "Then take her to the I.S. morgue."

Ivy smiled to show her teeth. "This is faster," she said. "Well, if *you* don't want it . . ."

That was my cue, and I lifted the box with one hand and brought it to the desk, dropping it with a heavy thump, sending the aroma of cheese and tomato billowing into the air. "Mmmm," Ivy groaned as she angled a slice in, hunched and giggling when the cheese pulled and snapped.

I didn't like this blatantly manipulative side of Ivy. It was weird. *And working,* I decided as Jack gazed longingly at the pizza.

"Ah, I don't have any space left for self-repair," he said, and Ivy beamed, the joyful expression looking wrong on her.

"She isn't coming back," Ivy assured him as she chewed, her eyes wide and blinking. "Tell you what. You sit here and enjoy what's left of my dinner, and I will pop her in the furnace. All you have to do is sweep out the bin and put her in a box for her next of kin."

I fought to keep my expression neutral. Ivy knew how to work the furnace? There were some things I didn't want to know, and that was one of them.

Jack glanced at the pizza again. "Constance did this?"

Ivy nodded as she pulled a square of paper towel from the nearby roll.

"And I'm not going to see any paperwork, right?" he asked, and I shook my head. I.S. sanctioned or not, it was still illegal. And easy. I didn't like easy.

Motions holding a heavy reluctance, Jack yanked open the top drawer of the metal desk, shuffling about until he found an old, overly thick key.

"You know the code to open the door?" he said as he extended it, and Ivy dropped what was left of her slice into the box to take it.

"Jack, you are a gem!" she exclaimed, pulling him across the desk to give him a quick buss on his cheek. Key in hand, she flounced to the gurney. "Rachel, I could use a hand."

"Sure." I jammed the crust into my mouth and pulled a paper towel from the holder, quickly wiping my fingers clean before dropping it in the trash. Jack had gone several shades to red, which made me wonder if Jack had done it for the kiss, not the pizza—even if he was now focused on it like a terrier on a bone.

Arms swinging, I followed Ivy through the second set of doors. There were four rows of drawers on either side, humans on one, vamps on the other, and everyone else where they could find space. As Jack had said, every drawer seemed to have a name tag, but Ivy was headed for the wide metal door set past the small waiting area.

"Hey, um, Ivy? How many times have you done this?" I said as she rolled Brice's body past the comfortable chairs arranged around the low table.

"Don't worry. The kiln is easy to operate." Ivy eased the gurney to a halt before what looked like a fire door, then tapped a door panel awake with one manicured finger. Without hesitation, Ivy typed a five-digit code into the keypad . . . and the lock disengaged with a metallic thump.

45202. My eyebrows rose. The building's zip code? Not much of a password.

I waited as she pushed the door open, flicked on the lights, and wheeled Brice into another low-ceilinged room. "That's not what I asked," I said as I followed her, taking a moment to make sure the unusually thick door wasn't going to shut on its own. The walls and floor seemed new, but the kiln itself was old, its corners softened under decades of black paint.

Ivy used the old, oversize key Jack had given her to open the waist-high, oven-like door to show a surprisingly modern-looking interior with smooth, tarnished walls and gleaming burners. A digital panel beside the door suggested it had been retrofitted sometime in the nineties. Below the large door was a smaller one to retrieve the ashes. Somewhere in between was probably a cremulator. It was hard to turn a body to ash unless the heat was hellacious, and this unit looked too old. Truth be told, the city morgue's kiln wasn't used that often, as there were far nicer crematoriums within the city limits. It was the city master's furnace. *And I am using it . . .*

She still hadn't answered me, and I took a quick breath at the thump of igniting gas and the whine of a fan. It was a stark reminder that she had once been Piscary's scion—until she had started saying no and Kisten had stepped in. And then Kisten had said no and had been punished.

I wasn't sure why I was even here as Ivy used the mitts hanging beside the door to pull out the tarnished rack as if preparing to bake some bread—and then angled the plastic-wrapped body onto it. Motions smooth, she pushed Brice in and locked the door using that oversize key. With a methodical quickness, she dropped to the second, smaller door, doing a quick check to make sure the ash from the last run was gone.

Finished, Ivy bowed her head. "You should have been smarter," she said softly, clearly speaking to Brice. "Your ignorance is your fault. I should have known you were ignorant and stopped you. That is my fault." Jaw tight, she hit the start button. Only then did the furnaces come on full with a muted lion's roar.

It wasn't a touching eulogy, but it was more than I would have expected.

Head down, Ivy pushed the empty gurney to the morgue. "Jack will make sure that her scion gets her ashes," she said. There was no victory in her voice, only a depressing knowledge that she was probably going to die on the same sword she wielded.

"Ivy, I'm sorry," I said as I walked beside her. This was why she had asked me to be here. To do this alone too often would break a person.

"For what?" Her voice was light, but I could hear the bound pain in it.

"That you have to do this to protect someone you don't even love."

"It protects you," she said as she pushed the set of double doors open.

A little huff of chagrin escaped me, and then I stopped stock-still, almost running into Ivy as she jerked to a halt. Jack was gone, and a young woman, almost a girl, really, sat in his stead, boot heels propped on the desk as if she owned it.

"Elyse Embers. This is a surprise," I said, and the tall, brown-skinned, straight-haired woman took a somehow . . . mocking bite of pizza. My guess put her heritage heavily slanted toward South America even though her accent was a hundred percent Midwest vanilla.

"Hey, hi." She dropped the slice back into the box. "An extra-large with everything," she said as she ripped a paper towel from the roll. "Is that the going price for cremation these days?"

"We brought a six-pack of Topo Chicos, too," I smart-mouthed. It might not have been the cleverest comeback, but I got bitchy when surprised.

"Where's Jack?" Ivy asked, the rim of brown around her pupils shrinking.

Elyse bobbed her head, acknowledging her. She would have looked like a collage freshman at a mixer if not for the money behind her light-weight black silk jacket, trendy jeans, and classy boots. The diamond pin in the shape of a Möbius strip on her lapel was her badge of office, and she wore it front and center as the coven of moral and ethical standards lead member. She was too young for the position. Again, not my fault. *It is not.*

"I sent him to find some real napkins," she said as she wiped her fingers clean. "He thinks I'm working with you," she added as she came out from behind the desk. "What a cutie."

I said nothing. We were too deep for me to reach a ley line, but Elyse probably could through her familiar. It made me vulnerable. Ivy, too, hadn't moved, and my neck was beginning to tingle from the pheromones she was kicking out. It had been Elyse who had tried to lure me into being a member of the coven of moral and ethical standards, promising me the spell to bring Kisten back as a ghost if I did. The deal sounded good on the surface, but they didn't want *me.* They wanted what I knew. I would be doing their bidding, when, where, and how they wanted—not be a real member with a voice.

It ticked me off that I was tempted, regardless.

"Looks like you took a beating." Elyse leaned back confidently against the desk. "No wonder you want to get rid of the evidence. I wouldn't want anyone to know how badly I fucked up a simple restitution chat, either."

Language, I mused, thinking the word made her sound less of a threat, not more. "What do you want? You gave me until June to uncurse Brad. I'm working on it."

Elyse sniffed in amusement. "Relax, I'm not going to bust your chops over a vampiric power struggle. You're simply hard to pin down and I figured you might be here." She tossed the mangled paper towel to the trash, missing. "You. Me. My office. Tomorrow," she said as she drew a business card from her jacket pocket and extended it. "Here's the address."

I let her hold it there for a good three heartbeats before I took it. Hard to pin down? She didn't want to come out to the church is all. I didn't blame her. My stronghold was formidable. "Carew Tower?" I said when I read it. "You're renting space from Trent?"

The tall, slim woman grinned. "Ironic, isn't it? But the location is central and it came with parking. Is three thirty okay? Yes? Good." She pushed from the desk, her nose wrinkled at the scent of the dead. "I'll see you there."

"Uh-huh," I managed, still trying to figure out how she knew to look for me here.

"Oh, and bring that book you used to curse Brad Welroe," she added, one hand on the door. "It will make the afternoon go smoother."

Ahhh, twist me to the Turn and back.

Ivy took a step forward and Elyse jerked, shoving herself backward through the double doors and into the hall. She was afraid—even down here where I couldn't reach a ley line and she could—but my God, she was good at hiding it.

"Oh, and if you go to the ever-after, we will assume you are fleeing justice," Elyse said from the safety of the hallway. "I will follow you there and drag you out, resident demons or not. Seems I'm the only witch on the planet who didn't get cursed. Thanks for that, by the way. See you tomorrow."

She let go of the door and it swung inward. Elyse was gone by the time it swung through again, the door closing in ever-shortening arcs as the sound of her steps faded.

"Is it a job offer or a ticket to Alcatraz?" Ivy asked.

"Does it matter?" I said, not sure which would be worse. Alcatraz I could escape. Probably. The coven? Not so much. I could show them the book and take the job to stay out of Alcatraz, but I'd have to abdicate my subrosa standing. "Constance isn't anywhere near ready. And even if she was, I don't trust her. Do you?"

Motions slow in thought, Ivy went behind the desk to replace the key. "No," she said softly, brow furrowed.

I stood with my arms wrapped around my middle, my entire night—my entire week, probably—ruined. There wasn't anyone I trusted to maintain the city except maybe Ivy.

And you had to be an undead or a demon to even be considered for the job.

CHAPTER

3

EYES CLOSED AND REINS HELD LOOSE, I ENJOYED THE SEDATE, SOFT thuds of Red's hooves beating the soft, grass-covered ground. The rocking motion was soothing and I was tired. Trying to mesh my natural body rhythm to Trent's crepuscular one made for early mornings. I'd been up since an ungodly eight thanks to Lucy and Ray, but it was hard to complain when morning meant real maple syrup, waffles toasted over a fire, and a ride through the ever-after to an unwatched ley line with two little girls. I had Ray before me, and the dark-haired, studious three-year-old was as comfortable on a horse as in her car seat.

The tall autumn grass of the ever-after tickled the horses' bellies, and the sun was shining. White-capped mountains rose to one side, a flat, tree-spotted plain ran on the other, and not a sign of civilization in between. Al was right. The ever-after needed a wild herd.

Tulpa's bluster behind me was a soft complaint, and I pulled the younger mare up, smiling as Trent and Lucy came even on the old gray. Trent looked fabulous on a horse at the worst of times. Today, though? His blond hair was almost white in the sun, his green eyes dark under the shade of his cap. He'd once had his ears docked—as all elves of his generation had—but a spell had returned them to their natural, pointy-arched elfness to match both Lucy's and Ray's. Slim and confident, he brought Tulpa even with us. Two trendy princess-and-rainbow-decorated backpacks sat behind him, holding what the girls would need for their weekend at El-lasbeth's.

Seeing him there, not just dealing with his life going off the rails, but thriving, my stomach gave a little hop. I loved him, and he loved me. Sometimes, it was that simple.

Trent guided Tulpa closer until our legs touched. "We should be seeing the ley line soon. Quen said it was clear of any FIB presence in reality." He frowned, squinting at the slight rise. "Eden Park would have been more convenient. This was a good twenty-minute ride."

"Perhaps, but you can't leave your car unattended there." I tightened my grip on Ray when the little girl pointed at the distant rise.

"See?" she said, her high voice clear, and I nodded, having brought up my own second sight. Not too far away, a ribbon of hazy red swayed and undulated at chest height. The ley line went deep into the ground as well as into the air, leaving only this narrow band that could be seen, shimmering like a heat mirage over the tall, unspoiled grass.

The sun seemed to dim as I used my second sight, and the hint of a cityscape wavered into existence within the tall grass; traffic and people moved silently amid the hard corners and dull colors. Grimacing, I dropped my second sight and reality vanished. Never in my wildest imagination would I have thought that the demon's ever-after would be an improvement from reality—but it was now.

"I need to walk." Trent gracefully slipped from his horse and helped Lucy to the ground. "Go pick some flowers for your mother," he said softly, and the little girl ran off, her straight blond hair streaming behind her. Still smiling, he reached for Ray, the quiet, dark-haired girl already leaning down to him. "You too," he added as he set her gently on the earth, and she beamed up at him before following her sister. The two girls shared not a drop of blood, but between Trent, Quen, and Ellasbeth, they were being raised as siblings, raised in love.

For a moment, I sat atop Red, feeling tall as I scanned the open grass-land. Despite the ever-after belonging to the demons, there was nothing here to harm them, and I swung my leg over to hit the ground hard. I hadn't been riding for a while, and I felt it. Trent's hand found mine, and horses in tow, we followed the girls as they raced from flower to flower.

Again, the beauty of the ever-after hit me, and I leaned into Trent until our shoulders bumped. It was probably the only place that the girls could run free like this, seeing as the ever-after was out of reach now unless you were an elf or a demon. And whereas the demons might enjoy making my life hell, they'd been giving me some slack lately. A thank-you, perhaps, or some respect after I had convinced them to bounce the witches' exile curse back onto its makers. It was the witches who had suffered, not the demons. All because, in their fear, the witches had broken the most important rule: first, do no harm.

"Rachel?" Trent lifted my hand and gave it a kiss. "I've said it before, but the ever-after . . . is amazing."

I swished my free hand among the grassy seed heads. My pearl pinky ring glinted, shining from its mate on Trent's hand being so close. "Thanks. I think most of it was from Bis. I never would have put in mountains like that."

An odd look of longing settled on Trent. "When Al has an afternoon, I'd like him to come to the stables. If he wants a semi-wild herd, he would probably appreciate choosing the lead stallion."

My smile was unstoppable. I hadn't known the demon's love of horses until recently. Perhaps it would bring the elves and the demons closer. God knew they needed something to fix the cracks as big as a canyon. "I think he'd like that," I said, my gaze rising to find the girls. Lucy was pulling a flower apart, singing at the top of her lungs, oblivious that she was re-creating a scene that had played out over the millennium, if not the exact words.

"Spelling on a Mon-day! Time is washed and hung. Little girls are running. All work done. Black pot in the sun. Sparkle magic lady. Run, run, run!"

"Little girls are coming," Ray corrected her, but Lucy had thrown away the denuded flower head and was chasing a dragonfly.

It was a little piece of heaven, and I sighed as my head flopped onto Trent's shoulder. I loved him, I loved my life—even if it was a little wonky at the moment.

And then my smile faltered as I remembered the corpse I had cremated to stall a murder investigation. Not to mention the illicit magic book Elyse wanted to see—the one that could land me in Alcatraz.

"Little girls are coming," Ray said, red-faced as she stood before her more vocal sister.

"Running," Lucy demanded.

"Coming!" Ray shouted.

"Running!"

I gasped, reaching out when Lucy shoved Ray down, the little girl landing with a thump on her butt amid the tall grass, her green eyes wrathful as they found her sister.

"Wait." Trent pulled me to a halt, focus intent. The girl had spells at her fingertips, thanks to Al. They were growing up elven, and the world would never be the same.

"Sparkle lady said *coming*!" Ray shrilled from the ground. "Say 'I'm sorry'!"

Lucy made a face, then relented. "I'm sorry," she said as she helped Ray up and gave her a hug that almost sent them down again. "Sparkle lady said running."

"Nu-uh." Ray gave Lucy a flower, then the two of them ran off together.

Grinning, I gave Trent a little punch on his arm. "I'm impressed. You let them handle it."

Trent exhaled, his gaze fixed on them as they ran to the ley line. "It's harder than it looks," he admitted.

"No, you're wearing how hard it is all over your face. Who is sparkle lady?"

"I have no idea." His shoulders lifted and fell. "The host of a kids' show? They've been singing it since coming back from Ellasbeth's last week."

"Mmmm." I relaxed against him, feeling good about myself and where

I was. The line was right there, but it was hard to leave. He had a long ride back with Tulpa and Red, and then he would be alone again. It was a blessing, I suppose, that he had an entire reality to escape to if he needed. "It's Saturday," I reminded him, and he turned to get the girls' bags. "Any plans?"

"I'm thinking . . . getting dressed up this evening, an overpriced dinner, mingling, then checking out the renovations at the new apartment." His shoulders slumped.

"Sure." I tugged him close in a sideways hug. "What will you really be doing?"

His gaze went to Lucy and Ray, both standing in the ley line and giggling as their hair rose in the magic's static. "Probably puttering about in my mom's old office behind the fireplace. I'm going through her books, winnowing out which ones need to go into the vault and which I can donate to the university."

"Sounds like fun."

"Sure, for the first fourteen hours," he grumped, then smiled when Lucy ran to us.

"Aunt Rachel? I picked you a flower," she said as she jammed the broken black-eyed Susan into my grip. Mystics from the line sparked between us, and I felt my own hair lift.

"Thank you!" I enthused, but she was already gone.

"You, ah, want to come over this weekend?" Trent asked hesitantly, his attention on my staticky hair. "I've enough in the fridge for two. Quen always stays with the girls when they're at Ellasbeth's. You and I will have the entire estate to ourselves now that the staff is gone. I could use some help with the books. You have a feel for them."

I twirled the broken flower, watching it flop from side to side as the mystics lost interest and returned to the line. They were the eyes and ears of the elven Goddess, and that they didn't recognize me anymore was a, ah, godsend. "Sure. If I'm not in Alcatraz."

Trent laughed—until he realized I was serious. "Because of Brice? I would have thought that Constance . . ."

"Yeah, no," I said, flower dangling. "Brice is fine. No one cares. Which is irritating all on its own. It's Elyse. I think she wants to show me that spell to bring back the undead." I hesitated. "Today, at three thirty."

"Mmmm." Trent's hand found mine again. "I thought only a coven member could see that particular spell."

"Which is why she wants me to bring the book with Brad's curse in it."

"Rachel," he started, and I cut him off.

"Relax, I'm not going to abdicate my subrosa position to become a co-ven member. I'd have no voice and end up doing their dirty work. But I *am* going to show her the curse I used on Brad. I owe it to Vivian." Vivian, who died because I wasn't honest with her, when a word from me might have given her the warning she needed. It was one of my largest regrets.

"Are you sure that's—" he started.

"If they try to put me in Alcatraz, I will take them apart." I leaned in and gave him a little peck on the cheek. Trent dropped his gaze, clearly not happy. "There's only four of them, and not one is older than me. Sorry in advance for any damage I do to the building. Did you know they are rent-ing space from you?"

He nodded. "Perhaps what they want isn't such a bad idea," he said, surprising me. "If you're coven, anything you do will be sanctioned. Past, future."

From the ley line, Ray sang, "All work done. Black pot in the sun."

"Sounds easy, doesn't it?" I said. "Maybe in a decade or two, but Con-stance isn't ready to run a city even with Ivy's and Pike's help. Besides, the coven doesn't want me. They want what I know." They wanted me to betray my demon kin.

Trent was silent. "I'm sorry about Brice."

I couldn't look at him. "The I.S. doesn't care, and the FIB doesn't have jurisdiction. It's done."

He took my hand to pull my attention up. "I wasn't sorry about the legal ramifications. I know you. Are you okay?"

My breath came in slow, and I nodded. "I am. Thank you." Taking

Brice to the morgue and cremating her without process was a warning to any other upstart vampires that challenging Constance would not be tolerated. It was effective even as it raised the question of how I was keeping the peace. Constance might be holding court, but I was the one in charge. Supposedly. That I had covered up Brice's death bothered me.

Or had I? There had been no attempt to hide what Constance had done. Ivy had taken Brice in the back door, sure, but she went through the entire building. Doing so had made Constance's actions public, in essence, divorcing Ivy from the actual killing. Ivy was saying, "I didn't kill her, but I will see that she is taken care of." And because I was with her, I was included in that.

My gut eased a little as I saw the sense behind Ivy's actions. "I'm okay," I said again, feeling Trent's warmth as he tugged me closer. Together we stared at the ley line, each of us reluctant to part. Like a tingling bolt of electricity hovering at chest height, the line would drop me and the girls downtown, right beside the parking lot where Quen had left Trent's SUV. I could almost hear the traffic.

"I used to stay at the estate for months without leaving it. Now I can hardly stand three days," Trent said.

"This, too, will pass," I encouraged him, and together we moved to the line.

"Quen is trying. We're hitting unusual roadblocks. I can't get my assets unfrozen, and what little I do have on hand is being treated like Monopoly money."

"Want me to make a doppelganger charm for you? We could go out to a movie."

"Yes," he said immediately, then, "No. But thank you. I can ask Quen to go with you to the coven if you like."

I could tell it bothered him that he couldn't come himself, and for a moment, I considered it. The dark elf had been Trent's security since before he was born, but Quen reacted too fast and too hard for my liking. "No. I'll be okay," I said, and I would be . . . until I wasn't.

"Let him know if you change your mind." We scuffed to a halt, the line so close I could hear it humming, feel it lifting my hair with the mystics who existed within it. The girls were impatient to cross, but Trent tugged me closer for a good-bye kiss. "Give me about an hour to ride back and get to my office so my phone will work. You'll call me, right? Before you talk to the coven?"

Still in his arms, I nodded. "Yep. And afterward, too, so you know how it went." Because if they put me in Alcatraz, he would help bust me out, warrant for trafficking in illegal genetic treatments or not. I reached for him and pulled him down to give him a lingering kiss. My breath quickened as a dart of sensation went right to my groin.

Shuddering with pent-up desire, I let him go. Trent was smiling. "You are amazing, you know that, right?" he said, and I flushed.

"Only on my good days. Ready, girls?"

Chattering, Lucy ran up to him, Ray quick to follow as they gave Trent little-girl kisses and promises to be good for their mother and not spell her cat into a frenzy.

"I appreciate you taking the girls to Ellasbeth," he said as he put their backpacks on them, and I smiled, trying to pretend it didn't bother me to walk away and leave him to make his solitary way back. "Quen will bring them home."

"My pleasure," I said. "Let's see. They have their things, I've got your keys, the girls. Car is there. Good to go." Unfortunately my reality was that after getting these two to their mother, I'd be doing a lot of soul-searching that would end up with me exactly where I was now: taking that book to the coven, showing it to them, then probably telling them to go Turn themselves in the nicest way possible. There might be a way to resurrect the undead, but Elyse was trying to bribe me into being their unpaid, underappreciated muscle. *Easy always bites me on the ass.*

"Okay, Ray, Lucy. Hands, please. Let's go!"

"Bye, Daddy!" they chimed out, and after bringing up my second sight to make sure we weren't going to appear in traffic, I took a step into the line, changing all of our auras to match the ley line. One more step and I released my hold on our auras, and the line spat us out, right into reality.

That fast, the whispering grass was gone, replaced by the familiar sounds of Cincinnati. One moment, we were there, and now we were here, walking briskly down the sidewalk to where Quen had left the car. It was cooler with the sun behind a thick cloud layer and the wind whipping up from the nearby river. November weather was fickle in Cincinnati, and I hustled, eager for Trent's heated seat and steering wheel.

"Spelling on a Mon-day!" Lucy chanted, jerking my arm as she skipped, one hand in mine, the other clenched around her wilting daisies.

"Time is washed and hung," I said, and she beamed up at me through her wildly whipping hair. My heart seemed to swell. I'd thought Trent might never trust me with the girls again, seeing as the first time he had, I'd been attacked by a Were intent on city domination.

"Nice transition, girls," I said, swinging their arms to get them to pay attention. "Let's get in the car. If we hurry, we have time to stop for a coffee at Junior's."

"Drive-through!" Lucy sang out.

"Hot chocolate?" Ray asked, and I nodded.

"Little girls are run-*ning*!" Lucy shouted, her hand slipping from mine as she jumped over the cracks in the sidewalk. The almost-three-year-old took after her mother but had the inborn magical ability of her dad. And maybe the cunning, seeing as she really wasn't the feckless, loud, energy-sucking kid that she pretended to be.

So when Lucy went utterly still and sent her gaze across the street, so did I.

All work done, I thought as I studied the man in jeans and a leather jacket watching us. Our eyes met, and he pushed off from his parked car. A flash of fear hit me when he looked both ways and crossed in the middle of the street.

"Damn it back to the Turn," I muttered, taking Lucy's hand again.

The whoop of a FIB siren echoed in the narrow street, and the man seemed to slump, hands going into his pockets as a Black man in a suit got out of the squad car and headed our way, pace fast.

I spun to the ley line, a quick check with my second sight telling me Trent was gone. It wasn't that far away. It might be better to simply jump back.

Until the FIB officer raised his hand in greeting and relief found me. It was Glenn.

"Aunt Rachel?" Ray asked, and I dropped down to put my face beside the girls'.

"It's okay," I said, my smile real. "It's Detective Glenn. He's from the FIB. He knows your daddies."

But even so, Lucy hid behind me when I stood, the little girl shy as the two men closed in on us.

"Stop right there," I said when the unknown man reached the curb, and he did, his youthful face holding a pleasant expression that I wasn't buying into. Annoyance was a quick flash over him when he glanced at Glenn, and that gave me strength.

"Hey, Rachel." Glenn scuffed to a halt beside us. His suit was cut for ease of movement, and his FIB detective badge was clipped to his pocket. He kept his hair cut close, and he had no beard. An earring gave him some bad-boy bling, but other than that, he could be the poster boy for the FIB force: collected, confident . . . and distressingly vulnerable when it came to dealing with Inderlanders. "I'm sorry about this. You go on about your day," he added as he turned to the man who had crossed the street. "This has nothing to do with you."

"I just need a moment," the guy said, his pale features and light brown hair making him utterly unremarkable. The worn amulets around his neck, not so much, and I didn't like that one of them was glowing. He had way too many rings, charms obviously. His pockets were weighted down, too. "Ms. Morgan, yes?" he added, voice pleasant.

Glenn pushed in front of me. "You don't have to answer that," he said tersely, adding, "Laker, I saw your warrant come through, and it has nothing to do with Kalamack's kids or his kids' driver."

Driver? I thought, then nodded. That was exactly what I was doing.

Laker stood with his hands in his pockets. He was human. He had to be. An Inderlander would know better than to accost me in the street when I had the girls. "I wanted to ask Ms. Morgan a few questions is all," he said, forced smile still in place.

Glenn grimaced, then eased his features when he realized the girls were staring at him.

"I won't take much of your time, Madam Subrosa," Laker added mockingly.

Damn wizards. There was nothing more dangerous than a magic-using human. They didn't know the meaning of the word *restraint*, always going too far and often miscalculating the effect of their magic. Eyeing him, I let go of the girls' hands.

"Whoa, whoa, whoa!" Glenn said, rightly reading my mood.

"It's just Rachel," I said, glad the girls had moved to stand behind Glenn of their own accord. Quen had taught them well. "Or Ms. Morgan. We keep the demon subrosa thing low-key when I'm escorting Mr. Kalamack's children to his, ah . . ." My words faltered. I wasn't sure what Ellasbeth was. She wasn't his ex, but she did have visiting rights with Lucy, and where one girl went, the other followed.

"How about you start by telling me what you want?" I said, my grip tightening on the ley line when Laker took his hands from his pocket.

"Just getting my documentation," Laker said when he saw my hair beginning to float. "What's with all the suspicion?"

"Kalamack's girls have been made into bargaining chips before," Glenn said, and I sighed when Laker handed me an official notice.

"I don't work like that," the nondescript man said, actually waving at them. "I don't need to. Rachel, would I be correct that Trenton Aloysius Kalamack is on the other side of the ley line in the ever-after?"

Glenn stiffened. "You don't have to answer that."

"He was," I admitted, fully aware that the girls were clustered behind me. "But he didn't stick around."

"Thank you." Laker seemed surprised I'd answered him. "How much to escort me over there?"

A laugh escaped me. "What, so you can bring him in?" I said as I gathered the girls' hands. "Not happening, Mr. Laker. If you will excuse me, I need to get the girls to their mom."

"One of them doesn't have a mom, if I understand it correctly." He simpered at me when I froze, aghast. "At least that's what my research says."

"Your research is wrong," I said, angry now as I walked away. Ray had a mother. Yes, Ceri was gone, but that didn't mean Ray didn't have a mother.

"Can I talk to you for a moment?" Glenn practically growled as he pushed Laker toward a light pole with his mere presence. "That woman does more in one week to keep Cincinnati's crime numbers down than the I.S. does in a month. You need to give her more respect or she is going to correct you."

"That sounds like a threat, Detective," Laker said, and I skidded to a halt, the girls' feet pattering as I spun. "Are you interfering with my attempts to bring Trent in on bail?"

Glenn's shoulders were hunched. "Not at all," he said, wincing when he realized I had stopped. "It's a public service announcement from me to you. You can sit at the curb. You can watch the church. But if you approach her door, or follow her, or show up at her favorite coffee spot, I'm going to drag you in for harassment, and your license to collect bail jumpers in Ohio and Kentucky goes away." He hesitated, lips pressed. "Say something so I know we have an understanding."

Laker frowned, peeved as he played with his amulets' lanyards. "Leave the witch alone."

The girls' hands felt small in mine, and I forced the energy from the line down before it could flow into them. "I'm a demon, Mr. Laker," I said. "Witches can't cross the ley lines anymore."

Laker shifted his weight to one foot, eyeing me in evaluation. "That's what I heard."

"And beyond what Glenn has said, if you touch either of these two girls, or talk to them, or try to ask them questions, I will give you exactly what you want."

"Yeah?" he said. "And what is it that I want?"

I felt tall with the girls beside me. "I will take you into the ever-after," I said. "And leave you there with the demons." I cocked my head while that soaked in. "Have yourself a great day, Mr. Laker," I added, then walked away, the girls' heels pattering along beside mine. He seemed a little cowed but not nearly enough.

"Sit tight," I heard Glenn say over the traffic. "I want to talk to you."

I sighed as Glenn's dress shoes quickly rasped behind me. "Rachel?"

Glenn came even with us, and I slowed. The girls were silent, and I smiled down at them as I gave their hands a little squeeze. Ray blinked up at me, clearly relieved.

"Rachel, I'm sorry about Laker," Glenn said. "I knew he was looking for Trent. How come he's not using the ley line at the church?"

I took a slow breath. Held it. Let it out. "Al is camped out in it, and Quen had their car seats here."

"I would have let you handle it, but you've got the girls . . ." he started in explanation.

We had reached the car, and I let go of Lucy to unlock the SUV with the fob. "No, your intervention is appreciated. Thanks." I glanced down the street to see that Laker was gone. "Is he going to be a problem?"

Glenn shrugged, embarrassed. "I don't know. He's new. From Chicago."

"Mmmm. They have a big wizard population there, don't they."

He nodded. Wizards were humans who used premade witch charms. The man who had raised me had been a wizard, using the spells my mom made to fool everyone into thinking he was a witch. Nick, one of my ex-boyfriends, had been a wizard, too, and it had ultimately killed him. Actually, pretending to be a witch had killed both of them.

Grimacing, I took Lucy's backpack off and lifted her into the back, where she scrambled into the second car seat. Ray was next, silent as I helped her in and buckled her up. Lucy, as she loudly informed me, could do it herself.

"Laker isn't FIB, but he does have jurisdiction to serve warrants and bring in bail jumpers," Glenn added, and I moved the girls' things into the car.

"Good to know." I didn't mean to be short with him, and I tried to soften my tone. That Trent was basically a prisoner in his own estate grated on me.

"Let me know if he harasses you," Glenn said as he waved to the girls. "Not to say you can't take care of it yourself," he added. "Good-bye, Ray and Lucy."

My lips parted when he lurched forward, leaning into the car to give them little sticker badges. "That makes you official FIB deputies," he said as the girls giggled and kicked their feet. Then to me, somewhat embarrassed, "It's a community outreach thing."

"Elves working for the FIB?" I questioned as I got into Trent's SUV and started it up. "I like it."

Glenn grinned, and I rolled the windows down so the girls could say good-bye again, but worry dogged me as I drove off. When I had seen Laker, I had assumed he was coming for me. That he was after Trent wasn't a surprise, really.

Sparkle magic lady. Run, run, run.

CHAPTER

4

"TINK'S TITTIES, IT'S COLDER THAN A TROLL'S TOE," JENKS SWORE AS I pushed through the narrow revolving door at the corner of Carew Tower.

"You could have made the trip in my bag," I said, and the pixy snorted, the noise loud, as he was sitting under my ear.

"I can't keep your ass above the grass from a purse," he muttered, but I thought it was more about the demon book that he'd be sharing space with than any worry he had over my safety. Once inside, I slowed, breathing in history. Carew Tower had been built during the thirties, when people lavished style and art onto their city structures. That Trent had bought it meant that the crumbling art deco building would be restored. *That is, if he ever gets access to his money again.*

Mood faltering, I worked my way through the general outflow of foot traffic to the elevators, stifling a shudder when Jenks plastered his wings against my neck to warm up. The pixy had insisted on coming despite the chance he might get stuck here. He couldn't fly when the temps got below forty-five degrees, and if the coven didn't let me walk out, he'd be living off French fries and pesticide-contaminated pollen from the flower shop until someone could come get him. November was too cold for pixies.

Chances were good that wouldn't happen. Not with my shoulder bag heavy with that demon book and my middle full from the Skyline chili I'd had for lunch. After dropping off the girls, I'd taken some time to prep. My boots were now scuff-free and my slacks roomy enough to kick ass in. My dark green jacket did double duty, both fashionable and spell-proof, as potions couldn't soak through the leather. I'd taken the time to wind my spell-straightened hair into a bun to hide a zip-strip clipper. As long as my hands weren't behind my back, I could get free.

"You good, Jenks?" I said, worried that he hadn't said much of anything. The sun was shining, but it was still cold.

"I need a minute," he answered, a thin dust of orange sparkles sifting down my front.

Angst flickered as I flashed Elyse's card at the security guy and was pointed to a smaller set of elevators. Thirty-third floor. Not so far up that reaching the ley lines would be hard, but not so low that you wouldn't have a view. Boots thumping, I jammed the card into a pocket and hoisted the book-heavy bag higher up my shoulder. Apart from the obvious, I had my splat gun, zip strips, and vials of salt water to break earth charms. My go-to, though, were the ley lines. That, and Jenks—soon as he warmed up.

I hit the button for the elevator, surprised when one was immediately available.

"Hold that, will you?" someone called, and I stuck my hand out and stopped the door from closing. Huffing, the woman hustled into the small, art deco–appointed lift. She had four cups of coffee in a tray, and I breathed in the scent of roasted beans as the doors closed and she hit the button for the sixteenth floor.

"Thanks so much," she said with a sigh, and I nodded and used my knuckle to light the button for the thirty-third. "Coffee run," she needlessly said, and then her nose wrinkled, and she sniffed.

I lifted my bag to explain where the faint scent of burnt amber was coming from. "Coven contraband," I said with a toothy smile.

"Oh." The woman's gaze flicked to the elevator panel, and she hit the button for the next floor. "Um, have a nice day."

The lift stopped, and she bolted when the doors opened, stumbling out to stand in the hall and stare at me until the doors closed and the lift continued on.

"Wow," I said sourly, and Jenks snickered.

"Relax, Rache." The pixy's dust was a bright silver as he took to the air, warm again. "You got this. It's a bunch of teenagers. How bad could it be?"

"Bad," I said. "My decision-making sucked until I hit twenty." I frowned, thinking. "Twenty-three. Maybe."

Jenks chuckled, wings sparkling with dust as he landed on the raised detail of the elevator's walls.

Fourteen, fifteen, sixteen . . . The lift eased to a halt, and the doors opened to a busy hallway. The woman at the distant reception desk didn't even notice us, and the silver doors closed and we continued up. "Do you think the coven really has a spell that can bring the undead back as a ghost?" I said, fidgeting. "A lot of everyday curses and spells are bastardized from heavy hitters, but she was *so smug.*"

"Elyse?" Jenks sat, feet dangling as he ate a wad of pollen he'd brought with him. "My guess is there's a reason she's trying to up your June deadline to uncurse Brad. They won't let you look at the spell unless you're coven, meaning you'd have to abdicate your subrosa position. Rachel, you don't need them. You don't need anyone. *They* need *you.* Remember that."

I nodded, wondering if he was saying I didn't need Kisten, either. No, I didn't *need* him, but I missed him. And if I could recover Kisten, even as a ghost, I wouldn't need to be the subrosa. Kisten had the clout and charisma to run the city. He had when Piscary had been in prison, and he'd been alive then.

Besides, it wasn't as if raising a ghost was unheard-of. I'd done it once myself when I'd been eighteen and tried to resurrect my dad for some desperately needed advice to my younger self. I'd gotten a witch named Pierce instead, and I'd stirred the spell so well that the ghost had been solid and substantial, alive, for all intents and purposes, until the sun came up. The coven's spell couldn't be that different, and if I could do it once, I could do it again. I would do it every night if needed. Kisten could serve as a figure-head better than Constance ever could. Because unlike Constance, Kisten had loved me, and he would never do anything to betray that.

"Rache, you got everything balanced," Jenks said as he came to sit on my shoulder, distracting me from my thoughts. "You have the DC vamps by the short hairs. Constance is behaving herself—within the framework of acceptable master vampire activity. Ivy and Pike are doing the real work. David's got the Weres. Zack and Trent have the elves. And witches . . ."

I shrugged, glad Jenks was with me. The witches were doing what they did best, sitting back and watching. I knew Elyse wasn't happy about their entire population losing the ability to cross into the ever-after. *Maybe that's what she really wants to talk about,* I mused as the elevator doors opened and I took a large step forward.

But I quickly scuffed to a halt when I saw Elyse standing before the reception desk waiting for me in a black suit, her hands clasped to make her appear far too young and cheerful to be in charge of an entire demographic of people. She was twenty at the most.

"Hi," the woman said pleasantly, her straight, long black hair swinging as she came forward, hand extended as though we were the *best* of friends. Eyebrows high, I met her grip, needing to shove the energy in my chi down so it wouldn't spark to her. "Did you have a nice morning? Security called and told me you were on the way up."

"That's great," I said, filing that little nugget away as I pulled from her. "I had a wonderful morning," I added, sublimely confident she had nothing to do with Laker finding me. "I was able to spend some time with, uh, Trent's kids." I wasn't sure how to define our relationship. They called me Aunt Rachel, but that was for convenience.

"That must have been pleasant." Elyse gestured for us to go down the hall, and the woman behind the lobby desk returned to work. "I'm glad you were able to make it here with such short notice."

"Like you had a choice?" Jenks muttered, unnoticed on my shoulder.

"We have a lot to unpack," Elyse continued, her steps silent on the flat carpet as she led me past the closed office doors. "I think you'll be pleased at what we have to offer you. We've set up in the library."

Offer? "Ah, Elyse," I began.

"Phew-wee!" Jenks said loudly. "Good thing you brought your good boots, Rache. The troll crap is gonna get thick!"

Elyse stopped short, her flash of ire quickly hidden. "Jenks," she said, tone flat. "I'm sorry. I didn't see you there. I assumed it was too cold for you to be out of the church."

Jenks rose up, wings a shimmering blur. "Naw, I can ride in a purse okay," he said, his hands at his waist in his best Peter Pan pose. "If you're warm enough, I'm warm enough."

"Mmmm." Still not moving, Elyse stared at him. "Could I ask you to wait in the lobby?" She smiled without warmth. "Coven business."

"No." Jenks smiled back, his hand dropping to the hilt of his garden sword. "Where Rache goes, I go. Kind of like a curse or an STD."

I sighed. Elyse was eyeing me as if I could tell him to stay—like he was a dog or a familiar. "Is it a problem if he joins us?" I asked, and Elyse's smile faltered.

"Oh, for great green caterpillar turds," Jenks complained as he bobbed up and down, dust a bright silver. "Rache, I'll be in the *lobby*."

"Great, Jenks. Thanks," I said. "I'll see you in the *lobby*."

All of which meant he'd be watching me from a light fixture instead of my shoulder. On the plus side, I wouldn't have to deal with his smart-ass remarks being whispered into my ear.

"Ah . . ." Elyse watched him fly back the way we had come, her furrowed brow saying she knew she'd made a mistake. If she had just let him join us, she'd know where he was. Now it was a crapshoot.

"Shall we?" I said brightly, but inside I was simply wanting to get this over with. I had until June to either get Brad uncursed or show her the spell, and changing a deal once struck was not only tacky but unprofessional. "I didn't know the coven had a permanent office in Cincinnati."

"It's new." Elyse gestured to a glass-walled meeting room at the end of the hall. "We recently signed a long-term lease, and we're nearly moved in."

"We? How many of you are staying?" Worry made a knot in my gut. "I thought the coven was based out of San Francisco."

"It is." Elyse seemed to have recovered most of her aplomb. "We maintain offices in many major cities in case of need. I doubt we will all be here by the end of the year, but chances are good one of us will stay." Mood lightening, she gestured at the frosted-glass door. "Here we are."

The glass-walled room was clearly a library, as books took up two walls and much of the third overlooking Cincy. Elyse opened the door, and the three young people and the one old guy waiting turned to us. They were standing between a circle of chairs and a low table holding an untouched tray of cheese and crackers. Napkins with the tower's logo in gold foil were arranged neatly beside little black paper plates. Four glass quart containers of what was probably cider were nestled in ice nests. Business-casual attire aside, it was obvious they were all coven, and their expressions ranged from wary acceptance to mistrustful.

A crow perched on a bird stand at the floor-to-ceiling window between two bookracks, the animal chortling when we entered, wings lifting as if to take to the air. The plaque screwed to the stand said that his name was Slick and that he would bite if he felt like it. I caught Elyse shaking her head, and the bird settled down. *Her familiar?* I wondered. Better than the cat that I had assumed. Crows were wickedly smart, and the better you were at magic, the smarter your familiar had to be—hence the logic behind demons stealing people. Smart, clever people.

"Hello," I said, managing to stop myself from making a stupid wave, but it was close.

No one said anything and Elyse pushed past me, all smiles. "Rachel, you didn't get to meet the team last time," she said, and my brow furrowed. *Meet the team?* Perhaps because they had just tried to curse an entire demographic from reality.

"I'm Scott," the old guy said, smiling as he leaned over the cheese, hand extended. "I'm the supporting ley line practitioner."

"Supporting?" I blurted, as I took in his gray hair, wrinkled eyes, and loose, unassuming clothes. Supporting meant he wasn't the junior member or lead, but the middle—not necessarily in power but in rank.

Scott grinned, flashing me his coffee-stained teeth. "You can't retire from the coven, but you can go out on disability. I'm filling in for Lee until June."

"Nice to meet you," I said, feeling my ergs rise to my skin where we touched. He was running low—or I was running high—and I let go when

I felt him draw on the ley line and our balances came to a pinging match. He was probably over a hundred, but seeing as witches averaged a hundred and sixty, it wasn't out of the question for him to be called back to duty.

"Ah, and this is Adan," Elyse continued, awkward as she took control of the introductions. "He's our junior earth magic practitioner."

"Hi," I said, remembering the gawky, slim blond boy from Fountain Square as I met his smooth, uncalloused hand.

"Rachel," the kid said as he quickly let go, a worried slant to his blue eyes.

"And Yaz," Elyse continued, looking at the only other woman in the room. She had the fresh face of a sixteen-year-old, with brown skin, wide shoulders, and a powerful build. "Yaz is our supporting earth witch."

"Nice to meet you." I extended my hand again, impressed by her firm grip. The scent of lilac drifted from her, and her nails were stained from chlorophyll.

"Rachel," she said, head bobbing. Her voice was higher than I would have expected from her large frame.

"Orion is our leading earth magic practitioner," Elyse said, and a young man, probably late teens by his sparse, razor-burned stubble, rocked forward and extended his fist.

"Hey," I said, remembering him as I bumped my fist against his.

"Nice to officially meet you." His gaze dropped to the bag still on my shoulder.

"Same here." I rocked back, one hand on my shoulder strap. The scent of redwood was growing, and all five of them were tapped into the same ley line I was. Even an earth witch knew how to set a circle. "We were kind of busy the last time for introductions."

The heartbeat of silence was telling.

"This isn't awkward at all," Elyse said sourly. "Rachel, help yourself to the cheese and crackers. Can I get you a drink? We've got a cider-tasting flight. Apparently they go from sweet to tart."

I glanced at the four decorative glass containers of cider with a new understanding. "Some tart cider would be nice," I said faintly, and the five of them began to move a little. It wasn't stuffy in here, but I felt trapped, as if I was one of the books they wanted to put on the shelves. Adan, the youngest earth witch, was wrinkling his nose, and I wondered if it was from the scent of burnt amber coming from my bag.

Elyse made a point to crack the seal as if to prove that the cider hadn't been tampered with. "I've been wanting to try this since it was delivered," she said as she filled two small sampling cups. "Anyone else?"

My lips quirked at the sudden rush. Everyone wanted something to do with their fingers, and I took a tiny black paper plate, putting three crackers and a couple slices of cheese on it. Heads were down and no one said much . . . but they were sneaking glances at my bag. Jenks hadn't shown up yet, and I scanned the freestanding bookracks behind them for a hint of pixy dust.

The old guy, Scott, sat down with a heavy sigh. As if it was a signal, we all found seats, the table between us as they held their little plates of cheese and crackers. I took the chair nearest the door, but I still felt trapped.

Frowning, I set my plate on the table and crossed my ankles. "Elyse, why am I here?" I said, my shoulders relaxing when I spotted a faint stream of pixy dust sift from a book-laden corner. "You gave me until June to get Brad uncursed," I added, not liking that that crow had spotted Jenks, too, the bird's head cocked and a questioning rattle escaping him. "I understand your impatience, but I'm working on it. I'm not comfortable showing you the curse until I have the cure." Yet there it was, stinking up the entire room from the bag at my feet as requested.

Elyse wiped a cracker crumb from the corner of her mouth with a forced casualness. "You brought it, right? Yes? Good."

I tugged my bag possessively closer, my next words lost when Orion pushed to the edge of his seat, the leading earth magic practitioner's dark eyes fixed on mine. "We've been over the ley line practitioners available to fill our vacant position," he said, his ring-decked fingers playing with the amulets around his neck. "Either they are too old—"

"Or too young," Scott said with a chuckle, his attention on the cracker-cheese-cracker-cheese-cracker sandwich he was making.

"Or too bossy," Elyse said, staring at Scott as that crow chortled from his perch.

"To be suitable candidates," Orion finished.

"As you said." Elyse firmly resumed control of the conversation. "We see no reason to wait until June when everyone's choices are obvious. Scott gives us a quorum, so we took a vote and I am pleased to offer the position of junior ley line practitioner to you with immediate induction. Here and now." She hesitated. "We can do it today."

Junior? I thought sourly as Jenks's warning trickled through my thoughts.

"Elyse," I began, my words choking off when Elyse leaned forward and stuck a Möbius strip pin on my leather jacket's lapel. "Um," I added as I pulled my coat away so I could see it. The stones weren't the clear purity of traditional diamonds. No, she'd gone for rubies, and the bloodred gems glistened from a band of bright gold. It matched my aura.

Annoyed, I tried to take it off, my gaze going from Elyse's satisfaction to Scott, his old face wrinkled in amusement. If I said yes, he'd be my boss. *Junior, my ass.*

"Uh, this is all very overwhelming," I said as I continued to try to get the pin off. "I thought I made my position clear weeks ago."

"You did." Elyse smiled, but I could tell this hadn't been a unanimous decision. Yaz and Orion were clearly unhappy. "Which is why we are offering it to you today regardless if the curse you used on Brad Welroe is deemed illicit or not." Her gaze dropped to the bag on my lap. "Once a coven member, you will enjoy a far greater leeway in what is deemed acceptable."

Scott snorted, and I gave up trying to get the pin off, my thoughts going to Brice. I had a lot of leeway right now, apparently. "Why did I bring it if you don't want to see it?" I said, touching the book through my bag, and Adan flicked his blond hair from his eyes.

"Oh, we still want to see it," he said.

"And any other demon tomes you have," Yaz added as she set her plate aside.

"As time permits, of course," Elyse said when I frowned. "Suffice to say that your team inclusion doesn't hinge on the legality of the curse you put upon Brad Welroe anymore." Her head tilted. "Just your willingness to show us your library."

My library? Not even if a second Turn was coming. "And my subrosa position?" I said as the thin trail of dust coming from the top of the bookcase brightened to a dull silver. *Jenks, keep your tiny little white butt up there,* I thought as I made the subtle finger gesture for "hold."

Elyse took a sip of her cider. "You'd have to let that go, of course," she said, and I bristled, wondering if the DC vamps were subsidizing this sudden generosity. "We have already agreed that you can remain permanently stationed here in these very offices, but Cincinnati *will* resume a more traditional power structure."

I'd be both under their thumb and out of San Francisco and their business. Interesting.

Elyse shifted, clearly not trusting my bland reaction. "You'd be the coven's plumber."

Scott smirked, the old guy saluting me with his cider before downing it like a shot of whiskey. It was probably his position, and he would clearly be glad to let it go as there was travel involved. Since being coven was a lifetime appointment and everyone here but Scott was younger than me, it would be nearly a hundred years before I could give it to someone else. Providing they didn't die early, which, actually, they had a pretty good chance of doing.

"Mmmm, yeah," I said as I tried to work the pin off again. "As before, I truly appreciate the opportunity, but due to time constraints and previous commitments, I will have to continue to decline your gracious offer." Grimacing, I tugged at the pin. She'd spelled it on, and it wasn't budging.

They were all fidgeting—that is, except for Scott, who slammed his empty glass onto the table, startling the crow. "Rachel," he said, and Elyse shot him a look to shut up. "It was a mistake trying to curse the demons into being unable to cross into reality at will. The coven is in real danger of falling apart."

"It is not," Elyse said, cheeks reddening.

"Scott," Orion warned, and the wizened guy's expression flickered with an old anger.

"I may be temporary, but I was a member before you were even born," he said. "And if none of you have the guts to say it, I will. The coven made a mistake." Scott turned to me in the awkward silence. "And it's not hard to see why. None of them were ready for the responsibility apart from maybe Orion and Elyse, and if they won't say it, I will. Please. We need you."

My lips parted in surprise. I would've said they had asked him to play Good Cop to their Bad Cop, but Elyse was staring at him as if she was about to drop live coals from her fingertips. The tension in the room had risen, and the unfocused energy they were dumping into the air was threatening to bust my topknot apart. From his perch, the crow flapped his wings, agitated and feeling it, too.

"You want my help?" I said as I gave up trying to take that pin off. "What if it came with an opinion you don't like?"

"Decisions are made by vote." Elyse glared at Scott. "That won't change."

"Well, I don't work by committee," I said, and Scott gestured as if I had confirmed something he already knew. "Seems to me you want what I can give you but on your terms. Kind of one-sided, isn't it?"

"Keeping you out of Alcatraz is not one-sided," Orion said. I had this all figured out, though, and was ready to walk out the door.

"Alcatraz is not the certainty you think it is." I took my plate of cheese and crackers in hand and reclined deeper into the chair to show them how unworried I was—even as my stomach knotted. *I had polished my boots for this?* "Scott is right. You made a mistake trying to curse the demons into exile, giving them the fuel to curse you out of the ever-after instead." I took a bite of cracker, fuming. "Do you have any idea what it cost to get them back in reality? The benefits to all of you of that? The crap I'm going to have to put up with from them if I join your little club?"

"Little club?" Orion's face flushed, stark against his black mane.

"Benefits?" Elyse practically barked, and her crow cawed. "For who? Not us."

I brushed the crumbs from my front, embarrassed. "It's not all about you, Elyse, or the witches, or even the demons. It's not an *us* and *them* world anymore. It's one. Big. Us. And a large chunk of *us* was hurting." I set my plate aside, done. Done with it all. "You seriously think you can bully me into signing a contract with you after what you pulled? Frankly, you all deserve to be excluded from the ever-after until you grow up."

Scott stifled a guffaw, and I wondered if I had gone too far as the pleasantry fell away from the rest to leave only a hard anger—and a little fear.

"You'd let the demons do what they want," Yaz said bitterly.

I leaned forward to take a sip of good, tart Cincinnati cider. "The demons aren't doing what they want. They are playing by our rules."

Elyse huffed. "Only because they want to."

"Only because she's making them," Orion added.

I bobbed my head. "And that is different from everyone else, how? No. Your collective problem is the same as Vivian's. You have been told for so long that you are the alpha to omega that you don't know how to handle it when you aren't. You have no ability to trust that someone will do what's right because that's how we *all* get our lattes and Friday nights out." I felt a faint flush creep up my neck. "And I will not be your reluctant muscle that you stuff in a closet halfway across the continent until you want something. Elyse, it's been lovely, but I will see you in June as we agreed."

I stood, tugging at that damned pin until the leather tore. Jaw clenched, I set the pin on the table, a long rip of leather dangling from it. *Son of a moss-wipe troll turd.*

"Elyse," someone hissed, and I yanked hard on the ley line until my aura sparked. Elyse had stood, and four wary faces watched me as the woman moved to one of the locked glass cabinets. Jenks stood on the light fixture, unnoticed by all but me and that crow, his garden sword in his hand.

"I'm glad you brought the book," Elyse said tightly, her back to us. "I have the one you are interested in right here. Perhaps we can trade."

I jerked, my gut seeming to fall to my ankles. "It's real?" I said, incredulous. "I thought you were lying."

"I don't lie." Elyse murmured a few words of Latin and the glass case unlocked. *Quis custodiet ipsos custodes?* I thought, memorizing the simple magic. *Who guards the guards?*

"Elyse. We haven't voted on that yet," Scott warned, and Elyse turned with a book, her eyes holding a mocking cruelty. "She wants to see it. I want to see the curse she used on Brad. We have to give her something or she's going to walk out of here. All for letting her see?"

"Aye," Orion, Yaz, and Adan all said, and Elyse dropped the book onto the table to make the cider in the cups jump.

"And with me, that makes four," Elyse said needlessly.

"That's coven wisdom," Scott protested. "We don't have a quorum. It's not a legal vote."

"Just because you lost doesn't make it an illegal vote." Elyse confidently paged through the book until she found the spell she wanted. Taking a napkin, she stuck it in like a bookmark and closed the tome. "Well? You want to see it or not?" she added, eyebrows raised mockingly high.

"You can look at it here," Orion said somewhat nervously. "As long as you show us the curse you used on Brad. Illicit or legal, you will still have until June to uncurse him."

There was something here I wasn't getting. Why the rush all of a sudden?

"Or," Elyse said, fingers sparking as they rested on the old leather, "you could agree to become a coven member right now, the legality of that curse aside."

Scott was frowning. I didn't trust this at all, but I really wanted to know how to recover Kisten. Yes, I loved Trent, but I missed Kisten's smile, his ability to say just the right word or know when to not say anything. Besides, he could run Cincy's vamps better than I ever could, a much-appreciated cushion to Constance's brutality. He'd been trained for it from birth, knew all the players through birthday parties and weddings. I was winging it.

Jenks's dust went a dismal blue as I inched forward, my hand shuffling into my bag. "Just so we're clear, I see the spell to bring the undead to life, and you see the spell I used on Brad Welroe. You don't get to keep my book, and I walk out with it whenever I feel like it. I have until June to break the curse."

"Or become coven. Refuse and you are in Alcatraz," Elyse said, and Scott stiffened at Jenks's tiny snort of derision, his eyes going wide as he spotted the pixy and Jenks shrugged. By the window, the crow bobbed his head up and down, clearly agitated.

I knew how the bird felt. I didn't trust Elyse. And I really didn't like how eager Orion and Yaz were to get their hands on my book. "You're looking only at the one curse," I said, and Elyse nodded. "I can do that," I added, and Yaz turned from Jenks, the pixy forgotten as she scooted eagerly to the edge of her seat, all grabby paws.

And still, it felt as if I was making a mistake as I sat down again, the book in hand. "Clean your hands first," I warned. "And dump the line. I don't want you stimulating it."

"I know how to handle demon texts," Orion muttered, and I quit leafing through the pages, staring at him until he dropped his eyes.

"It's three pages including the countercurse," I said. "Hodin concealed the illicit ingredients and how it worked from me until after I'd used it."

"We understand," Elyse said, but I wasn't sure they believed me. Licking my lips, I spun the book to Orion and Yaz and pushed it across the table.

"This is it," Orion said, tone muted, and only then did Elyse reopen her book and slide it across the table to me.

My pulse quickened as I drew the book close. I wouldn't lie to myself and say that I didn't miss Kisten. I'd had relationships with ghosts before, and if it took me twisting the curse every night, I would. Not to mention Pierce had eventually parlayed his ghostly existence into a real one with the help of a demon. It hadn't ended well, but that's what happens when you try to kill a demon. Perhaps I could do something like that here. I'd become quite good at modifying curses.

And yet as I set my fingers atop the cramped print, my hope turned to an annoyed confusion.

"This is ancient elven," I muttered, peeved. "I can't read this." I looked up, angry at Elyse's self-assured smile. "You are sucky. All the way through."

Scott grimaced where he sat, hunched over his widely spaced knees. He didn't seem happy. I think he had known. I think they all had.

"The deal was see, not read," she had the audacity to say, then moved to peer over Orion's shoulder. The two earth witches were whispering excitedly, flipping back and forth as they dissected the curse. They weren't appalled at all, which made me feel a little ill. It was an illicit curse. It did ugly things. And they were as excited as if they had found a way to make ponies pink.

"Elyse, she wasn't lying," Orion said as Yaz shifted the pages, his fingers hovering over the now glowing print. "The countercurse requires an Atlantean mirror." Expression holding a heavy satisfaction, he turned to me. "You can't break this."

My face warmed as I rested my hand on the spell I couldn't read. Elyse had asked me here to trick me, tempting me with something I couldn't have. *And they called me a demon.* "I'm trying to find a substitution," I said through my gritted teeth.

"There isn't one," Scott said, and Elyse looked up, brow furrowed for him to stay quiet. "The only Atlantean mirror known to exist was in the possession of a demon named Newt."

"Scott," Elyse warned, and the old man ignored her.

"Yeah? Well, that would make sense, because I think she wrote the spell," I said sullenly.

"Yeah?" Orion mocked. "Seeing as the ever-after was demolished, you have a problem."

Oh. Right. I leaned back, ticked. "Not everything was destroyed when the original ever-after fell," I said. "We got all the people out. And the demons got their books and most of their stuff." I jumped when Elyse yanked the book out from under me and closed it, bookmark still in place. "Hey, I'm not done with that. Let me get a picture of it. Trent can read ancient elven."

Smug, Elyse had handed the book to Orion, who went to put it in the cabinet and lock it with a whispered word. "The deal was see, not copy," Elyse said, practically singing the words.

You little canicula . . . "Al might have Newt's mirror," I all but growled. "He hasn't been through all her things yet. There's like an entire room of her stuff." Which wasn't true. A box, maybe.

"Rachel . . ." Elyse coaxed me mockingly as she came closer. "Why are you making this so difficult?"

I stood, done with them. "I have until June. Someone might have the mirror."

"June." Elyse stretched to flip my curse book closed, and both Orion and Yaz grimaced, annoyed. "I don't think so. Decide now."

I stared at her, forced my hands to unclench. Suddenly, I knew what it felt like to be a demon trapped in a circle. "This wasn't the deal," I said, voice low.

My breath came in smoothly as I felt Elyse and Scott pull on the ley line. Yaz and Orion were fingering charms, and one of Adan's rings was glowing a hazy red. It was five on one. The odds were not in my favor.

Wait, I have Jenks, I thought when he darted down, sword unsheathed and wings rasping as he hovered beside me, eyeing that crow. *Even odds.*

"And you are still making mistakes," I said, voice holding a bitter threat. "Elyse, you gave me until June. You don't want to change the deal. Trust me on this."

"Elyse," Scott whispered. "She has until June."

Elyse's lip twitched. "I didn't promise anything," she said, and Scott shook his head.

"Vivian did," Scott said, and I thought it odd he was letting Elyse run this pony show. He clearly had the most sense. "If she can't find a mirror, then I will vote with you, but until then, I don't, and confining someone to Alcatraz has to be unanimous. That curse isn't anything worse than you've done yourself and you know it."

Elyse broke eye contact with me, flushing. "Shut it!" she shouted, sounding like a kid.

Scott shook his head, grim and determined. "Rachel might have twisted the curse for selfish reasons, but I think it benefited the public greatly."

Orion winced, his sigh saying he agreed.

"She is already in service to the city," Scott said. "If she's going to be coven, I'd rather it be a real choice, not one between Alcatraz, exile, or us. And not because we reneged on a deal and forced her into it."

"We can't stop her from vanishing into the ever-after," Yaz said nervously.

Elyse cradled my book on her hip. "Which is why we are going to keep her book as collateral."

Wait. What?

Jenks shook his head as he hovered beside me, a thin trail of silver dust escaping him. "And that is your second mistake," he said. "Three strikes, and you're out."

"Don't do this, Elyse," I warned again, my thoughts resting lightly in the ley line they all had a death grip on. The air was practically sparking, and my hair was threatening to spill from my topknot even as that crow of hers cawed and flapped his wings when the woman carried my book to her shelf, sliding it into an open spot and locking the glass behind it.

My hands slowly fisted. I exhaled, pushing the line from me. If I did anything, they would react. She was being stupid, but that didn't mean I had to be. *Pause, think, then beat the hell out of them. Be the demon.*

"Rache?" Jenks said, and I made the finger motion for retreat. Yeah, I was going to walk out of here without my book. That didn't mean I was going to leave it here.

"Come on, Jenks," I said as I shouldered my much-lighter bag, and Yaz stupidly relaxed, apparently thinking they had me by the panties.

Jenks dropped down to stab a piece of cheese with his sword. "You guys are really dumb. The first rule of dealing with demons is never break a deal with them. Ever."

The second rule was don't piss them off—which kind of went with the first. Angry, I pushed the glass door to the library open with a stiff arm and walked out, leaving a sudden conversation in my wake. There was no way in hell I was *ever* going to work with these people.

And there was no way in two hells that Elyse was going to keep my book.

CHAPTER

5

THE MID-NOVEMBER WIND PUSHED ON THE CHURCH, SCATTERING the last of the leaves and swirling them to beat against the sanctuary's stained-glass windows. The heat was on for the first time of the season, and I could smell the dust burning off the furnace as I sat on the couch and went through the last box of Newt's things.

"I'm fine, woman!" Jenks barked from the lampshade, and Getty rose, a flush pinking her cheeks.

"You didn't wear the scarf I gave you, did you!" the dark-haired pixy yelled back, her gossamer wings invisible as she hovered. "I'm not your wife, but you will, by the Turn, try out my weavings. I twisted those stitches so they would better block the wind and keep you warm with maximum mobility. I can't keep the garden alone, and if you kill yourself by falling into a hibernation stupor, I will dump your body over the wall and leave you to the sparrows!"

"I wore your scarf," he griped, wings a fast blur. "It worked great. I'm just trying to get warmed up, okay?"

"You wore it?"

I smiled at the pixy woman's surprise, my head down as I pushed to the bottom of the box, fingers tingling. "Perhaps you should explain to her why you're so cold, Jenks."

"Because I'm not going to ride in your purse like a package of gummy trolls!" Clearly peeved, Jenks left the heat of the lamp, still trailing a faint blue dust as he darted over to me and landed on my shoulder. "Tell her the scarf is pretty, will you?" he whispered.

"You tell her," I said, and he slumped as Getty bobbed up and down before darting out of the sanctuary, silver sparkles of indecision coloring her dust.

"Last time I told her something was pretty, she cried," he said, and I began to rummage again. Getty was desperately in love with him, but her upbringing left her feeling as if she didn't deserve love in return, especially from Jenks, whose heart still beat for his deceased wife. It had become just as obvious that Jenks could love her but that he wouldn't allow himself, worried it might mean he loved Matalina less. All I knew was that the two of them had better figure it out, or it was going to be a very long, tumultuous winter.

A sudden cramp of magic jolted through me, and I jerked my hand away from a sealed black envelope before cautiously taking it up and setting it on the low slate table. This was the last box that Al had inherited from Newt when she became the elven Goddess in my stead, my last chance for finding that damned mirror. I wasn't happy that Elyse was hiding behind definitions like a lawyer, and sure, I was furious that she had kept my book. But what really burned my toes was that Elyse had known exactly what button to push to get me to do something stupid.

Kisten.

Jenks's wings rasped as he landed atop the edge of the box and looked down, his pixy curiosity getting the better of him. Getty was banging about in the kitchen. And seeing as she was only four inches tall and weighed less than an ounce, that took some doing. "Ah, we are going to get your book?" he asked, clearly reluctant to go into the kitchen and make everything right quite yet.

"Tonight, yes." I carefully shook out a silken dusting cloth. It had the glyph for purity on it, and I set it aside to keep for myself.

Jenks hesitated for a moment. "So why are you mad?"

I couldn't bring myself to look at him, and I opened a wooden box to see neatly arranged puzzle-like shapes. Snapping it shut, I set it on the table to continue to search. "I didn't appreciate Elyse dangling Kisten before me as if he was a carrot," I muttered. Kisten was gone. I had mourned him and moved on. *And yet* . . .

"Yeah, that was kind of a jerk-ass move," Jenks said. "You fell right for it."

"Hey," I protested, my words faltering when I felt an odd draw on the ley line out in the graveyard. A soft *bong* came from the steeple, and I froze, senses reaching. Someone had done something magical, and it wasn't me.

"That was Al." Jenks dropped into the box to look under another silk scarf. "He's trying to reinstate that toadstool ring around the church."

"For protection?" Curious, I stood and went to peer out of one of the stained-glass window's lighter panes and stare at his colorful wagon parked in the graveyard. It had to be over twenty-five feet long, and would need a team of oxen to pull it. Maybe two teams. Not that it would ever move. He may as well take the wheels off and burn them for firewood. "How is it coming?"

Jenks's wings rasped. "Slowly. Apparently mushrooms have a natural connection to the ley lines. It's like making a circle without actually being connected to the line. Or at least that's how he explained it to me."

I turned, surprised not that Al had attempted to circumvent his current lack of ability to do ley line magic, but rather that he was using his limited skills to protect the church and, in turn, me. A demon who couldn't tap a ley line was vulnerable—more than one who couldn't jump the lines. It felt bigger than that, though.

"You told him about the coven's threat?" I said, shoulders slumping when a burst of dust blew up and over the top of the box. "Jenks," I complained, and he rose, wings laboring, and his arms wrapped around a knife as long as he was tall. "I feel bad enough as it is that he can't tap a ley line because of me. This just points it out."

"It's winter. I'm not going to say no to a little extra protection," he said, and I took the knife before it brought him down. "You can see your reflection in it," he said. "Maybe it's an Atlantean mirror."

"It's possible." I set it aside to ask Al. As much as I complained about the demon being this close, it did make teasing information out of him easier. I wasn't his student, but I did learn from him. He wasn't my protector, but he gave protection just by being in the garden—his current lack of ley line magic aside. He'd once been the demons' premier supplier of fine familiars, which meant he had been both a slave trader and an instructor all wrapped up in one. Now he wasn't much of anything—even as he was still rightfully feared. He was tired, as they all were, of maintaining the mystique of all-powerful. Especially when it kept him alone.

Which might be why I had made only a token protest when his RV/ wagon had shown up in my garden a few weeks ago, parked right in the ley line to make a fast getaway if needed.

Jenks rose from the box at the sound of the porch door opening. *I don't think I'll ever get used to him using the door instead of popping in via the ley lines,* I thought as Getty's voice sounded in a tart greeting and I went back to shuffling through Newt's things.

"Hey, Al. Was that you pulling on the line?" I said as the demon's boots scuffed to a halt at the top of the hall. "I didn't think you could get toadstools to grow this time of year."

"Their roots are in the ever-after," Al said, his slightly supercilious voice still holding a remnant of his affected proper British accent. "It's warmer there. At the mo-o-oment."

My attention rose at the drawn-out word, expecting him to be dressed in his crushed green velvet frock coat with the long tails, lace at his cuffs and throat, or perhaps his ornate spelling robes with bells on the sash and an odd, flat-topped hat. But apart from his boots, he was going twentieth-century businessman casual today, and I gave the tall demon a nod of appreciation at his black slacks, vivid red silk shirt, and elaborately embellished vest. No hat, but he had stuck his blue-tinted glasses on his hawkish nose, either to hide his red, goat-slitted eyes or, more likely, to peer over at me when I was being, in his words, "uncommonly stupid."

"Well, thanks for the extra protection," I said as I returned to shuffling around in the box. "If the coven was going to do anything, they would've done it while I was standing in their offices. I might need it later, though."

Jenks grinned, his young face brightening as he touched the hilt of his sword. "Let's hope they are that stupid."

"Mmmm." Al inched closer, his stylish boots skirting the body-size pentagram burned in the old oak flooring. I hadn't made it, and Al wasn't the only one who refused to walk over it. I knew I'd seen Vivian's visage appear from it, and seeing as she had died there . . .

Al settled in behind me. A short cane I was sure held a purchased spell or two thumped in accusation, and he peered over my shoulder. "You are wasting your time. The mirror is not in there."

His low voice rumbled about my thoughts, and I stifled a shiver. "Doesn't hurt to look," I said, then jumped, startled when he took the black glass globe I was scrutinizing right out of my hand.

"Look, no. But touching might," he said as he tucked the orb into a pocket. "That shouldn't have been left in there for you. It can burn you to ash where you stand when startled."

Whatever. I scooted closer to the box, wondering why he was here. Asking wouldn't convince him to tell me, but if I pretended indifference, he might spill—if only because I was ignoring him. "This is the last box, isn't it?" I said, frowning when he stuffed the silk scarf that I had wanted into his sleeve. "The coven thinks that Newt had the only Atlantean mirror."

"She is the only one of us who both recognized and utilized it," he said, enunciating every syllable with a biting precision. He leaned forward to put his attention more deeply in the box. "You shouldn't have this, either," he added, plucking a silver-coated bowl engraved with Latin from the mess. "Too dangerous."

Jenks's wings hummed. "She's madder than a jilted troll that Elyse tricked her."

I sat back with a huff as Al began pawing through the box, taking an interest in things now that I was threatening to do the same. "I showed them the curse I used on Brad in exchange for seeing their spell that Elyse said would return the undead."

"And will it?" Al squinted through a flat stone with a hole in it.

"I don't know. It was in ancient elven. I can't read ancient elven."

Al eyed me over his glasses as he slid the stone into a tiny vest pocket. "Your dealmaking is usually so tight," he said sourly, having been on the wrong side of it a few times. "Did you take a picture?"

"They wouldn't let me."

A smile, almost proud, quirked the corners of his lips. "They? You met with all of them? Four coven members against my itchy witch. Your reputation is serving you well."

"Yeah, well, it's five now. They pulled some old guy out of retirement. I'm going in tonight to get my book. I'll take a picture of the spell to bring back the undead then."

"You left your book with them?" Al said dramatically, and I glared at Jenks. The pixy beat a hasty, dust-ridden retreat to the kitchen, but it was probably better that Al had heard it first from Jenks. I pushed deeper into the couch, planting my arches on the table and crossing my arms over my chest.

"Yes, I let them *keep* my book," I said, peeved, as Al continued to sort and sift. "I left before I did something stupid, like blow a hole through Trent's building. I'll get it tonight."

"This is all junk," he said as he straightened. "You may keep what's left."

"Gee, thanks," I muttered as he primly sat on the couch across from me.

"About the curse to recover the undead," he started, and my focus sharpened on him.

"You already know it?" I blurted, angry that he hadn't told me, and he shook his head.

"One hears rumors," he said lightly. "I suspect Elyse is either lying or it will not work as you wish it to." Al settled himself, reclining indolently along the length of the couch to gaze at the heavy beams at the ceiling. "Still, as much as I would appreciate someone coming between you and your . . . mmmm . . . understandable infatuation with elf flesh—"

"That's not why I'm doing this," I interrupted, and his gaze darted to mine.

"As you say," he mocked, then turned back to the old-oak beams. "Let's assume the curse is bastardized from the one you used to bring Pierce's soul from purgatory. True, he would have mass, mobility, and a sense of purpose. But you would have to perform the curse nightly because I am not going to provide him with a real body as I did with Pierce." Al fussed with his collar as if to try to convince me that he really didn't care how far up shit creek I was. "I only did so with Pierce because I needed a skilled familiar." His eyes met mine mockingly. "And I doubt you will perform the needed curse yourself as it requires you to outright kill someone for a body. Not if you are bending yourself into knots to avoid the coven's wrath."

"I'm not hiding in the ever-after," I started, and Al huffed, interrupting me.

"Let's agree that Kisten's nightly ghost will be solid enough to serve as master of the city. True, it would solve the problem of Constance, but have you considered the carnal pull—"

"I'm not trying to bring my old boyfriend back," I said, face warming.

"No-o-o?" he drawled, his thick fingers clasped and an exaggerated expression of wonder on him. "I just *assumed*—"

"No," I said again. "I was an idiot when I was dating Kisten. I was an idiot the entire time I was living with Ivy. I mean, I do love her, but I do dumb things when I'm around her too much, and it's not Ivy's fault." It was my own. It had always been my own. I simply didn't do well around vampires. They smelled too delicious to resist. That's how they survived: convincing smart people to make dumb decisions.

A small noise of disbelief escaped Al as he stretched out on the couch and stared at the ceiling, watching the swirl of descending pixy dust. Jenks was up there, eavesdropping. "And you think that by recovering Kisten's ghost, you won't return to said dumb state?" he asked.

My brow furrowed. "He never should have died like that. Piscary made him into a party favor." I tilted the box, and a handful of marbles rolled. It was all that was left. "Killed him because he had become better at managing the living vampires than Piscary had ever been. He wasn't a threat until he said no to Piscary, and Kisten never would have stood up to him if not for me." I took one of the marbles in hand, and then dropped it back into the box with a rolling rattle. "I owe him everything."

"Mmmm." Gaze on the ceiling, Al dipped his fingers into that tiny pocket of his vest. "And the curse to do so is in elven?"

My pulse quickened. This was why he'd come in from the garden. "Can you read it?"

Al snorted. "Who do you think was responsible for teaching it to their brats? Tell me why you let the curse to wake Kisten's ghost leave your hands?"

"Because they had the book to uncurse Brad and I was standing thirty-three floors up."

He sat up. "People heal. Stone can be rebuilt," he scoffed.

"It was a library," I said, and Al's expression pinched in understanding. "Honestly, though, I was concerned about what a bunch of scared magic users would do," I added, remembering Elyse's smug expression and Scott's worry. "And then blame me for it. Why risk it when I can simply get a picture of the spell I want and walk out with my book? That was the deal: I walk out with it after I showed them mine and they showed me theirs."

"She reneged on a deal? You are within your rights to take every and any action to retrieve it."

Within my rights. Yeah. I was still breaking in, though, and that's not how they would see it in a court of law. Demon logic didn't hold water in a Cincy court. I'd found that out the hard way, and from the rafters came a tiny snort of agreement.

I leaned over the box, staring at those stupid marbles. Depressed, I began to gather them to give to Jenks's grandkids. But as I chased the glass around the dusty bottom, my thoughts drifted back to Kisten.

I hadn't thought of Kisten in weeks, and now, thanks to Elyse, I couldn't get him out of my head. It had really messed Ivy up when Kisten had found his second death on the heels of the first. Usually, when a living vampire dies, his or her soul waits in purgatory until their second, true death and the mind, body, and soul can move on together to whatever waits—purgatory being the ever-after. It had been a shock to find out that what I'd been calling surface demons—the vicious, half-starved, ragtag monsters in the ever-after—were really the tortured souls of the undead vampires. They existed apart and separate, having little agency other than a will to rend and tear. But seeing as the entire species of vampires had been created by the demons, it made sense. They had to put their souls somewhere.

"Al?" I jiggled the marbles in my hand, sending a trace of ley line energy through them to make sure they weren't spelled. *Just empty glass.* "Where do the souls of the undead go now that the original ever-after is gone?"

Al continued to stare at the ceiling, his hands laced over his middle, boot heels on the armrest. "They are in the bubble of reality you and Bis created. We moved the curse to keep the souls of the undead from rejoining their minds prematurely to forestall the mess you created the last time their souls were pulled into reality."

Yeah, that had been a mistake, and I dropped the marbles into a bowl Al had said I could keep. "How come I've never seen one?"

The demon shrugged. "I expect they are in the mountains, enjoying the reality you and Bis created. It doesn't look like hell, so they probably assume they are in heaven. And when in heaven . . ." He turned his red, goat-slitted eyes to me, a wicked smirk twisting his lips as he left his last words unsaid.

"You act like an angel," I finished for him. "Not a demon. Is that why—"

"No." Al sat up, his attention going to the front of the church. "Your demonic kin are behaving themselves because they realize they are both outnumbered and embarrassingly out of touch. Give them a hundred years to adapt and they will apply the full force of their presence upon the elves to bring them back under our collective heels."

I sighed, my own gaze going to the double doors at the sound of a motorbike. Al had heard it long before me.

"Personally, I can't wait for them to catch up." Al thumped his boots on the floor and tugged his sleeves down. "Rachel? I have decided that you will indeed retrieve your book tonight. I'll assist you with moving the church to the ever-after if the coven attempts to put you in Alcatraz for recovering what is yours. The toadstool ring is thick enough to handle the shift. Earth magic is amazing. Unfortunate that it takes too damn long to prep it."

Leave Cincy? Is he serious? I thought as Jenks dropped down on wings and sparkles. I was not about to abandon reality. I was Cincy's subrosa. Until June anyway.

"That's Ivy," Jenks said as there was a thud at the door followed by a gust of air blowing through the church.

"Hey, Rachel?" Ivy called as she closed the door behind her. Her low voice brought my shoulders down in a wash of remembrance as the church suddenly felt complete. Her confident steps in the dark foyer scuffed to a halt when Al half turned where he sat, his eyebrows high as he took in her leather-clad svelte form and the pizza box she had in one hand. How she had gotten it here on her bike was a marvel of balance. But that was Ivy.

"Hi, come on in." I stood to brush the rest of Al's rejects from the table into the box to make room for the pizza, my motion faltering when I realized Al wasn't following protocol and leaving, instead settling back with a copy of my *Witch Monthly*, his glasses pushed low, so he could see over them.

"Getty!" Jenks darted into the kitchen. "We got pizza. You want to split a tomato?"

"I heard you had a rough day." Ivy sauntered in looking like a frat boy's dream in her sexy leather and carrying a boxed pizza. "Al, if I had known you were here, I would have brought two," she added, her voice holding a hint of antagonistic jealousy. I wasn't a cookie for them to fight over, but they each had their claim on me and neither of them shared well.

Al flipped a page. "Good evening, Ivy Alisha Tamwood," he intoned, his focus firmly on the magazine.

Ivy dropped the pizza onto the still-cluttered table with a loud pop. "I know what using all three of my names means," she said, and I cleared my throat, warning him.

Expression shifting, Al beamed up at her. "Ivy," he said, voice dripping sarcasm. "It's good to see you." Using one finger, he lifted the lid and breathed deep. "Ah," he added as he helped himself to a slice. "The sauce has not been the same since your lover cut Piscary's head from his neck and he truly died, but this smells good enough to sell my soul for."

Ivy shifted her weight from one foot to the other as she eyed me for direction, and I shrugged. Satisfied, she pulled the box away from him and sat beside me. "I take it your meeting with the coven didn't go well?"

Wings humming, Jenks came back in, a pair of tiny chopsticks in hand. "How can you tell?" he said with a little chuckle as he descended upon the pizza.

Ivy glanced at the empty box. "She's looking for something to spell with."

Al turned another page, silent.

"So." Ivy flicked a tomato for Jenks off a slice before angling it between her perfect teeth. "They coming to put you in Alcatraz? I didn't see anything on the news."

Eating anything with a vampire was an unspoken invitation to become dessert. Ivy knew that wasn't the case here, but I was still hesitant in my reach for a slice. "June," I said, and her eyebrows rose in surprise. "Unless I can uncurse Brad. Which will be hard if I can't get my book back from them. I'm going to retrieve it tonight. Want to come?"

Ivy leaned deep into the cushions with her pizza. "That's why I'm here," she said, her network of informants clearly having done their job. "You got to see the spell to recover Kisten, right? Do you need his ashes?"

Al made a low growl, his attention in the magazine.

"Maybe?" I admitted. "It was in ancient elven. I'm going to take a picture of it while we're getting my book back. If Al won't help me decipher it, Bis or Trent will." I shoved the table into Al's knees, and he grunted in surprise. "Well?"

He beamed. "I'm always interested in coven magic."

Which wasn't exactly an answer, but I slid the pizza down the table to make a clear spot. "Okay, let's see it," I said, and Ivy blinked at me. "You wouldn't come here empty-handed."

"She brought pizza," Jenks said as he used his chopsticks to peel a flake of bacon free.

I held a hand out. "I need to see the tower's blueprints so I know what spells to prep."

"Thought you might." Ivy reached behind her jacket for her phone. "I don't have them, but I can get them if you want. I brought the layout of Elyse's short-term rental."

"Not her office?" Worried, I leaned closer as our weights slid us together and the scent of happy vampire washed over me, soaking in like a shot of tequila.

"She's in Circle Bluffs," Jenks said as he dropped down, hands on his hips and his dust blanking the screen when it hit it. "Fancy."

I stifled a shudder and Ivy sort of scooted back a little, the vampire eyeing Al in annoyance that he hadn't left. "It's an easy job," Ivy said, but I was not excited about breaking into someone's home. Business, sure. Lab, why not? Where someone lived and loved and slept? That was a different story.

"Yeah, Ivy's right," Jenks said, expression serious as he used two hands to move the screen. "If the coven took the time to bring you into their offices, show you where the book is, and even give you the word to unlock the cabinet, you can bet it's not there." He chuckled. "Infants."

"You can bet that they will be waiting for you, though," Ivy added.

"Yeah." Jenks's wings rasped as he stood on Ivy's phone. "Elyse is itching for a reason to put you into Alcatraz without that six-month waiting period. It's a setup. Come on, Rache," he coaxed. "If you stole a book from a demon, would you leave it in a library or take it home?"

I glanced at Al. "Home," I admitted, but it still felt wrong—even if Elyse had reneged on our deal. "Circle Bluffs, huh?"

Ivy gently blew Jenks's dust from her phone and scrolled to a screen detailing the security measures for the tenants. "She's renting the visitor bungalow. It has fewer safeguards than most of the homes out there."

"I didn't even know they had a visitor bungalow," I admitted, and Ivy smirked.

"That's what a neighbors' association can get you if you can stomach someone measuring your grass twice a month."

Jenks scrolled to the camera section. "And what color of car you can have."

Al's harrumph was loud, and again I wondered why he was lingering. He never took more than a cursory interest in my life—unless it was crashing into his.

"It's a very easy-in, easy-out run," Ivy said, her long hair falling like a fragrant curtain between us. "As long as you can get around any safeguards she might have put in. Anything too complex or permanent will violate the lease agreement. It's short-term and very specific."

Which I doubted Elyse cared about. I glanced at my bag by the door. The lethal-magic and strong-magic detection charms on my key ring were old but still worked.

"I'll put the cameras on loop," Jenks said. "No one will ever know you were there."

Ivy froze, and my eyes flicked up to her. As one, we shook our fists, ending with her going for paper, and me rock. *Damn it back to the Turn.*

"No, you won't," I said, and Jenks predictably bristled. "It's too cold." He rose up, wings rasping, and I tapped a line to make my hair float. "Jenks, it's November. Don't make me say that someone should be here to guard the church!" I shouted, and he backed down, his furtive gaze going to the top of the hall and Getty's bright singing in the kitchen. He must have made up with her already.

"Good. We will wait until after sunset and Bis is awake." Ivy settled deeper with a slice of pizza. "He's gotten good at recognizance."

Al cleared his throat. "And when they discover your book missing? What then?"

"I will laugh in their face and remind them she changed the deal, not me." But I knew that wouldn't stick. Not with the coven. Not if I snuck in and took it.

Thick fingers slow, Al set the magazine down and reached for that tiny vest pocket again. "Or you can take both and they will never know you have either of them," he suggested.

"I only need a photo of Kisten's curse," I said, and Ivy went still.

Jenks snickered. "You saying you're going to help Rachel? For nothing?"

"Oh, not nothing." Al grinned a not-nice smile. "I will help her theft remain unnoticed for a time, but in return I want the book that *Madam Coven Leader* tempted you with. The one in elven script that contains, as you say, *Kisten's curse.*"

I bristled. "Why? So you can keep me from doing it?"

Al glanced at Ivy. "No. I have a suspicion that Newt wrote it, elven script withstanding. I want the entire book, not simply the curse." He waved his hand. "Besides, a photo won't do. There's likely hidden text."

I frowned. He was right. A picture would help, but Newt often put a key component under lemon juice, so to speak. "If I steal it, it's my book," I said, and he took a breath to protest. "I will, however, let you hold it in trust for me if you help me twist the curse to raise Kisten's ghost."

Ivy swallowed hard, listening to Jenks whisper something in her ear. Her hands clenched with a white-knuckled strength, and Al studied her carefully before making a slow, deliberate nod.

"Done." Al scooted forward, his fingers dipping into that little pocket to set the flat, round stone with a hole in its center on the table with a loud click. Jenks went to investigate, and I leaned in, interested, when his dust brought a faint scratching of runes into bright relief. My reach for it hesitated, then became surer when Al flamboyantly gestured to have at it.

I picked it up. More runes were on the other side. I could feel it connecting to the ley lines through me, and I wondered what it did. It had a hole. Maybe I could see magical threats through it. "What does it do?"

Al's gaze slid to Ivy and Jenks, the two of them as quiet and unobtrusive as he had been, now that the shoe was on the other foot. "Mmmm," he hedged, clearly uncomfortable talking magic around them. "It overlays the image of one object or person onto another."

"A doppelganger charm?" Jenks scoffed. "Rache knows how to do that."

Al's lip twitched and he took the stone from me. "It is *not* a doppelganger charm," he said haughtily. "It is a transposition glamour. Like most glamours, it can be seen through with a deliberate scrutiny. It's limited. You cannot disguise a cat as a teacup. But making one cat look like another, or turning a children's book into a demon tome?" He gauged the stone's weight in his hand. "That, it can do. And fast."

"You're saying I could overlay the image of another book onto the one with Kisten's curse? She won't know I took it."

"Until she opens up the false one," Al said. "The stone makes a connection between the curse and your visual cortex, enabling you to perform the transposition glamour as many times as you want as quickly as you can speak it. Right now the stone is sensitized to Newt, but I can link it to you." He hesitated expectantly. "I'm curious. What do you propose to leave in its stead?"

A slow sigh sifted through me. I wouldn't be stealing only my book back from the coven but also one of theirs. The book he wanted. A rude chuckle escaped me as I glanced at Ivy. "I think I know just the thing."

CHAPTER

6

"YOU WANT TO TWIST A VISUAL-CORTEX CURSE WHERE?" I DROPPED the book I wanted to leave at Elyse's onto the small slate table in the sanctuary with a dull *thwap*. It was the vampire dating guide, and I thought it the perfect thumb in your face for when Elyse figured out I'd gotten my book and left a dud in its place.

"The pool table." Al stood before it, his feet spaced wide as he dramatically pondered the table set in the corner of the sanctuary. My cue sat propped against a window frame, a cube of chalk on the sill. I didn't play often, and not at all since Lee had cracked it. It was Kisten's table, and it reminded me of him. It was also why I kept paying to get it fixed.

"Is this a problem?" Al drawled, elegant voice mocking.

"It's cracked. The slate table on the porch is pretty big. It won't take me maybe a half hour to get a fire going out there. Warm it up. Or we could bring the table in here."

The demon spun, but the fast movement lacked his usual pizzazz without his customary long frock-coat tails. "It will take a good day for the stone to warm up and lose the moisture from being outside. No." Al gestured at the pool table. "This is perfect. Crack and all."

Peeved, I scuffed closer. I'd used the table to spell on before. The slate was from an ancient lake and it made for a very nice surface. That Al wanted to rip the felt off made me glad that Ivy had gone to borrow a car for the evening. Apart from her memories and an urn of ashes, the table was all she had left of Kisten.

Al stared at the green felt as if it was an insult. "Your choice of a replacement book leaves much to be desired," he intoned, and I quashed a flash of annoyance.

"Rynn Cormel's dating guide? I think it's great."

"It's superlative, but you're not thinking beyond short-term personal satisfaction," Al said distantly. "It's a textbook on vampire blood sex. When she opens it to do a little light reading, which you know she will, she will see through the glamour. A transposition charm changes what the outside looks like, not the inside. Not to mention it won't smell right. The book containing Kisten's curse reeks of burnt amber, does it not? You do not want to give yourself away because of someone's nasal clarity."

"Now that you mention it, it did not," I said slowly, and Al looked at me over his blue-tinted glasses in question. Either the coven found a way to deodorize it, or it had left the ever-after before it became a polluted burnt-amber hell.

Jenks darted in from the kitchen, clearly having heard our conversation. "So? She needs to learn that Rachel is better than her," the pixy said as he landed on the eight ball, his dust briefly turning it silver.

"No, he's right." Disappointed, I began to roll the pool balls into the pockets. "I'll just glamour something she has there." But yeah. It would have been nice to have thumbed my nose at her.

The last of the balls went rolling out of sight, and I turned to Al. "Okay. What do I need to link the curse to my visual cortex?"

A wide, truly pleased smile found Al. He was, at his heart, a teacher, and he didn't have much of a chance to indulge himself now that he wasn't abducting high-end magic users and training them to be demon familiars. "Other than a suitably large space to work on?" Back straight, he began to tick things off on his fingers. "Salt with which to scribe, white sage and rosemary to help promote purity and remove negative energy. A copper or rosemary stylus, saffron-infused wine, magnetic chalk . . ."

His red, goat-slitted eyes met mine over his glasses again. "And your blood," he intoned, his overdone drama quickly dissolving into a smirk. Blood was a common ingredient in spells, charms, and curses to link the magic to the user—and it still scared the crap out of humans for some reason.

"You sure you don't want to do this in the kitchen?" I tried one last time. "That's where most of my stuff is."

Al ignored me.

"Pool table it is," I muttered as I walked away. It wasn't an extensive list, but as sure as hell is hot, it wasn't complete. He'd left out much of what I'd need to prep the charm, leaving it to me to figure out as part of his ongoing instruction. Stuff like a bowl, and a ceremonial knife to get the blood from my finger. "Jenks, we got any saffron?" I shouted over my shoulder. I knew we had saffron. I just wanted him to stop making annoying circles around Al.

"On it," he said eagerly as he flew past me and into the kitchen.

My pace slowed as I followed him into my brightly lit kitchen, the space a wonderful blend of a state-inspected facility and home-spelled chaos. The recent rebuild had focused on keeping our emergency paranormal shelter status. It was mostly for the tax break, but it also meant the city had subsidized both the twin stoves and ovens as well as the huge fridge we used only a third of, apart from the solstice and the Super Bowl. There was a large center counter to bake at, and a long eat-at counter that looked out onto the porch through a wide pane of glass. French doors opened to the covered porch, which was really more of a three-walled room, with the original fireplace taking up one entire rebuilt wall. It could be used as additional eating space in a pinch, which was how we sold it to the city, but most times it was a pleasant place to sit outside with all the comforts of inside.

Beyond the porch, the damp, windy night had turned the garden into a black expanse of nothing. Al had left a light on at his wagon/van amid the tombstones, and it made the night seem even colder.

"Jenks?" I called, not seeing the pixy. "Ever-loving pixy piss, you didn't go outside in this, did you?"

"No, I didn't go outside," a high, muffled voice came from inside the cabinets. "I stashed the saffron in here away from the fairies."

Jenks exploded out from a drawer, his dust flying when he sneezed. "Saffron," he said as he set a glass vial the size of his thigh on the counter. "Apparently they think it's an aphrodisiac."

"Ah, thanks." I took the vial and dropped it into a pocket.

"That's why you can't ever find any." Jenks's downward angle to alight on the counter bobbled when a loud ripping sound came from the sanctuary. I was *really* glad Ivy wasn't here, and as Jenks went to watch Al, I got the wine and three-pound bag of spelling salt from the pantry. The copper stylus was in a drawer, and I grabbed my silver snips just in case. The magnetic chalk was in a coffee mug with a bunch of pens and pencils, and from the herb pantry I got a sheaf of white sage and a sprig of rosemary. At the last moment, I dug through the junk drawer for a fingerstick in case I didn't need the knife.

"He didn't say you needed the fingerstick," Jenks said as he darted back in, wings pink in anticipation. Unlike Ivy, he liked my witchy magic.

"He didn't say I needed the knife, either." Hands on my hips, I studied the growing pile and tried to anticipate. Sage meant smudging—which meant fire. I'd probably need something to burn it in, and I added a crucible—the copper one, since he'd made a point of asking for a copper stylus. Nodding, I put it all in my largest spell pot, then added my Srandford bowl because of the wine, a length of silk to dust the free ions from the table with, and finally Ivy's spray bottle of enzymatic blood remover—for not-so-obvious reasons.

Jenks snickered, and I included a spray bottle of salt water to remove any residual spells from the slate. One last look, and I grabbed the roll of paper towels and a second black scarf.

"That's all I can think of," I said as I shifted the pot to my hip and headed for the sanctuary, wincing as a second, longer rip echoed through the church.

Jenks flew ahead, his sour comment an inaudible nothing as I passed the two bedrooms and adjoining his and hers bathrooms now converted into a communal bath on one side, and a more family-oriented bath and laundry on the other.

"Tink's titties," Jenks said as I entered the sanctuary, his hands on his hips as he hovered over the damage. "You couldn't just magic it off? Even Hodin had the decency to magic it off."

"You should leave," Al practically growled. Cutting the felt from the bumpers was Al's only recourse, seeing as he couldn't tap a line yet—thanks to me. Al insisted that burning his synapses to unuse was a small price to pay for imprisoning his brother, but he'd done it to protect me while I'd done the actual imprisoning—and I still felt bad. Hence me not complaining about him setting up in the garden.

And still, I had to stifle my annoyance as I took in the damage. It was Kisten's table and everyone kept shitting on it.

"It is what it is, Jenks," I said, more to me than him, as I set the bowl at one end of the table. "Al, do I need to change into a spelling robe or am I good?"

"You are fine as you are." Al sniffed, clearly surprised—and grateful perhaps. "We are not working with auras. It's a simple spell. Minimal smut." Red eyes narrowing, he squinted at Jenks. "Keep your dust clear of the table or I will put you in a box."

Flipping the demon off, Jenks flew backward to land on the tip of my pool cue.

Please stay there, I thought as I began unpacking the bowl. Jenks didn't entirely trust Al, but I did. And truly, it wasn't that long ago that spelling with a demon would have scared the crap out of me. Al, though, had mellowed when he regained the ability to come and go freely in reality—all the demons had—and with the pain had gone a lot of their need to punish. Al was an exceptional teacher, and I'd caught him calling me Ceri on more than one occasion. I took it as a compliment, seeing as the powerful elf had been his student and companion for over a thousand years before she died protecting Ray and Lucy from a demon bent on dominating two realities.

But what I think I liked most about Al's teaching style was how it forced me to think. His list had been everything I'd need even as it was absent on what I'd use for technique. I'd have to think through the spell, decide if silver snips would work better than iron, or if I could use a finger-stick instead of a ceremonial knife. Copper bowls gave you a different result than, say, a walnut one, but sometimes it didn't make a difference. Knowing when it did was a matter of instinct, and developing that instinct would ultimately lengthen my lifespan. A poorly twisted curse could kill you. Not to mention that most demons left things out of their written spells and curses as a way to keep their secrets. The ability to parse out what wasn't written down was priceless.

Which was why I took the time to layer a heavy spray of Ivy's enzymatic no-blood on the entire de-felted table.

Al, though, frowned at the scent of citrus. "What," he said flatly, "are you doing?"

I didn't feel even a twinge of overkill. "The charm links to me through my blood, right?" I said as Jenks snickered knowingly from the tip of my cue stick. "Do you have any idea what Kisten and Ivy have done on this table? You want me to get the black light?"

The demon hesitated. "Continue," he muttered.

"Thought so." But the mist had puddled long enough, and I used the paper towels to soak up the excess before putting another layer of salt water down.

Al sighed impatiently as I wiped it dry and threw the waste into the empty copper pot.

"Hey, you're the one who wanted to use a nonspecific spelling table to spell on," I said.

"Rache, I gotta get some air." Jenks hovered before me, his dust a fading gray. The citrus scent was getting to him, and I nodded. Path bobbling, he flew to the kitchen.

"If we may begin?" Al intoned, and I snapped the black silk scarf out, carefully dusting the entire table for free ions.

"Absolutely," I said as I tucked the silk into my waistband, and he rolled his eyes.

"You are being excessive," he said. "Don't expect brownie points."

I stood at one end of the table with my things, he at the other. "You said it is Newt's charm, yes? And I'm trying to connect it to my visual cortex? My brain, basically? I don't want to screw it up because I was in a hurry. And besides," I whispered, "it got rid of Jenks."

Al shot a glance at the empty hallway and nodded. "So it did." He took a slow breath, and I could almost see his teaching hat go on. "The charm is already contained in the stone. What you will be doing is utilizing three pentagrams to firstly burn away its previous link to Newt, secondly to reconnect the stone to yourself, and finally to seal the spell so it does not unravel. To destroy Newt's connection, you will need to prepare a pyre of three smudge sticks made of white sage wrapped with a binding of rosemary. To apply your own link, you will need to make a paintbrush of your hair and the copper stylus. And lastly, you will need to soak that saffron in about a quarter cup of wine to carry your linkage into the stone. If you can warm it, all the better."

Of course I could warm it, but as Al went to drag a cushy chair closer, I used my magnetic chalk to draw a line just under the crack from one still-felt-clad bumper to the other, in essence dividing the table into one-third prep space and two-thirds spelling.

"What are you doing now?" Al said in wonder as he finished arranging his chair.

My motions to wipe the chalk from my fingers faltered. "Visually separating my work area from my spelling area. Why?"

The demon frowned. "I've never seen anyone do that before except—"

His words cut off, and his focus shifted to the stone amulet on the table.

"Who?" I said as I handed him the bottle of wine to open.

"Never mind," he said, his wispy voice holding a tired annoyance. "Continue."

It could be that I was bringing up unwanted memories. No need to pry. "A quarter cup?" I asked to distract him when he set the open bottle at my elbow.

"As I said." Annoyed, he settled himself where he could watch, one knee atop the other.

The saffron would have to soak, so leaving the smudge sticks for later, I poured an estimated quarter cup of wine into my Srandford bowl. It was glass and consequently neutral, and my brow furrowed as I took up the tiny glass vial. There weren't that many strands in there, but that wasn't the reason I shook only three out into my palm. The charm involved three pentagrams to remove the old, install the new, and seal the charm. Three aspects, so therefore three strands.

"Three?" I guessed, and he made a pleased-sounding grunt and a frivolous wave for me to get on with it.

My exhale was louder than I'd meant it to be, and I dropped the saffron strands in and warmed the wine with a quick thought.

Making the paintbrush was next, and I used my silver snips to cut a lock of hair, then plucked three long strands to tie the bundle to the copper stylus with three different knots. Finished, I glanced at Al to see if the three knots should have been the same, but he didn't seem to care—which meant it didn't matter, or I had done it right, or he was going to let it blow up in my face.

Mood sour, I soaked the makeshift paintbrush with a heavy layer of salt water to get rid of the hair straightener charm on it. The entire wad immediately twisted into a perfect curl, but at least I knew it was clean, and I blotted it dry with the ion-free scarf.

"Adequate," Al said, his nose again in my *Witch Monthly*, and I felt a wash of relief. I needed this to work and not be simply a lesson on what not to do.

Satisfied, I took up the white sage and began plucking leaves from all but three of the dried stems, then tightly folding the picked leaves into a packet around each and binding them with a denuded stem of rosemary. "Gordian knot?" I guessed, wanting to be sure.

"If you can manage it," Al said superciliously, a single finger slowly turning a page.

Obviously I could, and the very fact that he wasn't watching meant I was doing it right, but he put the magazine down and stood when I levered myself up to kneel on the table, chalk in hand. Eyeing the open space before me, I set the three smudge sticks down at the top to give myself room to draw three pentagrams total.

Al shook his head, his gaze at the center of the space. "You will be nesting the pentagrams," he said, and I made a small noise. This was something new. "Hence needing the large table," he added. "Put the first in the middle of your space."

"Okay. Thank you." Grateful for the new technique, I set the three unlit smudge sticks in the center. Nodding once sharply, Al set the stone with the hole atop them.

"Keeping your work small, sketch a pentagram of purity around the stone," he directed, and I jumped when he dropped the bag of salt beside me. "Use salt for clarity."

I should have known that, and I tucked the magnetic chalk into a pocket before stretching for my black silk cloth and working it quickly into a cone. Using it like a pastry bag, I carefully traced a small pentagram around the stone. "Runes?" I asked, relieved when I'd finished. I wasn't good at free-drawing pentagrams, but I was getting better.

"Yes, of purity at the points," Al said, nodding in satisfaction when I started at the bottom right leg and moved clockwise. "Very good. The pentagram surrounding it will be of connection," he continued as I worked. "The glyphs commonly used in calling circles are sufficient. Use your blood without the paintbrush. It will not work if the lines of the first pentagram touch the lines of the second."

Finished, I reached for my silver knife.

"And if you use that damned silver knife, I will be most disappointed," he added, throwing something at me.

It was a knife as well. I caught it by instinct and took a moment to study it. Unlike mine, it was copper, the soft metal almost useless. I didn't have one of these. "Jupiter finger?" I guessed. The point was dull, but it would work if I used enough pressure.

"Of course," he drawled.

It took some doing to open the skin enough to get a good flow. Finger moving, I sketched a blood pentagram around the first. Most practitioners equated them with illicit magic, but if it was my blood, what was the hurt? It would make a very secure connection to me, and that was more important than what everyone thought.

The glyphs I could sketch in my sleep, and I inched off the table and wiped my finger clean using the black silk cloth. The final pentagram would be enormous, and I could sketch it with my feet on the floor. "Good?" I said, asking for the next step, not his approval.

"As before, it is adequate." But the smile quirking his lips said different. "You have left yourself barely enough room to sketch the third and final pentagram of permanence around it using the magnetic chalk."

It felt almost done, and I hadn't tapped a line yet other than to warm up the wine. The smudge sticks, though, would need to be lit, and I set a faint ribbon of my awareness into the lines, relishing the warm tingle of power as I drew the final pentagram.

"Ahh, crap," I whispered when I noticed that I'd stained the chalk with my blood, and Al made a noncommittal huff. The pentagram was okay, but the chalk itself was ruined. Fortunately there was about a quarter inch unsullied with which to finish the spell.

"Wait," Al said when I reached to scribe the glyphs of permanence.

"I have another chalk in the kitchen," I said, and he shook his head.

"The chalk is fine. You will scribe the runes mid-spell." Al hesitated. "Can you tell me why?"

I thought about it for a moment, frowning. "Because if I do it now, the permanence will adhere to the table, not the spell? Seeing as it's nested?" I guessed, and the demon grunted in satisfaction, his thick fingers reaching to tug at lace that wasn't there.

"Correct!" he said. "You will now begin the spell. Do not work ahead of what I tell you to do. You have set it up properly, and as a reward, I will ensure that you finish it such that you have a functioning transposition charm."

I couldn't help my grin. "Thank you." And whereas showing any appreciation had once been fraught with a sullen annoyance, it now was laced with true gratitude. It felt like a win even if this last part was going to be fed to me as if I was a child. If I hadn't shown the level of proficiency he expected me to have, he would have let me screw it up. He had before. Once. And then I learned to think.

Al came closer, the scent of redwood and burnt amber a pleasant mix. "Light the three smudge sticks with your thoughts, but do not contain the smoke in a circle. Leave it free to disperse as it will—because . . ." he prompted.

I had no idea. "To allow for the impurities to escape?" I guessed.

His held breath slipped from him. "Possibly. Try it and see."

Al had already assured me that I would end up with a functioning charm, so I pulled deeper on the ley line, letting the tingling potential fill me until I pushed a wad of the energy into my hand and flicked it at the smudge sticks. *"Flagro,"* I said softly to harness the black-and-red-smeared ball of energy arching through the air, giving it agency and focus. Giving it magic.

The spoken spell hit the smudge sticks, and they burst into a bright flame, which quickly dulled into a billowing black smoke.

"Ah, the smoke detector . . ." I said, surprised at how fast it was burning.

But then I realized that the smoke and ash were settling only within the area defined by the second pentagram, in effect rubbing out the lines of the first.

"Oh! Cool," I said, unabashedly delighted as I glanced at Al. *Nested and self-erasing.*

Al leaned forward to eye the settling soot. "Newt's connection is now gone and the stone is open. Seeing as the outer pentagram is not sealed with glyphs and the innermost is nulled, you may enter the middle pentagram and use the copper stylus to apply your blood to the stone, thus creating an additional point of connection to you."

"One side okay?" I asked, seeing the logic behind it. I pricked my pinky this time, using my homemade brush to apply three drops of blood to the stone.

"One side is sufficient." He tapped the Srandford bowl to make the wine ripple. "Douse it. Saffron filaments and all."

The wine would probably carry my blood into the stone. It was going to make a mess, though. Wincing, I poured the quarter cup of wine onto the blood-painted, ash-smeared stone.

"Good," Al said, a hint of pride showing when the wine flooded the middle pentagram, the outermost . . . and then stopped at the chalk lines. It had defined the outermost pentagram while washing away the second. "Now apply the runes of permanence."

I knew them, obviously, and I quickly put them at the points, whispering their names and feeling the strength of the ley line grow as a stronger link was forged between me and the stone.

"All that is left is reciting the three phrases used to make the charm work," Al said, and then quietly pushed a strip of paper to me.

I smiled when I took it up, quickly reading and recognizing the Latin as the same inscribed on the stone. But the thrill that spilled through me was because he had trusted that I was going to do this right, so much so that he had written down the words ahead of time.

"*A priori*," I said, hoping my pronunciation was right. It meant "from the former," and a quiver went through me when I saw the glyphs engraved upon the stone begin to glow. "*A posteriori*," I added, and the glyphs brightened. "From the latter"—easy enough.

"*Omnia mutantur*," I said, nodding. It meant "everything changes," and I remembered it from another transference curse I had used before.

The writings on the stone burst into a horrific brightness, and my pulse quickened when a pinging sensation seemed to arch into me, quickly fading.

Al reached for the stone, rubbing the last of the ash from it before handing it to me. "It's yours," he said. "And yours alone." He hesitated, then added in a lighthearted voice, "Well done. A glamour can be seen through by anyone with a sharp enough intuition, but to break it entirely, use *finis*. Because it's linked to both you and the collective, you can glamour more than one thing at a time. I would be cautious in that regard. I've always found less is more."

I couldn't stop my grin. The stone was warm in my hand, and I wanted to try it out.

"Go on." Al waved a hand at me as if shooing chickens. "Tap a line, look at the object you want to lift the image of through the stone, and recite the first incantation."

What to copy . . . I spun a slow circle, raising the stone to my eye when I saw my *Witch Monthly* magazine. *"A priori,"* I said, and a quiver of line energy rippled through me.

Al dropped the vampire sex guide onto the table with an attention-getting smack. "Gaze upon what you want to disguise and recite the second."

Beaming, I peered through the hole at it. *"A posteriori,"* I said, then lowered the rock. It hadn't changed.

"And invoke it by speaking the third phrase through the hole, thereby carrying the spell to it?" Al suggested, and I felt myself warm.

Of course. "Omnia mutantur," I whispered through the hole. My breath streamed through the stone, pulling a haze of energy straight from the ley lines to settle over the book and soak in.

Slowly my smile faded. "It didn't work," I said, disappointed, but Al chuckled and swept Cormel's dating guide up, riffling through it in interest.

"It did," he said, lingering over an illustration as he turned the book on its side. "Since you cast it, you can't see the changes unless you look through the stone."

Curious, I brought the stone to my eye, excitement tingling to my toes as Al was suddenly holding a magazine. "So it's kind of a spell checker, too," I said, and the demon snorted.

"It's a transposition charm. You see things that are transposed. Magicked things appear as they truly are, and things the stone has glamoured appear as everyone else sees them. Don't ask me how it knows. It's like a thermos." He let the book drop with a thud that a magazine never would have been able to manage. Expression pleased, he grabbed the open bottle of wine and started for the kitchen. "I suggest you put it on a lanyard, but don't run anything through the hole. You'll ruin the spell."

"Thanks, Al," I said, getting a half-assed wave as he continued on, shoulders hunched.

Tickled, I opened my fist and ran a finger over the warm stone. I'd loop some wire around it and put it on a length of chain. "Hey, Al?" I called after him. "Do you think someone might have disguised the Atlantean mirror with a glamour?"

Al drew to a halt in the hall, his silhouette ominous as he half turned to me. "No. You can't transpose things that reflect. I'm sorry, Rachel. You have until June, and then it's Alcatraz, the coven, or me."

And as he spun to go out to his wagon in my graveyard, I began to wonder why I was working so hard to stay here.

IVY HAD BROUGHT THE LEFTOVER PIZZA, STILL IN ITS BOX, IN CASE
we wanted to play pizza delivery to get into Elyse's bungalow. Cold or not,
it smelled delicious, and I nibbled a crust down to nothing as we sat in the
curbside parking and waited for Bis to return from his recon. The narrow
two-story had a postage-stamp yard, but it was more elaborately landscaped than the others in the old-school neighborhood. If I had to guess,
I'd say it was the original show home to help the developer sell as-yet un-
restored properties.

The area was quiet despite the plethora of cars parked on both curbs,
having a busy nightlife just a street over with eateries, a niche market, and
a couple of trendy bars. Clearly the developers were taking a page from the
Detroit rebuild and were trying to create a small-town feel in a large me-
tropolis by keeping the buildings low and fostering a mix of chic com-
merce and residences. Which, when you broke it down, was really an old
idea given new life. More to the point, it was working to keep property
values high by restoring much of Cincy's old architecture. Unfortunately,
until there were more of these "recovered" neighborhoods, everyone wanted
to be here and the bars were servicing more than the small community.
Parking was dear.

Ivy jumped at the thump on the roof, her pale hands on the wheel
tensing at the sliding hiss of wings as Bis craned his neck to look into the
car. The cat-size gargoyle's red eyes were eager, and his pebbly black skin

only made the white tufts on his ears and tail stand out all the more. His great leathery wings were extended for balance, and he beat them once when he slipped off the roof and lurched to find a perch on the open window like a drive-in-eatery tray.

I'd felt his presence before he had landed, and that our mental link was slowly returning was a huge relief. Maybe in a decade or so it would again be strong enough that he could teach me to jump the ley lines and I wouldn't be so damned vulnerable.

"I didn't go in," the gargoyle said, now a rosy pink for having slipped. He was only fifty, barely old enough to be out from under his parents' watchful attention. That he had bonded himself to me was an honor, but I was scared to death that I'd fail him. As usual, he wasn't wearing any clothes. He didn't need them, being able to create his own heat at will. He was lightweight despite his stony mien and could triple his size and weight by absorbing water much as a bridge troll did.

"The TV is going," Bis added, angling his white-tufted ears to the townhome. "Elyse isn't there, though. It's a little boy. Maybe ten?"

I glanced at Ivy as Bis's great claws carefully pinched the open window. "Elyse has a kid?" I guessed, immediately dismissing it. She was only twenty herself—best case.

"Brother, maybe," Ivy said, her focus going distant in thought.

My brow furrowed as I had second thoughts as well. Our assumption that the coven would be waiting for me at the offices seemed right, but we hadn't planned on a kid being here. Violating the sanctity of her home, as temporary as it was, didn't feel like an option anymore.

"I don't know about this," I said, fiddling with the transposition stone around my neck. I had spent some time wrapping it in a copper wire and attaching it to a lanyard, and the strand of black gold was cool in my fingers.

Bis's tail curved around his feet, the tip twitching. "He's asleep in front of the TV with a spell book. I think it's the one you want."

I heaved a sigh, torn. If the kid wasn't there, it would be a no-brainer. But a small part of me wondered what a ten-year-old was doing reading a demon text. "I don't want to scare anyone," I said, looking at my bag with its splat gun. "Or be seen."

Ivy reached for the door handle. "You need the spell to recover Kisten." As if that was all there was to it, she pushed open the door with her foot, grabbed the pizza box, and got out, shutting the door hard. "It's not breaking and entering if they open the door," she said through the open window.

Bis grinned. "That's unlawful entry," he said, and with one wing pulse, he was in the air.

Uneasy, I grabbed my bag and got out. "It's still breaking and entering if it involves coercion or deceit," I grumbled as we crossed the street. "The place was supposed to be empty."

"Relax, I do this all the time." Ivy's boot heels clicked smartly. "I ring the bell, you hit him with a sleepy-time charm. I catch him. He'll be fine. No drama, no trauma."

Perhaps, I thought, head up as I fumbled in my bag for my cherry-red splat gun. I hadn't counted on leaving a witness, much less a minor, and I wondered at Ivy's zeal. She was usually overly protective of kids. *But this is about Kisten,* I realized. The way she probably saw it, the coven was withholding Kisten's resurrection from her.

A gust of wind blew an escaped strand of hair into my face as Bis hovered over us. "I'll get the camera," he said, gravelly voice eager—and then he was gone until his black shadow clung like a bat to the peak of the roof and he tilted the camera away from the steps. It wasn't as slick as when Jenks put them on a loop, but it worked.

Confident and sure, Ivy strode up the front steps and rang the buzzer. "Maybe you should . . ." she suggested, making a nod toward the shrubbery by the door, and I slid out of sight.

That ugly feeling rose at the sound of light feet inside. It was too late to change our plan, though, as the door opened to show a kid dressed in a pair of jeans and a Howlers' hoodie.

"Ah, I didn't order a pizza," he said, his high voice holding a questioning lilt. "You have the wrong house."

KIM HARRISON

From the other side of the door, Bis pantomimed shooting him, but he was ten, and I was not happy with this.

Sighing, Ivy looked at the box as if reading a label. "Is this 12A Walnut Street, Mount Arrie?"

The kid rocked back. "Right street, wrong subdivision. This is Circle Bluffs."

Ivy's lip twitched in annoyance, probably because I hadn't shot him yet. "It's cold, anyway," she said, buying time for me to move. "You want it?"

"That's from Piscary's, isn't it?" he said, his eagerness sounding nothing like a ten-year-old, and then he hesitated, his mood becoming suspicious. "You're not a witch. Why do I smell witch?"

Bis winced, and I stepped forward. "Because she's with me," I said, and the kid's breath caught. If he was ten, he was a small ten, black hair and hazel eyes. Slim.

"Morgan!" the kid blurted, shocking all three of us. "I knew it!" he crowed as if pleased.

Ivy moved, eerily fast as she took a step forward and shoved him inside. "Quiet, Junior," she said as the kid pinwheeled over the threshold, his shock melting into anger.

He knows me? I followed Ivy in and shut the door. Bis was a white shadow on the ceiling, having shifted his color to remain unnoticed. Stumbling, the boy caught his balance and stood in the hallway as if to bar our way.

"Relax." Ivy dropped the half-eaten pizza on the hall table. "We don't want you. We want a book."

I couldn't bring myself to shoot him, and I held my splat gun behind my back and tried to find a soothing smile. That is, until someone tapped the nearest ley line. Hard.

"It's the kid!" I said when he dropped into a stance, arms moving dramatically as he gathered enough ley line energy to fry a cow. His short black hair lifted, and his focus fixed on me with an odd, anticipatory gleam. "Ivy, he's packing!"

94

Definitely one of the coven kids in waiting, I decided as I yanked on the ley line and his gaze shot to me.

"Do something, Rachel!" Bis said from the ceiling, and the kid's attention shattered.

Line energy sizzed to make my hands tingle and my legs a wobbly mess. I knew better than to engage the coven using magic, and so I swung my pistol up instead.

The kid's eyes dropped from Bis. *"Rhombus!"* he shouted, and a thick circle rose up around him. Purple and green, his aura-tainted circle took my first two shots until he rolled and broke it. I followed, hoping that when his circle fell, I might get a shot in.

Every single one missed, and I pushed past Ivy to follow him into the townhome.

"Why didn't you shoot him at the door?" Ivy practically snarled, ghosting past me with her vampiric speed.

"Kid gloves, Ivy!" I shouted as I got a glimpse of a cozy, well-appointed living room, a gas fireplace going before an overdone couch and chair. The TV was on to the news, which I thought was odd, but it was the thick, ratty book on the end table that kept my attention. The faint scent of burnt amber tickled my nose, but it wasn't coming from the book Al wanted. It still had the black napkin in it to mark the curse that could bring Kisten back as a ghost. *One down, one to go.*

Ivy had pinned the kid against a wall of leather-bound books with her hand around his biceps. "Where's the book to recover Kisten's ghost?" she demanded as she hunched over him and showed her small, sharp fangs.

"Bad move, Tamwood," the kid said—and then Ivy cried out as a purple and green haze shocked through her, shifting her aura into the visible spectrum for an agonizing instant.

Ivy fell to the floor, and suddenly I didn't have a problem shooting him.

"That was a mistake," I said as I pointed my splat gun at him and inched toward Ivy.

The kid looked nothing like a ten-year-old as he snickered, hands wreathed with line energy while he backed away from Ivy. "I told Elyse you wouldn't show at the office. Glad I drew the short straw."

"If you have hurt Ivy, I will not be gentle," I threatened. She was at my feet, but I didn't dare take my eyes off him to see if she was okay.

"Good." He squared up and beckoned me closer. "Show me what you got, demon girl."

Demon girl? I thought, jerking clear when the kid threw an unfocused ball of energy.

I hit it with my own, and the two fizzed and popped until they spent themselves on each other. It had been a test throw, both to see my reaction time and to find out if I could sense how much energy he was packing. This was not ten-year-old behavior, coven apprentice or not.

"You and me. Right now," he said, sounding like an old man despite his high voice.

"I got her, Rachel," Bis whispered. "She's okay."

That was all I needed. "Now works for me," I said, then threw a ball of raw energy to his right.

The kid predictably turned to get it, almost missing the real spell I threw at him. And I say almost, because he managed to catch it after deflecting the first, holding the second in his hands as if to take control of it.

"*Voulden,*" I intoned, giving the raw energy we both claimed direction. The spell was elven, and I was betting he didn't know it.

Shock lit through him at the delayed invocation, and then the spell triggered, racing over him with little sparkles of my aura until they soaked in and shorted him out. Choking, the kid dropped, out cold before he even hit the floor.

"I don't have time for you," I said, angry as I spun. "Ivy?"

"She's breathing." Bis stood at her head, a craggy hand touching her forehead. "Her aura is fine. What did he hit her with?"

I glanced at the kid to make sure he was still out. "I think I know what this is," I said as I put a hand to her as well and a tingling hint of the spell he used whispered through my thoughts. "Vivian tried it on me once." I exhaled and ran a light trace of ley line energy through both of us. Feeling it, Bis pulled his hand away. "There's a reason Vivian and I argued without bringing the lines into it. Until she quit trying to impress me with her magic, she taught me oh so many good things," I added, then focused on Ivy. "*Corrumpo*," I whispered, letting only the faintest hint of the demon curse race through her.

It was one of Newt's. I'd seen the insane demon take down one hell of a circle with it, and I figured it would break anything the coven would know. Sure enough, it did. I eased back on my heels when I felt the charm flake away and Ivy took a deeper breath. "Give her some space," I warned as Ivy sat up in a quick spasm of motion.

A shudder raced through me at the utter blackness of her eyes, pupil dark until she realized where she was. "He shocked me, the little shit," she said, fingertips pressed into her head.

I stood, hand extended to help her rise. "I told you he was packing. You okay?"

"I'm fine." Clearly peeved, she let me pull her up and she glared at him on the floor, only the barest rim of brown about her pupils. "How long was I out? Did you find Kisten's book?"

"I haven't had a chance to look yet," I said, answering both questions with one answer. "I'm pretty sure the one on the table has Kisten's curse in it. Mine has to be here somewhere."

"On it!" Wings flapping once, Bis flew to the bookcase, landing to hang upside down and run a gnarled finger over the titles. "These aren't even spell books," the gargoyle said, his white-tufted ears pinned, and Ivy went to help look.

"It's a good place to hide one, though," she said as she began tilting them forward to make sure nothing was hidden behind.

I breathed deep, studying the room. Burnt amber was a hint, so faint I couldn't place where it was coming from. The feel of the room was less home and more glorified hotel. The overdone scalloped woodwork didn't seem like Elyse's style, and the overstuffed couch and chair too dark for her. Annoyed, I grabbed the remote and clicked the TV off. I would have liked to have left a lighter footprint, but with Junior here, that was a boat long sailed.

"You think he was watching the news to see if we got caught breaking into the coven's offices?" I said as I dragged the kid to the chair and hoisted his limp form into it.

"Maybe." Bis turned from inspecting the books. "Something is off with him."

"You mean other than his magic?" Ivy said, her back to me as she searched.

"He's probably the coven's next whatever." In a moment of pity, I shifted his head so he wouldn't wake up with a stiff neck.

Hoping we hadn't made a mistake, I picked up the book on the end table and thumbed to the spell marked by the black napkin. It *looked* like the right book, the illustrations and cramped handwriting being the same as what I'd seen in Elyse's office. The subliminal tingle from the ley lines rising through it to meet me were familiar, too. But I couldn't read elven, and I didn't trust Elyse any farther than I could throw her.

"Bis, you want to take a look at this?" I set the open book on the coffee table with a thump. "Make sure it's the right one before we walk out with it?"

The little gargoyle perked up, his lionlike tail switching. "Sure." His wings flashed open as he pulled a book off the shelf and staggered into the air. "This one is about the right size to replace it," he said as he beat his wings thrice and landed heavily on the table, a *Reader's Digest Condensed Books* leather-bound doorstop in his arms. "That kid is going to tell them you were here. I don't think glamouring it will help much."

Brow furrowed, Ivy looked from replacing the couch's cushions. "You could dose him into forgetting," she suggested.

"No, too risky." There was no way I'd dose the kid into forgetting we had been here. That was a one-way ticket to Alcatraz. "Well, Bis?" I asked, and he glanced from the book splayed before him.

"Looks legit," he said as he closed the book and backed away, that little black napkin in his hand. "Spell 'em."

Easy enough. I took my new transposition charm from around my neck and stared through the hole at the book Elyse had tried to lure me with. *"A priori,"* I said, and a quiver of line energy rippled through me, the power going nowhere but simply pooling, waiting for direction.

I turned my attention to the doorstop of that *Reader's Digest. "A posteriori."*

The energy tingling at my fingers doubled. *"Omnia mutantur,"* I whispered, speaking the words through the stone. The magic poured from my lips, visible like a smoky fire as it settled over the red, gold-gilded monstrosity and soaked in. As before, the book looked the same to me. "Did it work?"

Ivy came over, impatience making her motions sharp. "Yes. Wow. If I hadn't seen you do it, I would never guess." She flipped one open to show stark white pages and a regular typeset monotony. "They look exactly alike on the outside." Expression closed, she took the black napkin from Bis, put it between the pages of the fake one, and shut it. "Make sure you take the right one."

"No kidding." But when I went to put it in my bag, Bis held his hands out, a wistful expression on him.

"Um, maybe I should make sure it's all there," he said, and I nodded.

"Good idea. Thanks," I said softly as he settled himself right there on the table, his black, gnarled fingers holding a book almost as large as he was. "Any luck on finding the one she kept?"

"I'm sure it's here. I can smell it," Ivy said, her back to me as she continued to search, and I shifted the decoy with the black napkin back to the end table.

"Maybe they left it at the office," Bis said, his head bowed low over the old text, and I moved to stand before the shelf, hands on my hips.

"Maybe." I fingered the transposition charm, thinking. "They could have disguised it," I said as I peered through the stone for a telltale sign of mischief. *Nothing,* I mused, turning on a slow heel to do a circuit of the room.

Again, everything seemed to be as it should be—until I gazed through the stone at the kid and he aged right before my eyes, suddenly buck-naked and sprawled in the chair with his legs stretched out and his head lolling. His cheeks were shaved, and he looked to be about sixty, which meant he could be as old as a hundred. It was a witch thing.

"U-uh," I stammered, glancing over the stone to see a slim ten-year-old in jeans and a hoodie, his sneakers dangling over the floor. "Guys?" Breath held, I tried to nudge his knobby, old foot with mine, my boot encountering nothing. He might look six-foot-two through the stone, but it was an image. Like a placeholder. "I don't think our little kid is really a kid." *Why is he naked?* I wondered as I handed the stone to Bis and the gargoyle peered through it.

"What am I supposed to be seeing?" he said, and Ivy took the stone from him.

Confused, I glanced between her and the, uh, kid. "You don't see an older man?" I said, deciding to keep to myself that he was also naked.

Ivy shook her head and gave the stone back to me.

"Me either," Bis said. "But his aura is wrong. It's too complex for a ten-year-old."

"Huh." I tucked the stone into a pocket. "He's been spelled younger. I'm going to say demon curse, maybe, because it's not a glamour." I flushed, remembering his smooth skin and, uh, yeah. I'd obviously seen naked men before, but only when the person in question wanted me to, and I felt like a voyeur.

"Why would they do that?" Ivy asked, and I grabbed a couch pillow and set it on his lap.

"To put us off guard?" I guessed. "I'm going to wake him up. He might know where my book is. Bis, make yourself and the book we're walking out of here with scarce."

Bis's haunches bunched, and then he launched himself into the air, landing awkwardly on the top of a bookcase, where he could watch everything and remain out of sight. Head down, he continued to read as I put a couple of zip strips on the guy, first around his wrists to keep him contained, and then one about a slim ankle. Their core of magicked silver would keep him from tapping a line. It wasn't hard to make a magic user impotent, which was why I kept my membership up at the local dojo.

He really was the size of a ten-year-old. But that was not what I saw through the stone, and I stood nervously before him. *"Honna tara surrundus."* I said the elven words to break the sleep spell, hoping I got the pronunciation right. The kid, or guy, I guess, came to with a snort. His focus shifted from the three of us facing him to the pillow on his lap and back again. I could tell when he reached for a ley line, not because I felt it but because his expression went ugly. Too ugly for a ten-year-old.

Smug, I crouched to put us eye to eye. "Hi. We're going to play a little game. Hot and cold. You know how to play that, right?" I pitched my voice as if I were talking to a kindergartner, and his expression darkened even more.

"You can go to hell on a stick," he said, his high voice holding a scary amount of anger.

Ivy put her hands on her knees and bent over him. "I'd smack him, but I don't like hitting people who don't have to shave yet."

"Mmmm, go ahead." I stood, not comfortable with my head that close to Ivy's. Not when her pupils were that big. "He's not ten."

Bis snickered. "Definitely not ten," he said from the bookcase, and the kid twisted, craning his neck to try to find him.

"Hey. Hey!" Ivy exclaimed, snapping her fingers for his attention. "Eyes forward, sport."

"You can see me?" the kid said, and I frowned as it began to come together.

"You knew me," I mused as I peered through the stone, glad I'd put the pillow where I had. "Which isn't unusual. Most of the city does. But why did the coven leave you here guarding a book?"

His gaze darted to the glamoured copy on the end table, and I set a gentle hand on it, feeling nothing from the disguised *Reader's Digest*. "You're coven, aren't you. Are you Scott?" I guessed, and the "kid" looked torn between annoyance and relief. "You were like a hundred this afternoon. What happened?"

"Yeah, well, now I'm ten," he said, high voice bitter. "I'll be older in the morning."

Ivy smiled, and a shiver crossed me. "If he's not ten, I can bite him."

Scott's nasty smile faded, and I shook my head. "And add a vampire scar to his misery? We are not that cruel." Head cocked, I considered him. *Older in the morning?* His body must shift with the sun, aging and youthing. I'd bet his clothes were spelled to shift with his body so he wouldn't have to change them when the sun rose and set. That was why he wasn't wearing any when I looked through the translocation stone. No wonder they put him on disability.

"That is a vile curse," I said, and his gaze darted to me. "Who did this to you?"

"That's funny," Scott said, sullen and ill-tempered. "I warned Elyse not to renege on the deal. Your book is under the couch. Take it and go. You take the other, and we will follow you to the ends of the earth for it."

"You put it under the couch?" I asked as Ivy pushed off from his chair, shifting it backward a few inches. Hips swaying, she dropped to the floor and stretched.

"Got it," she said as she backed out from under the couch, my book in hand.

I turned to Scott, aghast. "You put it under the *couch*?" I said again, and Scott winced as Ivy set it thumping onto the end table beside the glamoured *Reader's Digest*.

"I wasn't going to answer the door with it sitting in the open." Scott looked like an embarrassed kid. "I knew you weren't going to fall for the 'this is where we're keeping your book and the word to unlock the safe' routine. But try telling a twenty-year-old anything."

He'd said the last with a sneer, and I felt a twinge of annoyance. "Don't sell her short," I said. "She's probably on her way here right now."

Scott flinched, and I felt my expression blank.

"Shit, we need to go," Ivy said, and worry clenched my gut.

"Ah, Rachel?" Bis said from atop the bookcase, his heavy brow furrowed.

"She's on her way, isn't she?" I said, and Scott simpered at me. "How did she know we were here?" I asked, and still he stayed silent. Crap on toast. If the warning went out when we rang the bell, she could be here in as little as twenty minutes. We'd been here almost that.

"Okay, let's pack it in," I said. "Bis, we gotta . . ." My words trailed off as I saw his sick expression.

"What is it?" Ivy asked for both of us, and Bis half fell, half flew to the floor. Leaving the book where it lay, he pushed down once with his wings to land on the end table, one powerful foot resting on the glamoured *Reader's Digest.*

"Did you know?" the gargoyle said to Scott, and my gut tightened.

"Know what?" I asked, and Bis's nails made an awful sound, scraping three lines into the table.

"You can't bring Kisten's ghost back with that spell," he said, his eyes darting to the book he'd left on the floor. "It requires an intact body, not ashes."

I froze, feeling as if I had gotten kicked in the gut. Elyse had known this wouldn't work even before she'd dangled it in front of me two weeks ago. She *lied* to get me under her thumb, *lied* to trick me into betraying my adopted kin.

And as I stared at Scott, the beginnings of a true hatred began an insidious trickle through me, tightening my spine vertebra by vertebra.

I jerked, startled when Ivy lunged for him, pinning him to the chair.

"Did you know?" she snarled, her teeth grazing his neck, and Scott shuddered, his eyes closing as the scent of his fear drenched the room. "Did you know!"

"Ivy!" I shouted as I grabbed her arm. It was dangerous to take prey from a vampire, but this wasn't hunger. This was heartache. "Let him go. Let him go! Ivy, this is not who you want to be. Let. Him. Go!"

She let go, giving Scott a shove that was hard enough to almost tip the chair over. Breath shallow, she turned away and tried to bring herself down. She had let him go for me—not for Scott, and certainly not for herself.

Scott wiped the saliva from his neck with his bound wrists, a cold sweat on his smooth brow. Bis glanced once at Ivy, then shifted himself to my shoulder. His firm grip grounded me and I exhaled, realizing how close I'd been to letting Ivy have her way. This wasn't who I wanted to be, either.

But still, anger filled me. The coven didn't want me for *me*. They wanted everything I knew, and they wanted it in a way that would not only give them control over me but remove me as a rival so their own skills would shine all the brighter.

"Ivy wants to know if you knew it wouldn't work," I said, one hand on Bis's feet. The kid was shaken, and the line running through both of us was soothing. "So do I. Did you?"

Scott glanced from Ivy's hunched back to me. "Yes," he said, voice soft. "If it means anything, I voted against it. Demons don't belong in the coven."

My lip twitched. "Yeah? That doesn't look as if it's helping you much, does it."

Ivy slowly pulled herself straight, her eyes haunted as she turned. She was working hard not to break anything, even as her world was falling apart. I hadn't seen that look on her face for a long time, and my heartache shifted and grew. She was in mourning. Again. It had been hard for me when Kisten had died, but it had been devastating to Ivy. He had been her confidant, her business partner, her lover—knowing everything about her and loving her anyway.

Motions slow, I picked up the book Ivy had pulled from under the couch. It was mine and I was taking it home as we had agreed. The soft leather was glowing in recognition. "Let's go," I said as I put it in my shoulder bag, and Scott scowled at the glamoured *Reader's Digest*, clearly thinking it was the one Bis had left on the floor by the door.

"Leave it, Morgan," he warned in his high voice, and I hesitated.

"Why would I want a spell I can't use?" I said, fighting the urge to smack the confidence from his smooth, young face. Making the semblance of a deal was not out of order, though, a way to claim it was mine when the subterfuge was discovered, and I exhaled my tension. "I came for my book, not yours," I said, tracing a light finger on the glamoured book to make Scott's lip curl. "Leaving with a second one wasn't in the original deal. But seeing as Elyse broke the first agreement and I had to come *fetch* my property, how about a new one?"

I stood before him, a ley line tinging through me by way of Bis's feet. "I renounce any claim I might have on that book right there. I walk out of here, free and clear. In return, I won't retaliate for you trying to buy my services with a curse you knew wasn't worth troll spit. Deal?"

"Deal," he said, and I nodded, satisfied that even when the switch I'd made was discovered, chances were good they'd drop the issue. *If it looks as if you're getting something for nothing, don't make the deal. Demons 101. Dumbass . . .*

"Rachel, we have to go," Bis whispered from my shoulder, and I nodded even as I hesitated.

"You voted against this, eh?" I said as I hiked the bag higher up my shoulder. "Good for you. Bad that you couldn't convince the rest of them. Here's some advice from me to you, old man, advice from someone who has been across the board and back again. Pawn made queen."

I leaned in, and Bis left my shoulder in a flurry of wings. "I am not going to hide in the ever-after and leave this reality to your coven's gentle mercies. I am not going to submit and be incarcerated in Alcatraz. And I am *never* going to be coven," I almost whispered, reaching to arrange the strings dangling from his hoodie. "It was rotten to the core when Brooke wanted to turn me into a broodmare to give her a demon child, and I don't see anything different with Elyse in charge, hiding behind a gossamer-thin claim of white magic. Vivian was the only decent person among you, and she's gone."

I straightened, shoving his shoulder to push him into the cushions. "If you were smart, you'd get out again before the shit hits the fan."

Done with him, I touched Ivy's shoulder and together we walked out, leaving Scott to wiggle free of his bonds or not. I didn't care. Bis flew out over our heads to make sure the way was clear, and I picked up the book Al wanted in passing, shoving it in my already heavy bag.

I'd gotten what I'd come for, and then some, but heartache followed us like an ill fog, coloring the night and those yet to come.

CHAPTER

8

MY FINGERS TINGLED AS THEY TRACED THE CRAMPED TEXT OF MY recovered book, but with both that bounty hunter Laker and Elyse's crow at the curb, I didn't dare let go completely of the ley line out in the grave-yard, and I simply made a fist to squeeze the extra energy out of my hand. The unharnessed power hit the page with a little hiss, and I shifted uneas-ily, glancing at the hall where Ivy lay sleeping in Stef's old room before turning to the kitchen counter where Getty and Jenks were busy stringing her loom.

I'd been in a bad mood all morning, and yet a small smile found me. Matti had always asked her daughters to help set up her loom, and that Jenks and Getty had found something to do together that didn't touch upon his wife's memory seemed . . . important. The dark-haired pixy was making a point of including him in her design concept, and I was hoping that he might buck pixy tradition and wear something his late wife hadn't made. The two of them needed each other, did better in each other's com-pany. Again important. It wasn't always about attraction—though that's what had moved me once, apparently.

Exhaling, I dropped my gaze to my demon book that held the curse I'd accidentally used on Brad. I'd been standing at the center island counter now for a good hour, head down as I yet again went through it carefully, page by page, looking for any hint of a substitute for that damned

Atlantean mirror within the multitudes of other curses. Newt's spell books kind of sucked. There was never a table of contents and she left things out. All the time.

The sliver of cold November sun that had been here this morning was gone, and yet a good feeling suffused me despite my frustration. The church felt different, more complete with the light scent of vampire mixing with the rich aroma of brewed coffee, the tang of burnt amber, and a hint of pixy dust. After seeing Ivy's grief, I had insisted that she spend the night in Stef's old room. My former roommate had wisely moved out shortly after getting her first paycheck from the hospital, and though Ivy had stronger ties across the river in the Hollows with Nina, it was more than reassuring having her here—not for my or Jenks's sake, but for hers.

There was no way Jenks or I was going to let Ivy go home last night—not with that old grief finding her anew. My excuse that I was worried about the coven showing up had been met with a sour, eyebrow-high expression, but she had stayed, and the scent of anxious vamp was now everywhere. Most might find it unnerving, but Ivy had always been uptight, and the tangy pheromones felt like home. My life in a nutshell.

Not helpful . . . I mused as I flipped from a curse that colored a lock of hair permanently gray. Time would do the same thing, and it wouldn't leave any smut on your soul. *And somewhat innocuous for Newt?* I thought, stretching until my spine cracked.

I collapsed back into myself, my gaze going to the plate of croissants. I'd picked them up for Trent, but he hadn't shown, and yawning, I took a bite of one before returning to the book.

"Oh, that's just nasty," I said as I realized the intent of the curse before me wasn't to lightly siphon off a person's energy to give to another in need, but to rip the person's aura away entirely and use it to extend the practitioner's life. *What an ugly bunch of hocus-pocus,* I mused, shuddering. It was clearly illicit magic, and I hoped that Scott hadn't seen it. I didn't need any more dings questioning my reputation.

"Hey, Rache." Jenks's wing hum gave me bare warning before he landed right on the pages. "Any luck?"

"Only bad." His dust was making the print glow. With a sudden thought, I flipped to Brad's countercurse and pulled my bag closer, rummaging to find that flat stone with the hole in it. "Is Ivy showing any signs of wakey-wakey?" One eye squinted shut, I peered through the stone at the pages. Jenks's dust vanished, but no secret words or phrases appeared to replace them.

"Yeah." Jenks used his chopsticks to pull a long flake of croissant from one of the untouched pastries. "This is your five-minute warning. She's going to want coffee."

"There's a cup still in there." Intent, I set my hand on the page and ran a light trace of energy through it. Again, the print seemed to burst into glowing relief, but nothing extra showed, even when I looked at it through the stone.

Slumping, I pushed away from the counter. Crap on toast, I wasn't going to let them put me into Alcatraz because I had trusted the wrong person—even if a significant fraction of the population there was incarcerated for that reason.

"How is she doing?" I asked as I picked at my croissant.

Jenks's wings went still, the veined gossamer angled low on his back. "She's handling it better than I would have thought. Which means her grief will show in inappropriate ways."

I winced. "Not necessarily bad, if it can be channeled." Cincy, though, had been on an even keel for a while, and now that Brice wasn't aiming to take over the city, there was no one for Ivy to take her grief out on. "I practically promised her I could raise Kisten's ghost," I whispered. "It's as if she's in mourning all over again."

Jenks's wings blurred into motion at the soft squeak of a door. "I'm glad you made her stay the night," he whispered as Ivy went into the bathroom.

"I know how she gets." Eyes down, I pulled my croissant apart. "She wouldn't have taken it out on me, but there was bound to be some stupid ass at Piscary's who would push her too far. And then she'd hate herself in the morning. Probably insist on cleaning up all the blood by herself."

The pixy's sharply angled features twisted into a bittersweet smirk. "Like I said, I'm glad you made her stay the night."

No one could *make* Ivy do anything, but the sentiment was there, and I pulled the book closer and studied it to at least pretend we hadn't been gossiping about her. Her empty expression last night at Elyse's bungalow had torn me up, all the way back to the church, all the way through a late, uncomfortable dinner. She'd gone straight to her old room afterward under the excuse of being tired, but I had heard her muffled sobs.

To say that I was pissed at Elyse for dangling a hope that didn't exist before us was an understatement. I'd refuse to work with them for that alone, and I was really glad I'd realized that the coven's half-ass invitation was in truth a calculated way to limit me. Still, I wasn't sure what I was going to do now. I was no closer to uncursing Brad. Come June, the coven would choose a sixth member and they would vote me into Alcatraz.

My attention rose when the bathroom door opened, but Ivy made a beeline to her room, and I exhaled, feeling as if we were already walking on eggs.

"I'll see how bad it is," Jenks said, and I bobbed my head as he took off.

Head down, I flipped through pages. I had half expected Elyse to show up on my doorstep this morning and demand her book back. Embarrassment might have kept Scott's mouth shut concerning our chat, and if no one opened the glamoured *Reader's Digest*, the switch might not have been discovered. *Maybe . . .*

Getty's warning wing rasp sounded like summer itself, and my pulse quickened in anticipation at the soft knuckle-knock on the porch railing.

It wasn't Trent but Al, and the imposing demon hesitated on the stair as my flash of libido died. Annoyed, he stomped across the covered porch, looking odd in an enormous bearskin coat.

Oh, yeah. The other book, I thought as I glanced at it sitting atop the counter. I should have taken it to him last night—a loan until he deemed my skills enough to handle it.

"Hi, Mr. Al," Getty sang out as Al opened the French doors and came in, an extravagant mood full upon him once more. But he had seen my disappointment that he wasn't Trent, and I was embarrassed.

"Hey, Al." I focused on my book as my neck warmed. "The book with the curse to bring back the undead is by the fridge. Sorry. I should have brought it out last night. You want a croissant?"

"No, thank you . . ." he drawled. Ignoring the book, he took off his coat to show a more typical thick wool slacks, pressed shirt, and embroidered vest, plus a handmade scarf I had never seen before. I couldn't help but wonder who had knitted it. Ceri, perhaps?

"I have coffee, too," I added when he tossed his heavy bearskin coat to the eat-at counter.

"Coffee, I will indulge in. It is much appreciated." He hesitated as if I might get off my dead ass and pour him a cup, and when I didn't move, he frowned and went to the pot. He hadn't so much as glanced at the book I'd stolen to pay for the translocation stone, and I wondered if I'd done something wrong.

The last of the brew chattered into his traditional rainbow mug. There was a pause, and then a sigh of contentment. "This tastes so much better without the bitter ash of burnt amber."

"Yeah?" Demons once reeked of charred sap, the scent clinging to them from their forced occupation in the hellish ever-after, the reality so abused and beaten by magic that you couldn't survive on the surface. But he wasn't showing any signs of making more coffee, and I finally flipped the book closed to make a puff of burnt amber and went to run the tap.

"Well done." Al's boots clicked on the tile as he went to the book I'd stolen for him and flipped it open. "Bold is half the battle and should be rewarded when real risk is required."

Our positions had been reversed, and I threw out the old grounds. "I wasn't bold, I was pissed." My elbow ached as I put a new filter in and added fresh coffee. "They lied to me."

"Did they?" he drawled, using one finger to flip from curse to curse until he settled on the one I'd been hoping would bring Kisten's ghost back.

I measured out the grounds, accidentally spilling them. "They knew the spell wouldn't work. Bis went over it. It needs an intact body, not ashes." I should have done more than walked out with a couple of books, and I slowly exhaled to bring my anger down. I'd have to play it cool if Elyse and her little gang showed up.

Al studied the book, his lips pressed. "Perhaps it is for the best. The spell you used to draw Pierce's ghost from purgatory is bastardized from this very stirring, and like the spell you stirred when you were eighteen, the price for giving a ghost enough mass to touch is that the magic only works when the sun is absent." He closed the book with a thump. "You would have to perform it every sunset."

The water went into the reservoir, and I hit the button to start the coffee brewing as he strode across the kitchen to the other spell book. "I could do that. I *would* do that."

A smile quirked the demon's expression as he flipped the book open—right to the spell to uncurse Brad. "Of that, I have no doubt, but tell me, Rachel. When would you cease preforming it and let his soul rest?" He eyed me over his blue-tinted glasses. "Five years? A hundred? Two hundred? You're not only making a choice to bring him to life but taking on the decision to choose when he finally moves on to whatever awaits all of us." He turned his attention to the book, studying it. "You will decide when he dies his final death. I see no benefit for the vampire in question other than him seeing you and Ivy happy."

My arms crept up over my middle. It sounded selfish when he put it like that. "Kisten deserves to have a life. Piscary cut it short because he stood up for me."

His head bowed, Al dipped his fingers into a small pocket in his vest to withdraw a smoky-gray glass. "No one knows you have it?" he asked.

"I'm not sure." I glanced at the empty hallway, hoping Ivy wasn't hearing this. "Ivy was right about them expecting me to burgle their office for the book, but they left some guy they pulled out of retirement to guard it." I hesitated, remembering the bitter anger on Scott's youthful face. "Seeing as the only person at the curb this morning is that bounty hunter looking for Trent, I'd say either they haven't opened it up yet or they are ignoring I have it." I leaned against the counter, watching Al run that smoky glass over the print to see if anything new showed. "Maybe Scott was too embarrassed to tell them we tied him to a chair and hasn't said anything."

Al straightened from his hunch over Brad's countercurse. "Since you risked everything to recover it, consider it yours fully and unconditionally." He grimaced. "You earned it."

"You mean the one I stole for you?" I blurted, warming in embarrassment as he eyed me over his blue-tinted glasses. "I mean, thank you."

He nodded, a soft smile flickering before he hid it. "Well. That was my last idea." He pocketed the glass and closed the book with a peeved flick of the finger. "Brad Welroe's curse can't be broken. Rachel—"

"I'm not hiding in the ever-after." Annoyance and a little fear trickled through me as I nudged him aside and flipped the book open again. "As tempting as that would be with Trent stuck there as well."

"It's not hiding," Al coaxed. "It's a short sabbatical in the ever-after to build on your skills. We all take sabbaticals. Say, a hundred years? Good round number?"

Jaw clenched, I stared at the book.

"A few more spells in your chi would put you eons beyond any upstart at Camp Wanna-Be-a-Ruler," Al said. "Your gargoyle, Bis, would assuredly be rebonded to you by then, and you would be able to jump the lines. My synapses would no longer be burned. This fuddling about as a half-ass demon is making us all look bad."

I spun, annoyed. "Then help me."

"That is what I am doing," he practically growled, and my shoulders tensed. "Home is where your books are," he added as he took a sip from that rainbow mug. "I can move the entire church. Pixies, gravestones, Vivian's ghost, and all."

"I can't leave," I said, amazed that, only two years ago, he had been trying to own me, because to own and dominate had been the only way he would allow himself to care for someone. The day I'd figured that out had been as scary as all hell. That we were now arguing as peers was a fragile candle I would fight to keep lit. We did not have an equal relationship. He needed me more than I needed him: to teach, to argue with, to stand with against his kin, who were still mired in the past. The responsibility of that scared the crap out of me.

"Al, I have worked too damn hard at getting demons in reality for me to walk away," I said softly. "This is my home. Tell me you wouldn't do the same thing."

The demon slumped. Slowly he lost his bluster, and his head bowed. "I would," he said as he stared into the depths of his coffee, and from the far corner of the room, Getty sighed.

Frustrated, I crossed my arms over my middle. All for a lack of a friggin' mirror destroyed two years ago with the original ever-after. Lost.

Al shifted, and my shoulders relaxed when he began to fiddle with the curse book again. "I'm surprised Elyse isn't banging on my door," I said sourly. "Scott might be too embarrassed to tell her what happened if he got out of those zip strips."

Al snorted, then flipped to the last few pages in the book where the index would be. But Newt never bothered to make an index, and it was only a curse to turn stone into water.

"He's got a really nasty curse on him," I said as I leaned against the counter. "Yesterday, at the coven offices, I'd swear he was over a hundred. Last night at Elyse's place, he was ten. And when I looked through the transposition charm, he was about sixty. It's hard to tell." *Even when he's naked.*

"Mmmm?" Al ran a finger down a line of text. "Glamoured to throw you off, I suppose."

"Maybe, but he said he'd be older in the morning. I think it's a curse. Young at night, old in the day." I rocked forward to top off my mug. "He looked sixty through the transposition stone, but I couldn't touch his foot. It wasn't really there. No wonder they put him on disability. I'm surprised they pulled him back into active duty. He was downright bitter when I asked who cursed him."

Al's brow furrowed as he studied the book. "I don't know any curse that does that."

"Newt's time and space calibration curse, maybe?" I offered, remembering how the half-mad demon had pushed the captured soul of an undead vampire forward and back to see if time and space were still running congruently. I had modified it to push a lily two years into the future to torment Constance with a super-scented plant. It had seemed like a good idea at the time.

Al shifted in a soundless sigh. "Perhaps, but Newt's curse requires direction. It does not wax and wane without prompting." His expression shifted to one of worry. "Ah, you still have that book, yes? I mean, you didn't loan it to your—ah, Trent, did you?"

I sipped my coffee, thinking. "Perhaps Scott tried to twist it and did it wrong and ended up sending his body back and forth through time instead of whatever it was he wanted to move." I frowned, remembering the ache of sending the lily. It had been connected to me, and it drew on my body's resources to stay alive through the spell. "He must have found a way to pull energy from the ley lines to survive."

And then Al's last question hit me. *You still have that book, yes?* But it wasn't his words as much as the concern he was trying to hide that struck me. He was worried? About that spell? Why? All it did was move things through time. Badly, if Scott was any indication.

But Scott had done it wrong.

Huh. "Do you think I can use Newt's calibration curse to return to when the ever-after was still intact?" I said, and his eye twitched. "I pushed that lily two years forward. Maybe I could get the mirror before the ever-after fell."

"Mother pus bucket!" he shouted, a thick fist slamming down on the demon book to make a flash of power spark. "No. Even if you could, you'd be trying to seduce something from an insane demon. Do you remember Newt's state of mind then? You will do your hundred years in the ever-after as penance for being uncommonly stupid. Why do you think I gave you two books if not to keep yourself occupied? Pay the price and go on with your life. Don't be uncommonly stupid again. Two stupids do not make a smart."

I glanced at the hall, my pulse quickening. "You think I could, though?"

Al took a breath to protest, then hesitated, making a soft groan as he pinched the bridge of his nose. "Let's say you go into the past until the original ever-after exists, then solve the issue of providing your body the two years of resources it will need to return. You will still have to bargain with Newt for the mirror, and she was absolute chaos. It's too dangerous."

"And Alcatraz and the coven aren't?"

"No," he said as Jenks flew in, drawn by our argument. "Newt's spell will not send your mind to fill your younger body. It will unwind your body to an earlier state. Your mind is fluid and would remain as it is, but your body will not. The energy demands alone to return will kill you."

Jenks's dust flashed an alarmed red. "Whoa, whoa, whoa! Rache, I know what he's saying here. Remember what happened when you made that lily grow two years in two minutes? There's no way you can take the long way home. You'd have to hide from everyone."

"So we add another spell or two to get around the energy needs," I said.

Al used a single finger to possessively draw the book away from me, closer to him. "And what if you find a way and are successful? Do you remember seeing another version of yourself during that time? No, because you were not there."

"Yeah, well, maybe that's because I stayed out of sight."

But as I paged through the curse book, searching for that spell that spindled auratic energy, I felt a drop of foreboding. "Soon as I get there, I'll twist a doppelganger charm. Make myself look like someone else. Or I could return to a time when I was out of the city. That trip up to Mackinaw, maybe." *When Kisten was still alive?* flickered in my mind. I could see him, but what would be the point other than giving myself more heartache? I couldn't risk possibly changing anything. He was gone—even his ghost was out of reach.

Oblivious to my thoughts, Al flung a hand into the air as Jenks dropped down, his tiny, angular face pinched in worry. "Rache, you could have died moving that lily."

"But I didn't." I found the curse to siphon energy and began studying it.

"Only because a plant has a tiny metabolic need," Jenks protested. "You're talking about a person. Do you have any idea what you consume in a week, let alone two years?"

"Here," I said as I pointed at the curse I wanted, and Al paused in his huff to glance at it. "I can use this to spindle my life's energy on the way out, stockpiling it to use when I come forward. Store it in the collective."

"Right from your soul, eh?" Al said sourly. "This curse is designed to kill, itchy witch."

"So I modify it," I coaxed as I waved Jenks's dust away. He was hovering far too close.

"Rache, I can't come with you." Red-faced, Jenks spun as Ivy's boots sounded in the hall.

I froze, sure she hadn't heard what we were talking about. She seemed far too lost in her own misery, her face puffy and pale as she took in Al standing at the counter. Her slacks were wrinkled and her shirt untucked, but it was the emptiness in her expression that tore at me.

"Good morning, Ivy Tamwood," Al said, practically baring his wide, flat teeth at her.

Ivy's eyes flashed pupil black in annoyance before regaining their usual brown. "What is she doing now?" she asked as she shuffled to the coffee maker.

I glanced at Al, peeved. "I've decided to give the coven what they want, proof that I cursed Brad with illicit magic," I lied. "I'll be in Alcatraz by the end of the week."

Ivy turned, coffee in hand. "Thanks for the heads-up," she said, clearly unconvinced.

A frustrated red and gold dust spilled from Jenks, and Al glowered.

"Yep." I turned to the curse in question. It didn't seem too complex, even if it was one of Newt's. It was likely already in the collective. All I had to do was say the words and accept the smut. "On second thought, perhaps I should become the coven's puppet. I'm sure I'll have time to keep Cincinnati together between fending off the coven's attempts at forcing me to give them every last demon secret I know."

Al cleared his throat, and Ivy numbly sipped her coffee, trying to wake up.

"Or I could go down rabbit hole number three," I finished.

Jenks flashed an alarmed red and Al's chin lifted. "Which is more likely than the other two to kill you," the demon intoned. "If you remember, I was hell-bent on owning you in the past."

"The past?" Ivy went to top off her mug.

"So I go far enough that you don't know me. Five years ought to do it." I took the demon book in hand and dropped it on the counter beside Ivy. She jumped at the loud pop and edged away. I knew she didn't like that I could do magic, but I wanted her to see this. "I can use Newt's curse to go back to when the original ever-after still existed and get an Atlantean mirror. Bring it forward, uncurse Brad, expunge my record, stick it to the coven." I took a breath, hoping I wasn't making a mistake.

Ivy's eyes flicked to mine, her hope and pain obvious. "The past? Kisten . . ."

"Five years," I said, feeling like a shit-heel. "I'd still be interning at the I.S. Ivy, I can't—"

"This is academic," Al said, pulling my attention from Ivy. "The energy needed to return forbids it. Newt developed that curse to test the balance of time and space within the ever-after. She used surface demons as visual markers because they are nothing but the souls of the undead in purgatory. Yes, they moved back and forth through time, but they have no caloric needs."

"You would be right there, and I won't be able to help you," Ivy whispered, and I pulled her into a quick hug. She stumbled, her grace gone.

"Look." I let her go and turned to the book. "It's a dark curse, yeah, but only because you are taking energy from someone. If I take my own, spindle it with this curse here . . ." I flipped through the book, my finger holding the place of the original curse. "Store it in the collective. Maybe the vault. No one goes in there. I can use it on the trip home."

"It's too dangerous when you can simply move yourself and all that you care about to the ever-after," Al insisted. "Give everything a chance to pass. There's no need to risk yourself."

"There is every need!" I shouted, and anger flashed across him. "I can *not* do that. I will not ask Ivy, and Jenks, and everyone I care about to move to the ever-after, exiled into taking little sips of life when they think they can avoid detection. This is my home. And I'm not leaving it if there is one shred of a chance that doing something bold, and inventive, and yeah, a little dangerous, will allow me to not only stay but make my place more certain."

Ivy slumped where she stood, Jenks's wings making an obvious hum until he landed on her shoulder. They both looked miserable, but I was more concerned about Al, his head down and avoiding me.

"Al, you hid for thousands of years, and nothing good came of it," I pleaded, thinking he looked depressed. "It's my risk. My decision. But I need help. Please."

For a moment, I thought he was going to walk out, but then he came closer, jaw set as he nudged me out of the way and he took control of the book. Head down, he silently studied it, his brow furrowing. "Your body will grow younger, but your mind will not," he said, voice distant as he talked about the curse I'd used to move the lily through time. "You will be limited to taking things with you that existed at your target date, or they will vanish en route."

"Yes!" I exclaimed, hearing his agreement to help me.

"I would also suggest not twisting the curse in the church. You need someplace hidden that hasn't changed in five years. The tunnels perhaps? Or Eden Park. There's a ley line there."

"Five years!" Jenks exclaimed. "Rachel doesn't have anything from five years ago. She lost everything when she quit the I.S."

"My shoulder bag is that old," I said, my enthusiasm faltering as I saw Ivy's fear. Jenks, too, was not happy, bobbing up and down in frustration.

Finding a place to twist it wasn't a problem. I could probably find money that was that old. I'd have to make the doppelganger charm when I got there, as I doubted the spell itself or the materials to craft one would survive the trip. My new transposition charm, however, should be okay, seeing as it worked through my mind and my mind would be unchanged. The stone itself was probably older than the sun.

"But the ley lines," Jenks protested. "You're using them to run the spell, right? What about when the Goddess destroyed them?"

Panic froze me, but as I looked at Al, I knew there was an answer. He looked reluctant to speak . . . and my jaw clenched.

"The day the lines went down will not be an issue," he admitted. "The curse will use the line it originates with until it's completed, blipping over the span of no-magic." His gaze turned to me. "You would use the new lines on the way out, and the old ones on the way back. I'm more concerned with finding something to indicate when you need to end the curse to arrive when you want." Al frowned, his mood bad. "A marker of sorts. Do you have anything that was broken five years ago? If you carry it with you, you can end the traveling curse when it becomes whole and be exactly when you want to be."

Adrenaline was a heavy wash, but there was nothing to fight, nothing to flee, and I jiggled on my toes. "I can go back in little hops until I get to the time period where I want to be."

Al's expression soured. "That is an extremely bad idea. Excuse me."

"Yeah, well, it's the only one I got," I snapped.

Al dropped the book and stomped away. "I can do this," I said, then jumped at the glass-shaking thump when he slammed the door to the porch. "Where are you going?" I shouted, but he never slowed, slogging out into the cold November morning as if on his way to war. "It's all here. All I need to do is dovetail it together," I said softly, frustrated and worried.

Until I realized Ivy was scared to death. Then I was just worried.

"Don't sweat it, Ivy. I'm going with her," Jenks said, and my head jerked up.

"No, you aren't," both Ivy and I said as one, and the sound of his wings shifted into an irritating whine as he flipped us both off. Matalina had been alive five years ago. It would break his heart to leave her, and it would break mine if he stayed there in the past.

I wouldn't be able to contact Ivy. Trent, either. Al was exiled into the ever-after five years ago and wouldn't know me. *Maybe this isn't such a good idea.*

"Try to stop me, witch," Jenks said belligerently. "Someone needs to watch your six."

"Truer words may never have been spoken, but you aren't coming," I said. "Ivy, I can do this," I added, but when I moved to give her a hug, she dropped a step back, clearly upset.

"Don't touch me," she said, voice raspy, and I jerked my hand away. Jenks froze in the air, and we stared at her as she quietly panicked. "Just because you survived the five years between then and now doesn't mean you don't go back tomorrow and get yourself killed."

"I have that same risk every day," I pleaded. "I have to try. How else am I going to get the coven off my case? I am not going to be their demon slave, and I'm not going to hide in the ever-after for a hundred years while they live out their lives and die!"

For three heartbeats she stood there, expression stricken. "I have to go," she said, then spun, head down as she strode from the kitchen.

"Ivy?" I called, but my impetus to follow her died when I realized Al was coming in from his wagon, arms swinging and shoulders hunched as he wove through the graveyard. Torn, I skidded to a halt. He was going to help?

"I got her," Jenks said, then darted out.

Lip between my teeth, I waited, nervously flipping the book to the energy-spindling curse. *Pentagram to contain the curse, linking object to link, words to access the demon collective.* The curse was there. All I'd have to do is set it up and run it.

"I thought you weren't going to help," I said as Al came into the kitchen, two lengths of a black gold chain dangling from his tightly fisted hand.

"I broke this about five years ago," he said as he held them out.

His mood was closed, and I gingerly took them, stifling a shiver as they coiled into my palm with a cool sensation.

"It will get you to your target date," Al said distantly, as if it didn't matter, as if he hadn't given me a real chance. "Travel back until it regains its unbroken state, then stop. I can guarantee you that I did not know you then. You should be safe. From me."

Safe from him . . . Elation was a heady wash. He thought I could do this. I could do this. "And to get back?"

"That's simple. Break something an instant before you leave and take it with you as a marker. It will mend on the way out. When it breaks again on the return trip, you are home."

Home, I thought. Odd. I'd be going somewhere without ever leaving it. "Thank you."

A tense, false grin crossed him. "Don't thank me yet. I suggest that you register how you twined these two curses into a new one into the collective."

"So I can make the return trip easier?" I guessed, and he shook his head.

"No, my thought is that by registering the blended curse in the collective, you can prevent anyone else from using it."

I bobbed my head at his logic. Without a cost-for-use clause, no other demon could duplicate what I did unless they independently invented it themselves. I'd never registered a spell with the cost-of-use clause, but I knew how in case I ever made a spell anyone else would want.

"I know your reasons for doing this, and they are worth the risk." Worry pinched his brow, making him look old. "Keep your presence light. Little changes will be absorbed, but anything large will settle in your mind and drive you mad."

Newt, I thought, stifling a shudder.

"You remember the words to register a spell?" he asked, and I nodded again. "Good. And stay out of my sight," he added. "If I encounter you with your current skill level, I will try to snag you as a familiar, regardless of not knowing you then."

"Okay." I flipped the book closed. I had so much to do.

"Jenks!" I shouted. "You up for a trip out to Second-Hand Charm?"

CHAPTER

9

THE INCONGRUITY OF CELTIC BAGPIPES AND DRUMS PLAYING "Sabotage" was an odd, wild, and decidedly stirring mix. But the modern beat blended into the ancient sound perfectly, and I tapped in time as I slid a wad of hangers down the rack with a rasp. Second-Hand Charm organized their clothes by color, not size, which worked surprisingly well, and I quickly sorted through the black tees to find something without sequins.

"Hey, Rache?" Jenks said, his wings clattering in the chill of the place. "Check this out."

He had alighted on a rack of red shirts and blouses. Beyond him, Trent stood in the men's area, one foot up as he held the bottom of a shiny dance shoe to the bottom of his boot. He had insisted on coming, and I had agreed, but only after I used the transposition stone to make him into Ivy. Which, now that I thought about it, might account for the odd looks he had been getting, and a smile quirked my lips as I closed the gap between me and Jenks.

"Whatcha got?" I said as I fingered the vibrant red short-sleeved shirt. It had a flattering V-neck, but I hesitated at the sequins making a surprisingly subtle pattern of a happy monkey on the sleeve.

"It's a Simation," he said, flitting over the monkey-adorned tag at the neck. "Witchwear bought them out seven years ago and they changed labels. It will last the trip."

Still not sure, I held it up to myself, and he nodded his approval. "How on earth did you find it?"

"It smells old."

My motion to drape it over my arm slowed. *I can wear something with sequins for a day,* I thought as I looked for the jeans. Trent had moved into the toddler area, a studious, wistful look on his face as he held up a jumper. *The man does like to shop . . .*

Smirking, I turned away. He hadn't been shopping since going into hiding last month. Never in a million years would anyone expect to find him here, at a secondhand store. My smile faltered. It was sort of my fault.

"Is that all you need? A shirt and pair of jeans?" Jenks asked.

The jeans were by the registers, and I pushed into motion. "I have socks and underwear old enough." Both of which either fell down or rode up because of elastic issues. I should have thrown them out, but you never know. "I have a jacket that old, too. I'm good." Not the one Elyse had torn but another, still serviceable even if it had a rhinestone pentagram on the back.

I checked on Trent before following the pixy's low-dusting trail weaving through the displays to the jeans. He had scoped out the entire store in the first three minutes we'd been here, and whereas I was concerned about the slight chill, Jenks obviously wasn't.

"Thanks, Jenks," I said as I settled in and began to dig through the stacks of folded jeans, only to hesitate when my phone hummed. My gaze shot across the store to Trent, but it clearly wasn't him, and I pulled my phone out, glanced at it, and hit the accept icon.

"Hi, Mom. Everything okay?"

Jenks's wings rasped as he eavesdropped, and I put her on speaker.

"I heard an undead passed at Piscary's," my mom said, her voice intent and anxious. "I wanted to make sure it wasn't Ivy's girlfriend."

Immediately I relaxed and Jenks darted to the other side of the table, his curiosity satisfied. "Oh! No. She's fine. I would have called you, but I didn't think it would make the national news." I lifted a pair of bejeweled jeans to check for size against my hips. "Constance was making an example out of someone." *These look familiar . . .* I thought as I ran a thumb over a missing stone. Flushed, I put them back on the table. I had too much bling as it was.

"I was worried," my mom continued. "They only said it was an undead vampire, and I couldn't find anything more online. I'm glad you're both okay."

Both, I mused, remembering Ivy's expression when she cremated Brice. "She's fine. I'm fine," I said, then mouthed to Jenks, "You want to talk to her?" to which the pixy violently shook his head, sparkles falling from him like rain.

"You sound tired. Are you getting enough sleep?"

I stared pointedly at Jenks, and the pixy laughed at me. *Fine.* "Hey, Mom, I want to talk to you, but I'm sort of in the middle of something. Can I call you in about half an hour?"

"Oh, no need," she said. "I simply wanted to check on Ivy." She went silent for a moment, then added, "Where on earth are you? I haven't heard 'The Sound of Silence' done in bagpipes since . . . You're at Second-Hand Charm? Rachel, you haven't been shunned again, have you? Do you need money? I can wire you—"

"Mom. No." Embarrassed, I glanced around the store, glad no one but Jenks was in earshot. Trent, though, was coming my way, a pair of shoes and two little-girl outfits in his basket. "I haven't been shunned, and I don't need money." *Not yet anyway.* I'm cleaning out my closet and am dropping some things off."

"Cleaning your closet?" my mom said in disbelief, and then, voice laced with pity, "Oh, honey . . . were you cursed again?"

Cleaning my closet? I thought, wincing. Yeah, that was hard to believe. "I was not cursed," I said, uncomfortable, as Jenks darted off to meet Trent halfway. "I'm prepping to go into the past, and I need clothes from the era or I'll show up naked."

My mom was silent for a telling heartbeat. "I think I'll tell Donald that you got cursed again; otherwise neither one of us will be able to sleep to-night."

I picked up the phone and took her off speaker. "Mom, it's okay," I said softly, but I knew I must have looked sick when I met Trent's worried gaze and he settled in beside me. "I'm joking. I'm shopping for something Trent wouldn't be caught dead in so we can go out to a movie or something." I put my phone to my leg to block the mic. "Say something to her," I whispered to Trent, and the man shook his head, eyes wide in alarm.

"I'm so proud of you," came distantly from my phone, almost unheard. "Don't give those coven bitches anything. How far are you going into the past?"

Sighing, I put the phone to my ear. "Five years," I said, wondering where Jenks had gotten to. "It's safer if I'm not on anyone's radar." Meaning Al, Trent, the I.S. hit squad. Vince's Were pack from Mackinaw. Though it might be nice to drop in on Nick and smack him up a little.

"Good." Her voice was heavy with pride. "Call me when you get back, mmmm? Don't make me worry."

I exhaled. My mom was a little unbalanced from what she had dealt with in her life, but on the rare occasion, that worked for me. "Okay," I whispered. "I love you, Mom."

"I love you, too. Be careful."

"I will." But my mom had disconnected, and I tucked my phone in my pocket. A thin trail of cold-blue pixy dust sifted down from the front window, worrying me.

"Your mother is amazing," Trent said as I turned back to the table, digging down through the folded jeans to find my size. Everything had artful rips and tears . . . which meant they were expensive, not old, and I glanced at the bejeweled pair of tens I'd probably left in a donation dumpster six years ago. "I found something for the girls," he added as he lifted his basket. "And a pair of shoes I don't need."

"Can't ever have too many shoes." Frustrated, I moved a stack. Everything was made to *look* old. I was going to show up naked. I knew it.

"Hey, guys?" Jenks's short stop before us sent a wave of dust over us. "We got an issue."

My heart gave a hard pound. "What is it?"

"Laker." Jenks landed on the bejeweled jeans. "He's in the parking lot."

"The bounty hunter?" I glanced at Trent. "How is he following us?"

Trent put my red shirt into his basket. "Maybe he tagged your car?"

"We parked three blocks from here," I protested, then ducked down below the table when the tall human pushed open the door and a fanfare of bugles sounded. "Jenks, is there another way out of here?"

"Yeah, but it's an alley, and I don't like it." He rose up, wings rasping. "Hang on. Let me get a squint at what he's doing."

"Jenks?" Trent whispered, and a hint of energy fizzed between us as he began to pull on the nearest ley line, slow and easy, filling his chi and making my skin tingle.

"Yep, it's Laker." Jenks stood on a stack of jeans, hands on his hips. "He's talking to the woman at the register. Showing her his phone . . ." His wings stilled as his dust shifted to a bright silver. "She's pointing to the kids' section. Tink's a Disney whore. She outed us."

Trent grimaced. "We can fight our way out," he said, sounding eager for it.

"I'd rather not." I glanced at the basket, uncomfortable. We needed to pay for this stuff, bare minimum.

Jenks dropped down to put our eyes on the same level. "No pixy in their right mind would be out here this time of year. He knows me. I'll lure him away from the door. Give you enough time to slip out the front."

But it was too cold for him to catch up if we went far, and a flash of anxiety furrowed my brow. We would all leave together, or none of us.

"Okay. You distract him." I pulled the bejeweled jeans out from under him and dropped them into Trent's basket. I was pretty sure they were mine, which would put them old enough. I'd gotten them when I'd been interning with Ivy. "Trent and I will stay low until he takes the bait, and we will meet you outside the door. From there we go to the car. Together."

"You both should walk out of here," Trent said. "I'm the one he wants."

"All or none, cookie man," Jenks said, and then he darted off, flying no more than two inches above the floor like a deadly shadow.

All or none, I thought, feeling a pang of belonging and gratitude. It hadn't been that long ago that Jenks would have cut Trent's Achilles tendons if I had asked him to. "It's too cold for him," I whispered, worried as Trent and I hid behind an endcap. "Even in here."

"Disguising me as Ivy might not have been the best idea," Trent whispered, then motioned me to stay put as he cautiously peeked around the endcap.

"Yeah, maybe." Crouched beside him, I renewed my grip on the ley lines, and with a whispered *"Finis,"* the glamour broke, little shimmers of light cascading over him. Trent seemed to shudder, and though he had never looked anything like himself to me, now everyone could see him as himself.

Jenks swore colorfully from the far end of the store, calling for me, and Trent's lips quirked. "Laker heard that. Let's go."

Trent's fingers found mine, drawing me to my feet and pulling me into motion as a thrill coursed through me. Pace fast, he strode to the register, smiling grandly as he line jumped to the front. The woman manning it glanced up, then did a double take, her lips parting when she recognized Trent.

"Put the change in the animal rescue jar," he said to the woman as he dropped two fifties on the counter and pulled me past her.

"Th-thank you!" the woman called, then added an irate, "Hey! You can't take the basket!"

I cringed. Laker might not have heard the "Thank you," but her shrill demand to leave the basket must have carried.

"Heads up!" Jenks shrilled, and I jerked from Trent, energy whooshing through me like liquid flame as I pulled on the ley line and turned.

Laker stood atop a table of puzzles at the back of the store, one hand gripping an amulet, the other wielding a staff. Energy rippled down the length of wood, and I shoved Trent toward the door when the wizard shouted a word of Latin and a spell shot from the end as if it was a gun.

"*Rhombus!*" I exclaimed, taking Trent, Jenks, and a rack of glassware into my protective circle. Laker's spell hit it . . . and a silent boom of sound reverberated out. Clothes blew into the air and people screamed. I dropped my circle even before the rack of clothes hit the floor.

Trent stood beside me, eyes bright with anticipation. "Out. Now," I said, and he shook his head, a wisp of pearly magic spiraling up over him as he faced Laker. "Get him out of here, Jenks!"

The pixy dropped down, his dust a brilliant gold in excitement. "Let's go, cookie man. And don't forget Rachel's stuff."

"All or none," Trent echoed, and I grimaced. I couldn't have it both ways.

"Okay, but don't destroy the store. My mom used to shop here," I said as the businessman fragmented away to leave only the elven warlord, seldom seen but always there. That veneer was paper-thin, and I stifled a shiver, liking it. Liking it a lot.

Thinking we had given up, Laker jumped from the table and started over, a second amulet in his hand as a purple glow began gathering along his stick. "Trent Kalamack, I am authorized to detain and bring you in for—"

"*Entrono voulden!*" Trent shouted, and I shuddered as his spell rippled over me like the touch of a lover, sparking with a sensation of silk.

Laker yelped, the glow on his staff vanishing as a protection circle snapped around him. Trent's spell hit a display to send a tornado of clothes to smother the man.

"Move!"

"Wait, my stuff!" I shouted, snagging the basket when Trent grabbed my arm and ran for the door. Jenks flew vanguard, and we burst from the store as the woman at the register began a shrill harangue.

"Stop him!" I heard faintly, and then we were gone, my boots hammering a thundering cadence up my spine.

"Jenks?" I called, relieved when the rasp of pixy wings became a cold spot on my neck. "Okay. Car. Let's get out of here."

"I got this." Trent took the basket, and our pace slowed as he shot a quick glance behind us. "You should have your hands free in case he follows." He winced. "You're a better street fighter than me."

"Thanks." What he meant was I was better at minimizing innocent bystander collateral damage. The street, though, was almost empty, dusky in the early evening. "He's not following."

"That's 'cause he knows what's good for him," Jenks said as we slowed at the car, and I froze when the lethal-detection charm hanging on my bag flashed a warning red.

"Stop!" I yanked Trent back as he reached for the door. "He spelled it." *Son of a moss wipe . . .*

Trent's gaze went from my car to me and then over my shoulder to the street. "Seriously?"

I nodded. "That's what wizards do. Less confrontation, more pregame. All he needed was to flush us out. Get us reacting. That's why he's not following us." Thank the Goddess that I had a death threat on me once, or I'd never have had the detecting charm to begin with.

"What a weenie," Jenks said, and I grimaced, wondering where the nearest bus stop was. At least they'd pick me up now. *You Nair a guy once on the bus . . .*

"We taking a ley line home?" Jenks asked, and Trent's focus blurred.

"There's one three blocks that way."

A feeling of being watched stole over me. "Let's go," I said as I scanned the street, my eyes widening when Laker stumbled out of the store, still shedding clothes. The woman from the register was with him, yelling loudly as she gathered what she could.

"Go!" I pushed Trent into motion, glancing back when Laker shouted at us.

"Kalamack!" the wizard demanded, shoving the woman off him as he bolted for us.

My skin was tingling as Trent ran beside me, the two of us meeting the pavement as one. I loved working with him, and I fought with the inane desire to take his hand in mine, even as we ran.

"Don't stop," Trent said as we turned the corner and he slid to a halt and pulled more heavily on the nearing line. *"Ta na shay, juncta in uno!"* he shouted, and my knees almost buckled as the nearby line pulsed with energy, racing through both of us when he gave it direction and aimed it squarely at the determined human.

Laker skidded to a stop, fumbling with his amulets as Trent's spell slammed into him and froze him to the ground.

Trent grabbed my hand and pulled me into a run. Wild magic pressed into me, tingling and suggestive. "The line . . ." I started. It had to be close. That last spell was like . . . wow.

"He broke it!" Jenks shrilled from behind my ear, his grip cold as he held on for dear life. "Rache, he's searching his pockets."

"He's free?" Trent said, clearly annoyed. "That should have held him for at least five minutes."

"Rache!" Jenks warned, and my hand slipped from Trent's. We weren't going to make it. We had to make a stand.

"Knock it off, or I will put you down!" I shouted, and Laker pinwheeled to a halt. He was half a block away from us, and we were half a block to the ley line.

"Go," I said softly, and Trent settled in more deeply beside me. "Trent, the line is like right there," I protested, and he shook his head as magic wreathed his hands.

"I'm just doing my job," the man said, winded. "Go ahead and spell me. The coven would love an excuse to bring you in, too, Morgan."

I pulled heavier on the line, my aura flashing into the visual range. The line was too far away to simply step into. I could feel it humming through me, though. Laker could probably see it.

"Rache, he's stalling for time," Jenks said. "Hit him with something and run."

"He's trying to figure out which amulet to use," Trent said. "He can't get both of us."

"He's not getting either of us." I ground my soles into the pavement.

"Laker?" I said, stiffening as the man gripped an amulet like a grenade. "Don't make me do this."

But he did, and as he pulled the pin on the ley line amulet, I tugged on the ley line and let it fill me. "*Quod periit, periit!*" I shouted, and Laker squealed like a baby as every last strand of his hair fell out. It was the same thing I'd done to get me kicked off Cincinnati's bus line, but this time, I'd meant to do it.

"Move!" I gave Trent a shove and started running. Once the shock wore off, he'd be really pissed.

"Oh, he didn't like that," Jenks said, and I ran. The line was just ahead, and Laker was still standing there, horrified.

"Rachel, that was—" Trent said.

"A nonlethal joke spell," I finished. "You only do six months' community service for it."

"Even when helping a wanted felon escape?"

I grinned at Trent as we slid into the ley line. "You aren't a felon. You haven't been tried yet."

The hum of the line's unbridled energy lit through me like home given a sound. "Thanks for a great night out," Trent said, and I grinned, standing almost on tiptoe to give him a kiss.

"You're welcome. But I'm coming with you." Trent's eyes went wide, and I added, "If that's okay?"

"Yo!" Jenks tugged on my ear, bringing me back to the present. "Whatever you're going to do, do it. He's staggering this way."

Trent's arm slipped around me. "I'd like that."

Together we turned to Laker, the man tired, beaten, angry . . . and bald.

"Morgan," he panted, glaring in hatred at me, and I gave him a bunny-eared kiss-kiss.

Shifting my aura, I felt reality dissolve, the cityscape blurring into nothing and the sound of autumn insects growing loud.

We were there.

CHAPTER

10

I STEPPED FROM THE LINE, LITTLE DRIFTS OF ENERGY PULLING FROM me to fall back into the humming energy stream in a delicious sensation of loss and promise to return. Jenks lifted from my shoulder in a burst of mystic-enhanced dust, wings humming as he darted into the ever-after darkness to do a quick recon. The shadows were thicker in this reality, the sun having been lost behind a distant cloud bank and a thicket of old-growth trees. I pulled the clean air in deep, glancing at Trent as he made sure we still had everything. The adrenaline rush of escaping Laker was like a roller-coaster ride—all thrill, no real danger—and I relished it even as I knew I shouldn't discount the wizard. I wouldn't say we were lucky, but if *he* had been, things might have gone differently.

Trent tucked the basket over his arm. "Laker knows every time I put a toe into reality. It has to be a spell."

His voice rippled over me, the low, almost musical tones going perfectly with the sound of late crickets and the wind in the trees. "Probably." I unfocused my attention and brought up my second sight, seeing Laker like a ghost among the outlines of buildings and shop fronts as he stomped away, phone to his ear. "You, ah, want to go back?" I asked, my thought hesitating when I eyed Trent. His aura, usually a brilliant gold with flairs of red, was showing more than a hint of smut. Now that I thought about it, there had been a whisper of black on his thrown spells, too. "Ah, I wouldn't suggest my car," I added as I dropped my second sight and his aura seemed to vanish. "But we could call a cab." *What have you been do-ing, my love?* I mused, worried. A smutty aura wouldn't get you in Alca-traz, but it would gain the interest of the coven, and that was often the same thing.

Oblivious to my thoughts, Trent shook his head. "I need to find out how he's tracking me," he said, red plastic basket in hand. "Until I do, I should probably limit my excursions to reality. I'll walk you home, though. On this side of the lines."

The rasp of Jenks's wings sounded as the pixy dropped to my shoulder. "That wizard should take the hint. Everyone else has."

The pixy's wings pressed against my neck and I stifled a shiver. It was warmer over here, but not by much. "I think he's trying to establish a name for himself. There are easier ways than this to make a living." I peered through the trees for any sign of the mountains with which to orient my-self. "Walk me home, huh? Good. I have no idea where we are."

"I do." Trent followed my gaze, then turned. "Church is that way." He pushed into motion, his hand finding mine with a comforting sureness. "Unless you're still up for dinner?"

"At the estate?" Jenks said brightly as he snuggled in between my neck and my collar. "Count me in. I haven't seen my grand-younglings in months. I bet they're flying by now."

Trent's hold on me tightened as he wove between the trees, awkward at first, then easing into his elven grace, which slipped like smoke through the trees, finding the easier path. "Sorry, Jenks. I'm talking soup over a fire here in the ever-after."

I stifled a quiver as a tingling energy slipped from him to me, our bal-ances equalizing. He smelled wonderful after all that magic. Like cinna-mon and wine. "Soup sounds great," I said, and he flashed me a smile, part relief, part eager anticipation. I knew he had been in and out of his estate since his buddy Saladan had implicated him in illegal genetic research, but I hadn't had an opportunity to check out his new digs at Al's grove in the ever-after yet.

"Where you been, cookie man?" Jenks asked. "You sure as Tink's a

Disney whore aren't in the garden, are you? I already gots a demon in there."

Trent's grin became mischievous. "No. I'm at Al's old place. Good water there."

Good water? Perhaps, but I thought it more likely that he had set up there to tap Al as a convenient babysitter and possibly buffer against the other demons. Al had since moved to the line in my backyard to avoid looking as if he liked Trent's two little girls. But he did. Al would die for them.

"Good water?" Jenks blurted. "You have a ley line running right through your estate as a foolproof escape tunnel. You could be eating someone else's cooking and taking hot showers, and you're eating out of a box, sleeping on the ground, and washing your boy bits in a cold stream? In November?"

"Jenks . . ." I cautioned, but Trent was smiling as he stepped over a fallen tree before extending a hand to help me cross.

"The girls and I do okay." Trent hesitated, his gaze distant for a moment as he placed himself. "Besides, the estate is empty except for the stables and a small maintenance crew for the gardens. It's funny. I used to stay months at the estate before feeling the need to go out. Now I can hardly stand being there."

Our way suddenly opened up onto a worn path, and I leaned my head on his shoulder, our pace easing as the night thickened about us. "True," I said softly. "But you had a full staff and lots going on then."

A small noise of agreement escaped him, and I flushed. "Sorry," I added, and he let go of my hand to slide his arm around my back and tug me closer as the path evened out. His father had died early, leaving Trent a legacy of illegal genetic tinkering needed to maintain his entire species. Now that the elves weren't in imminent danger of becoming extinct, he'd been free to find out who he wanted to be. It hadn't left him searching as much as one might think.

His mother had been rather wicked, I was finding out, and Trent had changed in the last few years, evolving in real time in front of me into something far more dangerous than his dad had ever been, playing with illicit magic the way he had once played with illegal genetic techniques. Society frowned on both of them. One they might forgive, but both?

But I had to admit his new dexterity with elf magic left him smelling delicious and pegged all my meters.

"It's okay," he said, voice intent as his breath shifted my hair. "I enjoy it here. Stop looking at me as if it's your fault. I'm the one with the genetic labs, not you."

But Lee never would have targeted him if it hadn't been for me. The witch had made a play for Cincinnati, going through my friends to get to me. Everyone else rode the wave to the shore, but Trent . . . His past had swamped him, and now he was rolling along the bottom of the ocean, struggling to find the surface.

My gaze dropped to the plastic basket in his hand. He was buying secondhand clothes for his daughters and used shoes for his feet. Ellasbeth was in her glory, and I worried every time Lucy went to fulfill her visitation rights that her lawyers would find a way to detain both girls.

"Hey . . ." Trent tugged me into him, trying to shake my bad mood. "I made some changes to the grove when Al left. I think you'll like it."

"I can't wait," I said, but I wasn't really listening, more concerned with how the next few days were going to play out. Going into the past to bargain with Newt for a mirror? What if I changed something and came back to find Trent and Ellasbeth married?

"Jenks, I put in some late-pollinator plants on the south end. Help yourself."

"Great. Thanks," Jenks said, his wings tickling my neck as a stream of greenish-blue dust sifted down my front.

"And I added an outdoor space," Trent continued, his pace slowing as the light began to brighten when the forest thinned. "Put in a tub for the girls . . ."

"Oh, really?" I stepped over a fallen log, recognizing where we were now. It was Al's old grove, though the protective ring of toadstools was gone, moved to my church, apparently.

"A tub?" Jenks scoffed, and I slowed at the edge of the clearing to take in the changes.

The three cherry trees in the corner were no longer in bloom, the leaves brown and crisping as whatever spell Al had on them had faded with his absence. Tulpa, Trent's gray horse and familiar, cropped the grass under them, his long, manicured tail swishing and his coat gleaming in the low light. Al's wagon was gone, but in its place was a large tent set up beside the stream. A patio of flat, rough stone made a pleasant cleared space around the fire. The flat stones continued into the stream to outline a deep basin. The river ran straight through it and on, but there was a nearby rock that could dam the openings, creating, as Trent had said, a tub.

"Oh, my gosh," I said as I rocked into motion to take a closer look. "It's a tub."

Trent grinned, his gaze following Jenks as the pixy went to scope out the place. "Yes. I stop the flow with a rock, and once it's full, it's easy to warm it up." His arm fell from behind my back. "Lucy . . ." he said, shuddering. "Lucy does not like cold water."

"She takes after her mom," I said, and Trent sighed, his fingers tight in mine as we crossed the glen. "Dinner sounds great," I said as the peace of the crickets took hold of me. I could forget everything for a few hours and just . . . be. "What can I do to help? Start the fire?"

He shook his head. "I've got it." His attention flicked past me to the stream. "You want to try the hot tub?"

Mmmm? "Sure, I don't mind warming the water." A quiver of anticipation shivered through me as I recalled his thickening layer of smut. Perhaps this was where it was coming from. Soaking in a puddle of hot water watching the stars come out would be a little slice of heaven. The only thing to make it better would be a fire, and he had that, too. "I'll find some wood for the fire first."

"No need. I got it. You can take a soak while I finish the soup."

"You sure?" I asked, and he gave me a gentle push.

"You, naked in my river? Absolutely," he said, and I grinned.

Jenks's wings clattered in annoyance. "Oh, for ever-loving, troll-humping fairy farts," the pixy said. "If you need me, I'll be with the horse."

Twenty minutes and a singed finger later, I had shimmied out of my clothes and was easing into a warm puddle of water, moaning as I settled my bare ass on a flat rock now radiating a gentle warmth. The sound of Trent fussing over a pot above the fire was incredibly soothing, and I felt my eyes slip shut. It was obvious now that—much like demons—his darkening layer of smut had been not from illicit spells but from him replacing his tech-rich luxuries with magic-based fineries. The entire glen felt safe, what with the lingering scent of burnt amber and the zing of elven magic.

My breath eased in and out, as relaxed as the day I was born, while the crickets sang their song of insect seduction. Trent was making me dinner, and I drowsed, lulled by the heat of the water and the peace of the place . . .

Until a soft ripple of water splashed, and the cool of the night hit me, startling me awake.

"Oh, hey!" I said, sitting up as Trent eased himself into the makeshift bath across from me, the water rising higher to rub out the chill the lapping water had left. His naked body was little more than a shadow, and I looked up, surprised that the stars had shifted. The fire, too, was now only embers. "Crap on toast," I whispered as he beamed at me. "I fell asleep?"

Moving slow to keep the ripples at a minimum, Trent eased closer until our shoulders touched and our feet intertwined. "You were tired." His arm slipped behind me. "I had to reheat the water."

My gaze went to the water, then back to his lightly stubbled face. "I didn't mean to fall asleep."

"Don't worry about it. The soup will hold." A sigh sifted from him, and he stared up at the sky. "This is *very* nice."

Behind him, a burnt-out candle sat between two covered bowls and a bottle of opened wine on a small table. "You should have woken me."

Trent's eyes closed. "I'm not going to wake you up for soup."

"Yeah, but you made it for me." I scanned the silent campsite for Jenks, finally spotting a faint glow over by the horse. "I can't believe I fell asleep."

KIM HARRISON

His eyes opened and he tugged me closer, his fingertips tracing a suggestive circle on my shoulder. "You fell asleep in my wooded garden," he
said, voice low. "That's dangerous, you know. Falling asleep in an elf's garden?" Water trickled as he shifted to give me a kiss, his lips tasting of broth
and wine. "You might never escape," he whispered.

Escape wasn't exactly on my mind at the moment, and a wry feeling
of disappointment rose through me when he eased back to settle more
firmly beside me. I was naked. He was naked, and his eyes were shut again.
What's wrong with this picture?

"Escape? I should be that unlucky," I said, even as I wondered again
why I was trying so hard to remain in reality. Al clearly wanted me in the
ever-after until his synapses healed and he could do magic again. Trent
was in exile, accessible and wonderfully bored. The coven was after my ass.
I could wait them out. A hundred years was all it would take, and as a demon, I had that to spare.

And yet I couldn't leave Cincy to the mercy of whoever was strongest.
Not when they fought only for themselves, not the weakest. I hated a bully,
and that's what many undead vampires were. Most had to be incredibly
selfish to survive in the first place, and that carried over when they died
their first death.

Trent's breath was slow and even, and I shifted, water sloshing. "I had
fun tonight." Sideways to him, I played with his hair, my entire side going
cold. "Evading Laker?" His skin was perfect, glistening with a sheen of
water, the firelight turning him into silver and gold under my touch. "Elven magic is so . . . earthy," I whispered, smiling as I saw goose bumps rise
behind a finger trailing down his neck. "Every time you pulled on a line, I
could feel it."

"Mmmm," he said, drowsy, and I sent a little surge of ley line energy
into the water.

Trent shuddered, a wrinkle of water echoing from him as his eyes
opened wide. They were almost black in the dim light, glints of firelight
making him a dangerous shadow under my touch. The softness of sleep
was gone, and a shiver traced down my spine when his gaze found mine.

"I didn't know you could sense me pulling on a line. Is that an issue?" he said, voice full of question.

I snuggled closer, my hand finding him in suggestion. "Only because it gets me more randy than a goat. Are you sleepy?"

"Ah, not anymore." Water sloshed as he shifted to tuck his arm behind my head, pillowing it. "What time do you need to be at the church?"

Sensation rippled over me as his hand found my thigh, tracing up and down in a gentle rhythm. "Hours ago." Tilting my head, I found his ear with my teeth, nibbling, tugging. "Ivy will be frantic."

A small sound escaped him, and under my hand, he became hard, his breath quickening. "I'm incredibly busy tonight," I whispered.

"I can see that." Again water sloshed, and suddenly he was over me, a heady, delicious feeling suffusing me as he nudged my thighs and I moved to make room for him. "This was not on my agenda, but I'll see if I can work you in."

Warm, he pressed into my entire length, and looking up at him, I could see only love. "That's my line," I whispered, then gasped when his reaching fingers sent little jolts of ley line energy into me, sparking against my skin and delving deep. My hold on him spasmed, and he leaned in, lips finding my neck.

"Oh, God," I groaned as he drew the smallest thread of ley line energy through me, running from my neck to my groin. It was almost too much, and I arched into him, reaching to guide him in. Foreplay? The entire evening had been foreplay, and I wrapped an arm around him, holding him close as a thrill flowed through me when I felt him enter me, the water making everything rougher than normal.

My breath left me in a rush, and I arched into him again, demanding more as he moved with me, slow at first, each motion meeting mine with an almost savage grace. My fingers grasped his shoulder, and when his teeth found my old vampire scar, I groaned, gasping as he worked it in time with our joined motion.

Water sloshed, and his hand cradled my head, cushioning me even as his lips and teeth savaged my scar, relishing the way he could make me feel. Sensation built upon itself, threatening to break. My breath came fast, and wanting everything, I sent a dart of my thought into his chi, smothering myself in him until I pulled the energy in his chi to me with a whip-crack snap.

Trent shuddered, jaw snapping shut on my ear.

Mine, I felt echo between us, but I wasn't sure whose thought it was first as a tingling rippled over us both, luring us into a deeper motion. Groaning, he arched forward to meet me, and with a sudden ping, I felt him climax, pushing deep into me with a sound of relief.

Wild with abandon, I shuddered, my hold on him spasming as his stolen energy snapped back to him, pulling a moan from me as it seemed to spark through the water like fire.

"Oh, God. Rachel," he whispered, as we clung to an electrifying bliss, each pulse of our hearts sending another jolt of passion through us both.

Until something went *kersploot* and a surge of cold water cascaded over us.

I gasped, my eyes flashing open as Trent swore, his weight coming down upon his elbow as he held my head in one hand and fumbled to replace the rock he'd knocked free with the other. He pulled from me in a sudden motion, biting back a yelp of pain as my muscles hadn't let go yet.

The mood utterly broken, he struggled to keep the freezing water out, rocks clattering and a muttered word of Latin joining the cricket-filled night until a warm wash of water blossomed once more and he looked down at me, water glistening to show every beautiful curve of muscle.

"I am so sorry."

Laughing, I pulled him down to me, holding him where he belonged until the water warmed us both again. "I don't know what for. That was amazing," I whispered, head against his shoulder, and an annoyed sound escaped him.

"I knocked the rock lose," he complained. "Completely broke the mood."

"And almost your manhood," I whispered, and he winced. Content, I played with the damp hair about his ears, liking the way the stars glinted past him and the way the water made glistening shadows against us. "Your aura is getting smutty."

"Is that a bad thing?"

I shook my head. "No. It, ah, might attract the wrong attention, though," I said, and his shoulders slumped in relief.

"Mmmm." Finally he eased himself back down next to me, and the world became even more right as his fingers traced a loving circle on my skin. "I've been doing a lot of magic lately. To take the place of technology." His eyes slowly slipped shut, and his motions slowed. "You sure it doesn't bother you? You're right that once I settle this and return to reality, there will be consequences. It's not as if I can hide a smutty aura."

"No." I studied the lighter dark against the top of the tree line. "Maybe you can convince someone to take it in lieu of giving you money."

He sighed, his muscles relaxing one by one. "It's possible, but I need the money more. And I kind of like it." A smile twitched his lips as he settled deeper into the warm water. "The smut, I mean."

Water drippled from my arm as I put it across his chest and rested against him. "It does give you a bad-boy flair."

He chuckled, eyes still closed. I wasn't sure I believed him, though as I looked over his camp, I saw nothing immoral here. Less businessman, more elf warlord suited him.

"Just missing a few things," he said, drowsy as his fingers' motion against me stopped. "You. The girls. But I get it. Living out in the woods is not for everyone."

A sigh shifted me, making little slices of cold skin as the water fell and lifted. "Yeah. As nice as this is, I would miss . . ."

Trent's eyes opened, their green lost in the dark. "What? Fighting for your right to exist? Your life on the line every day for someone else's problem?"

I snuggled closer, feet twining with his. "Honest? I'd get bored with this every day. Though tonight?" I sighed again, my focus on the stars beyond the dark trees. "This is perfect."

The water sloshed as Trent's arm tightened about me. "You're right. It's a pleasant exile, but I'm missing the game as well." He was silent a telling moment. "And my mother's library. Seeing a new generation of breeding cross the finish line. Coffee at the top of Carew Tower with the sun turning everything gold and black."

Guilt pulled through me as I lay twined with him, the soft noises of Tulpa and the ever-present crickets a soothing balm. Trent's arm around me was proof that I was loved, and that I loved in return, in so many ways. It made me wonder why I was trying so hard to stay in reality.

"Wow," Trent said, a hint of pride in his voice. "Did you know they did that?"

"What?" I said, and he took my hand in his, showing me our twin pearl rings glowing against each other. He'd spelled them himself, and if either of us took our ring off, the other ring would become black. Worst case, the ring was a call for help, but he'd made them to be a live-time reassurance that we were both all right. If my life wasn't in danger every four months, I'd say he was being overprotective, but I'd personally found a huge sense of relief in them every day.

"Oh, yeah." I felt myself warm as I snuggled closer. "They do that when we, ah, do that."

"I never noticed." A frown crossed him. "That reminds me. Don't move. I want to give you something before I forget."

I stiffened when he pulled away, water falling from him in a sheet as he stood and made his graceful way to his inlaid-stone patio. Fast from the cold, he padded to his tent, giving me an excellent opportunity to ogle his well-toned body lit by the dying fire until he vanished inside.

But his hands were empty when he came back out. "What is it?" I said when he quickly slipped into the warm water, exhaling as if he'd been holding his breath. One of his hands was clenched into a fist, and I sat up, scooting closer when he opened it.

"It's for you," he said as I looked at the small, child-size ring lying in his wet palm. "I want you to take it with you."

"Oh!" I glanced between the rings. "It's tiny," I said as I picked the new one up, smiling at the red stone and the whisper of hidden magic prickling my fingers. "What does it do?"

A smile quirked his lips. "I have no idea. I want you to trade it for the mirror."

My hand closed around it. "I'm not going to give it to Newt. Especially if I don't know what it does."

"If she wants it, give it to her." His hand took mine, opening it to take the ring and put it on my pinky, where it fit perfectly. "It was my mom's. I know it will last the trip."

The tiny red stone glinted wetly on my finger. "You think Newt might know what it does?"

He shrugged. "It's possible. I have a sneaking suspicion that my mother knew Al. There have never been many demons who let their summoning name be known. And, ah, if you run into me, seeing it on your hand might slow me down enough for you to escape."

I reached to tug it off. "Right after you accuse me of stealing it. Trent, I'm not trading your mother's ring for a mirror."

But his hand curved about mine, stopping me. "Yes, you will. If I don't know what it does, it's just a pretty ring." He paused. "And I like seeing it on your hand."

I angled it until the light made it shine. "Your mom had tiny fingers."

"Not really. She wore it on her pinky, too." He hesitated. "I could resize it if you want."

A flash of worry spiked through me. "No, pinky is fine," I said, and he tugged me closer and gave me a kiss.

"You're funny," he whispered. "If I was going to propose, I wouldn't do it naked in the middle of a forest."

"Trent . . ." I started, and he leaned in to give me another kiss.

"Give it to Newt," he whispered when our lips parted. "I can't sit here and watch you leave without trying to help. You wearing my mother's ring doesn't mean anything is changing."

But that's not what it felt like. Change was inevitable, especially if I couldn't fix things with the coven, and I forced myself to smile as I eased back into his arms and stared up at the stars. What he had here was wonderful. I knew Al wanted me to abandon reality, exchanging my chancy existence and the stress of balancing a city's wants for the pleasant expansion of knowledge. The coven would forget about me, and Ivy would be okay. Jenks, too.

But as I sat beside Trent and traced glyphs of protection on the palm of his hand, I knew that wasn't my path. I wasn't going into the past to keep the coven off my case. I was going because I had cursed someone, and it was my responsibility to uncurse him even if I lost everything in the process.

Full stop.

CHAPTER

11

"PERHAPS IF WE COULD HAVE THE AIR ON?" AL MUSED FROM THE back seat, and I met his pained expression through the rearview mirror before glancing at Ivy riding shotgun.

"We're almost there," I said, and Al made a rude noise. If I put the air on, Jenks would be cold. Same with opening the window. But when Al began to fuss with the driver-locked window switch, I compromised and cracked the windows, then turned up the heat.

Al made a neutral huff, and Ivy twitched in annoyance. It wasn't cool air the demon wanted but filtered or fresh. The anxious vampire was filling the car with the scent of sex and candy, her bloodred manicure making a steady, silent staccato on her knee as I drove a sedate thirty-five miles per hour through Cincy's night-emptied streets to Eden Park.

My long good-bye with Trent might have been a mistake as Jenks and I had returned home to find Al, Ivy, and Bis waiting for me, Al with a demon book in hand, Ivy with the couch covered in things from five years ago that I might need, and Bis tense and worried as he silently followed me around the church while I went over the last of the prep. Jenks, though, had been worse than all three of them combined, angry as Getty tearfully put layer after layer on him as he told me to shut up and go with it. It was too cold for him, especially with the blustery wind, but I couldn't stop him. The pixy still wasn't happy with me, currently sitting on Ivy's shoulder for warmth, bundled up so tightly that he could hardly fly.

I had decided to do the spell at Eden Park, not, as Al pointed out, because it would make it easy for Trent to attend my send-off but because the ley line there meant I wouldn't have to spend any time in reality before popping over to the ever-after. I could be home in an hour if all went well.

Please, God. Let this go well.

The scent of anxious vampire slowly dissipated in the odd mix of warm and cool air buffeting my face as I drove up the long drive to the overlook. My five-year-old underwear was riding up, and I squirmed, trying to get comfortable.

"Where did you get the ring?" Al asked suddenly, and I started, my gaze going to my new pinky ring snuggled up to the pearl ring, both glittering in the lot's lights.

"Trent. He thinks Newt might want it. It belonged to his mom." I paused. "She didn't get it from you, did she?"

"He gave you his mother's ring?" Worry pinched Al's expression.

"Relax, glitter poof," Jenks bad-mouthed. "It's on her pinky."

Al scowled, muttering, "Felicia Eloytrisk Cambri did not get it from me. What does it do?"

I slowed as we neared the overlook. "He doesn't know."

"You want to give Newt a ring whose magic is hidden?" Al blurted, and I winced, agreeing with him. But if it got me the mirror to free me from the coven, then it would be worth it. Probably.

Eden Park was empty, thanks to the early hour and the November chill. Three a.m. usually had witches in bed and the vampires at their local hot spot. I had my choice of parking, and yet my shoulders were tense as I pulled into a spot directly facing the Twin Lakes footbridge. "Bis, you want to do a perimeter?" I said before Jenks could volunteer.

"On it," the kid said, his red eyes glowing in the light from the dash as he hopped to first my shoulder, then the window, his cat-size body slipping through the crack like an octopus.

"Don't forget to check the bathrooms, pigeon spots!" Jenks shouted as the gargoyle launched himself and was gone.

Bis's silhouette cut a sharp shadow through the ambient light bouncing from the bottom of the low clouds as I turned the engine off. There'd been no sign of the coven when we'd left the church, not even Elyse's crow, but that was no guarantee that they weren't keeping tabs on me.

"Jenks is right. I don't like you going alone," Ivy said suddenly, and I forced a smile.

"I'll be fine." I pulled my bag from the back, narrowly missing smacking Al on the way.

"Why doesn't Al go with you?" she said as if he wasn't sitting there, and the demon made a tired exhale. "He'd be able to do magic five years ago."

"I can *do* magic now, vampire," Al grumbled.

"Because Al told me not to trust Hodin and I didn't listen," I said, guilt a soft twang.

Immediately Al opened his door and put one booted foot on the cold pavement. The night's chill rolled in as he got out and slammed the door shut. "I will assist your gargoyle in ascertaining that the area is clear," he said, voice muffled through the closed window.

"Thanks, Al."

But the demon was already walking away, his jauntily moving cane and his bearskin coat making him seem as if he'd stepped from the 1920s. Clearly unsettled, he went to the top of the bridge, placing his cane and hands atop the thick railing to stare over the shallow, man-made pond at the ducks sleeping at its center. Tension laced his stance, and worry. *Thanks a lot, Ivy.*

Perhaps I was being foolish risking my life to find a mirror to break Brad's curse. I had a feeling the only reason Al was helping was because it would also break the hold the coven was trying to put on me. Because if I didn't, I'd choose self-exile and there'd be nothing stopping Trent and me from making our relationship more . . . binding.

My gaze dropped to the two rings snuggled up to each other. Sighing, I worked them both off, not surprised when the pearl went black. Somewhere on the other side of the ley line, Trent's ring would have gone dark in response, but he was expecting it and wouldn't freak out. Brow furrowed, I dropped the pearl ring into the cup holder for when I returned, put the little ruby ring back on, and rolled up all the windows but for a crack for Jenks. I reached for the door to get out, hesitating when Ivy showed no sign of moving. Jenks looked miserable on her shoulder.

"I have to do this," I said, and Jenks scowled, not a flicker of pixy dust making it past his scarves and layers. "I'm going five years. No one is targeting me. Not even Al. If anyone sees me, all they will remember is a tall blonde once I get a glamour in place, Newt included."

Ivy cracked a smile. "You aren't that tall."

"You know what I mean." I gave her hand a quick squeeze over the console. "I'll be there an hour at the most. Al's line is like ten steps from the bridge, and from there, I shift to the ever-after. I bargain for the mirror. I come home. Al would stop me if he didn't think the time displacement curse will work."

"I'm not worried about the magic." Ivy stared out the front window, her expression utterly empty. "I'm worried about you. If you find yourself in trouble, come home, mirror or not. We can figure it out."

Jenks bobbed his head, clearly uncomfortable with his layers.

"Deal." But when I reached for the door handle again, Ivy touched my arm.

"Rachel . . ." She blinked fast, her ironclad control cracking. "We've been talking . . ."

I leaned across the space between us until our foreheads touched. I put a hand on her shoulder, a single finger curving around Jenks's back. "I will be careful," I whispered.

For a moment, no one moved, each of us worried about the same thing for different reasons. The delicious scent of vampire rose high in me, and pixy dust tingled at my fingers. Ivy's calm face held a ribbon of tension. In contrast, Jenks wore his mood on his sleeve, his eyes narrowed in frustration and his jaw clenched.

But there was nothing I could change, and so I got out.

Ivy was fast behind, a quiet murmur between her and Jenks as he shifted to wedge himself between her neck and coat. My breath steamed, and I tossed the keys over the car to her. She caught them in one hand as if expecting it, but the emptiness in her face tore at me. She had never liked the witchier aspects of me, and shifting through time was a big one.

"Oh, good. Kalamack made it," Al said sarcastically, his gaze on the ley line as Trent stepped out as if from nothing. His pace sure, the elf started our way, his slim outline marred by a full-length coat and scarf. The ley line was a wavering force behind him, and little rills of its energy spilled into me, making me jittery. I could do the charm anywhere, but having the line close was convenient.

Bis dropped to Trent's shoulder, and my adrenaline spiked. Everyone I loved was here.

"This is as far as Jenks and I go," Ivy said, and I pulled to a halt at the foot of the bridge.

"Okay." Loss spilled through me, and I hadn't even left yet. Al had already scoped out where I'd do the spell. The bridge supports rested on two squares of concrete. They were generally above water, and it was unlikely that anyone would be there at any given time. I could do the spell there and arrive in the past with no one the wiser.

Ivy's dark gaze flicked under the bridge. "We can see you from here, and it's only going to take a few seconds, right?"

"In theory." Though for me, it would be hours, best case. Worst case . . . I didn't want to think about the worst case. But for them? Yes. A moment.

I gave her another hug, ignoring Jenks's dramatic yelp as she gave me an unusually tight squeeze and then let go, head bowed. I felt as if I was leaving Cincinnati forever, and the odd thing was I'd never be leaving the city at all.

"Be right back, Jenks," I said, and he gave me a casual salute, most of him lost behind Ivy's collar.

My hand trailed from Ivy's shoulder as I turned away. The scent of unhappy vampire clung to me as I went to join Al at the top of the bridge. Head down, I hiked my shoulder bag higher. Inside it was just over a hundred bucks, all of it dated at least five years ago, my empty splat gun since the charms wouldn't make the trip, a wad of expired, paper-wrapped syringes to make more splat balls with, my new translocation stone on a length of black gold, an old phone of mine that didn't work anymore now but might in the past, its charger, and the spell book with the know-how to do the curse in case I lost my connection to the demon collective by going into the past and I had to twist the return curse from scratch. All my clothes were outdated and worn, but they were from five years ago and would last the trip.

"The far side of the bridge will put you closer to the ley line," Al said, and I nodded, my attention fixed on Trent as he closed the gap between us. Bis had left him to sit on Ivy's other shoulder, wings drooping. "Oh, for little green apples," the demon added when Trent took my hands and pulled me close. "Rachel, I will wait for you under the bridge."

"Thanks, Al," I said, and he brushed past us impatiently.

"Bis says that the park is empty but for one man in a taxi at the entrance having a smoke," Trent said. "I'll feel better once you get under the bridge and no one can see you."

"I'm not the one wanted for dealing in illicit genetic drugs," I said, trying to be funny, but my throat was tight and my gut hurt. "What do you think?" I added cheerfully, spreading my arms and doing a quick spin to show off my bejeweled jeans and matching jacket. "Retro."

Trent smiled and drew me back to him. "I always liked you in rhinestones."

"Yeah, but they don't belong on jeans," I said, my expression blanking as his smile vanished. His pearl ring was black, and a feeling of foreboding took me.

"Rachel," he started, and I shook my head.

"I have to do this." I pushed into motion, and he followed.

"Yes, but I don't know you five years ago," he cajoled.

"Hence the reason for going back that far," I said, head down as my worn boots found the dirt path to the bridge footings. "I'm a peon in the I.S., so if I run into anyone, nothing changes." I'd be a ghost. I couldn't contact anyone. Not Trent, not Ivy, not Jenks. No one at the I.S. or FIB. It had been a long time since I'd been on my own like this. Fortunately all the magic skills I'd gained between joining the I.S. and now would stick with me. At least that's what Al had promised.

Arms out for balance, I skidded down to the water, the worn path made by ducks and those wanting to feed them, but my steps faltered when Trent pulled me to a halt at the water's edge. Al made a muffled groan from under the bridge, frustrated.

"There has to be another way," Trent cajoled. "Maybe we can find a descendant of Atlantis and teach him or her how to make a mirror."

"Trent . . ." I took a slow breath. "This is it," I said, looking across the pond to where Ivy and Jenks waited. "I will be back in like five seconds."

His grip reluctantly fell away. There wasn't enough room for him under the bridge unless he wanted to stand in the calf-deep, duck-poop-green water.

"If you aren't, I'm coming after you," Trent said, and I leaned in, eyes closing as I gave him one last hug.

"Nothing will go wrong," I whispered, the scent of snickerdoodles and wine filling me. But I honestly couldn't say that for sure.

I gave him a kiss, long and lingering. Emotion tingled down to my toes, carried by my love and maybe a little ley line energy. "I have to do this," I said as I broke from him, my arms around his body holding him close. "I love you, but I need to fix what I did to Brad."

He exhaled, breath shaking. "I love you, too. Desperately," he said as he brought our clasped hands up between us. "I like who I am when I'm with you. Selfishly, please come back."

"Yes," Al interrupted with a caustic harrumph, "we all like who Trenton Aloysius has become. Let's get on with it before the moon crests and you are fighting nature itself."

My pulse quickened. It wasn't what I *could do* that would keep Newt from knocking me over the head and making me her familiar. It was what I knew. Resolute, I pulled my shoulder bag closer and picked my way to Al. I'd been down here lots of times to chase away the bridge trolls when I had worked for the I.S., not that I had ever had the heart to actually kick them out, but the area appeared empty. Either Sharps was gone or lurking in the deeper, warmer water.

"Circle," Al said tightly, the demon probably uncomfortable with his head brushing the underside of the bridge, but as I set my bag down to stick my finger, a bubbling froth rose up from the chattering water.

"Heyde-hey," a gurgling, wispy voice whispered, and I smiled, genuinely pleased as an ever-changing, water-covered face lifted from the green muck. One eye was a blind white from a past fight, telling me it was Sharps. The bridge troll had been in residence for as long as I could remember, and he pulled almost his entire upper torso from the polluted water, his blue limbs and algae-stained hair dripping. It was hard to say how big he actually was, as his size depended upon how much water he contained at any moment, but here, now, relaxed and not under threat, he was about six feet tall . . . and really skinny.

"Heyde-ho," I answered back. "Hi, Sharps. Glad to see you where you belong."

"Oh, for sweet everlasting banshee tears on a stick," Al complained. "Is there anyone else you need to say good-bye to?"

"I didn't recognize you in those old boots trip-trapping over my bridge," the troll said, a long purple-hued arm rising to pluck off a piece of concrete from under the bridge and eat it. It was no wonder the I.S. continually tried to drive them out, but I was of the opinion that everyone needed to be somewhere. "You need some help?" he asked.

"No. Just keep a lookout and let me know if the I.S. or coven shows up."

"I can do that." Sharps sank down, becoming a part of the water itself before flowing into the deeper pond. That he was watching was actually a relief. He had saved my butt in the past, giving me warning that could have made the difference between walking away from a conflict and being dropped by a spell before I had even known there was one.

Never ignore the chance to be nice, I thought as I nodded to Al that I was ready, and he smacked the hilt of a ceremonial knife into my palm.

"Circle," he prompted again, and I wiped my Jupiter finger clean against my old jacket. Crap on toast, the thing had a rhinestone pentagram on it. What had I been thinking?

The blade was so sharp, I hardly felt the cut, and I whispered a spell to keep the blood flowing until I had the admittedly big circle drawn. Chalk would have been easier, but blood was more secure, prudent in the current situation. Everything in the circle would move seamlessly through time. Five years of winter snow and spring flooding wouldn't wash it away.

Bis dropped down, uneasy as he landed on Trent's shoulder while I finished my circle and stood. The kid was clearly unhappy as he whispered in Trent's ear. Something was wrong.

"Don't stop," Trent said even as he turned to lurch up the embankment, Bis's wings wide behind his head for balance. "That guy moved and Bis lost him. I'm going to check it out." Trent hesitated. "See you in five minutes. Be safe, my love."

"Five minutes," I echoed. But a frown took me when I realized Ivy and Jenks, too, were gone. A trickle of unease tightened my spine. All that was left was tapping into the demon collective and reciting the words. *Easy*, I thought, not liking it. I'd be paying for this. I just hoped I had the street cred to cover it.

Nervous, I stepped into the circle and set my bag at my feet. I'd memorized the invocation, but I fumbled for the paper I'd written it down on.

"Rachel," Al said as I angled the paper to the chancy light. "I would not let you do this if I thought you didn't have a decent chance of surviving it."

"Surviving the curse or being five years in the past with no one watching my back?" I asked, and his brow scrunched in concern. I didn't see that very often, and it was worrisome.

"Stay clear of me," he continued, voice stern. "If we meet with your present abilities, I will try to take you as a familiar. Do not let Newt trick you."

I nodded as I remembered what he had been like before he had set aside his bitter hatred. Maybe not so much set aside, but replaced it with something he hadn't dared have for over two thousand years: hope.

"These are memory curses," he added as he dipped a hand into a pocket of his coat and withdrew three vials glinting with a hint of aura. "They were in Newt's things, so they will be as potent as they are old and will withstand the journey. Once the deal is struck and you have the mirror, use them on her so she doesn't remember you. She won't mind. She's already crazy from them."

I exhaled in relief. "Thanks," I said as I dropped them into my bag. I hadn't been eager to rely upon a purchased doppelganger disguise charm to hide my identity from an all-seeing demon. One problem solved.

"I know the temptation to warn yourself or Vivian concerning Lee's betrayal will be high, but don't." Again his brow furrowed, and I rubbed my thumb against my pricked finger, smearing the blood away. "Let the past be the past," he said cryptically. "Speak truth only to the dead."

Wise old man crap, I thought, nodding. *Speak truth only to the dead.* Sheesh.

"You have your return marker?" he added.

I took a stained redwood stirring rod from my pocket and broke it. The sharp snap jolted through me, and I had a flash of regret. It had been one of my dad's and was nearly a decade old if it was a day. Even now, he was helping me survive, and I tucked it into my jeans pocket as if it was gold.

"See you in a few," I said, and he started when I leaned out over my circle and gave him a hug. His grunt of surprise made me smile, and I let go when he patted my shoulder. Faint, so faint was the scent of burnt amber that I thought I might have imagined it.

"If you do not return, I will kill every single one of them. Children or not," he said.

"Al . . ."

"Go." Al took a symbolic step back. "Find your mirror. Find your way. And don't forget to register the curse to move through time, so no one else can do it."

It was sort of a "name it to bury it" kind of thing, and I nodded. Throat tight, I withdrew the coil of chain that was to be my outgoing marker.

When it mended, I should be far enough in the past. Holding it in my palm, I again studied the Latin on the scrap of paper. My hands shook, and I flushed, embarrassed. It was bad enough I was going to bargain with Newt. That I had to go into the past to do it made it a hundred times worse.

I took a breath, catching it at the sudden frothing by my feet.

"Rachel . . ." Sharps foamed, and from the parking lot, Ivy shouted, angry.

"Rache!" Jenks zipped under the bridge. "Get out of here. It's the coven!"

I spun, shocked, when Bis's wings beat about my neck and the kid landed on my shoulder. "Elyse is here," he said as he grabbed Jenks before the clothes-laden, struggling pixy could hit the water.

Al's expression went ugly as he turned and strode up the embankment. "Find the mirror and get back here to help," he demanded, and then he was gone.

He wants me to leave? I started at a boom of light and sound, my lips parting when Trent tangled Elyse's feet in a spell and brought her down. The charm threw the park into short-lived relief, and my eyes narrowed as I spotted Laker running from tree to tree, trying to get closer. *Son of a moss wipe.* Laker had followed us here, then called the coven because there were too many magic users for him to handle.

"Bis, drop a rock on that guy with the stick. He's after Trent," I said even as Orion took Elyse's place, beating Trent into a grudging retreat with thrown spell after thrown spell.

"Got it." Tense, the gargoyle held Jenks close and took to the air.

Ivy was struggling with Yaz and Adan. Al quickly joined her, joyfully bellowing obscenities as he doused the charm they had downed Ivy with. Wrathful, he stood over the shocked vampire and shouted ley line curses he couldn't invoke at the sky, scaring the youngest coven members into retreat.

"Do the curse, Rachel!" the demon demanded, magnificent as he swung his cane in threat at the two coven members to hit their incoming spells as if they were baseballs. "Go!"

It was hard, but if I did this right, I'd return in time to do some good.

Breathless, I checked to make sure I was within my circle. *Rhombus,* I thought, and a molecule-thin barrier stronger than the universe flickered into existence. *Damn it, Elyse. There's a difference between giving me an impossible task, and giving me an impossible task and then trying to stop me.*

"Morgan!" Elyse exclaimed, and I spun at the rattle of rocks and dirt as she slid down the embankment, eager for a fight. "You will desist all magic and put yourself under the coven's immediate control. I will not allow you to flee into a ley line."

I cringed as Trent shouted something and a boom shook the ground, wrinkling the smooth water. "Sorry. Gotta go."

She couldn't stop me. I was in a circle. The sooner I was gone, the sooner I'd be back, and I fumbled for the paper. My eyes closed as I sent my mind into the demon collective. A little ripple of presence caressed my soul, and my mind expanded as little whispers of conversation intruded into my psyche. If I was quiet, no one would know I was even here.

"I said stop!" Elyse shouted.

A thump rattled my circle, and I winced as one, then a second demon within the collective took notice of the raw power flickering through me. *Sorry. Got an issue here,* I muttered as I eased my grip on the collective and opened my eyes. Purple and red energy skated over my circle, foreign and unwelcome. It was Elyse's spell, but I had drawn a blood circle, and anything she could throw at it would only make it stronger.

"You overstepped yourself," I said, a feeling of pride taking me as I saw Ivy and Trent on one side of me, Al on the other. They were keeping the rest of the coven at bay. And Elyse? Elyse didn't have a chance breaking my circle alone.

"You will cease!" Elyse's black hair rose as she pulled deeper on the ley line, little rills of purple aura sparking from the tips. Smug, I shook my head and closed my eyes, sending my awareness deep into the demon collective once more. A smile found me, growing as I sensed the spells, curses, and charms that the demons had stockpiled through the ages, curses of war, spells of deceit, magic created by demons long dead. I could use them—provided I paid for them.

"*Ab aeterno,*" I said to pull the right curse into me. I shuddered as everything in the circle suddenly made a little hiccup. It meant from outside time itself, and it felt as if I was now moving in tandem with but apart from reality. The line I was holding glowed brighter, as if there were now two of them. I opened my eyes, jerking when Elyse slammed a roundhouse kick into my protection bubble.

"I never understood why Vivian trusted you," the young woman said bitterly. "You are a demon trickster."

"I'm not trying to escape. I'm trying to find a friggin' mirror!" I said.

Behind her, Al had fallen to one knee, almost in the water, with a hand outstretched as he shook his head, warning the rest off. The remnants of a preprepared spell flickered about his fingers, dying quickly. Bis was on his shoulder, wings spread and hissing at Adan. Sharps rose up, bellowing as he sucked in enough water to become the size of an elephant. Cowed, Adan retreated. *Crap on toast. I have to get out of here so I can get back.*

"*Obtineo et teneo,*" I said, my anxiety growing. With a sudden pop, the power in the line doubled, a dizzy, heady mix. To obtain and keep: it was the spell to spindle my life's energy as I moved backward through time, and I had to dovetail it into the first spell so they would work together, or I'd never have enough energy to make the return trip.

"I will have you out of that circle!" Elyse shouted as she held her singed hand close.

"*Iuncta iuvant,*" I said to bind the two curses—and my conviction that this was going to work grew as I felt the two curses twine about each other, little rills of energy knotting them together like twisted wool.

Elyse had given up trying to take my circle. Bowed almost double, she dragged a knife across the worn cement to make a second circle outside my first. My breath caught as Bis pinwheeled to evade Elyse's crow. Jenks was in his arms, and torn, I looked at my friends fighting to give me this chance. I had sworn I would never let anyone pay for my chances again.

"Rachel, go!" Al shouted, utterly magnificent as he threw another earth charm and Bis barrel-rolled himself and Jenks to safety. "Return to end this!"

He was right, and feeling ill, I turned my attention inward to finish twining the spells and make a new one. A curious prickling was rippling over my skin, and my circle had begun to pulse.

It's Elyse, I thought as I saw her within her invoked circle, nesting outside of mine. What the hell was she trying to do?

"You will not run away this time," she said as our eyes met, and then her hand touched my circle's surface and pushed.

"Be right back." Head bowed, I dropped my mind into the collective. *"Respice in icta oculi,"* I whispered.

And the spell invoked.

CHAPTER

12

I YELPED AT THE UNEXPECTED DROP IN THE LEY LINE, FALTERING TO a knee when vertigo hit me. I mentally scrambled to renew my hold on the line. It tasted different, angry maybe, that I was trying to bend the rules of time so far, if energy could be thought capable of such. Eyes clenched shut, I forced my mind past the resistance until the rough connection smoothed and the flow renewed.

I was still connected to the demon collective by way of the spell itself, and I could feel the energy-spindling curse gathering up my life's force as I sloughed it off, moving backward through time. The twined spells were working. All that was left was to register the process.

"*Evulgo*," I whispered to drop what I'd just done into the collective as a unique expression of magic. I was sure no demon would ever even think to look for it, seeing as my actions were being spread out over who knew how many years. I could feel them, lightly in my mind, their collective thoughts rising and falling like the tide as the days and nights passed. "Jariathjackjunisjumoke," I added to set me as the originator of the spell, and finally, "*Ut omnes unum sint,*" to seal it. It was done. Now all I had to do was survive the trip.

My breath came in with the dry choking feel of sawdust filling my lungs, and I held it, squicked out by the continued, utterly weird sensation of my body's energy spilling from me as if it was being pulled into a tube. My head began to hurt, then ache.

"I can do this," I whispered as my fisted hands pushed into the damp cement. The length of black gold that Al had given me to gauge my passage shook in my grip, the two ends glinting. Five years. He had broken it five years ago. When it mended, I could stop. Not a moment sooner. Too bad my head was beginning to feel like a migraine and a heart attack had a baby.

The booms and crackles of a magical fight were gone, replaced by an odd rise and fall of that headache-inducing whine. I slowly pried my eyes open, panting as I tried to figure out where the light was coming from. A big nothing hung past the red-sheened bubble that protected me. It wasn't dark, and it wasn't light. My mind had no reference. It was as if the entire universe was in this small bubble, and perhaps for me, it was.

It was almost like being stuck in a line jump, but unlike a line jump, I still had my body. I could feel the cold of the cement and the grit between my fingers. The scent of blood from my circle was thick in my nose. I was here, present.

"I can do this," I said again, teeth clenched. The chain in my hand was slowly losing its tarnish, but it was still broken. My vertigo was awful, and worried I would collapse and break my circle, I drew less on the line to slow my passage down.

"Morgan," a high voice rasped in pain. "Oh, God, let me go."

I spun, my butt hitting the cold cement as I lost my balance. It was Elyse, curled into a tiny ball behind me. She was in my circle.

Shocked, I stared. "How the hell did you get in here?"

Elyse struggled to find my gaze, her focus distant. "Let go. You're pulling on a line through me. Burning. Let go . . ."

Through her? I thought, realizing now why the line felt wrong. "How did you—" I caught my next words. "You're not supposed to be here!" I said as I figured it out. My circle was down. Elyse had taken it, and now it was Elyse's circle that contained the spell, not mine. She must have assumed control of my circle right as the spell invoked. It was no wonder she was in pain. She was channeling the entire ley line.

"Let go of me," she groaned again in agony. "You will rot for this. I promise you. Stop the curse. Stop it!"

"You idiot!" I rolled to my knees, startled when her coat winked out of existence. "What did you think was going to happen?"

"Stop the spell!" Elyse screamed, eyes mere slits. "I can't let go of the line. It's burning!"

"Then maybe you shouldn't have tried to take control of the spell!" Frantic, I looked at the length of chain. It hadn't mended, but Elyse . . . Elyse was shaking in anguish.

"You're burning me alive," she rasped, head down.

Son of a moss wipe, I thought. *"Stet!"* I shouted, my sympathy warring with my annoyance as I let go of the ley line running through both of us. *I should have known when the taste of the line shifted,* I thought as the spell ended with a soul-snapping thump.

I jerked, choking down a gasp of surprise when a burst of white light slammed into me. Elyse's protection bubble had fallen, and I pulled the scent of warm, mucky water deep into my lungs as my eyes teared and I coughed the sensation of dust from my lungs. I blinked as the light dimmed and the world slowly became understandable again. It had only been the light of the moon, but it had seemed as if the sun had gone nova.

Lips parting, I stared out from under the bridge at the softly lit park, only now believing what I had done. Thirty seconds ago, the moon had been a bare sliver almost below the horizon. Now it was nearing full and hanging high among the trees. Shocked, I reached for the bridge's support. The stone was warm under my shaking hand, and as I straightened, a sharp *ting . . . ting, sploot* drew my eyes as something bounced to the edge of the footing and into the ugly green water. Whatever it had been, it was gone.

"It worked!" I exclaimed, then winced when the couple walking their dog noticed me and continued on, heads close together as they gossiped. I'd done it, and I touched the outside of my pocket to make sure the snapped stirring rod was still there. It was, and I exhaled in relief.

"What the hell did you do with my clothes?" Elyse croaked from the base of the footing. "I think I'm going to be sick."

I turned to see Elyse kneeling over the water, trying not to throw up, stark naked apart from her socks. She was younger, too, her dark hair long and having a simple cut. I closed my eyes in a strength-gathering blink. I looked pretty much the same. *Almost,* I mused, sighing at the demon mark decorating the underside of my wrist. *At least I still have my clothes,* I thought as I shuffled my jacket off and draped it over her.

Elyse clutched at it, but I wasn't going to hold her hair back as she fell into dry heaves.

Al's chain lay on the cement like a broken promise, and I picked it up. I stood, slipping the necklace into a pocket, and tried to figure out how far I had managed to get. My hair was longer, bound in a braid I recognized needing at least eight pixies to make—Matalina must still be alive. Then there was that demon mark, a single slash through it, a promise to pay Al back for saving my life. If I had one on my foot, that would narrow the time down as well, but I wasn't about to look now. I ran my thumb against my fingers, feeling a prickling of smut on my aura, but it was the tentative touch on my neck that gave me the best idea of when we were as the flash of arousal nearly brought me to my knees, flaming all the way to my groin.

"Crap on toast," I whispered, breathless and kind of ticked. It was my vampire scar, and it was full and potent, almost new. Five years? Not a chance. *Two maybe,* I thought as I peered out at the world, worried.

Elyse had gone quiet, and I rested one shaky hand on the bridge, the other on my neck, as I wondered when we were. It was warm. There were leaves on the trees. *Summer.*

"Where is everyone?" Elyse wiped her mouth, glancing at my heavy shoulder bag before peering up at me. "You think it's funny? To spell my clothes off? You are an ass, Morgan! You hear me? An ass!"

What, by Tink's little pink rosebuds, am I supposed to do with her? "I didn't take your clothes, and your friends are fine."

Elyse staggered to her feet. If she wasn't so haggard, she'd look like a frat boy's dream in my bedazzled leather jacket hanging mid-thigh. "Oh, so they just magically vanished for no reason? What is your problem!" she shouted, and then she cried out in sudden, unexpected pain, her face creased as she staggered, reaching for the curved wall of the bridge. "You singed me!"

"Elyse, wait," I said as she stomped to the embankment.

"Orion?" the woman called as she picked her way up in her white socks. "Yaz!"

For one moment I thought I'd let her just go, and then I hiked my shoulder bag higher and started after her. She hadn't gone far, and I found her at the base of the bridge, mouth agape as she stared at the moon peeking through the trees thick with leaves. "How long was I out?" she whispered, fear pinching her expression. "What did you do to me?"

"I didn't do anything," I said, then put up a hand, asking for patience. "This is not my fault," I added as she slowly inched away. "You couldn't just let me go back and get the mirror."

"Go back?" she echoed, and I nodded. "You mean like in time?" she squeaked, her attention darting to the moon.

"As far as I know, Orion and Yaz and Adan are fine." Sympathy and a little guilt tightened my chest. "Ah, how badly are you singed? I didn't know that would happen."

Elyse smacked my reaching hand away and retreated two more steps into the bushes. "You are in so much trouble," she said, her eyes on my demon mark.

"For what?" I glanced at the two people pushing a stroller to the parking lot. "I haven't done anything illegal," I said softly. "I think. I need to find out when we are. I swear, if I didn't get far enough into the past, I will leave you here to take the long way home."

But I wouldn't. She could do too much damage, and worry tightened my chest as I looked for a trash can and maybe a receipt with the date. I doubted the charm to spindle my life force had spindled hers. She might not have any other choice than to take the long way. Stasis charms only lasted three days before they spontaneously broke to prevent death by dehydration. At least, the contemporary ones did.

"My God, you really think you can go back in time?" Elyse said, half hidden in the bushes to make her white socks stand out. "Are you serious?"

"Yeah." There was a trash can twenty steps away, but I wasn't ready to walk away from her yet. "I honestly didn't know it would hurt. I'm, ah, sorry about that, but you shouldn't have interfered with the spell."

Elyse's eyes narrowed. "Why am I naked and you aren't?"

"Because I spent two hours yesterday in a secondhand shop finding clothes that existed five years ago. Ah, you don't happen to know when you bought your socks, do you?"

The woman pulled my jacket tighter about herself and glared. "Take me back. Now."

"Um, right. Just sit and let me find out when we are." Motioning her to stay, I edged away, my new-again boots thumping as I strode to the overflowing trash can at the water's edge. It wasn't my fault if she was stuck here, but I still felt responsible.

"Slick?" Elyse shouted for her familiar, and I grimaced, ignoring her. She wouldn't get far in only my jacket and a pair of socks. Head down, I began to pick through the trash for something with an expiration date, finally finding a yogurt cup: August 20, 2007. It wouldn't be the exact date, but it would be close.

I exhaled as I dropped it into the trash bin. August 2007. Upside: the original ever-after still existed. Downside: both Newt and Al would know me. I'd have to get Newt alone, get the mirror, and dose her with her own forget charm without her caretaker/familiar Minias knowing.

"You have to undo this," Elyse said from the bushes. "I can't do eighteen again!"

A familiar, cheerful *ping* came from my bag, and I swung it around, trash forgotten. My old phone had connected to a tower. I had the date. *Gotta love it when things go right . . .*

"Where's my pin?!" Elyse shouted. "Morgan, did you take my pin?"

Seriously? She is worried about a pin? Hands shaking, I dug my phone out. My lips parted. One fifteen a.m. July 28. I had just missed my birthday. But that didn't throw me as much as the text. It had posted a while ago and was from David. He was frantic. Three of his one-night stands had committed suicide.

"Oh, crap on toast," I whispered, my breath leaving me. Staggering, I felt for the bench and sat down. It wasn't August. It was late July.

Kisten is alive, my thoughts sang, but my gut hurt as I stared at the moon, feeling betrayed. This was bad. Al was actively trying to abduct me. Ivy's girlfriend Skimmer wanted to kill me. Trent was trying to blackmail me into being his lackey. In about forty-eight hours, I was going to arrest him at his own wedding. But the worst? Kisten was still alive. I couldn't warn him. I couldn't stop it.

"I can't do this," I whispered, gaze unseeing on the townhomes across the park. Elyse was worried about having to do eighteen over? How about sit and do nothing knowing the man you loved was going to die twice to keep a monster from eating you alive and enslaving what was left?

Hand at my middle, I stared at David's frantic texts. I'd seen them first two years ago, and they still filled me with fear. He would be jailed for manslaughter, the church would be condemned, and Kisten . . .

I forced myself to take a breath, vision swimming.

Kisten would be made into a blood gift before the night was over. I wouldn't know he had died for days. But I knew now, and it hurt. Bad.

"How did I ever survive my life?" I whispered. But it was obvious. I had my friends. Ivy, Kisten, Jenks. The pixy kids. Ceri across the street, and Keasley. David, who was about to have the worst week in his life. I couldn't talk to them. Any of them. Not to help me. Not to help them. "This had better be worth it," I whispered.

And then my head snapped up at Elyse's angry shriek.

"Don't touch me! Back off!" she shouted, and I got to my feet, hand fumbling in my bag for my empty splat gun. Two men in uniform stood before her as she backed farther into the bushes.

"Ma'am, we are not going to hurt you," one said, and my reach for my gun faltered. It was the I.S. Me and the I.S. were not on the best of terms at the moment, and I shrank deeper into the shadows. "We only want to make sure you're okay. Get you some help."

"I don't need your help," Elyse snapped. "I'm the lead member of the coven of moral and ethical standards, and you will turn and walk away. Better yet, go arrest Rachel Morgan. It's her fault I'm here."

Non constat, I whispered as they sent their gaze to follow her pointing arm. Relief was a quick flush as I felt my mind dip into the demon collective and the curse to make me hard to see invoked. I hadn't been sure if I'd be able to. It was only my body that changed. My mind and all the connections I'd made were still there.

I blinked fast, refusing to let the tears of relief start as the two officers spun back to Elyse, the fun and games clearly over. Al had given me the curse so I'd stop using the elven equivalent that Trent had shown me. Al was a thought away, and I wondered what he'd do if I reached out and summoned him here. Right now. I could do it. The demons were still cursed.

Something akin to grief clenched my gut. *Damn you, Elyse.*

"Ma'am, come with us," the taller officer said as the second made a quick call on his two-way. "We'll get you some clothes. Something to eat. A warm cot."

"I am not crazy, and I'm not homeless," Elyse said, then gasped as one reached for her. "Let me go. You will take your hands off me. Stop it! Let me go!"

But it would be days before Elyse could tap a line, thanks to me, and the two I.S. officers had her easy.

"Morgan!" she shrieked as she struggled, and I slid even deeper into the shadows, my heart pounding when I hid behind the tree, unable to watch them wrestle her into submission and tote her to their car. She screamed and fought, but I let them do it. I wasn't sure why, only that I was confused and angry, and maybe a night in the drunk tank would do her good. That, and if I got caught or seen, it would cause a lot worse trouble.

"Just down her. Down her!" one of the agents exclaimed, and then Elyse's protest cut off. Her silence was almost worse than her protests, and I peeked out from behind the tree as they pushed her into the cruiser and shut the door.

"Hollows Mental Health?" the second officer asked, and the first shook his head, little more than a silhouette under the chancy streetlight. "She thinks she's coven."

"Indecent exposure and resisting," he said. "A night in the spell-drunk cell. If she still thinks she's coven in the morning, someone else can deal with it."

"Works for me." Head shaking, the man crossed to the other side of the car and the two got in. I could see them talking, but the car didn't move, and I stayed where I was, wondering if perhaps I should have done something. If she contacted Vivian, it would complicate matters. But to be seen would be worse. If they recognized me, they'd show up at the church wanting answers my other self couldn't give. I could maybe down them from behind, but the risk they'd see me was too great.

Still, I gave it some thought, startled when a soft frothing in the water behind me turned into a watery, purple-veined face.

"Rachel," Sharps said, nothing more than two eyes and a mouth. "Everything okay?"

I hesitated, my initial reaction to flee faltering. He thought I was my younger self. Not only that, but he was seeing through the demon's unnotice curse. "Ah, hi, Sharps. Heyde-hey."

"Heyde-ho," he answered, his body taking on more definition. "I didn't hear you cross the bridge. You get new boots?"

My gaze went from the parked squad car to my old boots, brand-new now and without a scuff. "Um, yes. I didn't mean to bother you. I was doing a spell under the bridge."

"So I saw." Sharps eased down in a froth of bubbles. "I would have come over sooner, but I thought the I.S. was here to jolt the pond. Who was that? You got a new partner?"

He obviously thought I was me from two years ago, and I began to relax. "No. Just someone I'm trying to help," I said, and he bobbed his head, algae falling into his one blind eye.

"She knocked this into the water. I thought you might want it," he said as a thin, purple-veined arm snaked from the water and set a Möbius strip pin on the retaining wall.

"Oh, my gosh, thanks," I said as I picked it up.

But he was already melting back into the pond, reluctant to let the headlights of the I.S. car find him as the engine started and they began to leave.

"Take care of yourself, Sharps," I muttered as I hoisted my shoulder bag higher and began making my way to the bus stop. I had to get to Fountain Square, where I could hop a bus to anywhere both sides of the river. Maybe by the time I got there, I'd know where I was going. Piscary's to beg for Kisten's life? The ever-after to bargain with an insane demon for a mirror to save my own? Or perhaps door number three, the I.S. to bail out Elyse before she contacted Vivian?

Either way, I was going to need one heck of a disguise.

Or maybe not . . .

CHAPTER

13

I STOOD WITH MY TOES EDGING THE YELLOW LINE BEFORE THE counter, trying to look reasonable, not annoyed. The not-annoyed part was getting harder. My red, sequined shirt and bejeweled jeans were doing me no favors, and I wished I'd found something else to wear. I didn't look like a hooker trying to bail her friend out, but it was close.

"I'm sorry, Ms. Atakat," the woman behind the plastic window said, clearly not sorry at all. "You can't post bail on a Jane Doe."

"But she's not a Jane Doe," I insisted. "She's Elyse Atakat, my sister." Elyse was wisely going with Jane Doe, and I thought it prudent I use my birth father's name instead of my own—Donald Atakat, or as the world knew him, Takata. Not a big leap to figure out, but things were different back in the sixties when he took the stage name.

"If she independently confirms that that's her name, I might be able to help you. Until then, she is retained."

"For indecent exposure?" I said loudly, but there wasn't a hint of play in the stony woman's expression.

"For resisting arrest. She won't be released for bail until we can verify her identity."

"I told you who she is," I complained. But I was getting nowhere. "Can I talk to her?"

"Check back later." Done with me, the officer focused on her screen. "She has some paperwork."

"Okay." I dropped back, knowing I was only pissing her off now. Paperwork meant they had someone coming in to see her before they pawned her off on another city service—probably a mental health group, seeing as they found her half naked in the park claiming to be a member of the coven of moral and ethical standards. "Can I wait?" I added, and the officer glanced at the orange chairs lining one wall and nodded.

"Thank you." My voice was listless, and I scuffed across the worn tile. I'd made a mistake in letting the I.S. take Elyse last night, putting my own safety before the greater probability that the woman was going to make matters worse. My first instinct that a night at the I.S. might bring the proud woman down a peg had been vanity on my part. It was far more likely that the I.S. would identify her even if she kept her mouth shut, and that they might be contacting Vivian this very moment had me antsy.

Cincy's overnight bail office was on the ground floor in a corner of the I.S. building, giving it convenient below-street access to one of the city jails. A wide plate-glass window looked out onto the sidewalk, just starting to brighten up with the first hints of morning. Traffic was almost nil, and at six in the morning, the awkwardly small short-time parking lot across the street was empty but for a single dusty compact.

I felt the early hour all the way to my bones as I sat down and set my bag on my lap. Crap on toast, I was sitting in the orange chairs, and I closed my eyes and let my head thump back into the wall. Elyse was probably more comfortable than me, and I stretched my legs out, stiffening at the sound of pixy wings.

My eyes slitted, but it wasn't Jenks, and I felt a moment of loss as I watched the winged four-year-old in a tattered smock hunt for sugar in the nearby trash can. Four years old and on her own. Life was hard for pixies in the city.

But at least I knew where Elyse was, and my pulse slowed as I relaxed. I hadn't been sure, having detoured to a convenience store before coming here. My hair was still curly, but now it was blond, thanks to an amulet. That was the extent of my disguise. I would have done more, but I didn't know how much of a dent Elyse's bail would put in my finances. I had no sleepy-time potions, no doppelganger charms. Nothing.

Except what I have at my fingertips, I thought as I pulled on the nearest ley line and a hint of power flickered about my fingers. I made a fist and the glow vanished. The place might seem deserted with its empty chairs, one attendant, and no spell checker, but there were cameras on the ceiling and only two doors: one leading to the street and one to the temporary holding cells. It took an ID card to open the latter. I was stuck.

My shoulders shifted in a sigh as I settled in to wait. Trent's mom's ring caught my attention, and I fiddled with it, spinning it until the red stone was hidden in my palm. I didn't care if Newt offered me three wishes. She wasn't getting this.

It usually didn't take this long to bail someone out, but they probably hadn't processed her yet. Elyse wasn't drunk, and once they unspelled her and realized that, it would be down to indecent exposure and resisting. That, and her wild claim of covenship. They shouldn't hold her for that. That she was underage was an issue, and I closed my eyes.

Immediately Kisten's smile intruded. My eyes flashed open, and I stiffened, pulling my shoulder bag higher up my lap. If I had my days right, I would find Kisten at the curb outside of Piscary's this afternoon, tossed out like last night's garbage.

"I can't stop this," I said, feeling breathless and unreal. Kisten was going to die. I had seen it happen. I couldn't change it.

Throat tight, I blinked fast and stared out the front window, gaze going to the flash of someone's headlights as a car swung into the tiny parking lot. A tall man in a thin, fluttery overcoat got out, fumbling with the keys as he locked the door. Glancing both ways, he strode across the street, pace fast.

"Someone's bad night is going to turn into a bad day," I mused aloud, thinking the sixtyish man looked especially annoyed as he stiff-armed the door and strode in. There was a light stubble on his face, and his short black hair was flat as if he'd been sleeping on it.

Then I froze. Holy crap on toast. *Scott?*

I pulled my stretched-out legs back under me, the new soles hiccupping on the dirty floor. It was Scott. Coven member Scott. Not old, not young, but the exact age I saw him through the transposition charm.

Ahhh, mother pus bucket.

I glanced at the door to the holding cells, then Scott making a beeline to the attendant. She must have been waiting for him, because she was already on the phone, her intent expression clearly for Scott, not whoever she was talking with.

They must have gotten Elyse's prints and connected the dots, I thought. Damn. I had to get her out. I'd thought I'd have more time.

"She's on her way," the woman said, and Scott bobbed his head, immediately taking his phone from his pocket and beginning to scroll.

I sat up, glad he hadn't noticed me. Pulse fast, I slowly rose, pretending to stretch as I gently, ever so carefully pulled more strongly on the ley line, spindling it so he wouldn't notice the draw. *Corrumpo,* I thought as I flicked a tiny wad of it at one of the cameras at the ceiling.

With a tiny puff of smoke, the little red light went out.

That, he noticed, and I felt his gaze land on me even as the door to the cells opened and a woman officer came out. Her smile was tired but honest as she went to greet him. Scott's attention returned to her.

The door to the holding area was arching closed. I had one chance.

I gathered my resolve. *"Corrumpo,"* I whispered, throwing another jolt of energy across the room. Scott spun, crouching as the gold and red ball smashed into the window, imploding it inward instead of out.

The officer's hand went to her sidearm as she shoved Scott behind her. Scott hit the dirty tile, a shimmering field of purple and green rising up from an undrawn circle to protect them from the falling glass. The counter attendant shrieked in alarm and dropped out of sight.

Desperate, I lurched for the door, just managing to get my hand in between it and the jam. Shoving it open, I slipped inside and pulled it shut.

"What happened?" someone shouted from the cells, and I pressed up against the yellow wall, my fear real as two uniformed officers ran toward me.

"It's a drive-by spelling," I said, hand shaking as I pointed at the closed door. "They need you out there. Front window is busted. I think someone's hurt!"

They pushed past me. I got a glimpse of the officer helping Scott up off the floor. Glass made an obvious ring around them where his circle had been, and I yanked the door to close it.

"Hey!" Scott shouted as our eyes met, and then I had the door shut.

"*Sub frigido.*" I touched the door panel, a smirk finding me as a thin trace of ice ran from it. Frozen shut. If they broke the lock to get through, I wouldn't be liable for damages.

I turned, stifling a shudder at the cells lining the corridor. "Elyse!"

"You have *got* to be kidding me . . ." came a high voice, and then stronger, "Here!"

I jogged past the holding cells, feeling like a kid looking for their mom in a grocery store as I paused at each opening, scanning for a familiar face. An alarm buzzed from deeper in the building, and someone began pounding on the door.

"Elyse?" I called again, and then an arm waved from between the bars. "Thank God. Why did you tell them who you were? Scott is here."

"Scott?" she echoed, seeming insufferably young and questionably innocent in a pair of thin gray sweats and an equally ugly pair of white sneakers. They'd let her keep my jacket against the chill, and there was a strap of charmed silver about her wrist.

"I didn't tell them who I was," she protested in a high voice as I tried to remember what the spell to unlock a cell in an emergency was. "They said a woman had come to bail me out. I thought it was Vivian."

"You let them print you," I said. *Apertus,* I thought, and nothing happened.

"I didn't have a choice! You really think I want Vivian showing up here? She thinks I'm at coven camp." Elyse hesitated. "I am at coven camp."

Quis custodiet ipsos custodes, I tried next, glancing down the hall at a sudden pull of power. Little rills of purple and gold energy were slipping around the door, massing into a dangerous field. My spell wouldn't last much longer. "Coven camp? You really call it that?" *Adaperire!* I thought desperately, and in a sudden tinkling, every lock in the hall broke under the demon curse—including the one I'd put on the door to the holding cells. *Son of a moss wipe . . .*

"Out!" I shouted as the main door slammed open. Scott was silhouetted in a smoky haze, the light bright behind him.

"Oh, shit," Elyse whispered, then bolted out of the cell.

"Stop!" someone shouted, and suddenly the entire hall was full of fleeing people.

"Not that way!" I grabbed Elyse's arm and pulled her free of the mass exodus. "We have to get out of here before they lock down the building," I said as the escaping detainees flooded the wider hall in a doomed attempt for the street.

She looked desperate, and I tugged her in the opposite direction, pulse fast as we jogged up a narrow corridor. Multiple alarms were going off and people were shouting. I jumped at the thump of a spell taking someone down.

"It's a dead end," Elyse said bitterly as we found the locked fire door, and the three people who had come with us skidded to a halt.

"Just . . . trust me." Hands shaking, I punched in a code. It would tell them where we were, but we had a ten-second head start. I could do a lot with ten seconds.

Elyse's eyes widened as the door alarm went off, and I shoved it open. "You know the code?" she asked as the people with us fled onto the seldom-used loading dock, exuberant with the promise of freedom.

"I used to work here. No, wait!"

But she didn't listen, and she followed them as they made the long jump to the pavement. Grimacing, I shot a bolt of raw energy at the camera, then took the awkward jump as well, grabbing her arm and yanking her back and down to crouch against the cold cement behind us. There was a metal lip just overhead. It was only a few feet wide. I prayed it would be enough. This was not where I had intended to wait out the next two minutes, but our ten-second window was gone.

"Shut up!" I hissed as Elyse struggled, and her hot retort died at the sudden scuffing of shoes above us.

"*Teneo!*" someone shouted gleefully, and I put my arm across Elyse's chest like my mom used to do when she had to stop the car fast.

"Got 'em!" someone else said, and the three fleeing people cried out as black coils of energy wrapped around them, yanking them into an unmoving knot . . . a scant few feet from the sidewalk.

"Not bad. You actually saw daylight," the first voice said, and Elyse cringed when two officers hopped to the pavement, inches from us. "The last you're going to see for months, numb nuts!" he added derisively.

But they didn't spot us, and as they casually walked to the still-squirming people, I drew Elyse to her feet and we slunk behind the dumpster. Again, not my go-to hiding spot, but it would work. *Please work.*

"Can you tap a line yet?" I whispered as we wedged between the filthy container and the cold brick wall, and she shook her head, hand trembling when she held up her wrist in explanation. There was a strip of charmed silver around it, and she watched, anxious, until I dug in my bag for my clippers and cut it.

The snap was loud, and we both froze as the two officers continued to cajole and berate the three people shuffling back to detention.

"How about now?" I asked, truly concerned, and Elyse winced.

"Not yet," she whispered. "Two days, maybe."

It was about what I had expected, and I exhaled as I leaned to see if the camera was still out. It was.

The fire door shut, and the alley became quiet. I worked my cautious way out from behind the dumpster, scanning for any more cameras. There'd been only the one when I worked in shipping my first six months in the I.S., but that was ages ago, even if I was two years into the past.

"Like you really care if I can tap a line," Elyse muttered, and guilt pricked me.

"I didn't know that it would burn," I said. "And I don't remember asking you on this magic carpet ride to begin with. And yes, I do care. I've burned my synapses before, and it's awful. Two days sounds about right. Don't push it. You'll make it worse."

"I know how to handle sensory burns," she snapped, and frustrated, I started for the bright rectangle at the end of the alley, knowing she'd follow. I was her ticket home. *I hope.*

"Ah, we can get a cab at the corner," Elyse said, voice subdued as she joined me.

"And go where?" My voice was harsher than I'd intended, and I felt a surge of sympathy as she took a long step to come even. She was cold, and alone, and in an ugly pair of sweats.

Speaking of which . . . "Hey, hold up," I said as we scuffed to a halt, the sidewalk and the rest of the world three steps from us. "You are a moving target dressed like that. I can glamour you if your coven sensibilities can tolerate a demon charm." Yeah, it had sounded a little bitter, but I had yanked her ass out of I.S. lockup, and she hadn't even said thanks.

"Demon?" She looked at me as if I was trying to entrap her. "I'm not taking the smut."

I rocked back, arms over my chest. "Wow. Just wow," I grumped. But I didn't want to get caught, and she was in institution gray sweats. Irate, I motioned for her to stay where she was as I dug about in my bag to find the stone. A sudden prick of pain lanced my finger and I jerked back.

Jenks! I thought, utterly terrified as I pulled my bag open wider. But it was only Elyse's coven pin snuggled up next to the glamour stone, and my shoulders slumped as I took them both out. The pixy had stowed away before. It would have been awful if he had again—awful even as I desperately missed him. Fingers shaking, I handed the pin to her.

"I think this is yours," I said, and Elyse's eyes widened as she practically snatched it away. "Sharps found it in the water. I'm guessing it fell off when you lost your clothes."

"Oh, my gosh," she said, sounding all of fifteen as she rubbed the dried muck from it. "Thank you."

That's what I get a thank-you for? "You're not going to wear it, are you?" I said as she began to fasten it to her collar. It would look utterly ridiculous on a pair of sweats.

"I am the lead member of the coven," she said haughtily, and I eyed her until indecision pinched her features. "But I see what you mean," she added as she fastened it to the inside of her sweatshirt instead, hidden.

Satisfied she wasn't going to move, I looped the glamour stone over my neck and peered out of the alley, studying the passing people.

A woman in shorts and a tank stood across the street waiting for her dog to finish his business. She was about the right age, and knowing Elyse would try to find a way to use it against me, I tapped a line and peered through the stone at the woman. *"A priori,"* I intoned, feeling the tingle behind my eyes as her image went into holding, so to speak.

I turned to Elyse, and her eyebrows rose in question. *"A posteriori,"* I said softly, then blew through the stone. *"Omnia mutantur,"* I finished, and a pulling sensation raked through me, stiffening my spine as a haze of my aura settled over her and soaked in, taking the image with it.

Elyse shuddered, clearly feeling it. *"That* is a glamour curse?" she said as I took a quick peek at her through the stone, satisfied by the result.

Head down, I tucked the stone behind my shirt. "Yeah. I didn't even have to kill anything," I said sourly. "You look like yourself to me, but everyone else will see her, right down to her shoes."

Elyse followed my gaze across the street. "The woman with the dog? That's got to leave a mark."

What she meant was smut, and I scanned the street, not liking how busy it was getting. "Your aura is clean, Madam Coven Leader. All the benefit, none of the cost. Your aura is *safe.*"

Okay, that last might have been a little bitter, but me taking the smut doing curses for their benefit was exactly her aim in trying to force me into the coven. *Rachel, you are a fool.*

Ticked, I pushed into motion, Elyse hesitating half a heartbeat before coming even.

"That's what you used to glamour that *Reader's Digest* into looking like a demon text," she said, and I eyed her, pretty sure what was going to come out of her mouth next. "I want that back. The deal was you look at it, not take possession of it."

"You holding my book hostage wasn't the deal, either," I said, my steps pounding the sidewalk. "Or you upping the June deadline for me to un-curse Brad. *You* broke it, so Scott and I made a new one. I walk out of your apartment free and clear, and in return, I don't retaliate for you trying to buy me with a curse that wasn't worth troll spit."

"You made him think the book on the table was my *demon text*," she ground out from between her teeth. "You tricked him. Do you have any idea how long it's been in the coven's possession?"

"You mean stolen?" I barked. "How about you disguising your grab for demon knowledge under a fake invite into the coven?" My fingers tingled, and I looked down, embarrassed at the flicker of energy wreathing my fist. Jaw clenched, I shook my hand out. *Calm your ass down, Rachel. You are better than this.*

"You think I'm stupid?" I said, softly now. "That I don't know you'd shove me in a closet only to trot me out when you don't want to get your hands dirty? That my aura would get more and more smutty while yours stays per-fect, and then when you're done with me, you throw me under the bus for it?" I ran a hand over my snarling hair to get it to lie flat. "Maybe you should count yourself lucky all I took was a book that never should have been in your possession and find something else to complain about." I exhaled to relax myself. "Unless you want me to bring Dali into this?" I finished sweetly. "He's generally the one who mediates the interpretations of a deal. But honestly, we specifically agreed that I walk out with my book, and you retained it." I looked at her, daring her to protest. *You feeling lucky, punk?*

Her lip twitched. "Fine. Keep the book. It will be back in my library come June anyway."

Right . . . I mused darkly.

"Scott said you could see through his curse with it," she added as if to change the subject. "The glamour stone?"

180

"And?" I kept walking, trying to outdistance the thought that I'd accidentally pulled energy off the line in anger.

"That sounds like more than a glamour curse."

"It is." I flicked a glance at her as we paced quickly to the big bus depot at the end of the street. "It also sees past transformations when I look through it. It won't work for you. I had to link it to my visual cortex."

Elyse lurched to keep up. "And you just used it. A spell stored in the demon collective."

"That technically makes it a curse," I corrected her, and she waved her hand as if it was one and the same, and maybe to her, they were.

"That means you are linked to the demon collective. Right now. Are you telling me you've been in the demon collective for two years?"

I hesitated, then deciding it really didn't matter, I nodded. Somehow her mix of horror and disbelief made me feel better. That she had agreed the book was mine didn't hurt, either.

"Since Friday . . . I think," I said casually, smug when her eyes went wide. And it was true. As of this morning, local time, I was in the collective with a brand-new summoning name in my effort to get Al from popping into reality to abduct me. And now that I thought about it, coming to this time might actually work better than my original five-year plan. Five years might have left me with fewer resources by far.

"I will not allow you to try to save Kisten. I know what day it is."

I jerked to a stop, my breath catching as she yanked my heartache from my chest and stomped it into the ground. Blinking, I took a slow breath, focused on the crosswalk flashing a warning red. The sun was up, and I had to squint through the low light. "You know," I said softly, carefully. "If you hadn't assumed I was running away and stuck your big nose in my business, I wouldn't be here. I'd be three more years down the timeline. I'm not here to save Kisten." Because I couldn't. I'd seen him die twice. That wasn't changing.

Elyse scoffed. "I doubt that."

"Yeah?" The light changed, and we stepped out together.

She peered up at me as we walked, arms swinging, her mood foul. "Yeah. It hurts too much. I'm not taking the pain on the way home."

My heart is breaking, and she is worried about a little pain? "I don't remember your ticket being round-trip," I said, refusing to look at her, instead studying the downtown bus depot strung out along an entire city block. There was a lot of activity, even for early rush hour. "If you don't want to take the long way home, you will stay out of my way and watch for when you can be helpful."

My hands were shaking, and I made fists of them. Totally uncowed, Elyse huffed.

"I'm not here to save Kisten," I said again as we stepped up onto the sidewalk. Though I wanted to. I ached to see him one more time. I wouldn't warn him. Just tell him I loved him and always would. "I'm here to find a mirror." Misery hit me with a cold slap. "That's it."

Elyse was tight at my heels. "I thought . . . Seriously? You don't want to stop him from dying?"

I jerked to a halt when I saw Scott and three officers going through a bus. *Looking for us . . .* The Turn take it, I was wearing red.

Adrenaline washed through me, pushing my heartache into the hidden folds of my brain to keep me awake at night. "Ah, change of plans," I said, taking her arm and turning us around. "Of course I want to stop him from dying. But anything I do would only put it off for another day. Piscary would give him to someone else, or Art would simply keep trying until he managed it. I'm not here for a rescue. I'm here to find a mirror and untwist Brad's curse."

My last words were bitter, and I didn't think I had ever disliked her more than at that moment, chaperoning her wanted ass through Cincy. I had gotten her out of jail, and she hadn't even thanked me.

"The ever-after hasn't been remade yet," Elyse said, voice distant. "My God. You're going to bargain with Newt?"

I nodded, shoulders easing when no one shouted for us to stop. I had to reorganize my day. The I.S. would be a major presence downtown for a while. Good time to catch some sleep. "I would have been home by now with that mirror if you hadn't butted in." I couldn't go to the church, but there were other places to catch a nap, and no way was I going to face Newt tired and fatigued. "This way."

Elyse's pace bobbled as she glanced over her shoulder at the bus depot before meeting me stride for stride. "Where are we going?"

"The library. Ancient book locker."

"For some spells," she guessed wrongly. "Good idea. But don't they usually keep them under lock and key?"

"Yep." Good thing I knew where Nick stashed it.

CHAPTER

14

I WASN'T SURE IF IT WAS THE SCENT OF COFFEE OR THE SOUND OF sliding pages that woke me, but I stayed where I was despite the painful crick in my neck, slumped in a chair and smiling at the thought that I must have fallen asleep in Trent's office again.

Until a feminine, very un-Trent-like voice whispered, "Oh, that can't be legal."

My eyes flashed open, my smile fading at the sight of the rack of old, musty books. *Not Trent's office.* It was the ancient book locker.

I sat up, stifling a groan as I patted my pocket to assure myself that the broken stirring rod was still there. I was sore, stiff from sleeping in one of the ratty rolling office chairs that had been dumped down here. Elyse barely glanced up from her book, her butt in the other rolling chair, her institute-bland sneakers on the round table at the center of the small room. My jacket hung from the corner of a low bookshelf. Guess she was done with it.

"Good afternoon," she said, her high voice only slightly mocking.

"Is it?" I practically whispered. The book in her hand had been written by a demon, if the lack of a title meant anything. She had two paper cups of coffee beside her, and a sticky-looking pastry in her hand. "What spell?" I asked when she didn't respond, and I took a slow breath. She was getting crumbs on the pages, and it bothered me. "What spell can't be legal?"

"Freeze someone's blood in their veins. I thought it was an expression.

I'll have to come back for this one," she said, her gaze never leaving the ancient text. "I know how to freeze inanimate things, but this one works past auras. I had no idea Cincinnati had such a treasure of illicit dark magic under her streets."

That tends to happen when you're one of the oldest cities in the U.S. I stretched, feeling my calves ache and my feet twinge from being on the cold concrete. My spiffy red shirt was wrinkled. One of the sequins was loose, and I jerked it free, flicking it to the filthy carpet. "What time is it?"

"Almost noon? You're the one with the phone." Elyse ate another bite, brushing the crumbs off when I pointedly noticed them. "I got you a pastry from the vending machine before the library opened. That coffee is yours, too, if you want it."

My neck cracked when I shifted my head, and I stood, feeling like a zombie as I shuffled over. "Thank you."

"I didn't know what you liked, so I got you a black, two sugars."

"Perfect." I dragged my rolling chair to the table. One of the casters was busted, so it took some effort.

"You're welcome," she added sullenly.

Wow. Just wow. I was too fuzzy to try to figure out what her problem was, and I sat down in my chair and took the coffee in both hands. The pasty was one of those nasty cinnamon rolls wrapped in cellophane, but it was the coffee I really wanted, and I tapped a line and warmed it up with a quick word. It had been sitting for a while.

Elyse's attention returned to her book. Her feet were still on the table, but I could sense a rising tension in her. The ancient book locker sat at the end of a long hallway in the basement of the university's library, safe behind a chain-link fence with a mundane lock and a magical deterrent they put in about a year ago after a particularly nasty break-in. Industrial lights hummed overhead, and my aura prickled at the hint of power.

A faint musty smell fought with the scent of burnt amber rising from the room's more valuable books. A cracked cement-block wall with a broken glass cabinet took up one side, books on the other three. Several more racks of books stood between our cozy ten-by-fourteen space and the chain-link fence and hall to give the occasional user less of a feeling of being in a cage. That was why the table and chairs. Nothing was supposed to leave the ancient book locker.

But it did, I thought, grimacing at the broken cabinet and the black stain below it as I wrestled with the pastry to try to get the cellophane to break.

Finally I got it open, and the scent of syrupy sugar made me a hundred times hungrier. "Thanks, I'm starving," I said as I pulled off a strand of dough and ate it.

There was a black hoodie on the back of her chair. It went with her gray sweats better than my sequined jacket, and my eyebrows rose. "You didn't get that from a vending machine."

"Nope." Elyse turned a page, playing with her coven pin as if it was a talisman. "I got it from the employees' break room along with your breakfast. And before you say anything, it was in the lost and found. They weren't even open yet. No one saw me."

I bobbed my head. If anything got us caught, it would be the scent of coffee.

Elyse slowly lost the chip on her shoulder at my silence, but the tension remained.

"Mmmm," she finally said. "I could do this if I had a snow crystal. I'll have to check Vivian's things."

Thinking she was baiting me, I ate another ribbon of dough. "That's not a spell. It's a curse," I said, and Elyse beamed at me.

"As long as no one dies, it's legal if you're coven," she said, and I took a slow, steadying breath. I was so tired of the hypocrisy.

I finished my coffee, lips set wryly at the last grainy dregs. My boots were unlaced, and I bent to tie them up. I had a busy day, and it would start with spelling her to sleep so she wouldn't follow me and muck things up.

"So . . ." Elyse's sneakers hit the floor and she pushed her rolling chair back a few feet. "I'm dying to know how you got the demon mark. I've heard rumors."

My gaze went to the cabinet Al had thrown me into, and I felt myself warm. "I'd think you'd be more curious as to how I got rid of it."

"I don't care how you got rid of it. I want to hear what you got in exchange for it."

I finished one boot and started on the other. "I got it because my boyfriend at the time didn't read the fine print." *Which might account for him being overseas at the moment.* I would have rather gone to Nick's abandoned apartment last night, but I'd be taking Kisten there tonight, and I didn't want to disturb anything.

Grief hit me, twice as potent as it was unexpected, and my fingers faltered on my laces. Crap on toast, he was going to die tonight, and here I was playing nanny to a coven member. I should have been in and out of here already.

But when I came up from my boots, Elyse was waiting for more, that little-girl look of hers on her face as she eyed me over her book.

"Oh, for the love of the Turn," I muttered. "Piscary sent a demon to kill me because he didn't like that Ivy thought I might be able to help her escape his hold on her. The demon caught up to me here, actually." Again I glanced at the busted cabinet. The glass had been swept up, but they hadn't bothered to get the wet-vac down here to pull the blood out of the flat, dirty carpet.

"That's my blood," I said, and Elyse lost some of the mocking lilt to her brow. "He busted my head against the cabinet there, then ripped open my wrist, all the while wearing the image of Ivy. Filled me with enough vampire spit to bind a cow."

"Merlin's mistletoe," she said, and I blinked at the odd curse.

"He would have killed me, but Nick circled him." I fiddled with my empty cup. "That broke the hold that Piscary had on him, and Nick made a new deal that rubbed out the one he'd made with Piscary. Ugly story short, the demon saved my life in the end by getting me back to my church, but I got a mark in exchange for it. So did Nick."

Mood sour, I stared at nothing. Nick was alive at the moment. If it wouldn't mess up the timeline, I wouldn't mind fixing that.

"The second mark I got was Lee's fault," I said, waggling my foot at her. "He abducted me, took me to the ever-after to sell me to the very same demon. But I didn't fight back and Lee looked like the more powerful magic user, so Al took him instead. You should have listened to me when I told you he was a dippy-doo."

Elyse's brow furrowed. "Wait. Al?" she questioned. "You're telling me the same demon who tried to kill you is now your *teacher*?"

"More or less, emphasis on less." Because as much help as he gave me in getting here, he felt more like a mentor. There was a difference. Teachers give you information and teach you how to use it. Mentors are simply two steps ahead of you, able to lift you up or bring you down by what they share. Avoiding her, I began going through my bag to make two piles: one to take while talking to Newt, one to leave here to pick up later. I wasn't going to risk bringing anything I couldn't replace. *Like the book that got me here*, I thought as I set it aside—then looked at Elyse with mistrust.

"Mmmm." Elyse scooted closer, her finger marking her spot in her closed book. "How did you get rid of them?"

Empty splat gun . . . stays, I thought, setting it on the book. Newt would only be insulted. "I thought you didn't care."

"Just curious."

Elyse was silent as I put a stick of magnetic chalk on the "take" pile. "Hey, um, can you snap a picture of this for me?" she asked.

She was holding out the book to that blood-freezing curse, and I gave her a look. "I'm not going to put an illicit curse on my phone for you to call me a dark practitioner with."

A hurt expression drew her childlike face in. "That wasn't my intention. My phone didn't make the trip."

She set the book on the table with a thump, frowning when I ignored it. "What are you doing?" she asked as I fingered my new transposition charm. If I left it here, anyone might find it, but if I took it with me, Newt might say I stole it, seeing as it was hers, or had been, or whatever. Grimacing, I reluctantly put the stone next to my splat gun, trusting the ancient book locker to keep it safe. Elyse might take it, but she was going nappies before I left.

"Prepping to trick a crazy demon into giving me something for nothing," I said, remembering she'd asked me a question. Maybe I could stop at the coffee shop on the way. Demons would give a lot for a cup of sweet coffee untainted by the stink of burnt amber. *Actually, that's not a bad idea . . .*

Elyse glanced at the two piles, her lower lip between her teeth. "I saw half a dozen good spells you could use."

"Newt has better ones." My fingertips touched my pocket with the snapped stirring rod. The necessity to keep it safe warred with the need to keep it with me, and I left it where it was. *Memory charms—take. Zip-strip snipper . . . definitely.*

"Not for trading, for fighting," she said with a grin. "I for one wouldn't mind stopping at a spell shop first."

Crap on toast, she thinks she's coming? I scowled at her. "You can't fight a demon. Ever. You get them curious enough not to drag you away immediately, then stall for time, wedging in what you really want amid your teasers."

"Sure, but—"

"But nothing," I interrupted, setting a second memory charm next to the first on the "take" pile. "At the moment, there aren't any laws protecting people against demons. That little gem won't come into effect until, oh, a few years from now, thanks to Trent."

I looked at the books surrounding me. One of them might interest Newt if it was hers, but all the really old ones had been in the glass cabinet and were gone. Stymied, I glanced at the one I had brought with me, the one that Newt had written. *No. I only have a few books as it is.*

"Okay, so what are you going to give her?"

I glanced at my new pinky ring, and my hand fisted. "Yeah. That's the question." I weighed my phone before setting it by the forget charms to take. "I woke up a few days ago—the me of this time period, not the one we belong in—with Newt in my head. She had possessed me so she could walk on hallowed ground to search the church. At the time, I'd assumed she was looking for the focus, which is currently in David's freezer turning the women he is having sex with into Weres, but now I think Newt was searching for a memory of when we first met." My eyes dropped to the filthy carpet. "I think she guessed I was a demon straight off. The only reason Al snagged me first was because Minias, her caretaker, probably dosed her with a forget charm, accidentally obliterating the information. She might trade that memory for the mirror."

"A memory of you is going to buy a priceless, one-of-a-kind mirror?" she asked, and I felt myself warm at the scorn in her voice. "Morgan, you are my ticket home, and I'm not risking you being abducted by a demon because you trust in the importance of your birthright. I'm coming with you. You need some firepower, and I'm it."

Son of a moss-wipe pixy pisser. My jaw clenched, and I forced it to relax. She was right about needing more, though, and I reluctantly moved the spell book to the "take" pile. I'd offer it as a last resort. Clearly I was connected to the demon collective and didn't need it to get home. I'd rather lose that than Trent's mom's ring.

"Ah, you *can* get me home, right?" Elyse asked suddenly, taking my silence for unease.

"Probably."

Elyse blanched. "You're not sure?" She sat up, shoulders stiff. "You came here and didn't have a way home? Were you planning on living those two years again?"

"It was supposed to be five," I snapped, thinking I was going to have to surprise her if I had any hope of downing her, singed synapses or not. "And no. *I* have a way home. *You're* the problem. You've *always* been the problem."

She was silent, her expression empty as I began shoving my "take" pile into my bag.

My eye twitched. It was going to require a defunct, ancient stasis charm to get her home, but if I told her that now, she would insist on coming so she could barter one from Newt. I knew Trent had one, but it was defunct, and not only would I have to steal it, I'd have to rekindle it, too—in front of a coven member. *Son of a moss-wipe troll hickey.*

"You can't get me home?" she asked, her voice high, and I felt a moment of sympathy. "Is that why it hurt so bad?"

"I don't know," I said truthfully. "The curse I used doesn't simply move you back in time. It shifts your entire body to an earlier state. That's why you're younger. You lose energy going into the past and require it going into the future."

"I'm hearing a big 'however,'" she said, her face pale.

"Yep," I said sourly. "It's not designed to move living things, so I twined an energy-spindling spell into the traveling curse to catch the lost energy. That part of the curse is illicit, but I figured since I was stealing my own energy, it would be okay. The energy is stored in the demon collective and will unspool on the way home. I didn't know you were there. I didn't include you in the, ah, curse."

"Then . . ." She studied the racks of books. "How the hell am I going to get home?" Her focus sharpened. "This was all a trick, wasn't it! You want me dead. If I'm stuck here, you get away with everything!"

Oh, for little flying pixy turds . . . She was starting to lose it, and I rubbed my forehead as if tired—which I was—hoping it made me look nonthreatening. Singed synapses or not, the woman was dangerous. "Relax, Elyse Embers. I can get you home with a stasis charm."

"You mean a stasis charm that spontaneously breaks after three days to prevent death by dehydration? Try again!"

I nodded. The auto-break was a coven mandate—for good reason. Stasis charms wouldn't work any longer than three days on the undead, either. "You're right, if it's witch made." I slung my bag, feeling confident at its book-heavy weight, though I would be loath to lose it if worse came to worst. "But I'm not a witch, am I."

Elyse licked her lips, eyeing my bag. "I'm coming with you to the ever-after."

"No, you aren't." I picked up my splat gun and the rest and took them to the shelves.

"Hey! I may look eighteen, but I'm really twenty!" she said.

Oh. My. God. "I'll be back once I have the mirror. If I wanted to leave you behind, I wouldn't have bailed you out of jail."

"You didn't bail me out. You broke me out. And if you screw any of this up, I'm stuck here! I'm going with you."

I tucked the splat gun behind a couple of tomes and turned. "You think you can play the part of my familiar?"

"Your what?" she said in repugnance. "I'm not going to be your slave."

Elyse had stood. Maybe I could knock her down, sit on her, and tie her to a bookcase. "It would be safer if you stayed here and went through the books for a stasis spell that will last longer than three days. I suggest the old ones without titles." Because if she couldn't find one, I'd be stealing one from Trent.

Elyse lifted her chin. "You can't stop me from following you."

She sounded like Jenks. Her expression was just as determined, and I went to get my jacket, seeing as she had her lost-and-found special. *Rhinestones . . .* "I could." I let that sit there for a moment. "You can't tap a line yet, and I doubt you spent your adolescence in the gym learning how to fend off creeps."

Her eye twitched. "I can help," she said, switching tactics. "I'll be quiet. It will be good experience. I bet Newt knows how to collect enough energy to live on for two years."

This was exactly what I had wanted to avoid, and I stiffly shoved my arms into my jacket and tugged it straight. "I know she does. Where do you think I got the spell?"

"Then I can bargain with her for it."

"That's why you aren't coming." I gathered myself to leave, not sure what to do anymore. "Stay here. Concentrate on the demon tomes. Maybe you'll get lucky. Because if you ask her, she'll want your soul. I guarantee it. Nice young coven member. She won't have to break you of any bad habits."

Bag over my shoulder, I strode through the freestanding racks of musty books. Her scuffing steps were right behind me, and I half expected her to try to hit me on the way out. I shoved the chain-link gate open and stepped into the darker hallway, senses tingling as the wire door scraped loudly.

And then I made a mistake. I turned to latch the gate shut.

Elyse was standing there looking desperate: desperate to help, desperate not to be left behind, desperate to be taken seriously. It was the last that broke me, and my grip on the chain-link tightened. Suddenly I couldn't bring myself to shut it. "Okay. Seriously," I said, and the light of hope brightened her expression. "Can you pretend to be my familiar? Do what I say? Take all manner of insults? Keep your mouth shut? I mean it. Can you? Because familiars take a lot of shit." But the real question was, would she?

"Yes," she said immediately, and my mood soured. *I am so stupid.*

"Fine, you can come. It's probably a good thing you can't do any magic, because if you did, Newt would flatten you like a bug. Let's go."

Elyse stepped into the hall and slammed the gate shut behind her. She had left her hoodie, but I was betting she didn't trust me enough not to lock her in if she went to get it. "You didn't prep anything," she said as I secured the gate with the mundane key.

"Okay, what would you do?" I said as I tucked the key into its hidey-hole where Nick kept it. "Summon Newt into a circle? Demand the information? Trick her like you tricked me?"

The young woman flushed.

"I saw her take down a three-ringed blood circle not three days ago local time. Anything you could spell wouldn't stand. Any information you gained from her wouldn't be a lie, but she'd leave something out that would make it worthless. You trick her," I said, voice gaining strength as I stared her down, "and she will kill you where you stand with no more thought than swatting a spider. There's nothing wrong with an up-front, honest deal, Elyse." I reshouldered my bag and started down the long hall, chain-link cages to either side. "Demons don't have to do anything, even if you circle them. And Newt? She's the worst. No one, even her, knows her summoning name. She just shows up wherever and whenever she feels like it, as if she was immune to the curse that imprisoned the rest in the hellhole of the EA."

I was telling Elyse how to survive, but I didn't think she was listening.

"It's not as if I can do any magic anyway," she said sullenly, and I stopped.

"Look, you wanted me in your coven to learn about demons, right?" I said. "I'm trying to tell you something. How about listening?"

Elyse stared belligerently at me. I knew she wasn't eighteen, but twenty wasn't much better. "Here," I said as I took the chalk from my pocket and snapped it in two. "Before we get started with Newt, draw a circle and I'll invoke it for you."

"Why not circle Newt?"

I shuddered. "Not her. Never her. That would only piss her off. She might laugh if you circle yourself. It won't last long if she wants to take it down, but I might be able to distract her in the meantime."

Elyse considered the chalk in her hand as if I'd given her a slingshot against a tank. "You're asking me to go against thousands of years of lore and trust you? Seems to me that a coven member for a mirror would be a damn fine trade. No one would ever know."

"I would." Somehow the dim lighting made her seem older. Or maybe it was her skeptical expression. "I told you to stay here, remember? Besides, Newt already has a demon for a familiar. You'd be a step down. Just because people have been circling demons for thousands of years, it doesn't mean that it's right or that there isn't a better way."

Elyse put the chalk into a pocket. "How are you going to find her if you don't summon her?"

I peered up the grungy stairway. "I have an idea," I said as I started up. "One that will keep Minias out of the equation, too."

Elyse's shoes scuffed on the cold cement as she followed me, the sound uncomfortable in the tight confines. I was beginning to think Elyse *should* see the ever-after, witness firsthand what five thousand years of a magic war does to a world. But then again, I didn't want to spend my life trying to free Elyse from a demon. Getting her free from the I.S. had been hard enough.

"You know," Elyse said from three stairs down, "we could end this and go home right now if you agree to be coven."

My grip on the filthy banister tightened. "I'm not doing this for the coven. I need to uncurse Brad. Evading the coven was always secondary. Besides, easy always bites me on the ass, and baby, you're easy."

Her heavy sigh turned me around and I winced at her gray sweats. Sure, she was glamoured, but it was a demon curse and Newt might be able to see through it. "Hey, ah, does Vivian give you an allowance when you're at coven camp?"

"Yeah, why?"

I glanced down at myself, cringing at the sequins. "If you are going to be my familiar, you can't go in like that. You need some style. We both do."

Elyse smiled. "There's an ATM in the lobby."

CHAPTER

15

"AH, IT'S A COSTUME SHOP."

I gave Elyse a sidelong look. The young woman was clearly unimpressed as she stood at the curb and stared at the store across the street. Everyone else saw her as a perky blond co-ed, but I got the ugly reality of gray sweats and sleep-flattened hair. My regret that I'd let her come had gone from thinking it was a mistake to knowing it was. Other Earthlings wasn't a costume outlet. It was a high-end image consultant firm . . . and in her glamoured image of shorts and tank, Elyse looked as if she was skipping out on her high school gym class. I wasn't much better in my sequined shirt and bedazzled jeans and jacket.

"It will have exactly what we need," I said as I waited for the light to change and we could cross. The old storefront was a quiet place in July, but come early October, people would be lined up down the sidewalk to get in, like a must-see movie or concert.

Elyse twisted her lips in doubt. "The University Spell Shoppe is a quick cab ride away. It will be hard to outfit with standard spells, but I've worked with less."

I tugged my bag higher up my shoulder. That it had lost two years of wear and tear was an unexpected pleasure. "And Patricia's is two blocks up," I said. The light changed, and I stepped off the curb. Glamoured or not, Elyse was still a person of interest, and I was nervous.

She jumped to keep up. "Why don't we use your glamour stone?"

"You mean the one I left in the library so Newt wouldn't take it?"

Elyse gestured as if in disbelief. "We need hard-core spells, not straight hair and four inches of height."

"Agreed." Boots thumping, I strode down the sidewalk and tried to hide my worry. Sylvia had recognized me the last time I'd come in, but that hadn't happened yet and it had been because of my hair, currently spelled blond. I should be okay. "It's not a disguise shop. It's an outfitter. Trust me on this," I said as we reached the door and I pulled it open. It was the off-season, and there wasn't a doorman/security. "They will have what we need," I added as the delicious scent of expensive coffee hit me.

"I still say a few gray spells would serve us better," she muttered, her expression easing. "Oh, that smells good."

But seeing as what we'd had this morning had come out of a vending machine, everything smelled good. "You can't out-spell a demon," I said softly, hesitating just inside to scan the quiet front. "We aren't arming for war." Well, we were, but it was a war of wits, not skills. Besides, I might run into myself at my usual haunts, and I knew I wouldn't be here.

Elyse wrapped her arms around her middle, her jaw dropping when she saw herself in the mirror. "Wow." Hand falling from her hair, she took in the high-end shop. "I don't know what you expect to find here. How elaborate a disguise do you think we need?"

"I told you, we aren't here for a disguise. We are here to be outfitted," I muttered.

"Well, if it's clothes you want, the mall is . . ."

I quit listening, smiling in appreciation as I soaked in the odd mix of upscale clothier and tattoo parlor. There were large fitting rooms in the back with couches and chairs where you could have a catered lunch as you built a costume, but up front it was all business with brightly lit mirrors and multiple computer consoles and tablets. They even had an image scanner where you could upload a three-dimensional image of yourself and then try on clothes and prosthetics to see what you'd look like without ever leaving your chair. There were a few racks of clothes here, mostly to get an idea of how much you were willing to spend, as in taffeta, or cotton, but most of it was in storage.

Some of the charms sold here were tightly regulated, but much of what was available could be found anywhere. The magic was in applying them together. It was a skill that used to be hidden in the makeup trailers in the back lots of Hollywood, and in truth, that was where the money still was . . . unless you went all out, becoming world-renowned as Sylvia had done.

"I didn't know Cincinnati had anything like this," Elyse said. "It's like Sammy's in LA."

"I think that's Sylvia's sister, actually." I turned at the sound of a small scuff to see Sylvia, clearly having been eating her lunch as she dabbed at her mouth and tossed a napkin away. Come October, the owner/operator would be busy with her more affluent customers, but in July, she was more hands-on. *Which bodes well as long as she doesn't recognize me.*

"Good afternoon," the smooth-faced woman in her sixties said pleasantly. "I'm Sylvia. Can I help you ladies?"

I smiled to hide my nervousness as Sylvia studied us, taking in our body shapes, our hair, noses, shoe sizes—and if we were spelled to look this way. If we were tracked here, the I.S. would get a very good description.

Elyse shuffled her feet. "I have no idea why we are here."

Impatient little brat, I thought. "Ah, hi. I'm interested in working up two ley line professors. Formal spelling robes, mostly. You stock them, yes?"

"Sure." Sylvia dusted her hands and reached for a tablet. "Have a seat."

My breath slipped from me in relief. She didn't recognize me. "Thank you." I followed the classy woman to a seating arrangement.

"Getting a jump on Halloween?" Sylvia folded herself onto the white couch and focused on the tablet. The large screen on the wall brightened with her logo, quickly shifting to mirror what was on her smaller screen as she searched their clothing options. "Good idea. We are already booked for two weeks before. Are you thinking silk or synthetic?"

"Silk," I said, and Elyse perked up, turning from where she'd been idly fingering a rack of fabric samples.

"We have a nice selection right now." Sylvia glanced up from the tablet. "Could you both step onto the imager? We don't keep our entire stock on hand, but I can have just about anything sourced between now and October."

"Ahh . . ." Elyse gave me a sharp look and I shook my head, not wanting to leave a digital footprint, either. "We'd rather walk out with it today if we can," I added, and Sylvia nodded.

"That will limit you. Let me see what we have."

Again the big screen shifted as Sylvia swiped and tapped, her slim fingers moving fast to fill the upper boxes with several choices.

"Do you have anything to match her aura?" I said as I inched closer, aching to try the tablet out myself. "Purple and red."

"Mmmm." Sylvia swiped everything in the trash and started again. "I've got three in stock that will hang right."

My gaze lifted to the large screen, and I stifled a wince at the price. "Um, the one that starts red and fades to purple at the hem," I said, and Sylvia moved the robe into the larger display box. There was minimal embroidery compared to the other two, but Elyse was going to play the part of the familiar.

"Kind of plain, isn't it?" Elyse said, finally interested.

"We'll up the pizzazz on the sash," I promised. "Mine should be gold deepening to black at the hem. If it has a little red in there, even better."

Sylvia sorted and clicked. "How about this?"

"Perfect," I said, though it had less decoration than Elyse's.

"Seriously?" Elyse hung over the back of the couch, eyes fixed to the large screen. "We're going to look like university dropouts."

"I'm not done yet," I said sourly, then turned to Sylvia. "Sashes. Any with bells on them?"

Brow furrowed, Sylvia cleared the search box of robes. "Better selection there. You want to match the robes or go with a simple black?"

I thought of how Minias had once put me in a robe identical to his, and then Al's flamboyant enthusiasm in dressing me as an individual. "Black," I said, and Elyse made a heavy sigh. "But something flashy for both of us. Embroidered, lots of little bells."

"Oh, this is going to be nice," Sylvia said as she brought them up. "We have stars, flowers, or esoteric symbols."

"Symbols," Elyse said immediately.

"I'm a flower kind of girl," I said, and Sylvia added them to the generic models on the screen. "Any chance of the hats having the robe colors and the scarf embroidery?"

Sylvia sighed as she scrolled. "If you can wait three weeks—"

"Those aren't right," I said as she brought up a screen of traditional pointy hats. Looking at them, I wondered if perhaps they were originally designed to thumb their noses at their demon kin. Demons wore flat-topped hats; witches wore pointy. "Ah, I need a flat-top, round, heavily embroidered . . ."

"Like this?" Sylvia said as she cleared her workspace and brought up the men's hats. "It's not a traditional hat for ley line practitioners."

"Yeah." I scrolled through the pages, searching. "I know. These are perfect," I said as I found two. They weren't the right color, but it was the best there was on short notice.

"Okay." Sylvia added them to the models, not caring one whit that we were straying from tradition. She'd probably dressed Weres as vampires and vampires as dryads. As long as she didn't know we were going for ancient demon, we would be okay. "We have enough to get you in a room," she added, smiling. "Want to try them on? It's easier to add to it from there."

"Absolutely." Eager to see how it would look, I stood.

"Great. I'll put you in the big room. You can try them on together." Sylvia handed me the tablet and walked to a wide arch at the end of the lobby. The hall was brightly lit beyond it, doors spaced in recessed alcoves like upscale hotel rooms.

I sighed as I saw the running total—which was probably why Sylvia had handed me the tablet. Elyse peered over my shoulder, snickering. "That's going to raise some eyebrows when it comes across Vivian's phone."

"Don't worry about it." I pushed into motion to follow Sylvia. "My treat," I added sourly.

Five steps ahead of us, Sylvia half turned. "We can also do this in synthetic fibers."

"Silk," I said, wondering if I had enough time for them to sew bells onto the hats.

Elyse swung her arms, apparently finding joy in the fact that I was broke. "Sylvia, can you bring out that red robe, too? Matching scarf. I don't care if it has bells on it."

"Of course!" Sylvia pushed open a door, glanced inside, and then slid the indicator to OCCUPIED. "Have a seat. I'll be right back with your items. Can I get you anything? Water? Coffee? Tea?"

Elyse pushed past me, making a beeline to the couch and flopping down into it, so ready to be waited on it made my lip curl in disgust. "Some of that coffee would be splendid."

I smacked her shoulder to get her to sit up and stop being such a prima donna. "I'd love a cup, too, if it's not too much trouble."

"No trouble at all." She hesitated. "Five minutes," she said, then shut the door, her heels click-clacking down the hall as she called for someone.

The door obviously wasn't locked, but there was no other way out and it made me nervous. I'd been here once before when I'd thought Trent had knocked up Ceri. He hadn't. It had been Quen, and the result was Ray. All of which hadn't happened yet, which was confusing all on its own. This room looked similar if a little larger with a small stage surrounded by three-way mirrors under lights. A couch and coffee table faced it. Racks and locked cupboards holding spells and props took up two more walls, all dimly lit to make the stage stand out.

A memory struck me of Trent standing on the stage dressed in a frumpy suit, charms about his neck as he tried to look like Rynn Cormel. Suddenly I found myself blinking fast to ward off the tears. I missed him. He was just across town plotting to buy the focus from me even as he was getting ready to marry Ellasbeth tomorrow. Slowly my melancholy vanished as I recalled his silent fury at me when I arrested him at his own wedding. He'd thanked me for it later, but at the time . . .

"I take it back." Groaning, Elyse stretched out on the couch as if to nap. "This is better than a spell shop. I still think we need to stop at one. I feel naked without my usual accoutrements. What we are wearing is not going to help. We should be outfitting our spell lexicon."

"I hear you," I muttered as I tugged at a drawer labeled EYES to find it locked. "But what we are wearing will be the difference between surviving the first fifteen seconds or not. If we do that, we have a chance to get what I need and get out. Which is why I am this close to spelling you into a closet and going by myself." Annoyed, I turned to her. "This isn't your fight. It's mine. You can't best a demon, and certainly not Newt."

Elyse smirked. "Sure I can. You've done it yourself."

I let my bag hit the coffee table with a dull thump, book and all. "You mean like circle them and make demands? Is that really what you want to be known for?"

"Kick 'em when they are down and they might hate you, but they will leave you alone." Worry marred her conviction. "And I need a stasis charm, one that will keep me alive."

I shook my head, wondering if she was going to survive being the lead member of the coven—if any of them would. She'd been fed a steady diet of "Be the boss" her entire life. There was nothing wrong with being the boss. Being mean about it was, though. Not searching for the nonaggressive solution was, too. There was nothing wrong with everyone walking away with something.

"Or you could go out for a coffee and come to an understanding," I said, and she snickered as if I was the one being naive. "Elyse, I'm going to make a deal with Newt, not subjugate her. Besides, a few days ago in this time frame I watched Newt blaspheme my church, then take down three blood circles. Magic won't best her. You have to play on her failing. Curiosity. And for that, we need to appear . . . intriguing, not dangerous."

Elyse brought her gaze down from the shadowed ceiling. "Always the hard way with you."

"The demons are hurting," I said, knowing she would never understand unless she saw it for herself. "Meeting their anger with mistrust and trickery only exacerbates the tension."

"Tension." She sat up. "You make it sound as if there is a way other than capture and force."

"And you wonder why I refuse to join the coven." Chin high, I slipped out of my jacket and set it on my bag, grimacing as two sequins pulled free from my shirt and drifted to the floor. "Let me get this straight," I said, voice hard as I went to the stage and the brightly lit mirrors. "You think the way to success is to go in, circle her, force her to give you a stasis charm and me an Atlantean mirror, and leave. Either she will kill us for the audacity of trying to circle her, or she will play along out of boredom and give us what we want, knowing it will make things worse."

In the reflection, I could see Elyse staring at the ceiling, hands behind her head and her feet on the arm of the couch. Silent. I wound my hair up so it would fit under the hat. "If you were half as open as Vivian was, you'd take the opportunity to listen to what I'm saying, look at what I'm doing— listen, learn." Bun held tight to my head, I reached for the spelled bobby pins. Elyse was silent as I wedged in three of them, then added one more. The messy blob was not as good as a pixy could do, but it would hold. "Maybe you should admit that you don't know squat about demons and consider that I might, seeing as I've worked with them more than anyone alive and that I am one."

"That's what I'm afraid of, Morgan." Elyse sat up, her feckless act gone. "A coven member might be worth an Atlantean mirror."

I met her eyes in the reflection. "*I* wanted you to stay in the library."

"Lee told us how you gave him to the demons. You have done this before."

I turned, flustered. "Lee has a skewed vision of what happened. I did not give him to the demons. He tried to give me to them, miscalculated, and was taken instead. I did, however, get him free." Or I would, in a few days' time. Which kind of sucked seeing as the man was now the architect of Trent's current legal woes.

Elyse gestured angrily. "Then why are you dressing me up like a doll?"

My next words hesitated as I saw things from her viewpoint. "I'm not dressing you like a doll. I'm dressing you as a valued asset. It will give us a good ten seconds to—"

"Not circle her," Elyse interrupted.

"Pique her interest." I got off the stage, wondering if I should go look for Sylvia. It had been a while. "I'm wearing the same thing. What is the problem?"

"Admit that giving me to Newt would be a win-win for you," Elyse said bitterly. "If I'm gone, no one will dare put you in Alcatraz and you get what you need."

I bobbed my head. "You're absolutely right, but when have I ever done the easy thing?" Silent, I came to sit at the chair kitty-corner to her. "Maybe you understand demons after all. You don't trust anyone, either."

Elyse pushed back into the cushions, arms over her chest as she stewed. I mirrored her in my stiff chair, thumping my boot heels onto the table in a silent rebuke to her mistrust. Kisten was sitting at the curb this very moment, given as a blood gift to someone, punishment for defying Piscary. Kisten would die twice tonight, and here I was, shopping with a coven member. I couldn't interfere. I couldn't change anything.

"This sucks," I whispered, and Elyse's attention flicked to me.

"Knock knock . . ." came cheerfully from the hall. I sat up and took my feet from the table as the door opened and Sylvia came in pushing a rolling rack with our robes and an assortment of hats, both flat-topped and pointy. Behind her was a young woman with the coffee tray. "This is Laura," the older woman said as she parked the rack beside the mirrors. "She's going to help me get you looking exactly the way you want."

Because Laura is a witch and can invoke any charms we might need, I thought. The scent of redwood almost rolled off her as she set the tray down.

"Coffee," Elyse said as she helped herself, taking a cookie as well. "Mmmm, thank you."

I stood as Sylvia unpacked the hats. "I brought an assortment of slippers, too," the older woman said as I came forward to finger the robes. There were more than two there, all of them the requested color but not all of them silk. "You're a size nine, right? And seven and a half, narrow toe box?"

"Damn, you're good." Elyse delicately nibbled the edge of a cookie.

"It's my job." Sylvia smiled. "I brought out the synthetic robes, too. They will look exactly the same."

"Looks aren't everything." I stood before the rack, touching each robe until a soft shiver lifted through me. *Silk* . . . "This is beautiful," I said as I fondled a gold sleeve. The shift to black at the hem was exquisite. Immediately I slipped it from the hanger and shrugged into it.

The silk robe iced over me like a cool breeze, lightweight and protective. I chose the sash with the most bells, wrapping the robe closed and tying it snugly. Immediately my shoulders dropped as I felt the new barrier between me and the world soothing my aura. "Perfect." I stepped onto the stage, delighted to see the faint pattern of a winding Chinese dragon in the silk. "Oh . . ."

Sylvia was right there, tugging at the fit around the shoulder. "If you can wait a few weeks, I can get one without the dragon."

"No, I like it." I suddenly realized I'd never bought a spelling robe for myself. Always they had been gifted, and satisfaction stole over me as I used the ties in the sleeves to bind them about my elbows where they belonged, making that little pocket as Al had shown me.

"And a hat completes the ensemble." Sylvia stood by the rack, a hand hovering over the traditional pointy hat, and I shook my head. "Flat-top it is," she said cheerfully enough, and I took it from her, feeling good as I fitted it on my head. I shifted one way, then the other, tiny bells ringing. The boots were off, but Sylvia had brought slippers, and I trusted her guesstimate fit.

"This is perfect." I got down so Elyse could get in front of the mirror. "Elyse, let's see."

Elyse looked up from the shadows, where Laura had been helping her tie her sash, bells ringing. She had a pointy hat on her head, and I cringed. Her institutional-white tennies stuck out more than my boots, and her sleeves were bound wrong, but at least it was the proper robe and not the flamboyant red she wanted.

"Under the lights," I prompted again, and the young woman gathered her robe and stepped up as if it was a waste of time.

"Good." I brusquely took the hat off and handed it to Sylvia. "Let me retie your sleeves."

Elyse yanked away from me. "I know how to tie sleeves."

Scowling, I undid the ties. "You know how to tie sleeves," I agreed as I twisted the fabric to make a pocket before tying them off. "You don't know how to tie them right. Hat?"

Sylvia handed her a flat-top and Elyse put it on—the wrong way.

"This is a man's hat," Elyse complained, her head down as Sylvia fingered her freshly tied sleeves. "I look ridiculous."

"That's because you have it on wrong," I said as I pushed it to sit squarely on her head instead of halfway off like a halo.

"What difference is it going to make?" Elyse complained. Until her gaze went to the mirror and she blinked. "Oh . . ." she said, leaning forward to hide her shoes. "Huh."

Pleased, I nodded. The hat did look better, but it was going to be the sleeves that would stop Newt's instinct to shoot spells first and ask questions later. Hats could be mimicked, but the peculiar twist and tie of our sleeves was unknown outside of the ever-after. Until now.

And as Sylvia continued to frown and finger Elyse's sleeve, I began to wish I had waited until we had left before I had tied them correctly.

"Laura, will you tend the front desk?" Sylvia said softly, and the young woman left, taking the empty cookie plate with her. "You've worn spelling robes like this before?" the woman asked when the door had shut, and I felt myself warm.

"Occasionally," I admitted as I arranged Elyse's sash so that the ends were the same length. Elyse was eyeing herself in a new light. So was Sylvia, making me wonder if she was seeing past the glamour. It was her job. "These are an exceptional quality."

Sylvia put a hand on her hip, a calculating gaze fixed on Elyse. "They are spell-worthy," she said, attention flicking to me. "Authenticity is what we are known for. Everything works."

"It's perfect." I jingled the bells on Elyse's sash, feeling like a demon all of a sudden.

"Perfect, except that neither of you look like a ley professor," Sylvia said. "The hat is wrong, and they don't utilize bells on the sash. We had these for the Arabian Nights courtesan."

Elyse stopped swaying, her gaze finding mine in her reflection. "She's right," she said. "What are the bells for? You asked for them specifically."

I cringed, not wanting to talk about it in front of Sylvia. "Ah, it's to confuse mystics that might be attracted to high magic? Or so I've heard."

Sylvia went to the table and picked up the coffee carafe. "If you tell me what you're trying for, I can be of more help." Silent, she poured out a cup of coffee, her expression waiting.

"Demons," Elyse said, and I stifled a wince. "We're trying to be demons."

"In spelling robes?" Sylvia asked.

"It's to scare someone," I blurted, thinking fast. "My roommate has been dabbling, and I'm hoping if we give her a good scare that she will knock that shit out."

"Oh." Sylvia sipped her coffee, not moving. "Then you will want a gender flip and red eyes. There are no female demons."

"No, this will work." I studied my reflection next to Elyse's. The young woman was cocky and sure of herself, but I clearly was in charge. "This will do nicely."

Sylvia's breath hesitated, her words unsaid as a knock came at the door.

"Sylvia? There's a man from the coven to see you?" Laura said, and I fought to keep my expression from changing.

The older woman took a slow, sedate sip of her coffee and then set the cup down. "Could you excuse me? I'll be back in five minutes."

"Sure," I practically whispered, my gaze darting over the room.

I didn't move until Sylvia had walked out and closed the door.

"Everything off." I undid the sash, bells chiming as I spun the silk into a roll around my hand and then pushed it off.

"It's Scott." Angry, Elyse stepped down from the stage and tossed her hat to the table. "It's got to be. He was at the I.S., and now here? How, by the Turn, is he following me?"

"Let's go. We have five minutes." I slipped out of the beautiful silk, and Elyse stared at me as if I was stupid.

"Five minutes?"

"That's what Sylvia said." I carefully folded the robe and tucked it in the hat. The scarf was next, and then I jammed the hat in my bag.

"You think . . ." Elyse glanced at the door, a hint of hope lighting through her. "Why would she give us a five-minute head start?"

"Because we gave her a brand-new authentic look," I said, impatient. "Didn't you see her fondling those sleeve ties of yours?"

"Yes, but these must cost a fortune."

I smiled as I went to the rack of robes and properly tied the sleeve of one. "Her reputation is priceless," I whispered. *As is mine.* "Move. Robe off. Put it in your hat with your sash. We'll figure out how he tracked us here on the way to the university ley line."

Elyse went to the door and cracked it, her shoulders tensing when Scott's pleasant voice filtered in, rising and falling against Sylvia's light banter.

I frowned at the clothes rack and the four pairs of slippers waiting for our approval. I didn't actually know if the clothes were included in Sylvia's "five minutes" comment, and a flash of guilt hit me. Grabbing a pen, I wrote a quick note. *I'll return them in a few days smelling authentic.* And if I didn't, I'd be dead, so feeling guilty wasn't going to change anything.

"Son of a bitch, she's telling him we're here," Elyse hissed.

"She's not going to risk Alcatraz for us." I snatched up Elyse's hat and stuffed it into my bag. I left the slippers, feeling as if it would overstep

Sylvia's offer. The coffee I had no qualms about, slamming half my mug before joining Elyse at the door. She'd finally taken off her robe and sash, and I jammed them into my bag as well.

"You first," I said, wanting to put myself between her and Scott. I could do magic. Elyse could not. "Out and to the left. There's got to be a rear delivery door."

Shoulders square, Elyse boldly walked into the hall. I was right behind her, whispering a word of Latin to lock the door. Energy lit through my aura, and my fingers tingled as the spell took hold. It was only a hint, but Scott must have felt it as both his and Sylvia's voices grew louder. She was trying to stop him from pushing past her. He was good. I was better.

"Hey! You!" Scott called, and Elyse and I bolted, the young woman stiff-arming the swinging door to the back and vanishing.

I followed, and together we jogged through the small break room and into the larger, dimly lit storage area. Racks stretched to the ceiling, filling the entire length of the building.

"Go, go, go!" I shouted. Scott was thumping in behind us, and Laura's complaint rose high.

"I just want to talk!" Scott said.

"Left!" I gave Elyse a shove toward the scent of cold concrete and spent gas. They had to have a loading dock. If we could make that, we might have a chance. My bag wasn't heavy, but it was awkward, bumping into the racks as we ran for the far side of the huge room, dodging left every time an opening showed.

"Just want to talk," Elyse mocked, and my breath caught when my hold on the ley line sort of hiccupped. It was Scott . . . pulling on the line.

"Down!" I lurched for Elyse.

"*Teneo!*" Scott shouted, and I slammed into Elyse, the taste of tinfoil on my teeth as I invoked a protection circle over us both. It was undrawn, but I was pissed, and it held long enough for the spell crackling above our heads to dissipate.

Purple sparkles faded on the old oak floor, and my eyes rose to Elyse's. "Go." I pushed her to her feet. "Find the door."

I stood, a tingle of energy gathering in my hand. Gold and black bands twined in my fingers, aching until I pushed the force to my fingertips. *"Implicare!"* I exclaimed, throwing the tangling lines of force not at Scott—who would know how to break them—but at the rack he was passing. Gold spun between us like fairy-tale spiderwebs . . . and then I yanked the spell back.

Boxes avalanched from the shelves, falling on him even as I broke the charm. But it wasn't enough, so I grabbed the nearest rack and pulled it down as well, filling the aisle between us. Scott slid to a halt, our eyes locking.

"Door!" Elyse shouted triumphantly, and I spun.

"I said stop!" Scott exclaimed as I ran for the scrap of light, a mountain of boxes between us.

I blew through the door, skidding to a halt in the sun. Elyse was already at the street, waiting, and I put a hand on the cold metal latch. *"Sub frigido,"* I whispered, satisfied when an icy ache flowed from my hand and froze the lock shut. Breathless, I spun and began to jog down the alley. Scott would have the counterspell, seeing as I had used the locking curse on him just this morning, but it might give us ten more seconds.

"Hurry!" Elyse demanded, and I tugged my awkward bag higher and shook the last of the spell from my hand. "I got us a cab." Her attention flicked behind me at the sudden banging at the door. "You should have melted the lock. Or don't they teach you that in demon school?"

"Funny." I tumbled into the cab and slid over to make room for Elyse. "Sylvia is already going to take a hit for this. She doesn't need a repair bill on top of that." I hesitated, my fingers rising to make sure my "disguise" amulet was still in place. "Can you get us out to University Commons, please?"

The driver eased the cab into motion, and I settled into the cushions only to clench my jaw in frustration. I'd left my jacket. Sure, it had been gaudy with rhinestones, but it had almost been classy. A collector's item.

Elyse looked at my stuffed bag. "I thought you said . . ."

"They will be going back." Not happy, I held out my hand. "Give me your pin."

She stared, not understanding. Then her lips parted. "I am the lead member—"

"Not two years ago you weren't," I interrupted, glancing at the driver. Us running into his cab like that was going to be remembered. All Scott had to do was talk to the cabbies to find out where we were going. "How long have you had that pin?"

Elyse took it from her collar, brow furrowed. "Since I was ten. Vi gave it to me."

"And I'm guessing two years ago, it probably had a tracker on it. Give it."

Her lips twitched, and in a flash of defiance, she rolled the window down and tossed it out. "Satisfied?" she said, sullen, and I nodded.

But I wasn't.

CHAPTER

16

"WOW." HANDS ON HER HIPS TO REMIND ME OF JENKS, ELYSE STOOD on the sidewalk and stared at the university's ley line as I paid the cabbie. "It's bigger than I expected."

The cab drove off, and I smiled as I took in the familiar old buildings. I'd gone to the local college, but I still felt a kinship here. The campus was almost deserted, probably because Al had been out roaming the city last night, causing chaos in his effort to convince me to testify for him in a demon court. The nearby ley line was hard to see, its unusually wide size and length diluting the typical red haze to a faint distortion.

"Dali made it." I hiked my shoulder bag up, bulky with robes, sashes, and hats. "It took him a long time to punch through from the ever-after to reality. The longer it takes, the bigger the damage, the wider and longer the line." A shudder rippled through me at a memory. "I made the one out at Loveland Castle. Or I will, rather. I couldn't tap a line for a week."

Elyse's twisted her lips in a wry expression. "I was talking about the campus."

My lips parted. Bigger than expected? What, she thought we were a little hick town?

"I thought it was propaganda that demons made the ley lines," she continued, oblivious to my dark frown.

"No. It hurts like hell, and if you can't manage it or your gargoyle can't find you and pull you out, you die."

"No kidding," she said as if she didn't care.

Let it go, Rachel, I thought, head down, as I started for a quiet corner of the massive ley line. I didn't think anyone was watching us, but I didn't want to make it obvious that we'd vanished into the ever-after—seeing as voluntarily going into the demons' realm was a veritable death sentence at the moment. "Ready?"

"Sure."

She was down to one-word sentences. Either she knew she'd insulted me or she was scared. I was betting she was scared. "Hold your breath," I said as the tingling of the line found me, warm and welcoming. Mystics played in my hair, and I twiddled my fingers, seeing them dance about my nails like living glitter. *Thank all that is holy they don't recognize me.*

"Hold my breath?" she said as if I was being stupid. "You can't breathe while you're traveling a line. What difference is holding my breath going to make?"

Because you know all about that, I thought sourly as I tweaked my aura to match the line's resonance and vanished. I wasn't going to shift her. She could do it herself, burned synapses or not.

For a moment, I was in the All, existing everywhere at the exact same moment. Time was marked not from the spinning of the earth or the expansion of the universe but from the decay of energy. I hung there a telling moment, listening to the universe chime, feeling it pulse through me like a great bell. Images of Trent passed through me, of Jenks and Ivy. *Kisten . . .* And then I gathered my resolve and let my aura shift back to normal, pushing myself out.

I jerked, breath held as I hunched against the sudden stinging wind. Slowly I exhaled, and then the scent of burnt amber hit me as I breathed in, the smell chokingly thick. "Crap on toast," I whispered, having forgotten just how bad it had been. It was misery made real.

"Elyse?" She was coughing violently, waving me off as she tried to clear her lungs. But the more she coughed, the more she took in. It was a losing battle.

Next time I tell you to hold your breath, hold your breath. Hand over my face, I peered through the stinging dust to the bloodred sun. It mirrored the one in reality, hanging a good ten degrees above the horizon. Broken buildings surrounded us, dissolving and re-forming as if in some bizarre lava lamp in reverse; the ever-after tried to maintain a reflection of our reality . . . failing.

"Oh, my God." Elyse's eyes were damp with tears as she came to stand even with me, squinting at the broken landscape. "Vivian wasn't exaggerating. This is . . ."

"Hell," I said for her, stifling a shudder at the red-smeared nightmare. The demons had created the bubble of existence to mimic reality long ago, but time had separated the two realities so far that maintaining any semblance of reality was gone. The open spaces were better, but there was little if any rain, and the grasses were dry and the trees leafless. To be honest, it looked as if a bomb had gone off.

No, it looks as if a bomb is actively going off, I decided. Some sort of weird bomb that melted everything. The scent of burnt amber was faint but persistent, and my eyes burned.

"We can't stay out here in this," Elyse said, arms clasped around her middle as she cast about. "Maybe one of the buildings."

I dropped my shoulder bag, digging in it to find my sash. Bells tinkled faintly in the blowing grit as I wrapped my head and covered my face but for my eyes. Immediately my discomfort eased, and I took a deep breath. "Only if you want it to come down on you," I said as I put that flat-topped hat on my head to keep my sash from blowing off. "I know somewhere that's stable."

I shrugged into my robe and then handed Elyse her sash. She held it for a moment as if I was crazy, then began to wrap her hair, bells ringing. "No wonder they don't live on the surface," she said. "This is a nightmare."

I'd never worn a spelling robe in the old ever-after before, but the moment the cool silk hit my shoulders, relief spilled through me. The lightweight fabric billowed and snapped, but silk naturally protected the wearer's aura, and a feeling of separation between me and the gritty wind eased into existence as I tied the sleeves tight about my wrists. After a moment of consideration, I retied my sash about my waist to leave enough to go around my face as well. With the hat, I was protected.

Which would blow off if it was pointy, I realized, seeing the sense behind it now.

"Wow, that makes a big difference," Elyse said as she shrugged into her own robe. "This is awful."

Which was an understatement. But the sun was too close to setting for my liking, and I resettled my much lighter bag over my shoulder and pushed into motion. "We need to get to the Basilica before dark."

"Because of the surface demons?" Elyse followed, bells jingling as she held the tail of her scarf over her face.

"They won't bother you if they know you're strong enough to fend them off. We're dressed like demons, but that's no guarantee." I studied the broken buildings as we walked, but it was the lay of the ley line that told me where south was, and I nodded at the dry riverbed and a hazy spire beyond. "That way."

Elyse slipped on the dusty rock, then shifted to walk close behind me. "I never understood how the souls of the undead could hurt anyone," she said, and I stiffened at the sliding click of a rock. They were there. I was surprised they hadn't come out. Either they were waiting for darkness or our demon robes had scared them off.

"Souls have substance here," I said, wondering if I might find Kisten's if I hung around until after he died. But no. He died his second death too fast. His soul had been spared the indignity of the ever-after, at least. "We're headed for that building over there."

"That big church in the Hollows?" she said, and I stifled a grimace.

"It's a Basilica, not a church, and it's one of the few places here that holds together. The demons have a protected database there. If I ping it, Newt will show. Alone. *I hope.* Minias is busy chasing Al at the moment." Annoyed, I stomped along, the sand stinging my hand as I held my sash to my face. I'd lost my nail polish when I'd traveled back in time and it was irksome.

"Sorry," she muttered, and I eased my pace.

"No, it's me," I said, relenting. "You remind me of Trent's onetime fiancée, Ellasbeth. Like you, she has lots of potential. Lots of ability to make the world a better place."

"Yeah?" Elyse brightened.

"Lots of passive-aggressive put-downs to protect herself," I added, and her eyes narrowed. "Laser focused on making the world what she thinks it should be instead of creating a space where everyone can be themselves."

Elyse scowled. "Yes, because demons are *so* understanding of personal boundaries."

A laugh burst from me, honest and true. I think it shocked Elyse, and my mirth vanished as we slid down into what, in reality, was probably the Ohio River basin. "The demons are understandably angry. Frustrated," I said when we reached the bottom. "Wouldn't you be? Stuck here, unable to leave unless some idiot forces you out. And then you're in a circle listening to total egomaniacs prattle on about what they want you to do for them. Not to mention making you pick up the cost." I frowned, remembering the few times I'd been summoned. "With only this to come back to," I finished.

Elyse silently slogged on beside me, her gaze going everywhere. "Why did they let it get so bad? I mean, can't they fix it?"

My boots looked odd from under my robe, and I tugged the silken fabric lower to hide them. "No. Al said it was once a paradise, a beautiful trap of sunny meadows and shady forests to snare the elves, who simply wanted to escape having to deal with humans. It worked, but the elves spun the holding curse around the neck of the demons as well, trapping them both here. While humanity developed alone, the elves and demons fought for eons, ruining their tiny artificial universe with magical waste. The elves enslaved the demons, and then the demons got the upper hand. That was when the elves escaped back to reality, leaving the demons to rot in the magic waste they'd both created." I took a slow breath, my pulse quickening as we slogged up the other side of the dry riverbed. We'd hardly be halfway across in reality, but everything was closer in the ever-after because the universe itself was smaller. "And since magic is basically changing the laws of nature, the waste from it is just that. Change. Constant, ugly, too fast for anything to survive it. Unless you are the soul of an undead."

I paused at the top, waiting for Elyse.

"Which you fixed," Elyse said as she tightened the sash around her face. "I've seen it. Sun. Grass. Big-ass mountains. How did you do what they couldn't?"

"I didn't fix it. I made a new one." I pushed forward and she followed. "You know Zack, right? The leader of the elven dewar?" I asked, and she nodded. It seemed as if all of Inderland's conventional rulers were children these days. *Not my fault.* "His predecessor convinced the Goddess to break the ley lines. They are what connects the ever-after to reality, and breaking them would destroy the ever-after and the demons with it. Bis and I used the demons' accumulated smut to punch a new, smaller reality into existence, and the demons scribed new lines to keep it running." I hesitated. "Or at least they will."

"That's what Vivian said." Head down, Elyse trudged beside me. "She also said the summoning curse broke when the lines went down. I thought she was kidding."

I slowed our pace as we found ourselves among buildings again. They were holding together better, but it only made me more nervous. Solid buildings meant places for surface demons to hide, and I started at a soft clink of stone. "I was out for almost a week, but it was that or the end of ley line magic. Earth magic, too, would have faltered in time. There were too many ugly things being held captive by magic. I doubt we have caught them all yet." I squinted up at the spires of the Basilica, my thoughts on Bis. Some of his kin still remained in the ever-after, and I missed him. "Besides, the demons needed a place of their own where they wouldn't have to maintain their all-powerful image and just . . . live. It takes skill to fit in, and they are several thousand years out of practice."

The shallow, wide steps of the Basilica were before us, and Elyse looked up from her feet. "That detail is amazing," she whispered, her gaze running over the grapevines twining in stony relief across the door. "Is it like that in reality?"

"Exactly." But the doors were probably chained shut in reality, and I reached for the handle, anxious to get off the street. I still didn't see any gargoyles. Maybe they were hiding from the scouring wind. "Go," I prompted as I pulled the door open, and she hustled inside.

I gave the broken pavement and slowly dissolving buildings a last glance before following her in and shutting the door behind me.

It was dark, as the only light came from the setting sun through the stained-glass windows, and those were coated in grime. The tiny bells on our sashes seemed loud, and I stiffened, ire flicking through me when Elyse took a ley line charm from her pocket and pulled the pin, invoking a pre-made spell to create a globe of light.

"Where did you get that?" I said, thinking she'd stolen it from Sylvia. We hadn't gone anywhere else.

"Library," she whispered, holding the globe higher to throw the broken sanctuary into high relief. "What happened? It looks as if there was a bar fight in here."

"I don't know." I unwound my sash from my face and retied it around my waist. "No one is talking." I picked my way down the center aisle past the broken pews, the heavy benches jumbled into the alcoves and in corners as if they were toothpicks. The stonework was heavily cracked and the pulpit coated in what had probably been blood but was now a black, scummy mold. The only thing clean was the statue of Mary, and that, of course, was the entrance to the belowground database.

"Don't. Touch. Anything," I said as Elyse followed me, sneakers almost silent. "Especially the statue. It's spelled and it will knock you right through a wall."

It smelled like old dust, and my gaze went to the low steps as I remembered how beautiful this space had been when Trent had almost married Ellasbeth here. I think he had been attracted to me even then, but it wasn't me who had interested him but his love of the dangerous.

"How did you find out about this place?" Elyse said, and I stifled a shudder as her voice echoed back in half-heard whispers.

"I've been here before. Or rather, I will be?" I halted before the altar, not sure where I should make a circle for Elyse to hide in. I hadn't noticed a drawn circle two months from now when Trent and I had stolen his DNA sample, but it could have been lost in the clutter, and I finally decided to put it tucked out of the way in the shadows.

I dropped my bag beside the stairs, bending double to rummage through it to find my chalk. Salt made a good base on a variable surface, or blood, but I wasn't about to cut my thumb. Magnetic chalk would do. Al's memory potions brushed my fingers, and I took a vial, tucking it into my pocket for an emergency getaway.

"The demons keep a genetic record of every familiar and demon in existence under the Madonna," I said as I straightened. "My dad died trying to get a sample of elven DNA to help Trent's dad repair the elven genome, and when they failed, Trent and I do. Did. Will. Whatever."

But we wouldn't have managed it, either, without Jenks's help, and I pushed the broken concrete from a roughly circular area with my foot, grimacing at the grime. "I didn't realize it at the time, but giving Trent the way to save his people took a huge burden from him." Exhaling, I bent over and began to scribe a circle. "That was when he became gentler, less of a world threat. People change when their fear is removed. That's the only way they can."

Finished, I began to draw a second circle nested within the first. "You're welcome for that, by the way."

Grit popped under her shoes as Elyse turned. "I thought you said Newt could take down a blood circle. What is that going to do?"

"Buy you ten seconds to say your prayers." I tucked the chalk into my sleeve pocket and held out my hand. "Give it."

Elyse's eyes widened as if surprised, but her neck was flushed. "Give what?"

"Whatever it is that you stole from Sylvia to snare Newt and demand a stasis curse."

Brow furrowed, she retreated a step. "I'm not going to stand in front of a demon in the ever-after totally helpless."

Too late. "Elyse, you already are." I wiggled my fingers in impatience.

"Whatever that is, all it's going to do is piss her off. Give it. I'll find a way to get you home."

"No." Hand to her middle, she backed away, feet scuffing in the debris. "You walk around as if you have this golden shield around you. That nothing can hurt you. How do you expect to survive the coven if you can't even survive a demon?"

"Survive the coven?" I laughed, not liking how bitter it sounded. "Elyse, the coven has been nothing but a mild irritant compared to the crap I've had to deal with concerning the demons." I dropped my hand, seeing as she wasn't putting anything in it.

"Let's take this week, for example," I said. "And I don't mean me trying to purchase a mirror from a demon. Tonight, I watch the man I love die twice—in my arms—because his guardian gave him to another vampire to kill for the crime of saying no. Al is currently chewing up the best Cincinnati has to convince me to testify on his behalf, the damage of which I get blamed for somehow. Piscary has been released from prison to deal with him, but all Piscary wants is to kill me, or better yet, force Ivy to do it to prove her loyalty to him. In a few days, I'm going to nearly drive myself mad trying to control an ancient Were artifact so Trent doesn't get it and sell it to fund his secret labs. And while we're on the subject of Trent, he is going to be so pissed that I arrest him at his wedding tomorrow that he would cheerfully kill me himself instead of sending Quen to do it."

I took a step forward and she retreated. "You want to know how I survived? Not my skills, because my paltry few years of learning spells mean squat to someone who spent eons developing war magic. I survived because of my friends. My friends are my golden shield. They kept me together when Kisten died. They pulled the focus out of me before it could make me insane. Piscary . . . well, I didn't kill him, but Ivy suffered his abuse instead of killing me. I survived a dark coven by exposing it, and Trent by finding out who he was, what drove him." I took a slow breath, my pulse racing as I bared my soul. "And once I understood that everything he did was to save his people, I found a way to stop hating him."

I held my hand out for whatever she had stolen. "Which is what happened when I began to understand the demons. That's why I work so damn hard to give them a chance. The only reason I survived Al was because I trusted him." My voice almost broke, and I blinked fast as I remembered Vivian. "Vivian understood that," I added, whispering now. "I didn't invite you. You forced yourself on me. If you don't trust me to get you home, I can't stop Newt from snagging you as her familiar when you do something stupid. Give me the damn spell."

For three seconds, Elyse considered it, her jaw set. I didn't think many people had ever told her what to do. But that was her problem, not mine.

"Give it, or I will let her abduct you," I added, deadly serious. "I didn't ask you to come, but I'll keep you safe. I can't do that if you're slinging spells behind my back."

She lifted her chin. "I don't trust you," she said as she extended what looked like a mass-produced wooden amulet. It was probably unprimed, seeing as I felt nothing when she dropped it into my hand. "All it does is make a circle. I got it at Sylvia's."

My shoulders eased as I read the instructions and decided she was telling the truth. It was hard to function with your synapses singed, but this little baby would help make up for it.

Flustered, Elyse yanked her robes higher. "Like it matters?" she grumped. "If that demon snares me—"

"I will die trying to free you," I finished for her.

Her jaw tightened. "Which means pixy dust to me if you fail."

But I was feeling better. She stole an amulet to keep herself safe, not to blow anything up. Then again, Sylvia didn't stock destructive spells. "Your best option here is to keep your mouth shut and your circle uninvoked." I tossed the amulet to her, and she caught it. "The more powerful you seem, the more she's going to want you." I waited for that to sink in. "Go on. Get in the circle. It won't stop her, but you'll feel better."

She hesitated only briefly, then stepped inside. "It's not big enough for two."

I moved to get between her and the statue of the Madonna. "I don't intend to get in it. It will give you about ten seconds. It would be better if you don't invoke it at all."

Elyse was silent. She was braver than I gave her credit for, going into the ever-after with nothing but a stolen circle spell to protect herself. Exhaling, I glanced at the ring Trent had given me, then made a fist. It was a link between Trent and his mom. He had so precious few of those. I wasn't going to trade it to a demon, and I spun it so the stone was hidden against my palm.

I was already connected to a ley line, and with a whispered word, I invoked a small globe of light, just enough for the stage area. "Here goes," I said as I balled up some raw energy in my hands and flicked the tingling mass at the Madonna.

Even expecting it, I jumped at the purple and black sparks, taking a step back when black snakelike threads exploded from the statue with a slithering hiss, snapping through the air to search us out. "Fire in the hole!" I exclaimed, cowering behind a hastily invoked circle. "Elyse?"

"Good!" she shouted, and I risked a glance. She hadn't invoked her circle, but she was fine, and the black threads had already retreated.

Exhaling, I stood and dropped my circle. "That could have been nasty," I whispered. And then my attention jerked to the ceiling at the sound of a rasping scrape: two red eyes blinked at me, and a hint of leather rustled. It was a gargoyle, and a big one.

Alarm washed through me. "Ah, I intend no harm," I said, and the gargoyle's white-tufted ears swiveled at the chiming of my sash. "I only wanted to talk to Newt and didn't want to summon her." Great. If he hadn't been sleeping, he would have heard my pregame pep talk.

"And yet you summon her nevertheless," the gargoyle said from the shadows, his gravelly voice rumbling like distant thunder. "If you try to harm her, I will stop you."

Oh, really? My lips parted. Perhaps I had stumbled upon Newt's gargoyle. She had to have one. Didn't she?

"I only wish to bargain," I said, bowing my head in respect. He had a dented sword in his thick-fingered grip, making me wonder if he was the same gargoyle I'd run into before, or would run into. Whatever.

"That does not negate the possibility of harm," he grumbled.

"Oh, God," Elyse whispered, clearly scared as a smattering of rocks pattered down, and then I lifted my head at the faint hint of spoiled green. Burnt amber.

I followed Elyse's gaze to the center aisle. It was Newt in a gold spelling robe, a flat hat on her head, and a red sash with no bells. Her eyes were utterly black, even the whites. It was said she gained them by staring into the bottom of a ley line too long. Her bare, bony feet showed from under her hem, and suddenly I felt like a fool. What the *hell* had I been thinking? She would recognize me, forget curse or not.

But as she came forward, not a hint of recognition marred her smooth face.

"Are we matching our auras and robes today?" the demon said, her androgynous pitch of voice pricking down my spine to leave a body-wide shudder in its wake.

"Ah, hi, Newt," I said, too alarmed to care that my voice broke.

"Adagio likes you." A glimmer of energy washed over her to shift her gold robe to a stunning black. "He normally drops rocks on interlopers." She paused, eight feet back, head tilted as if listening. *No hair,* I mused. It was about fifty-fifty that she ever had any. "But you don't seem to be normal," she finished, voice low.

"Perhaps he remembers me." I couldn't beat her magic. I had to baffle her with bullshit.

"Remembers?" Newt's gaze flicked past me to Elyse, the young woman blessedly quiet for a change. "I don't remember you, but that's not unusual." She squinted. "Possibly because you are both . . . glamoured?"

Oh, yeah. I'm a blonde. I exchanged a nervous glance with Elyse before taking the purchased amulet from around my neck and tossing it to my bag. I wouldn't be able to reinstate Elyse's disguise until we returned to the library, but if we got what I came for, we could go home as soon as we got there. *"Finis,"* I said boldly, and Newt's lips twitched.

"You dabble in demons, little witch?"

"No, but they tend to dabble in me." I tucked a strand of hair behind my ear, glad it was its usual color again. *Now, if only I can get rid of this sequined shirt.* "It's good to see you," I said, surprised to find it was true. I did miss her, as odd, dangerous, and erratic as she was. By becoming the elves' Goddess, she had saved my life. I could never repay her.

Newt glanced up at Adagio as she came forward another step to study Elyse behind her double circle. "I think you mean that. You brought me someone to play with?"

Elyse took a breath, and I put up a hand, wanting her to stay quiet. "You have something I need. I'm here to bargain for it. She's not for sale; she's here to hopefully learn something."

But Newt was shifting, her body growing smaller, thinner. A shock of red hair mirroring mine grew, and her robe vanished. Dressed in shorts and a white T-shirt, she leaned her scrawny arms on the railing circling the stage, freckles melting into existence as she grinned at Elyse. "Is she fun?" Newt said, her voice now high and young. "I'd give a lot for fun."

"Sweet mother of God," Elyse whispered, and I grimaced when she pulled the pin on that over-the-counter spell and a flimsy circle rose up around her. *Great.*

"She's not for sale," I said again. "She's here to learn how to stay alive while dealing with demons."

Newt laughed, the high giggle changing to a mature chuckle as she pushed off from the railing and became herself again. "How is that going?" she asked coyly.

"So far so good. But she imagines she knows more than she does. She doesn't speak for herself. I speak for her. And I will continue to do so until she stops thinking that the best way to deal with a demon is to circle him and make shitty demands."

Newt cocked her head at my obvious bitterness. "Mmmm. And what do you think?"

I dropped back, inviting her up onto the stage. "It's complicated, but as you see, she's the only one in a circle."

Newt eased up a step and halted. Her black eyes narrowed, and I felt my heart stutter. "That's my book," she whispered, and I followed her gaze to my shoulder bag tucked behind me.

Pulse fast, I snatched it up, scrambling to catch the book when it fell free. "It's not yours yet."

But Newt had moved, and she now stood on the stage, her hem shaking. Unfocused magic snapped in her robe, and it was only the unknown of my talents that kept her from spelling me. "You stole it," she intoned, a black haze spilling from her fingers. Mystics sparkled at her fingertips, and I felt my face go cold. "Give it back."

"It's still on your shelf," I said, refusing to move. "It's yours until you give it to me. Finder keeper, writer weeper."

Newt's jaw clenched as I tried to confuse her. "Indeed . . ."

"This isn't working," Elyse whispered.

"Are you alive?" I muttered. "It's working."

A patter of stones fell from the ceiling, and Newt glanced up at Adagio. "I will consider the incongruity that my book can be in two places at once as a possibility. What do you want?"

My grip tightened on the book. That she'd recognized it would help if I needed to give it up. I think. "I, ah, twisted one of the curses in it in error. I need an Atlantean mirror to break it."

"And a stasis charm," Elyse blurted, sash bells jingling.

Newt's lip curled up in a smile. "All that for a book I apparently still have?"

I shook my head. "I'm keeping the book. You don't need two, and this one is mine. The stasis charm isn't a must-have, but the Atlantean mirror is."

"It sure as hell *is* necessary!" Elyse exclaimed, but Newt had dismissed her, her expression calm as she leaned against the Madonna statue.

That is, until a high-pitched whine sounded, and the demon's aura flashed into existence.

Newt pushed from the statue, little arcs of black lightning popping as they snapped around her. "I don't remember you. I'm done here."

"Wait! Newt, the mirror," I blurted.

"Make your own mirror." Head bowed, she stomped down the stairs.

"I don't know how." I reached out after her, jerking to a halt when a stone cracked at the ceiling. "Newt, tell me where one is. I can tell you the future!"

"Blah, blah, blah." Her gaze roved over the sanctuary in horror as if only now realizing it was in ruins. "I can tell the future, too. It's easy when every day is exactly the same. You don't belong here and you will die before you escape it."

"I know what you were trying to find in that church!" I shouted, and Newt spun.

She started for me, arms swinging. Panicked, I retreated, only to trip on my robe and fall against the steps. "Tell me now! No deal. Tell me!"

"Me!" I squeaked out, flat on my back on the stairs. "You were looking for your memory of me!"

Newt jerked to a halt, pain in her eyes. The book against my chest sparked, and uncertainty lit through her. It didn't want her, and that, more than anything, I think, was saving my ass.

"Minias is destroying your mind to keep you pliant," I said, thinking the information wouldn't change anything since she eventually figured it out for herself. "He's been writing down everything you remember, then making you forget."

"This is a different kind of future," Newt said, jaw tight as she stared at me with those black eyes. "Who are you?"

I slowly sat up, my book clenched to me, scrambling for anything that would satisfy her and not give too much away. "You will ride across the paradise you destroyed," I said, and confusion flickered, familiar and hated. "And though you will not see the ever-after renewed, your horse will run across it through amber fields and cool forests. You will see the elves reborn and the demons saved, and they will both fear you for your greatness."

"I will ride?" she said wistfully, and from above came the crack of a rock—warning me.

I sat up more, finding strength in her bewilderment. "A mare so fiery that even the finest elven horseman can't break her. A gift from a hated name." Yeah, that was vague enough. If she ever figured it out, it would be in hindsight.

Newt's focus sharpened in distrust. "I see what you want me to believe, but you are no one. Nothing. I killed all my sisters."

"I saw Ku'Sox dead," I said. "Poor child."

"Ku'Sox is not dead," Newt said, and I put a finger to my nose.

"It depends on when you look." She was scrambling now, and I felt a flicker of hope.

"My sisters all have mirrors. You are not my sister."

"No," I admitted. "As you say, I'm nothing." I had to keep her talking, thinking, interested until she gave me what I wanted out of sheer confusion.

"I don't remember," Newt said. "Was I there when Ku'Sox died?"

I slowly got to my feet. "You will be," I promised. "Do we have a deal?" I asked, though no deal had been made.

Newt's mood shattered. "An Atlantean mirror for a delphic vision of my future? No." Her black gaze flicked past me. "For her, maybe. So many spells, I sense, and not a whisper of hesitancy to use them. No wonder you singed her before dragging her to market."

"Rachel . . ." Elyse warned, and I grimaced as she named me.

"Not nothing. You are a *Rachel*," Newt said coyly as if having gained points.

"You can't have Elyse," I said, using her proper name, seeing as she'd used mine, and the woman flushed, only now seeing her mistake. Demons could use your name against you, but she wasn't getting all three so it was a moot point. "She doesn't wear my smut. She has her soul," I added, and Newt smiled to show perfect white teeth.

"Then nothing will stop me from taking her."

Book in one arm, I fingered the forget potion in my pocket. "I will," I said boldly. "And as you say, I'm nothing." Little ribbons of hair that had escaped my hat were floating in the mystic-charged air, magic discharges snapping. Maybe this was why Newt chose to rock the bald look. "Don't press me, Newt. If I tell you too much, you won't survive what's coming."

Newt sent her gaze to my hand in my pocket, not a clue as to what I held. She could best me, but she hesitated, lest she ruin exactly what she coveted. "And what is that?" she asked.

My pulse was fast. "Freedom."

"From this hellhole?" she said dryly, and I shrugged. Bored now, Newt considered me. "Perhaps. I will give you a mirror, but I want something in return."

She had one, and I stifled my excitement. "What?" I asked, and Newt smirked. The expression seemed surprisingly right on her.

"A night away from this," she said, rubbing her fingers together to sift dead magic from her like pixy dust. "You summon me to reality, and I will tell you what you want to know."

"What about my stasis charm?" Elyse said, panicking.

"Okay," I said, and Newt batted her black on black eyes at me. "But I don't need to summon you. You can take us there right now."

Newt stiffened, her entire demeanor shifting. "How do you know that?" she said, almost frightened. "I hardly know that."

"I told you. I am the future."

She went still, so still I wasn't sure she was breathing. "I won't deal with those who don't trust me. Drop your circle," she said, and I followed her gaze to Elyse standing under the utterly useless protection of a ley line circle charm.

And yet Elyse shrank in on herself, clearly frightened. "No."

"Humm." Newt adjusted her sleeves as if preparing to leave. "You are not serious." Glancing at the book in my arm, she sauntered down the stairs. "Maybe you *are* nothing."

"Wait!" Elyse was pale and shaking. *Damn it to the Turn and back . . .* "I told you not to come," I said, cross. "Take it down, or I will embarrass you and take it down for you."

"Oh, I'd like to see that," Newt said, hesitating at the bottom of the stairs.

Elyse shook her head, and I glared at her. "Vivian trusted me," I offered.

"And it killed her," Elyse shot back.

I exhaled slowly, marveling at Newt's craftiness. She was getting a lot from this conversation. "That's not what killed her. What killed her was me not trusting her. Don't make the same mistake I did. Please. Let it go."

Chin high, Elyse gathered her courage and stepped forward. The charm broke as her aura hit it, shimmers of energy flaring before they disappeared.

Newt chuckled, and the young woman went pale. "Nicely done," she said, voice sly. "You took her circle without magic. Are you sure you're not one of my sisters?"

"No." Newt had killed all her sisters. It was a sorority I did not want to be included in. Worried, I dragged my bag sitting on the top step closer and put my book into it. That I hadn't brought that glamour stone had probably been a good choice, even if Elyse and I looked like ourselves again.

"You both need a change of clothes," the insane demon said, and then I gasped as I felt all three of us wink out of existence.

CHAPTER
17

PANIC TWISTED MY THOUGHTS AS I FELT MYSELF YANKED INTO A LEY line. Quick from practice, I snapped a protection circle around not just me but Elyse as well. There was a whiff of erratic, confused thought . . . and then Newt's mind was gone, walled off. She hadn't expected that, and I felt her heavy presence hesitate as we hung in the high-energy haze of a ley line.

Until she shoved us out and the slow rise-and-fall thrum of the universe's energy shifted to a bland, suggestive, rhythmic thumping.

My breath hissed in as I caught my balance. Elyse swung her arms wildly, almost going down. She was terrified, and I tugged at her until she looked at me. "You're okay!" I exclaimed, almost embarrassed by the woman's fear. But then again, she had probably thought we were dropping into Newt's oubliette to be forgotten—or not. And from the scent of cheap alcohol and rude catcalls, I doubted that's where we were.

"Where are we?" Elyse whispered, her eyes wide and scanning.

I let go of her arm. It was a bar, mostly men at small tables all facing the stage. Women and men wearing almost nothing moved between them as servers. Newt stood out amid the black wood and scratched floor in her robe and flat-topped hat, but then again, we all did.

"Dalliance?" I blurted, recognizing the living vampire on the stage, gyrating and playing with the crowd.

Newt's attention flicked from the hidden speakers to me. "Dalliance?"

she said, her black eyes blinking in an unusual surprise. "You've given yourself away. If you know Dalliance, you are an escaped familiar."

"Familiars aren't allowed in Dalliance," I said as I figured it out. We weren't in Dalliance. We were in reality. And not just any reality but the strip bar that would eventually become a memory in Dali's jukebox. "Besides, this one isn't in Dali's jukebox yet." I smiled at her, trying to be mysterious and esoteric. "Is it."

I had only the one card. I wasn't sure how many times she'd let me play it. As soon as she thought she had me figured out, the game would be over. If I didn't have what I needed by then, both Elyse and I would be up the proverbial creek without a boat, much less a paddle, and I stood in the strip bar's foyer and tugged the hat off my head, trying to look as if I belonged there.

At least we're back in reality, I thought as we began to get noticed. Chin high, I took off my robe and snapped it out. Dust flew, and I stuffed it into my hat along with my sash. The scent of burnt amber became obvious, and more heads began to turn. Elyse followed suit, though admittedly not as flamboyantly, and I held my bag open for her to drop her robe in as well. *Not my slave, my friend,* I thought, hoping Newt saw the distinction. The robes had done a great job in keeping the red dust off us, but my boots were caked with it, and Elyse's white tennies were even worse.

"The scent of despair tends to linger, does it not?" Newt eyed my sequins and rhinestones. Sighing, she turned to the patrons, studying them a moment before dissolving into a mist to re-form wearing an upscale black dress suit. Hair grew as she ran a hand over her head, the red curls flowing to match my own unspelled locks. The scent of burnt amber began to ease. "You know of Dalliance, yet claim you're not a familiar. Who are you?" she said as she flicked a pair of sunglasses out and perched them on her nose to hide her black eyes.

"No one." I needed to start watching my mouth. The game was playing out faster than I wanted, giving Newt way too much information to make this last.

"There's a table by the stage," Newt said, and I went the other way to a quiet booth against the wall. It was one of those half-circle things so every-one faced out, but I wanted it because I could see the door.

Elyse hesitated, then lurched to follow. "This is reality?" she whispered, exhaling in relief when I nodded. Chances were good we were not just in reality but somewhere in the city limits, seeing as the walls were covered with Cincinnati Howlers' paraphernalia. "How?" she added. "Demons can't cross the ley lines unless summoned. I didn't summon her. Did you?"

There was a thread of panic in her voice, but I was feeling pretty good. I was in reality. I still had my book. Elyse was at my side and I had a demon in tow. If I had my history right, my other self had made a deal with Minias to come get Newt if she ever showed up this side of the lines again. *Two cards to play* . . .

"Newt can." I glanced over my shoulder to see the imperialistic demon garnering stares as she sauntered behind us as if this distant table was her original intent. "The banishment curse didn't work on her. Maybe because she's female. Maybe because spells don't stick to crazy." I slid into the booth and settled my bag beside me. *Maybe because she was the one who cast the spell* . . . I wondered silently. "You want the aisle?"

Elyse nodded in unease, and I slid to the middle.

A woman in what might generously be called a bikini top and short shorts followed Newt to the table. Her scars put her as a living vampire, and the elaborate lace collar around her neck invited bites and nips. Actually, now that I took the time to look, most everyone here was a vamp, mostly the living, but there were a few clearly contemporary undead risking the early night and the chance to make a claim before the really old undead showed up. They were getting a lot of attention at the moment, but I knew that would change when someone who died before the Turn arrived.

"I've never been in a vamp strip club," Elyse said as Newt gracefully settled to my right and the server set three tiny black napkins down.

"What can I get for you?" the woman asked, and a flicker of unease crossed Newt. She didn't know.

"I'll have what they're having," the demon said, beaming to show the long canines of the undead. They weren't hers. She was trying to fit in.

"Bloody Mary," Elyse said immediately. "Easy on the Cholula."

I glanced over the clientele. Not everyone was staring at the stage anymore. "Orange juice. No pulp." We needed to settle this and get out of here. The artists onstage were off-limits. We, however, could be considered fair game—which might be why Newt had made a show of fangs. *Worldly cosmic powers, and you drop us in a vampire strip joint. Really, Newt?*

"One tab," I added, and the living vamp returned to the bar, hips swaying as she took the long way to engage her clientele. I had enough in my wallet for three drinks and a tip. Probably.

My gaze lifted over the tables, and the skimpily clad guy onstage waved to me, gyrating in invitation to come stuff a bill in his thong as our eyes accidentally met. Well, it was an accident for my part of it, and I shook my head no, only to have the man dramatically blow me a kiss.

Grimacing, I dropped my eyes. I'd never been here before—apart from the version in Dali's jukebox—but there were lots of places that catered to vamps that I was oblivious to. It was a quiet venue even with the too-loud bass. The line at the bar seemed a mix of one-night bites and living vamps there to relax without having to be anything other than what they were. Piscary's on a slow day had a higher pheromone level. My scar had been sensitive two years ago, and it was hardly twinging.

"I brought you both, hon," came a high-pitched voice, and I looked up to see the server dropping off the drinks. There were four, since Newt hadn't made it clear exactly what she wanted. "Let me know when you want another."

"Thank you." They'd put mine in a champagne flute to look like a mimosa, and Newt cleared her throat, lifting her orange juice as if to make a toast.

"To elves, eels, and strawberries," Newt said, and Elyse and I stared at her, not daring to clink our glasses. A frown flickered across the demon's brow. "If you don't know why, I'm not going to explain. You can have Elyse or the mirror, but not both."

"I am not for sale," Elyse said hotly, and from a nearby table, a chuckle rose. The man watching turned away, and with that, we were accepted and ignored. Vampire norms sucked, but now, at least, I understood Newt's choice of venue.

I took a slow sip, relishing the tangy juice. "Elyse is not mine to bargain with. She's here to learn something, not serve as collateral. She is her own person."

"Learn? As in how to be a familiar?" Newt offered. "Love, don't befuddle yourself," she added to Elyse as she gulped her Bloody Mary. "I like the screams crisp and nuanced."

"What the . . ." Elyse set the drink down, angry. "They gave me a virgin!"

I clinked my orange juice against her red. "You look like a kid."

"I am *not* a *kid*!"

"Your body is," I said, smiling at Newt. *And a little more confusion . . .*

Elyse pushed back into the bench seat with her virgin Bloody Mary—stymied.

"I must have something you want," I said. "Other than Elyse and a book you still have."

"Then produce it," Newt said. "I don't understand your reticence. You're going to give her to me. You need the mirror more than you need her." Newt closed her eyes and breathed deeply. "She has more spells at her fingertips than you. She's stealing from your larder. Is that why you singed her synapses before tricking her to come before me? It makes her almost helpless. So much easier to drag to a line."

Elyse pulled her drink closer. "Touch me, and you'll see how helpless I am."

Newt leaned forward to look at her around me. "I intend to."

I thought of my dwindling cash, then motioned for our server to bring me another orange juice. "Both of you, stop it. Newt, I told you, she's not my familiar. She's here to learn stuff."

"And get a stasis charm," Elyse grumbled.

The demon arched her thin eyebrows. "I enjoy dealing with people who are foolish enough to treat me as an equal. I will tell you what you want to know, and then I will take Elyse, since you won't give her."

"Try it . . ." Elyse said, glowering.

"It's for her own good," Newt continued. "She needs her reset button pushed. A few hundred years to reassess where she sits in the world order. We can call it a loan. I'll return her when she knows something. You are not going to survive whatever it is you are running from without a mirror to see yourself: what you are, what you were, what you will be."

"For the third time, Elyse is not an option. I have a book—"

"Which is already mine." Newt chuckled, eyeing me over her glasses as I'd seen Al do hundreds of times. "How about this? I will give you a hint, and if you can figure out what it is, the mirror is yours."

My pulse leapt. I couldn't lose, and so I nodded.

"Good." Newt smiled, chilling me. "It will cost you nevertheless."

"Ah, Rachel?" Elyse murmured as Newt leaned over the table and breathed on it. An eerie, icy mist coated the cheap Formica and rolled onto the floor, where it warmed and dissipated. Using a single finger, the demon drew a finger-squeaking circle on the table.

"The Atlanteans were said to have existed but for an instant of time before even the elves," she said as she scribed a neat pentagram within the circle. "A failed trial of glory, of wisdom." Glyphs of memory went at the points, one by one. "They might have been demons, or what demons came from. We don't know, as it was long before my time. It doesn't matter. They don't matter. All that they knew was lost, though it existed. All that they were is gone, though it once was as obvious as the writing on this table."

Silent, she watched her work fade in the heat of the room.

"Transient." Newt touched her chin with the back of her finger in satisfaction. "A fleeting clarity vanished as if it never existed. And yet . . ." She leaned forward and breathed again, bringing the pentagram back to light for an even shorter moment. "Exist it did."

Elyse frowned, her smooth brow furrowed. "Atlanteans were transient. Okay."

But Newt wasn't talking about a people. She was talking about the mirror. The mirror was named after the people. The mirror itself was transient. Something that comes and goes. *Like the moon? The tide? A comet? A puddle of dark water?*

Newt eyed me, making me feel not stupid but untutored, and where once it would have left me angry, it now only made me glad that there was more to learn. *Thank you, Al.*

"If you can find the mirror, you can have it," Newt said.

Find it? I glanced at the pristine table. "How do you find something that is there and isn't?" I said, and Newt smirked.

"That's not my problem," she said. "Now. As we agreed. Your familiar?"

The demon reached across me for Elyse.

"Stop!" My grip on the ley lines sharpened, but I didn't pull anything off them. So far, Newt was being passive, and I didn't want to change that. Sure enough, Newt felt the connection and drew away. "Elyse, maybe you should wait outside."

"I'm not going anywhere," she said, looking young as she shirked away. "Soon as I'm out of your sight, she snags me." Brow furrowed, she stared at Newt. "There are laws."

"There are no laws but that might makes right." Newt sipped her Bloody Mary. Hers probably had vodka in it.

Not to mention the man who would pen them, sponsor them, and lobby for them would, at the moment, like to see me dead.

Newt sighed as if tired. "Tulpas that haven't been made, laws that don't exist, age that hasn't happened. You're from the future. Boring. And there are laws?" Newt drummed her nails once on the table, right where she'd scribed the pentagram, invisible once again. "Human laws. Witch laws. I follow demon law. And only when it makes the game more fun."

"Is this a challenge, Newt? Is this fun?" I said, letting a faint glow of nothing drip from my fingernails and puddle against the table. The Turn take it. She had given me a riddle. *Time? Does time come and go?*

Newt took a sip of her drink. "It could be."

I shook my head, channeling my inner Al. He could manipulate Newt into anything. "It might be a mistake," I said, letting a hint of warning lighten my voice.

"Perhaps." Newt eased back and watched the server approach. "This is too easy. But I did give you the mirror. There will be an accounting."

"The deal was the mirror for a girls' night out. And we are out." But the server stood before us, and I daren't say anything more at the moment.

"Is it National Orange Juice Day?" the woman said as she hesitated, waiting to see if we wanted anything else. "There's a guy at the bar who ordered the exact same thing."

"What?" I stiffened, leaning to look past her.

Newt beamed, drink in hand as she saluted the bar. "You aren't the only one who can see the future," she said cryptically, and then I froze at a familiar pained cough.

Kisten?

My heart hammered and I flushed, even as my knees went watery and my gut flip-flopped. I stood, recognizing the hunch to his shoulders, the way he sat at the bar with his back to the stage, his foot on the rest. His hair was damp from a shower, and he was in a faded pair of sweats from Nick's closet. I had left him at Nick's place to go make a deal with Piscary, only to wake up in the church thinking Kisten was still there.

I couldn't move. It was Kisten. He was there. Alive. Hurting. Beaten bad. But it would be worse tonight.

"I left him . . ." I whispered, unable to look away. I couldn't breathe. I wanted to go to him. I knew better, but he was right there. I wouldn't warn him. Just say good-bye. I could not sit down and pretend I hadn't seen him.

"Don't leave me. Don't leave me with her!" Elyse begged, one of my hands in her grip.

The server had walked away. It was all I could do to stand there. "He's supposed to be at Nick's apartment," I whispered, numb with indecision.

Newt sipped her drink. "If you look forward far enough, you can see the past. But you seem to have learned that lesson already."

"Excuse me." My words were breathy. He was there. He was hurting. Sometimes, it was that simple.

"Don't." Elyse yanked on my wrist. "You'll screw up the timeline."

I pulled from her, angry. What if I did? What did anyone care? "You're only worried about yourself." There was a small bag at his feet. Was he running?

"Rachel, no!" Elyse whispered, her eyes haunted as they fixed on me. "You walk away, and she takes me! You know it. You promised."

It was as if someone had hit me in the gut. Breath held, I turned to Newt, reading the surety of that in her smug confidence. "You knew he'd be here," I said, voice shaky, and she shrugged, content to wait and see.

And though it hurt like a thousand knives, I sat down. I had loved Kisten, but Elyse needed me right now. Here. And I had promised.

It felt as if my heart was breaking all over again.

"Thank you," Elyse said, voice ragged, and then Kisten lifted his head.

I stared, my heart hammering as he turned on the barstool, following the server's pointing finger to me. I couldn't seem to get any air.

"Rachel, please," Elyse begged. "Don't change anything. Just pretend you're you."

"It's too late," I whispered when Kisten got to his feet, clearly in pain as he picked up Nick's borrowed overnight bag and came over. An unsure smile was on his freshly shaved face, as if we had been caught playing out "The Piña Colada Song."

"How did you know?" he said, and I blinked fast, trying not to cry as his voice rumbled through me, sparking memories. Lacerations decorated his arms and face, and his cheek was still swollen from the beating he'd taken this morning, but it was him. "I wanted to be sure I had a safe way out of here before I called you. Everyone knows your little red convertible."

He thought I was me, and I stood, shoving past Elyse to give him a hug. *I can do this,* I thought. *I can pretend to be me. Nothing has to change. I just want to hold him. Say good-bye.*

My God. It hurt.

"Kisten," I whispered, and then I had him, hands trembling as I pulled him tight enough to make him grunt in surprise. Vampire incense puffed up between us, and I almost lost it. It was him. He was alive, and I couldn't let him go. "You were supposed to wait for me at Nick's apartment," I choked out.

"You were right," he said, low voice pulling through me, and I closed my eyes, breath held until I knew I wasn't going to cry. "I called my cousin. He's going to meet me here. Let me borrow his car."

He pushed me back, and I gazed at him, soaking him in as I carefully touched his bruised face, remembering him, remembering every little thing. "I missed you," I said, voice soft so I wouldn't cry. "I missed you so much."

My heart was aching. I didn't care what was going on behind me at the table. All that mattered was this moment. This now.

Oblivious, Kisten wiped my eyes. "Love, it's only been half an hour. It's going to be okay. You're right. Even an hour is better than nothing, and maybe they won't find us. Maybe."

My shaking hand fell from him, tightening into a fist. He was running. How did he end up on his boat?

"Rachel?" Kisten tilted his head, trying to catch my eyes. I couldn't speak, confused. This was not what I remembered. This is not what happened. *What have I done?*

"Rachel."

It was firmer this time, and I looked up to see him studying me. Slowly he rocked back, one bruised hand falling from my shoulder, the other still clinging to my waist.

"You are not my Rachel," he said, and I tensed, feeling as if I'd been socked in the gut.

"I am," I said, voice shaking as I glanced at Elyse's muttered curse and Newt's satisfied smirk. "We need to go. Now. My friend will help us get out of Cincinnati."

"I will not," Elyse said sharply, but Kisten had reached out and I couldn't move as his swollen and cut fingers gently went through my hair, arranging it.

"You love someone else," he said as if mystified. "How can that be? How could you fall in love with someone in half an hour?"

Panic iced through me. "I love you," I asserted, and he cocked his head, confused.

"No," he said slowly, then, "Yes. You do. But you are *in* love, and not with me." He turned to the bar as if in thought, then back again. "You are my Rachel, but not. Have I slept?" Horror crossed him, and he let go of me. "Am I undead?"

I reached for him. "No, you're living," I said, blinking fast to keep the tears at bay as I fiddled with the collar to his sweat suit, touching his neck, his chin, his face. "And we're going to keep it that way," I finished, voice warbling.

"Rachel, you can't change this," Elyse said, and my throat closed.

"She isn't changing anything," Newt said, an ugly, knowing expression tightening her face. "This is her answer. This is her truth. And truth pays all bills."

Truth, perhaps, but I couldn't tell him anything. "You're alive," I said, hands gently cupping his face, and he blinked at me, still trying to figure it out.

"I'm alive," he agreed. "I have not slept. But you are not you." He glanced at Elyse and Newt. "I'm going to die. You are . . . you are from the future?" he guessed, and my eyes shut, unable to look at him anymore. "Is Ivy okay? Does she live?"

Speak truth only to the dead. That's what Al had said. Maybe . . . maybe he was right.

My eyes opened and I sniffed back the tears as I wiped my face. "She is okay," I said, and Elyse groaned as if pained. "Piscary can't hurt her anymore. She's found love. She's happy."

Relief eased the band about my chest, and I met his smile with my damp eyes. Kisten would still die, but he would die knowing Ivy was okay. Maybe it was enough.

"And you have found love, too," he said, head down as he studied our twined fingers, his strong and scared, mine pale and shaking. "Deep, abiding." He drew the air deep into his lungs. "True," he added, his blue eyes dark with unshed tears as he beamed at me. "Look at you. Look at how strong you are, sitting with the coven and a demon both. You are my Rachel of the future. Look what you have become without me."

"I never said . . ."

He put a gentle hand on my face, stopping my words. "I am gone. I see it in your every breath. And if I had been there, if I had survived, you'd be smaller. I know it."

I'd wanted to give him comfort, not this, and my agonized smile faded. "No. That's not why I'm here."

"You would be smaller," he said softly, and then my heartache redoubled as he pulled me into a hug, his body relaxing as he sighed against me. "You would be smaller, my love . . ."

"You don't know that," I sniffed into his collar, and we parted.

Eyebrows high, Kisten ran a finger down my neck. Only a faint hint of passion rebounded under his touch—and he knew it.

"I do," he whispered. "And I'm proud of you," he added, pulling me into a crushing embrace again. "I want you to go back. Become the mortar between the coven and the demons." He shifted against me as he considered my scent. "And the elves?" he added, surprised.

I pushed away, blinking fast and biting my lower lip between my teeth.

"Kalamack?" he guessed, and I couldn't speak.

Kisten sighed as he drew away. He had ferreted it out of me, and now I was someone else's love . . . not his.

"Kisten," I started, and he shook his head, letting go of me and picking up his bag. "Kisten, we can run," I said. "I don't need to go back."

"But I do." He leaned down and kissed my forehead. "Good-bye, my love."

"Wait." I gave Newt a look to behave herself, but she was clearly content to watch my life fall apart in a cruddy little bar in the Hollows. "If you return to the boat, you will die twice."

"I was twice dead the moment Piscary got out of jail," he said. "Running will only make it worse. I have to go. You're better without me. The world is better without me in it." He took a steadying breath. "Thank you for this. Now I know I'm making the right decision."

I caught his hand and stopped him. "That's not true."

He ran a thumb across my jawline. "My death makes you stronger. The person you are now is sitting between a demon and a witch."

Which was sort of where I'd always been—sort of. "No." I shook my head, not believing this. He had been ready to run. With me. And now he was going back?

Newt sighed, and suddenly I understood. He'd been ready to run until he saw me, knew that Ivy had found love, that we both had. He thought his death made both of us stronger. So he went back to die. Because of me. I had been here. I. Had. Been. Here.

"Kisten." I wouldn't let go of his hand, and he reluctantly halted. "The world needs you. Ivy needs you. I need you. I need you to run Cincy."

"Rachel, shut up!" Elyse exclaimed, then yelped when Newt slammed her fist on the table.

"I won't warn you again," the demon intoned. "Let this play."

Kisten's gaze softened as he ran a hand through my hair. "Go home. Be strong and beautiful in your choices. The world is safer with you free to act within it, and I am proud that I had a hand in helping you find your potential."

"You dying does not make me better. Kisten, please," I begged, and he pushed my hand from his wrist. "I know where you are going," I said, frantic. "I'm going to stop Art. You don't deserve to die for saying no to Piscary!"

He scuffed to a halt, uncaring that the nearest tables were listening. "Take care of her so she can take care of everyone else," he said to Newt and Elyse, and Elyse made a sad huff.

"Good-bye, my love," he whispered. "I will always love you."

"Let him leave," Newt said, and I froze, not because of her words but because my heart was breaking all over again.

"Kisten?" I called as he headed for the door, bag in hand, his head down when he threw a bill on the bar and walked out. "The world is not better without you. Kisten!"

But he was gone, and I didn't know how to breathe anymore.

"I can't . . ." I whispered as I turned to the table. "He was ready to run and I ruined it."

Elyse shook her head. "They would have caught him. Killed both of you."

"But he thinks he's worthless!" I shouted, hating that the music had started up again. Everyone was going back to their lives, oblivious or un-caring that mine had ended again.

"Not worthless." Newt stared at nothing, focus lost behind her black glasses. "He deems that leaving helped make you. And now I know who you are. I wasn't sure before."

I looked at the door one last time, then sat down, sick to my stomach. This was intolerable. I couldn't stop Kisten from dying, but I'd be damned if I let him go to his final rest thinking that he was worthless, that he was nothing more than a foil to make me stronger. I needed him. I had always needed him. The world needed him. And I was going to get his body and raise his ghost and tell him so. Every night if I had to.

My head came up, and I pulled my bag closer, ready to walk out the door. "We're done here," I said, and Newt smiled.

"Give me Elyse, and I will give you what you need to save your vampire."

"What?" I stammered, shocked, and Elyse went still, suddenly afraid.

"He doesn't have to die twice tonight," Newt mocked. "Just once. He could take the long way home. What's two years to the undead?"

"You need to shut up," I said, feeling as if she'd socked me in the gut.

Newt sniffed, peering over her dark glasses at me. "Stand and do noth-ing as I take Elyse, and I will jump you to him. You could get him under-ground before the sun comes up. Who knows how long he will linger fighting Art's virus."

"You are a true demon," I whispered, knowing I couldn't. I saw him die. There was nothing to change. *But what if he hadn't been truly dead when I left him, a flicker of life still there . . . Had I left him to die when the sun rose?* Heartache tore at me as I stifled a groan.

"You can't . . ." Elyse whispered, her expression pinched.

"Be silent!" Newt shouted, and we both jumped. "She can. I think she will. What does she owe you anyway? All you've given her is misfortune and distrust."

"No," I forced out through my clenched teeth. "Kisten dies. He dies on that boat. I saw it. I can't change that. Elyse wins. You lose, Newt." It hurt.

I knew better, though. Newt wouldn't offer unless it was possible, but something would intervene and I'd be bereft of everything. Demons were like a wish, and wishes always bit me on the ass in the end.

"As you say. But if you change your mind, come see me. That is, if you survive the next five minutes."

My head snapped up. "Survive what?" I said, then followed her gaze to the door.

It was Scott, a crow on his shoulder. The bird saw Elyse and began bobbing his head. It was her familiar. *Son of a troll turd's moss wipe.* He tracked Elyse down through her familiar.

"Rachel is right," Newt said casually. "You have far too much to learn to survive a night alone in the Hollows. What are your other names, Elyse?"

Newt moved liquidly fast, snaking a thin arm around Elyse's neck and yanking her close.

"Hey!" I shouted as Elyse shrieked. "Hands off!"

Newt's eyes glinted behind her glasses, knocked askew by Elyse's struggles. "Don't ruin my new view of you, Rachel," she said as I tapped a line and energy roared in. "Us girls have to stick together," she whispered into Elyse's ear. "You can't help it if you are ignorant, unless you fail to learn when given the opportunity."

"She is not for sale!" I shouted, angry at my own naivety. I had trusted Newt to play by the rules, and Elyse was going to pay the cost. *Not happening,* I thought, ready to rip the bar apart to keep Elyse this side of the lines.

"Lucky for you I just found someone better," Newt whispered as she shoved Elyse out of the booth and onto the floor. "Be smarter," she added as she stood up and stepped over her, an odd glow with gold flickering with black sparks at Newt's hands.

Elyse rolled under the nearest table, her bruised wrist held tight to her chest. Her synapses were burned. She couldn't tap a line, helpless.

But she's free, I thought, wondering. "You let her go? You agree she is not for sale?" I said, and Newt stood amid the tables, her robes misting into existence as everyone scattered, stampeding to the doors at the sudden scent of burnt amber.

"No," she said as I felt her tap into a ley line. She ran a hand over her hair, and it vanished. "I don't want her now. *He* knows more."

I tensed as I realized she was looking at Scott. *Aw, for ever-loving pixy piss . . .*

Teeth clenched, I yanked on the ley line, understanding why Newt was bald half the time as my hair sparked and haloed. "Everyone down!" I shouted, and then, *"Corrumpo!"*

A pulse of air slammed into the four walls and ceiling, knocking everyone standing to the floor. From the ceiling, an ominous crack sounded, and dust sifted from the old beams. *Oh, no. Not again,* I thought as Newt got to her feet, her black eyes wrathful. I hadn't attacked her directly, which was probably why she was staring at me instead of slinging spells.

"Run!" I shouted at Scott, waving violently at him. "Get out of here!"

"Implicare!" Newt exclaimed, and Scott backpedaled, his aura fizzing as he failed to evade the black field settling over him. Newt made a fist, and it tightened. Gasping, the coven member dropped, a hand to his chest.

"Honna tara surrundus!" I countered, throwing the break spell at Scott, not Newt. It was elven, but it worked, and the man got in a gasp of air.

"Hinc et inde," the man croaked to join his will to mine, and Newt shrieked in anger as our combined strength broke hers and the curse fractured.

"Who the hell are you?" Scott got to his feet, white-faced as Newt shoved a table out of the way to make more room. "A demon summoner?" he added, and then his gaze flicked behind me as Elyse scuffed to a halt at my shoulder. "You can't be Elyse. I just talked to her."

That bird of hers was on her shoulder, bobbing and cawing. That, I decided, was how he had found us, and I frowned as she put up a hand to soothe him.

"You *are* Elyse. You traffic with demons?" Scott added, and Elyse's soft words to her bird faltered. "That's the only way you could have gotten here this fast. What have you done?"

Elyse sidled closer. "There goes my career. Thanks a hell of a lot, Rachel."

"It's not over yet." I fingered the forget potion in my pocket. I was going to need two, and I flicked a glance at my shoulder bag. "Think you can distract him for a second?"

"Are you serious?"

"Would you rather fight Newt?" I said, yanking her closer as Newt made another play for the man and Scott snapped a protection circle about himself. Exuberant, Newt stomped forward to hammer on it in delight.

"She'll never break Scott's circle. We need to get out of here," Elyse said.

But I knew Newt would, and I yanked my bag from the bench seat, digging through it to find another forget charm. The two vials felt small as I turned to Newt pushing a fist into Scott's circle, plumes of energy rising from her hand like solar flares, black and gold and Scott's own purple and red. The strip club had emptied, but someone would have called the I.S. We had to be done by the time they arrived.

"Do it!" Elyse shouted, and I shook my head as I inched closer. Timing was everything, and why should I singe my synapses when Newt could bring Scott's circle down for me?

"Mine!" Newt cried out in excitement as Scott's circle pulled over him like a shirt . . . and was gone. Shocked, Scott stood there, white-faced with nothing between him and Newt but a slowly dying sparkle. "It's been ages since I've had a coven member to bring me my morning tea," she added, one hand reaching.

"Newt! Look out!" I shouted as I popped the lid to the first forget charm and threw it into her startled face.

Newt gasped, backpedaling as she pushed ineffectively at the spell soaking in. "Why?" she exclaimed, but it was her last lucid thought, and I grasped her arm, wanting to be the first person she remembered when her thoughts realigned.

"We girls have to stick together," I said. "Run!"

Hesitating, Newt scanned the nearly empty bar, taking in the stage, the low lights, everything. A flicker of fear was a bare hint in her black eyes . . . and then she vanished, leaving only the scent of burnt amber.

"My God, thank you," Scott said, ragged as the glow about his hand flickered and went out. "Elyse . . ."

"Is at coven camp," I said, and flung the second vial at him.

"Hey!" he yelped, struggling to get it off him, but it was too late, and I snatched up my bag, grabbed Elyse's hand, and pulled her to the door. Her crow took to the air, beating about our heads until it landed in the rafters.

"Slick!" she called, and I pushed her out the door.

"Your bird is giving us away. Run. Don't let Scott see you," I said, glancing back once at Scott, who was still wiping the potion from himself. Crap on toast, I'd used a memory charm on a coven member.

But Elyse had fled, and I raced to catch up and yank her behind a nearby dumpster.

"I thought you said—" she started, and I inched forward to peer around the cold, stinking metal bin. I could hear sirens, but we had a moment.

"I want to make sure Scott gets out okay," I said, and she sort of slumped where she stood, shaking from the close call. I knew how she felt, and I held a hand to my middle as the I.S. roared up and sent three witches into the building. I had a riddle instead of a mirror. Worse, I couldn't stop what was going to happen tonight and it was my fault. Kisten had been ready to run, and seeing me convinced him that the world was better without him in it.

I couldn't let that stick.

Elyse was trembling when she came up beside me and looked past the edge of the dumpster. "I can't believe we got out of there," she said as Scott was helped into the back of a squad car. They left the door open; he wasn't being detained, only given a place to recover. "You got your mirror. All we need now is a stasis spell."

Kisten . . . "I do not have a mirror, I have a riddle." I took a slow breath, hoisted my bag higher up my shoulder, and then slipped out into the night, head down, heart aching.

"Rachel, you can't." Elyse followed, her steps quickening as she glanced over her shoulder at the amber and blue lights playing against the bar's facade. "You have to let him go."

"You're right. I'm letting him go." Jaw clenched, I studied Cincy's skyline across the river to place myself. "But the world isn't better without

Kisten, and if there is the chance that he survives the night as an undead, I'm not going to let him die twice thinking it is."

Elyse's steps hesitated, then she hustled to catch up.

I had come to the past with one goal. Now I had two. Three if you counted Elyse's ancient stasis spell. Once an undead, Kisten could not survive biting another undead—the two virus strains would battle each other, and no undead vampire survived longer than three days without feeding. No soul meant no aura, and if he didn't take in blood and the aura it carried to replace it, he'd starve. But if Kisten was undead, even for an hour, I would not let the sun burn him.

Coffee first, though. It was almost midnight, and I had a long night ahead.

CHAPTER

18

JUNIOR'S WAS UNUSUALLY QUIET, BUT SEEING AS AL HAD BEEN tormenting the city last night, it was understandable. Mark wasn't behind the counter, which was a relief. That might have been awkward, though the guy was used to me acting odd and might never know the difference. The coffeehouse was the only place I was pretty sure I wouldn't run into myself. If I had my timing right, I was either already knocked out at my church or, more likely, still at Kisten's boat, trying to convince him to run away with me. It was all a little fuzzy, seeing as Jenks had hit me with a forget potion. Soon as I was sure I wouldn't run into myself, I was going out to check on Kisten and cry ugly tears.

"How did I ever survive this?" I whispered as Elyse paid for our drinks with a twenty I had given her. It was odd, hurting this bad and wanting nothing more than to find Trent and have him fold himself around me, tell me everything was going to be okay—when it was Kisten I was hurting for. I loved Trent. Kisten being alive didn't rub that out.

All I had wanted was to get the pixy-piss mirror and go home, and now I was further from it than before. *Damn you back to the Turn, Newt.*

My old phone hummed from my bag, and I ignored it. It wasn't for me. David was currently having the worst week of his life. Maybe his second. I was already doing what I could for him.

Elyse had apparently gotten over Newt, seeing as she was flirting with the barista. I could have given her to Newt and been done with it. Solved two problems at once. But no-o-o-o-o, I had to do the right thing, and I slumped deeper into the thin cushion, angry and miserable, angry because I'd gotten a riddle instead of the mirror, and miserable because I couldn't help Kisten. He thought he was worthless, that Ivy and I—that the world—was a better place without him. I'd found a way to accept that he had died because of some inane vampire custom, but that he died thinking the world was better off without him? No.

Elyse's red, dust-stained shoes scuffed closer, and I looked up as she set a small coffee in front of me. Numb, I took it in hand, fingers warming. It didn't smell like a skinny latte with a pump of raspberry and a dusting of cinnamon, but if I had wanted my usual drink, I should have told her what it was.

Elyse sat down, silent as she sipped what appeared to be a blond mocha. "She took Scott's circle as if it was nothing," she said, her expression heavy with disbelief, laced with fear. "She almost had him—if it hadn't been for those memory curses, she would have."

Illegal memory curses are okay when they save your career, eh? "Yep," I said. "Demons are stronger than coven once you get them out of a circle. And it's only that summoning curse that keeps them in one. They can wield more power than anyone except the elven Goddess." *Or an elf petitioning for her help.* But no right-minded elf ever would, seeing as nothing good happened when a Goddess took an interest in your life.

Elyse scuffed her chair closer and put her elbows on the table. "All the more reason for you to join with us. Help us grow. Become as powerful as them."

Are you serious? "Sure." I took the lid off my cup to add some sugar. "You got a thousand years or so? The demons became strong by fighting a losing war. Personally, I'd rather get my wisdom from the library. Slower, but a lot less destructive."

Elyse fiddled with her coffee's sleeve. "The elves beat them? Elves are stronger than demons?" she said, her doubt obvious.

"Not anymore. If ever. They relied a lot on the Goddess, and the Goddess is seldom accommodating unless she sees a chance to make mischief."

Elyse pushed back. *"Pffffft,"* she said insultingly, and my focus sharpened on her.

"She's real," I said.

"Yeah. Okay."

I dumped the two packets of sugar into my coffee, debating the wisdom of arguing with her. "Believe what you want. But you just met her."

Elyse thought a moment. *"That* was the Goddess? Newt?"

I stirred my coffee, missing Jenks for some reason. "Not yet, but she will be. When the mystics become aware of, ah, intelligent mass, Newt will be the vessel that they pour their collective visions into to understand." Newt had saved my life, and I took a sip, smiling as the rich, and now sweet, coffee slipped down. "If you thought she was erratic now . . ."

Elyse chuckled as she sipped her almost white drink. "Thank you."

I set my cup down, surprised. "For what, exactly?"

Her gaze flicked to me and away. "For not letting Newt abduct me. Or Scott. For erasing his memory that I was here dealing with demons. Talk about awkward."

A sigh escaped me. If I had let Newt take one of them, I might be on my way home by now with a mirror instead of a riddle. "You're welcome," I said, but it sounded grudgingly given, even to me.

"I, ah, don't worry about those memory curses. It was in the service of the coven. You're good," she added, and my attention sharpened on her.

I'm good as long as it is to their benefit? Double standards suck. "Yeah? How about dropping that inane demand that I become a coven member and give you my demon books?" I hunched over my coffee like a bird over prey. "That would be really helpful."

"I'm thinking about it," she said, and my gaze came up in suspicion.

"If it means we can get a stasis curse and go home right now, huh?" I prompted, and suddenly she couldn't look at me. Leaving now meant abandoning Brad to a slow slide into nothing, and she knew it. Newt had given me a riddle, not an answer.

"We don't belong here," she finally said.

"We used to." I sipped my drink, actually considering for a moment what she wanted. "No. Even if you could convince the rest to go along with it, I'm not leaving until I get an answer about that mirror. Not for you, but for Brad. I made a mistake. I'm fixing it."

Lips pressed together in annoyance, Elyse pushed back into the chair until it came up on two legs. "You don't have to prove to me you're a good person. I'm kind of over that."

Coffee in hand, I stared past her at the night. "That's nice."

"You have to let Kisten go."

"This isn't about Kisten," I snapped, frustrated. I had unwittingly convinced him to return to that boat and let that butcher of an undead vampire kill him because he thought his death made me a *better person.* How was I supposed to live with that? Face Ivy knowing it? *What if he hadn't succumbed to Art and I had just left him there to die in the sun? Art lasted three days in the dark.*

"Rachel." Her voice was soft. "You can't save him. When an undead bites another undead, both die. Always. They can't feed if they aren't awake, and once the aura they take in with a donor's blood is gone, their mind realizes they are dead and the body dies."

"You don't think I know that?" I said, voice hard. "Shut. Up."

"Sorry." She sipped her drink, eyes on the night.

Yeah, that's what she said, but what I heard was, *Why can't we leave?*

I took a slow breath, hands laced about my warm cup. "You think we should leave," I said, but it wasn't a question. "Take Newt at face value about the mirror and hope I can figure it out when we get home?"

Elyse lifted a shoulder and let it fall. "I never wanted to be here, so yes."

"Funny. I never wanted you to be here, either," I muttered.

"Oh, for God's sake." She turned to face me. "This isn't about a mirror anymore. You want to see Kisten. Make sure he's dead twice before we go. So go see him already."

For a moment, all I could do is stare. "Are you serious? Why do you even care how I feel?"

She shrugged, eyes going everywhere but to me. "I, ah . . ." Her gaze met mine for an instant, and her grip on her cup tightened. "I shouldn't have tried to trick you using Kisten as bait," she said softly.

My lips parted in surprise, and she hunched forward, brow furrowed. "I am *so* sorry," she said intently. "I knew you loved him, but I didn't care about what that meant, only that I could use it against you. And seeing you react to him, and then watching Newt try to do the same thing . . ."

My anger flared, and her expression pinched, becoming contrite. "I am so sorry," she said again, and I wished Jenks were here so he could tell me if this was an act or not. "It was cruel and self-serving, and I know having the chance to say good-bye doesn't make up for that, but you could find some closure maybe. And we could go home? You said you knew where to get a demon stasis charm."

Closure? I didn't like how she said that, as if the one act would tie the box with a bow and put it on the top shelf in my closet. Not to mention her thinking it meant I'd forgiven her for trying to bribe me with Kisten in the first place.

"You need to go to the boat," she said, eyes darting. "Say good-bye if nothing else."

She just wanted to go home, but as I eyed her guilt and embarrassment, I wondered if I could trust her long enough to at least make sure he was twice dead. That I might have left him for the sun was a guilt I didn't want to live with.

My gut tightened and my foot began to jiggle. Jaw clenched, I tilted my head to study the dark sky and moon. *We have a few hours to sunrise.* "I'm probably not at the boat anymore. Art came to kill him before midnight. It happened fast."

I blinked as the tears threatened, coming from nowhere. *I am not going to cry in front of a coven member.*

"Come on." She stood, cup in hand. "I read Kisten's file. It's like a ten-minute bus ride to where his boat is. You should find out if Newt was lying." Her lips twitched and she forced a smile. "And if nothing else, we can get something to eat on the way. I'm starving, and coffeehouse pastries aren't going to do it."

I sat and stared at her, wondering if she was doing this not because she believed what she was saying but because she had to have that demon stasis charm and I was her only source.

Lips pressed together, she took my cup—as if it might lure me into following her. "You can't help him, but you can say good-bye," she said. "Once you know for sure, we can go home."

My stomach hurts. This was something I wanted to do, but I was likely to walk away even more messed up. "After we get the mirror."

Elyse put a hand on my shoulder and smiled. "And that demon stasis charm, sure."

19

THE BUSES DIDN'T RUN OUT TO TUCKER'S LANDING, AND THE RUSTY beater that I had magically hot-wired from a used-car lot was burning both oil and antifreeze. I had driven so Elyse could eat, and the takeout bowl of Skyline chili in her hand gave me the twin feelings of hunger and nausea.

I could tell even before sunrise that the day was going to be hot. There wasn't a cloud in the predawn sky, now just beginning to show a hint of light at the horizon as we drove in from the main road. I wasn't sure if I should be thankful or creeped out that Elyse knew where Kisten had tied up his boat for his deadly rendezvous on the Ohio River. So I settled on suspicious.

Uneasy, I brought my gaze down from the skies as I parked at the outskirts, among the stored, tarp-covered boats that hadn't seen water in years. Kisten's yacht was at the nearby docks, set apart from the rest. The small cruiser was Kisten's sanctuary for when he needed space from Piscary. Or at least it had been. It was usually berthed at the quay outside the restaurant. Here, tied to a rickety, moss-covered dock, it looked huge.

"You okay?" Elyse asked, and I got out. The woman glanced at her chili, then awkwardly followed, bowl in hand.

"Peachy," I said softly as I walked to the dock, certain I wasn't on the boat. Art had fled immediately after Kisten had bit him. I'd left shortly thereafter, finding my way to the church to get some stakes to kill some vampire ass. My life might have ended right there if Jenks hadn't downed me with a forget charm. *Thank you, Jenks.*

My feet were silent on the damp boards, Elyse's steps fast and out of sync behind me. Memories flooded me as I paced to the stern, where it was easier to board, memories of Kisten, his smile, his blue eyes bright with love—dark in desire, how he made me feel . . . But mostly, how helpless I'd been when Art had attacked him, the way the boat had moved with his weight when he came aboard, how the water had lapped, chattering out a warning, Art's bloodlust, and then anger when Kisten had died before he'd gotten even a taste—and lastly, Art's fear when Kisten had sacrificed his undead existence to protect Ivy and me.

Exhaling, I grasped the railing for balance and swung my leg over it. "Don't touch anything," I said as the boat moved and I drew my other leg over and stepped down into the luxurious cockpit. "The I.S. couldn't care less about what happened, but the FIB sweeps for evidence and there was no sign of you."

The cushions were still out, damp with dew, and I blinked fast, sealing everything away.

Elyse scuffed to a halt behind me. "Maybe this isn't such a good idea."

But it was too late, and I hiked my shoulder bag higher and looked through the glass doors. Kisten's kitchen and living room were dark and tidy. Breath held, I slid the doors open and stepped into the galley, resisting the urge to call out to him.

And then I hunched, physically pained as Kisten's scent washed over me.

For a moment I couldn't move, my arm wrapped around my middle as a thousand feelings sifted through me. It was almost worse than seeing him in the bar. This was where we had dreamed, and planned, and lived.

"Rachel?"

"I'm okay." I forced my gaze up as the scent of chili plinked through me. It was her dinner, and it jolted me from my heartache. Grim, I forced the lump from my throat. "You probably shouldn't bring that in here."

Elyse held her takeout dish of Skyline chili tighter. "I won't spill anything."

"If I can smell it, so will the I.S.," I said as I forced myself to go into the short hall to the bedroom. *Closure. She thinks I needed closure?*

"Two days from now?" she questioned, and I ignored her. The place already smelled like the pasta Kisten had made for us—for my birthday. As long as she didn't drop it, we'd be okay.

What the hell am I doing? I thought again as I passed the tiny bathroom. Kisten's door was open, and I scuffed to a halt. I'd already done this with Ford, the FIB's psychologist. Or rather, I would. Course, by the time he'd brought me out here, Kisten had been cremated and the investigations had been shelved.

I forced myself to take one long step to settle in the archway to Kisten's low-ceilinged bedroom. It was dark, the curtains pulled back to let in only the faintest hint of the coming dawn.

"Don't turn on the lights," I whispered, my expression twisting as I saw him propped up against the bed where I remembered him being, his head slumped to his chest, one knee askew, the other leg out straight. His hands were in his lap, and my eyes closed in a strength-gathering blink. *Elyse, you are either a very good friend or a sadist.*

My breath slipped from me, and I went to him, my legs like water.

I fell to a kneel, reaching to touch his face, to brush his silken hair from his forehead. He was still fucking warm, and my throat tightened. His eyes were closed, and tears spilled from me. They weren't tears of grief or loss, but at the stupidity of it all. I had loved him, and there were still times when Trent would find me staring into space with a wistful look. I'd always miss him, but my heart had mended, slathered with Trent's devotion and utter love for me. I had found a way to live past his death.

"I'm so sorry, Kisten," I whispered, taking his hand in mine and brushing his hair back. Newt was wrong. There was nothing here for the sun to burn. I'd come too late.

And still . . . I could not bring myself to leave. "I wish I'd known what I know now," I whispered, unable to let go of his hand. "Been braver. Maybe I could have worked something out with Piscary and saved you. But I am glad you lived to know that Ivy finds love," I said, thankful that

Elyse had the decency to give me some privacy. "She found a woman who makes her whole. And I find not only love but someone who believes in me. We are both okay. You saved us."

Kisten's fingers moved in mine, and I jerked.

"Kisten?" Shocked, I gripped his hand and leaned in. Newt had been telling the truth, and I froze, gobsmacked. "Elyse? Elyse, he's still alive!" I shouted. "I mean, undead!"

Elyse landed in the doorway, that Skyline bowl in hand, her focus darting from Kisten to me. White-faced, she put a hand over her mouth. "Shit, I'm sorry."

Sorry? I thought, and then got it. Sorry because I was going to have to walk away and let the sun end this. *Well, fuck that!* I thought, giving him a shake. "Kisten? Kisten!"

"Rachel, stop." Elyse came forward and set her chili down. "I am *so* sorry. This was not my intent. I was hoping you'd find closure, not a false hope."

"But his fingers moved," I said, holding them to my chest as I studied his face.

Elyse inched forward, awkward and slow. "Bodies move as muscles let go."

"That wasn't a relaxing muscle." I gave his cheek a little slap. His face was ashen, but the undead didn't really have a pulse but for once every minute or so if they weren't active. *His aura,* I thought, quickly unfocusing my attention to make his aura visible. My breath came in shakily. His aura was still there, but it would be for up to three days after he lost his soul.

"Even if he was still undead . . . Rachel, he can't survive biting another undead. The virus mutates from host to host, and when they mix, they fight for supremacy, killing both."

But he wasn't twice dead yet, and my hope quickened. "Art lasted for three days." I held his hand, waiting for it to move again.

Elyse was silent, and I fought the urge to slap him again. Kisten's eyes had silvered that night. I'd seen it. But he was still here. I could not walk away and let the sun end it.

"Rachel, I am so sorry," Elyse said again, voice plaintive now as she hovered, clearly wanting to leave. "Giving you this false hope was not my intention. You can't change anything."

"Yeah?" I let go of his hand and lurched to my feet. "Maybe I was here to save him, huh?" If I didn't get him underground before the sun rose, it wouldn't matter if he was still undead. He'd be all-the-way dead.

"You can't save him," Elyse insisted, voice high. "You didn't. Ivy has his ashes."

But my resolve was growing, and I scanned the room for something to wrap him in. *Comforter, check.* "Ivy has someone's ashes. Maybe they aren't Kisten's."

"Rachel Morgan, stop this!" she shouted, going silent when I pulled the comforter off the bed and spread it on the floor beside him. "What the Turn are you doing?"

"Sorry, Kisten." I shoved him over, straining to roll him into place. The man was heavy with muscle. "Ivy might not have Kisten's ashes," I said breathlessly. "We never got to identify him. He was cremated at the city morgue before we could." Which was SOP for a master's mistake, now that I thought about it. I'd done it myself.

I dropped my bag onto Kisten's chest, feeling the early hour all the way to my bones. "I could use some help here."

"Whoa, whoa, whoa." Elyse raised a hand in protest. "You find him here. Dead."

"Not until Tuesday. That's two days from now."

"And then?" she said, still not moving. "What then?"

Crap on toast, why wasn't she helping me? The bloody sun was about to come up. "If he's still undead Tuesday morning, I will put a doppelganger in his place. Maybe they cremate a John Doe."

She made no move to help, even when I flipped the ends of the blanket over him and began to drag him to the narrow door. It was undignified, and I hated it, but Kisten wouldn't care. He'd laugh, probably.

"This would go faster if you would help," I said, looking past my hair at her. "We've got to get him underground before the sun comes up."

Elyse exhaled loudly. "They check for body authenticity before running the furnace. Ivy has Kisten's ashes."

I shook my head, grunting as I got him another foot closer to the door, and stopped. "I helped Ivy cremate one of Constance's city lessons three days ago. No one checked the body. They took us at our word." Frustrated, I let go of Kisten's shoulders, leaving his head propped against my legs. "It was your idea for me to find closure. I'm closing. The virus is still alive in him. Until it isn't, I'm keeping him away from the sun. You going to help me or not?"

"There are only two seats in that truck," she tried next, but Kisten wouldn't mind being put in the truck bed.

"Please," I said evenly, begging her. "Help me get him underground and we can talk about the ramifications all day. You're right he's not going to make it, but once he's gone, really gone, I can bring his body home under the same stasis spell you're going to need and do that stupid curse you dangled in front of me." And if this worked, I *was* going to use a stasis spell on him. To do otherwise would have him a decayed corpse by the time we got home. "You owe me, Elyse."

She flushed. "I don't owe you anything—" she started, but I'd have none of it.

"Nu-uh," I said, eyes narrowing on her. "You said you were sorry for using Kisten's death to manipulate me. That you saw how cruel it was when Newt did it. If you really meant that, prove it. Help me move him underground and find a body to take his place so I can bring him home and use that curse you tried to trick me with to protect Cincy when I have to go into hiding to avoid Alcatraz." I took a slow breath. "Or were you lying that you were sorry about that, too."

"Fine!" she shouted, clearly frustrated, and my pulse quickened as she dropped her empty chili bowl on him beside my bag and grabbed his ankles. "If we both need the same charm, you might actually twist it."

"You are a piece of work, Elyse." Head down, I took his shoulders and we maneuvered him into the narrow hall, elbows knocking.

"He's not going to wake up hungry, is he?" she asked.

Oh, if only, I thought, then shook my head. "Not with his aura still clinging to him," I said, then added as I snuck a glance at her, "Thank you. I really appreciate this." Because if I managed to get Kisten's body home intact, I could do that stupid spell and slip the coven. Sure, I'd be bringing Kisten's ghost back every night, but he could maintain Cincy's vampire population while I hid in the ever-after. *I don't want to hide in the ever-after . . .*

But that's where I'd be if I couldn't uncurse Brad.

"I'll help you stash Kisten and find a replacement body," she said. "But after he's underground, I want to get some sleep. I am so tired, I could hibernate. And we are even after this, Rachel Morgan," she added, face red. "You can't hold me manipulating you with Kisten over me again. Got it?"

I puffed a strand of hair out from before my eyes, thinking I would manipulate her with anything I wanted, any damn time I felt like it.

"Sure."

CHAPTER

20

ELYSE AND I HAD ALMOST COME TO BLOWS OVER HOW TO GET
Kisten off the boat. She'd been afraid of falling in, and I had finally agreed
to toss him to the dock like a sack of dirty laundry. *One, two, three, fling*...
After that, it had been embarrassingly easy to lug Kisten into our borrowed truck and from there to the library. I needed someplace safe underground, and using one of the nonprofit emergency shelters was out of the
question. All city buildings but the I.S. and FIB had been closed due to Al
rampaging through Cincy last night and had yet to be reopened, and the
rare-book vault seemed the logical place.

I had found myself missing Jenks again as we broke in at the delivery
door, and it was more than me needing to short out the cameras myself
with a well-flung spell. A long book bin and the freight elevator had gotten
us all down into the basement—though I was a little peeved at Elyse for
not helping me shift Kisten out of the rolling bin and into a more dignified
position once we got there. "He doesn't care," she said. But I did.

Unfortunately, he was too heavy for me to lift on my own, and tipping
the bin to dump him on the floor wasn't going to happen. So there he had
sat as we caught a few winks, his head uncomfortably wedged in a corner,
the backs of his knees draped over the side, feet dangling. After several
hours, he was chalk white, his blood having pooled in his extremities. His
aura, too, was growing thin, and that was a problem.

No soul meant no aura, the nebulous energy field not only serving as the body's first line of defense but also functioning as a conduit of communication between the body, soul, and mind to ensure that when the body died and the soul left, the mind would follow, thereby keeping all three together when they moved to whatever came next.

Not so with vampires. The vamp virus tricked the mind that the body was still alive after death, and as long as the vampire could take in enough aura-laced blood to bathe the mind, the mind never figured it out. It wasn't blood that the undead vampire truly craved but the aura contained in it, a clever link the demons who created the first vampires played upon to prevent the newly undead from destroying their aura source. You take too much blood/aura, the person passes out. You know to stop.

Kisten's soul was indeed gone—transitioned to the ever-after to wait until his mind figured out it was supposed to be dead. The aura from his soul was rapidly vanishing, and without an influx of new, aura-carrying blood, he would die his second death when the remnants of his aura dissipated. I might had saved him from the sun, but nothing could stop him from starving to death as his and Art's virus battled for supremacy, and my soul ached. *I'm sorry, Kisten,* I thought as I stifled the urge to arrange his hair. *But you are alive, undead, whatever.*

My gaze shifted to Elyse, drawn by her hand darting out to catch a blob of cheesecake that had fallen from her fork. "You look better," I said, and she bobbed her head, hair dripping from her shower.

"I could have slept for four days, not four hours," she said around her full mouth, then washed it down with bad vending-machine coffee, grimacing at the taste. The slice of cheesecake had come from the employee fridge, stolen, obviously. Elyse had helped herself as if it was hers. The woman ate with the abandonment of a teenager. But then again, she was one.

My stomach hurt too much to eat, and I studied her as her fork rhythmically moved, reading her lingering fatigue, her frustration that I hadn't gotten the stasis charm and taken her home yet. She hadn't said a single bad word about us stealing that truck or busting the library cameras. It had been her suggestion that we raid the employee fridge. I would have thought breaking into the library alone would have put me on the naughty list, being neither moral nor ethical. But perhaps the coven was only concerned about the spells used to manage mischief, not the mischief itself.

"Ah, hey. Thanks again for helping me get Kisten underground," I said as she plowed her way through someone else's cheesecake.

Her eyes flicked from Kisten to me as she ate another bite.

"Everything you said about not being able to keep him alive was a hundred percent valid," I added. "Good news. We can use the same stasis curse to get you both home." *Maybe she's mad I'd circumvented her plot to force me into the coven?* Unless she was lying about everything and all her promises vanished when I got her home.

"That's good. I'm glad you're interested in getting the charm now," she said, and my lip twitched. I wasn't the one breaking all our deals.

Seeing my disgust, she leaned back, fork dangling as she washed the last bite down with her coffee. That, at least, she'd paid for. *With my money.* "I'm sorry, but could you remind me who you are doing this for?" she asked.

She was looking at Kisten, and heartache was a sharp pain. *No wonder my stomach hurts.* "Isn't it obvious?"

She pointed her fork at me. "No, I want to hear it. You're not doing this for Kisten. He's not in a position to care. He basically committed suicide returning to that boat."

I clenched my teeth. The man was right there, probably hearing this on some level. "Having second thoughts, Elyse? I might not have the mirror, but once I get Kisten's body home, I slip your snare, Madam Coven Leader."

Peeved, she took a breath, her hand coming to rest on the table between us as if in placation. "I told you I'm not pursuing Alcatraz for you anymore, and once I talk to the rest, our demand to uncurse Brad will be rescinded. Which all makes me question why you still want to bring him home. I mean, Ivy has remade her life. To make her deal with this again? Who are you really doing this for?"

I could do nothing but stare. Was she trying to get me to change my mind and leave him to die alone? "Cincinnati," I said shortly, well aware that I might be dumping Ivy back in the morass of heartache we'd worked ourselves out of once. "*You* might have agreed to overlook what I did to Brad, but I'm telling you right now the rest won't. If I can't get Brad uncursed, I'm going to have to go into hiding to avoid Alcatraz. Kisten will be solid enough to do what he needs to do if I raise his ghost every sunset. He can keep Constance in line and the DC vampires out. I vowed to keep Constance safe. Kisten can do it. He practically ran Cincinnati when Piscary was in jail."

Uncomfortable, I ran a finger over the pentagram gouged into the tabletop. "Which is why I really appreciate you helping me find a body to put on Kisten's boat." My gaze flicked up to hers. "You're not backing out on that, too, are you?"

"The coven will do what I say—" Elyse began warily.

"Until you tell them to do something they don't want to," I interrupted, and she pinched the bridge of her nose, eyes closed.

"Fine. You're bringing Kisten home to chaperone Cincinnati's vampires. This is your town. Where do you suggest we go to find a body no one will miss?"

My relief was short-lived. Maybe it was a morality test. She was the leader of the coven of moral and ethical standards, after all. Not sure if I was doing myself any favors, I leaned over the table. "I was thinking the safe-haven drop box at Spring Grove. We can catch a bus from here. Be out there around sunset . . ."

My words tapered off as Elyse shook her head. "Bad idea. I almost got caught using a safe-haven drop box. There are no cameras, which is nice, but they generally have a silent alarm sound when the lid opens. The bodies don't stay in there for more than twenty minutes. We'd have to wait and intercept a corpse, and the people who use the safe-haven service can get . . . twitchy."

"Okay." I reminded myself she was a few years older than the kid sitting across from me. *Almost got caught?* "What do you suggest?"

"Hospital or city morgue," she said confidently. "Hospitals keep a close tab on their undead, but occasionally someone walks out unexpectedly, so missing bodies are not unheard-of. But if it was my decision, I'd go with the city morgue."

I grimaced, not trusting this. "Just how often do you do this? And why?"

"The I.S. is always finding John and Jane Does at crime scenes," she said, not answering me. "Whoever left them doesn't want them to be found or identified. You find a dead undead who has been unclaimed for over two weeks, you got yourself a good candidate. Someone already did the hard part for you by separating them from their relatives, if they even had any. Not to mention they are already bagged. No fuss, no muss."

"I ask again, how often do you need an unclaimed body, Elyse Embers?"

"Join my club, and I'll tell you," she said, meeting my gaze straight on, not a hint of embarrassment or shame.

I leaned back, head cocked in suspicion. "I can get us into the city morgue," I said, deciding to take this at face value. "I know how to run the furnace there, too," I finished softly.

"The city morgue has its own furnace?"

My gaze sharpened on her. What had she thought Ivy and I were doing with Brice's body? "That's where the city's master vampire's mistakes go?" I said, making it into a question.

Elyse bobbed her head. "We'll do that, then. With Piscary on the streets, there's bound to be one or two vampiric John Does."

For a moment, I just stared. "Just when I think I know you, Elyse . . ."

She tossed her damp hair from her eyes. "That only leaves the problem of getting a stasis curse that lasts longer than three days, because there is no way I want to show up at Eden Park with a two-year-old corpse."

I had to work hard to stifle my urge to walk out. I mean, she was right, but she didn't have to be so callous about it. The man was lying right there.

I must have looked kind of pissed, because she was staring at me. "What?" she finally asked, then her expression shifted. "You said you could get one. You can't, can you. You're going to leave me here?"

"I know where one is. I'm not leaving you here," I said sourly. Though it would make my life easier in the short run. "We simply have to go get it."

Unsure, Elyse ran her fork over the paper plate to get the last of the cheesecake. "I thought it was in the demon collective. You can't just say the words and poof?"

I shook my head, trying to decide how much I wanted to say. "It's not demon. It's an elven ley line charm stored in a circle of metal. Pre-coven, older than even the collective. Probably medicinal, so I'm guessing it holds minimal smut." I took a slow breath, reluctant to admit this next part. "It's been used, but it still has its invocation pin and I can probably rekindle it." Even if the charm *was* elven, it would dovetail with my demon spell to get home. The two schools of demon and elf magic were practically interchangeable—not that either would admit it.

"It's used?" she predictably blurted. "You can't rekindle ley line charms. Once they're done, they're done!" And then Elyse sort of froze. "*You* can rekindle ley line charms? Is that a demon thing?"

Wincing, I traced my nail over the etched pentagram. "Yes, and yes. It's in Trent's rare-item vault." Two-years-ago Trent would be pissed if he caught me, ah, borrowing it. Getting it would be hard, and she was going to have to trust me. I was going to have to trust her. *Oh, God, can I survive trusting her?* I glanced at Kisten, wondering how he could have gotten it so wrong. I was sitting beside a coven member scrambling to survive, not direct the course of events. "I've been helping Trent catalog his artifacts and I remember seeing it there. Our best chance to break into the vault is when he's getting married tonight. The wedding is after sunset so the undead can attend. We have loads of time to prep."

But in all honesty, I'd spent the last two years prepping to break into his house. I knew all his passcodes, his SOPs, everything.

"You want to steal it? Merlin's mangos. He's an elf!" Elyse exclaimed. "You don't steal from elves! And sure as hell not one of their ancient artifacts."

I stifled a shudder at the memory of dogs baying for my blood. Under my gaze, Kisten took a slow breath, then went still. "I intend to give it back, so technically I'm borrowing it." But local-time Trent wouldn't see it that way, and I totally understood her alarm. "He'll never know it's us," I insisted.

"You're in coven camp and I'll be arresting him at the time of the, ah, borrowing."

Elyse's eyes narrowed in suspicion. "And you can reinvoke it?"

"I don't see why not. It's elven. They used to put people into long-term storage all the time." I went to the table to sort through my bag. I was dead tired but not sure I would be able to sleep. I wasn't really stealing anything so my ethical concerns all revolved around invading Trent's space. I'd promised I wouldn't do it again, but I actually hadn't made that promise yet. Either way, he'd never know, seeing as he would be busy not getting married—and that he would never know seemed the most important consideration. "The hard part will be getting into his labs," I added as I touched the glamour stone around my neck.

Her gaze fixed on the innocuous-seeming amulet. "Labs that don't exist." She hesitated. "He keeps his rare-item vault in one of his labs?"

"In a manner of speaking." *Robe, hat, sash, splat gun, forget charm, lethal-detection charm . . .* "The vault is accessed through a ley line pulled into the earth with a magnetic resonator. It's really a two-person job. You up for it?" I doubted she'd stay here with Kisten.

"He uses a ley line as a door? He'd have to go through the ever-after to use it."

I nodded, satisfied she understood the danger when she stiffened, her expression shifting from gratitude that I wanted her there to suspicion that I'd use and lose her when things got tight. "Wouldn't miss it," she said flatly.

"Great." I stood before her and continued to go through my bag, but all I really needed was a smile and my new glamour stone. I already knew all Trent's SOPs and codes. "Once we get the magnetic resonator going, I could use someone to watch my back. I won't have a clue what's going on while I'm in the ever-after."

"My God. You're serious," she said softly, and I glanced up from my bag.

"Two steps, and then I'm back in reality and in the vault." I hesitated. "We good?"

"No, we are not good. But I can get myself out of anything you get me into." Again her gaze went to that stone. "We're going to use that curse again?"

I shrugged. "I suggest we access the grounds around sunset. He should be gone by then."

Because once I arrested Trent, Quen—his security advisor and best man—would be too preoccupied to do anything but delegate any action taken at the estate.

"Okay, I'm excited about this," Elyse said sourly. "When do you want to get a body to put out on Kisten's boat? Before or after?"

I looked at the racks of books as if I could see through them. She had agreed to help, but I didn't know if I could really trust her. I knew she wouldn't do anything to get me caught, but I had a hard time working with someone who might turn on me the moment they felt safe.

Still, I didn't have much choice. I doubted she'd sit with Kisten while I found a body. "Later, but I wouldn't mind seeing what's available so when we're ready, we can move fast." I closed my bag and draped it over my shoulder, and Elyse chuckled as she cleaned the last off her fork.

"You don't need to plan picking up a body. You go, find, and shove into a van."

She was sounding like me, which meant I was sounding like Ivy. *Good.* I yanked my phone from the charger and pocketed it. "Yeah, but I'd feel better having culled one from the herd. I suggest we check the hospital morgue first. They're not busy during the day, and I know how to access the undead area. If they don't have what we need, we will hit the city morgue."

Elyse stood, patting her pockets for her nonexistent phone or wallet. "And then?"

"Once we locate a body, we get him and Kisten in the same room, glamour the John Doe Vamp, and move Kisten's doppelganger out to the boat to be found by the I.S." I glanced at Kisten slumped in the cart. It was so undignified, but he wouldn't care. "The I.S. will move John Doe Vamp to the morgue on Tuesday thinking it's Kisten. We break in, pop the man into the crematorium before they do a positive ID. Ivy gets his ashes. We go home."

"After we get the stasis charm," Elyse said as I decided against bringing my bag and shoved it behind some books.

"And rekindle it," I agreed softly as Elyse started for the hallway, not a flicker of worry or regret at the idea of stealing what we needed, not caring about the people we would inconvenience or the laws we would break in order to get what we wanted. And that, I think, was what worried me most.

She might be helping me, but it was obvious she didn't trust me, and I, sure as pixy dust glowed, didn't trust her. Worse, I was giving her a front-row seat to the laws I had to break to do my job—and there was nothing I could do about it.

CHAPTER

21

"RACHEL, WE'RE HERE."

I started awake, surprised to find myself on the bus until I remembered. People in scrubs and jeans were making their way to the rear to get off, and new passengers dressed about the same were getting on at the front. I stood, stifling a yawn as I joined the line to the back and shuffled to the steps. Four hours of sleep hadn't been nearly enough. The coffee I'd had for breakfast wasn't helping. I was tired, my gut hurt . . . and a part of me was foolishly worried that Kisten might wake up and that I wouldn't be there.

But he was not waking up, not ever, and my throat closed against my heartache. He was starving to death, his aura slipping away as he tried to fight off Art's virus. This, too, I could not stop.

Elyse hit the sidewalk ahead of me, obnoxiously awake and alert. I planned on picking up our glamours on the way in, seeing as she was still a person of interest and I . . . Well, too many hospital workers knew who I was. Not to mention sequins and rhinestones didn't do it for me anymore. Much.

Head down, I didn't notice when Elyse veered off, and I scuffed to a halt when she shouted an annoyed "Hey!"

"This way," I said, seeing her standing halfway to the main entrance, hand on her hip as if I was a dunderhead. She stared at me for a heartbeat, then jogged forward as if four hours was enough sleep for anyone.

"Not the front?" she said as she slowed to meet my ambling stroll, and I shrugged. I'd left my bag at the library and felt naked without it. It was almost as recognizable as me.

"The undead's ambulance entrance," I said. "We'll find someone to lift a glamour from and work around not having the right ID."

Elyse's gaze fixed on the steady stream of employees leaving, the woman nodding at the predominance of red scrubs. I'd timed it perfectly. "The undead have their own entrance?" she asked.

"For convenience. Cincy has had a second emergency room since before the Turn," I explained. "They keep the languishing undead in a separate facility, which we can access more easily from there. The entire floor is slow this time of day."

She made a little huff. "It's your town."

"Yep, and you just keep remembering that," I said, not liking her doubt. "Slow up, I want to lift her image. We won't have her ID, but she's about the same build as you."

"An intern?" Elyse complained as I tapped a line and peered through the stone's hole at the woman in red scrubs, clearly eager to get to her car and the rest of her day.

"*A priori*," I said to capture her image in my mind, and I felt a twinge of connection.

I turned to Elyse . . . choking back the next phrase. She was gone. "Elyse?" Crap on toast, she was jogging after the woman in question. Worse, Elyse rammed right into the woman's shoulder, both of them crying out in surprise as Elyse caught her arm and kept her from going down.

"Oh, my gosh!" Elyse gushed, her brow furrowed in worry. "I am such a klutz. Are you okay?"

"I'm fine," the woman said in annoyance. "Just don't drive like that, okay?"

"I'm so sorry." Elyse began to back away, the woman's ID going into her pocket.

Clever, I mused when Elyse sauntered to me, as smug as a snake.

"Now you can spell me," she said, and I gave her a nod of approval.

272

"*A posteriori*," I said as I peered at her through the stone, then blew through it at her, thinking, *Omnia mutantur.*

Elyse shivered, and I looked through the stone again to see not Elyse but the athletic blonde, right down to her red scrubs. "You're good."

Elyse frowned as she peered at the woman's ID. "Mandy Manning. Tell me who you want and I'll get their ID."

"Her," I said as I targeted a short brunette. She was somewhat stockier than me, but I liked her black slacks and white blouse. She was probably an office manager, but with the right attitude, she could be from the I.S. "Leave her," I added when Elyse rocked into motion. "An I.S. employee wouldn't have a hospital ID. We'll get in on yours."

"You sure?"

"Light footprint," I said as I did the spell, shivering when it settled over me.

Glamours in place, we walked into the underground drop-off as if going into work. The cool of the garage was pleasant, and the elevator would get us downstairs. *And from there . . .*

I yanked on the door, frowning as it gave an inch and stopped with a metallic thud.

"You're up," I said, fully aware of the camera pointed at the door. No one would check the tapes. At least that's what I told myself. Getting out with a body might be another story. Might be easier to bring Kisten here, leaving him in the John Doe Vamp's place. One body in, one body out, and as Elyse scanned her ID, I winced, images of a wheelchair and a pasty-white man flitting through my head. Car. We needed a car. The bus would be too . . . memorable.

"So far, so good," Elyse said as the door opened, and I slipped in past her.

My shoulders slumped at the heady scent of the undead, the spicy mix of sex and power going right to my groin and rebounding to make the scar on my neck tingle.

"Wow." Elyse blinked, taking it in as she looked over the taupe walls and tiled floor. "That's strong. And we aren't even downstairs yet."

"Elevator." I raised my chin to point it out, feeling like Ivy as I hit the button in a quick staccato, trying to hurry the lift.

"Hey, Mandy," a masculine voice called out, and Elyse spun. "They call you back?"

"Ah, no," she said, and I pulled her stumbling into the elevator when the doors slid open. "I forgot something. Don't tell anyone I'm here. Okay? I don't want to get roped into anything."

Safe in the elevator, I watched the man turn his attention to his tablet with a chuckle. "I know nothing. I see nothing," he said, and then the doors slid shut.

Elyse exhaled, puffing out her cheeks to tell me she wasn't half as confident as she wanted me to think. "L-3?" she guessed with an overly bright smile, and I hit the button for the floor right below that.

"L-4," I said, steeling myself for the coming assault. I'd been to the undead emergency floor before, and it was rife with pheromones despite the massive airflow designed to remediate it. I'd been able to handle it then, but now? With a new vampire scar and a body sans two years of practice in saying no?

I winced, missing Jenks. Not only could he short out the cameras, but his smart-ass commentary would have gone a long way in keeping my libido in check. But when the elevator dinged and the doors opened, it was only the scent of antiseptic and comforting taupe walls that met me. Either the floor was empty of patients, or they made a point to keep this one clear of pheromones.

"Impressive." Elyse strode forward, oblivious that I had seen her momentary lapse of confidence. Maintaining that took a toll, but admitting to yourself and others that you were vulnerable was a strength she needed to learn herself.

"That way," I said, eyes on the small placard stating UNDEAD ASSESSMENT. They didn't like to use the word *morgue* until it was obvious they weren't coming back, and we needed an undead vampire who had recently passed. The window wasn't as small as one might think.

"Gurney?" Elyse suggested, and I shook my head.

"We're just window-shopping," I said as we slowed at the twin metal doors. Again, a tug got no response, and Elyse grinned.

"I bet Mandy has access," she said as she held her ID to the scanner.

A bland buzz sounded, and I pulled the door open, my steps slowing at the reception desk. Actually, it appeared more like an office than a receiving area, the desk being cluttered with papers, racks of filing cabinets against one wall, and a shallow fish tank with a turtle taking up one corner. A rotary landline phone from the seventies sat to one side like the insult it was. The lights were bright and potted plants were everywhere, as if whoever they had stuck down here pined for an aboveground office.

A collage of Cincy's bridges through the decades hung on the wall facing the desk, the pictures ranging from grainy brown-and-white to drone shots of the remodeled bridge twinkling with colored lights. Unlike the city morgue, there was no comfortable waiting room. This was someone's office, and I studied the heavy redwood scent overpowering the faltering vampire pheromones and embalming fluid. Whoever sat at the desk was a top practitioner. What were they doing down here?

"I'll be with you in a moment!" came a distant call, and I froze, recognizing the voice. I'd talked to her only once, but I'd know that bitter, angry, sarcastic tone anywhere.

"Um, it's Dr. Ophees," I whispered, and Elyse looked at my hand gripping her arm.

"She knows you?"

I let go, not sure why I'd grabbed her. "Yes. I mean, no. Not yet." *Relax, Rachel. This isn't a problem.* "We interacted for about five minutes. I'd bet my life that she didn't recognize me then, but she . . ." My voice trailed off in a sudden thought. "She has a spell that separates the aura from the blood that carries it."

Elyse's eyebrows rose. "Seriously? That can't be legal."

My pulse quickened, and I stared at the open archway where Dr. Ophees's voice had come from. "It is. Technically. I almost accidentally made a donation once. You can administer it to an unconscious vampire like a pill or salve."

My gut hurt. *Kisten.* He wouldn't be able to replenish his aura via a draft of blood as long as he was battling Art's virus. Sure, he would starve of aura depletion somewhere between now and home even if he was under a stasis curse, but that didn't mean he had to starve right now.

Elyse took in my silence, her eyes widening. "Rachel, no," she whispered as she followed my train of thought. "We are here to see if they have a body. Not some miracle cure. You can't fix this. No undead survives mixing their blood with another undead. He is going to die whether you give him an aura or not."

"I know that, but I'm not going to watch him starve if I don't have to," I said bitterly. "Why don't you check out what's available while I keep her occupied."

Elyse groaned, eyes closing. "Please don't do anything stupid."

That was my line, but hope had slashed my heartache wide open. If Dr. Ophees had the charm, I could what? Save Kisten? I'd never be able to get him home undead even with the stasis curse. It would keep him from decomposing. That's it. And even if I could, he'd be in a coma, reliant upon bottled auras for the rest of his comatose, undead existence. That's not what he would want. The best I could do was keep him comfortable until he died, and as Dr. Ophees came scuffing out from the back room, I decided that sometimes that was enough of a win.

"I could get home faster if I walked," Elyse muttered, beaming at the tall dark-haired woman tossing her blue gloves into the nearby trash can.

"Can I help you?" she asked, and I shifted to get her attention off Elyse. Dr. Ophees might have been going for professional in her dark slacks and pressed top, but a ratty cardigan and slippers ruined it. I couldn't blame her. It was unlikely that anyone ever came down here unless they were picking up or dropping off. Even so, she looked eminently qualified with her glasses, trendy haircut, and perpetually annoyed expression.

"Ah, hi," I said when Elyse cleared her throat. "I'm from the I.S., checking for unclaimed bodies to move to the city morgue."

The tall woman's lips twitched and she went to her desk, done with me. "I take my Does to the morgue myself. Though if you had been here on

Friday, I might have made an exception." She sat down and shook her mouse to wake her computer. "He should've gone there from the get-go, but rules are rules, and until their auras hit critical, they are mine. Good-bye."

An unclaimed vampire at the city morgue, twice dead from a declining aura? He'd be there at least a month to give someone the chance to claim him. This was better than we could have hoped for, and I glanced at Elyse, thrilled until I remembered that whoever it was, he had been important to someone.

Elyse made a directive nod to the hallway, jaw clenching when I inched closer.

"Ah, when you say 'critical.' What is that?" I asked, worried about Kisten. "Thirty percent aura?"

Dr. Ophees furrowed her brow, suddenly wary. "Who did you say you were?" she asked, and Elyse's grimace flicked to a smile when the doctor's gaze landed on her.

I had a heartbeat of panic. "Stef Monty," I said, borrowing the first name of my last roommate, and my dad's first name for my last. "I think there's been a mistake. I just made street runner, and hazing week sucks." I came forward, hand extended. "It's great to meet you. Mandy was nice enough to show me the way down here."

"Oh. Well, sorry you made the trip for nothing." Dr. Ophees stared at her screen, and I let my hand drop. "Have a nice day."

Elyse cleared her throat. "I'll walk you upstairs," she offered as she came closer, and then in my ear. "You got what you came for, let's go."

True, but how I wanted something else, and I stepped to the open archway, both women stiffening when I glanced into the morgue. It was all drawers, at least ten rows, and they all were wired for audio and visual by the looks of it. "It's only the undead down here?" I asked.

"Yes." The chair creaked as Dr. Ophees leaned back in suspicion. "But only after they lose eighty percent of their aura. Theoretically they could recover, but by the time they reach me, they don't have a chance."

Eighty percent. Kisten was not that bad. Yet. "Well, there are ways around that." I turned and leaned against the wall.

"All of them illegal," Dr. Ophees said mildly. "Ms. Stef Monty from the I.S."

"Not all of them."

Elyse shifted nervously. "Ma'am, let me escort you up." She gave Dr. Ophees a nervous grin. "Sorry to have bothered you, Doctor."

My arms crossed over my middle, making me into an immovable lump. "Go ahead. I know the way back if you're busy."

Dr. Ophees met my eyes, clearly annoyed as I settled in. "You need to leave," she said, voice hard. "I run a clean morgue. No illegal curses. They come in. I do what I can. They either wake up hungry or they don't."

I stifled a wince. She hadn't come up with the spell yet. *Crap on toast,* I thought, recognizing her anger now as frustration. *Well, maybe I was the one who taught it to her?*

"It's a spell, not a curse," I said, and Elyse cleared her throat in warning. "Bastardized from illicit magic, but it pulls the aura from donated blood, not a living person, freely given. No harm, no foul. You can store them on a shelf, administer them like a blanket to give the undead's body time to repair itself before a lack of aura kills them twice."

"There is no such thing," Dr. Ophees said with a bitter confidence. "I'd know about it."

I shrugged. "Now you do."

Elyse cleared her throat. "Stef, I really think we should leave."

Brow furrowed, Dr. Ophees stared at me. "So tell me."

Yes! I thought in triumph as Elyse stifled a groan. "You want me to simply give it to you?" I said. "For nothing? A charm that could make your entire career? I want something in return."

The woman shook her head and glanced at her phone. "I'm not giving you a body."

"Nope," I agreed. "You're going to save one."

Elyse bowed her head and pushed her fingers into her temples.

Silent, Dr. Ophees put the flat of her arms atop her desk.

"Consider it, Dr. Ophees," I said, feeling like Al—or Trent maybe— offering a heart's desire for what felt like nothing. "You will be pioneering a new field of emergency medicine, one that will save hundreds, thousands of undead lives its first year. *You*, not me. I don't want any credit." My gaze flicked to Elyse. "Neither does she. I simply want one man saved." I hesitated, thinking, *And maybe ten percent of any aura gathered to go to Kisten so he doesn't starve before Art's virus kills him twice.*

"Then you do it," Dr. Ophees said as her gaze on me went indistinct, then cleared. "Your aura is smutty, and you have at least one demon mark. Get out of my office."

"Where do you think I learned the cure?" I said. "I can't do the charm because I don't have the equipment. And I can't get it past the Federal Spell and Charm Association because, as you say, my aura is smutty and I have a couple of demon marks. You, though, with your reputation?" I let that hang for a moment, playing on her pride. "I need that aura, Dr. Ophees. I'm not going to break the law and hurt people with an illicit curse when you have the tools and I have the know-how to get it legally." I nodded at the first hints of belief in her. "I keep the man I once loved from starving, and you pioneer a new, legal method of providing emergency aura care to the undead."

"From donated blood?" she said, gaze going into the back room and probably a cache of fresh blood, on hold should someone actually wake up. "It can't be legal."

"I can assure you it is," Elyse said sourly, drawing both our attentions.

"And I should take the advice from an intern?" Dr. Ophees mocked, and Elyse flushed. "It's my reputation on the line, not yours. I'd need to see said charm. Judge for myself its moral ramifications."

My pulse jumped. The woman hated the futility of her job. She'd risk a lot to get out. I knew how she felt. "Absolutely. I need a pint of blood still containing its aura, two small scrying mirrors, wax candle." I hesitated. "From the fat of a fetal pig if available."

Dr. Ophees nodded. It sounded awful, but when dealing with the undead, anything that hadn't seen the light of day simply worked better.

"A glass jar about this size that can be sealed," I continued, holding my hands just so. "Big silver knife."

"Knife?" Elyse questioned, and I lifted my shoulder in a half shrug.

"To clean the wax off the scrying mirror when done. You don't want anything impure to embed itself in the surface."

"That's it?" Dr. Ophees hadn't stood up, instead looking at me through her glasses with an intensity that made me wonder if she was seeing past the glamour: sequins, rhinestones, and all. "I despise working down here," she said sourly. "Do you know there's only a three percent chance of recovery after they reach me? They call me Dr. Death."

I said nothing, waiting as she thought it over. *Please, please, please . . .*

"Okay," she finally said, and I stifled a jump. "Give me a second to lock up and collect what you need."

"Great." I exhaled to try to hide my relief as Dr. Ophees returned to the back room. The sound of drawers opening and closing could be heard, and Elyse inched closer.

"This is not a good idea," she whispered, and I grimaced. "We came here to scout for a body. We found one at the city morgue. What are you doing this for?"

I rocked away from her, fidgety because I knew she was right. "I thought you'd be interested in seeing how close the charm walks the line between moral, ethical, and Alcatraz. She can do some real good, but she needs your stamp of approval." Not to mention if it works, Kisten wouldn't die of aura depletion while waiting for Art's virus to kill him.

"You want to take her down there?" Elyse looked mortified. "What if she calls the I.S.?"

There was a series of beeps from the other room, followed by a soft sucking sound of an air seal breaking. "She's not going to call the I.S. She's under patient-doctor privilege."

Elyse grabbed my elbow in warning. "It doesn't work that way."

"She wants to go." I gestured to the back room. "She's a doctor. He needs care. Besides, she has this spell in the future. You think she figures it out on her own?"

Grimacing, she dropped away. "How come everything you want to do has already been done, and everything I want to do will break the timeline?"

"Maybe because *you* weren't supposed to be here." I found a smile as Dr. Ophees returned with a small, clearly used shipping box. The handle of a big knife poked out over the edge, and I felt a quiver of hope—quickly followed by a flash of anxiety. I was going to be inventing this charm on the fly, but I'd seen the pentagram she'd used in the future and I knew the original curse it was bastardized from. There might be years of tweaking to make it efficient, but it was a good start. Even if it only collected a small portion of aura, it would help. It had to work.

"Ready?" I said, looking for my bag. But I'd left it with Kisten, and I felt foolish.

"This is my lunch break," Dr. Ophees said. "You have two hours."

"Okay, but you're driving," I said as the tall woman ushered us out into the hall and locked the door.

Two hours. It had to work.

CHAPTER
22

"THE LIBRARY?" DR. OPHEES'S HANDS GRIPPED THE WHEEL OF HER electric convertible tighter as we stopped at a red light.

Elyse, who had insisted on taking the front seat, beamed a comforting smile. "It's closed. But we have a way in. Go left here. There's parking at the delivery bay."

The older woman's fingers tapped a frustrated staccato, and I leaned forward, uncomfortable at her obvious mistrust. It had followed her like a stray dog ever since leaving the hospital. Not that I blamed her. "Is this a problem?" I intoned, feeling like Al as I sat in the back and glowered.

"Yes, it's a problem," Dr. Ophees said. "I can't claim a published charm as my own."

"Oh!" Elyse immediately relaxed. "We aren't here because the charm is. We're here because that's where she stashed her old boyfriend."

I wasn't sure what Kisten was, but "old boyfriend" sounded so . . . in the past, even if it was correct. *Who are you doing this for, Rachel?* "It's a new charm. I guarantee it."

"You guarantee." The light changed, and after a telling moment of hesitation, she turned down the less busy street. "Your guarantee means goose slip," she added, grip easing.

Whatever . . . "Down that alley," I said, and the car slowed to make the sharp left.

"Better and better," Dr. Ophees muttered, but I could see her relief when the tight drive opened into a large paved courtyard between four buildings. There was another alley exit right in front of her, plenty of room for deliveries—or a quick departure.

She brought the car to a halt beside a dumpster and shut off the engine. "Okay. Clock is ticking," she said as she pulled her purse onto her lap and opened the door.

I scooted to follow her out of the little two-door, hesitating when the woman slammed the door in my face. Annoyed, I shifted to the other side of the car, vowing never to put Al in the back seat again. Elyse was already out, striding up the smooth, stained cement steps to the delivery bay door, leaving me to manipulate the seat by myself. Ruffled, I got out and slammed Dr. Ophees's door shut right as Elyse yanked the rolling gate up in a noisy, somehow-comforting clatter.

Dr. Ophees was decidedly wary as she popped the trunk to get her box of materials. I guess having me and that big knife alone in the back had been too much for her.

"I can't believe she came out here," Elyse said as I scuffed up the stairs to join her. "We could mug her and steal her car and no one would know." She watched Dr. Ophees stand at her closed trunk, box at her feet, her phone in her hand. "I'm not saying we would, but damn! I thought you were trusting. How did she survive this long?"

The whoosh of an outgoing email sounded, and I smirked. She survived because she was a badass. "Have you felt how much line energy she's packing?" I said as Dr. Ophees headed for the steps.

"Yeah. I get that, but it's almost too easy to nullify a ley line practitioner."

Tell me about it.

"There could be five big men waiting to jump her," Elyse continued, whispering as we went inside and hit the call button for the freight elevator.

Dr. Ophees lingered in the sun coming into the open bay as the old machinery clattered awake, the woman pulling in line energy slow and easy in case we went too deep and she couldn't tap a line. *Smart.* "Okay." I turned my back on the older woman. "First of all, picking your take from the basement of the hospital is stupid when there are a dozen trusting people wandering the streets. Second, even if we wanted to mug her, your synapses are singed, and since I'm pretty sure she's seeing past our glamours, she knows I have a big vampire hickey, telling her I'm stupid and therefore easy to overcome. Third, she just emailed someone where she was. Fourth and most important, she deals with the undead. Alone. They wouldn't put her down there by herself if she couldn't handle a surprise attack from someone potentially stronger than her."

The elevator clunked into place and I wrestled the gate open as Dr. Ophees joined us.

"And lastly, if you try anything, I will flatten you to the walls, sweet thing," the doctor said pleasantly as she pushed past us to confidently take the back of the elevator.

"She also has really good hearing," I said as I joined her there to leave Elyse to fumble the gate down and hit the descend button.

The lift hummed and clunked into movement, and we all stared straight ahead as the floor seemed to rise over our heads and darkness took us. "Sorry," Elyse said, clearly uncomfortable. "I just think this is a huge risk for you for little benefit."

Dr. Ophees scrolled through her social media feed until she lost connection and put her phone away. The ley line, though, remained secure as I knew it would. "I did an aura check before I got out of the car. There's no one alive in the building bigger than a mouse. The undead won't touch me. I am their last resort and they know it. I think that makes me safe enough."

Damn . . . I was starting to like the prickly woman, and I eyed Elyse as if to say, *See?*

"Oh, I agree that this is stupid," Dr. Ophees continued. "But I didn't become a doctor to watch people die, even if they are already dead." The stuff in the box shifted as she moved it to her hip. "I was put in charge of the undead after I saved the second life of someone a colleague misdiagnosed, and I work *so well* with the occasional survivor that they decided to keep me down there."

It was bitter, and Elyse jumped to open the gate when the lift ground to a halt.

"At least it pays well," Dr. Ophees muttered, and I stifled a sigh, going first into the dimly lit hallway. They probably moved her there because no one wanted to deal with her ego; the woman was smarter than them, and she knew it.

"He's in the rare-book locker," I said, not liking the whispers our feet were making.

"I've never been down here." Dr. Ophees's pace slowed as she noticed the books we were passing. "Can you check these out?"

"No." Elyse flashed her a smile. "Most aren't even supposed to be here."

I ran my hand across the chain-link fence embedded into both the ceiling and the floor, the quick *thump-thump-thump* against my fingers grounding me. "The university has an annoying tendency to steal things they think should be for their eyes only," I said sourly. "Which is why I don't have a problem sneaking down here and availing myself when I need to."

"Mmmm." Dr. Ophees studied me as if considering I might not be the vampire junky in rhinestones and sequins that she was probably seeing. I didn't really care what she thought as long as she listened. At least I wasn't in sweats and red-stained sneakers.

"Doctor," I said as I swung the gate to the locker open and she hesitated, waiting for Elyse to go first. I pulled the chain-link shut behind me, not surprised when the older woman ran her hand along the titles as she passed. That she could still tap a line down here was probably a relief.

"I didn't know this existed," she whispered as she paused at a title. "Stef, if that's your real name, I owe you some consideration if only because you brought this to my attention."

"Just don't spread it around. I don't want to come down here and find people," I muttered, my attention going right to Kisten when the short passage opened up to the small, ugly room defined by bookracks and one cold stone wall. He hadn't moved, and a sliver of panic iced through me. *Is that good or bad?*

Dr. Ophees set her box on the table. "Well, let's see how he sits."

I stood just inside the room, arms over my middle. Guilt swam up from a growing sense of responsibility. I should have been able to take him to the emergency department, not hidden him in the basement of the library. Vampire politics sucked.

"I still think this is a bad idea," Elyse said softly as Dr. Ophees whispered some Latin and a hazy spell sifted over him, flashing through what remained of his aura before it waned. "We have things to do tonight."

I fidgeted as Dr. Ophees took his pulse or, at least, waited for one. It might be a while. "We can't even be on-site until seven," I said. "She'll be out of here in less than an hour."

Still waiting for a pulse, Dr. Ophees said, "What did he die of?"

That damned lump was back in my throat. "An undead threw him into a wall and snapped his neck. He was a blood gift."

"Ah, there it is. Nice and strong," she said, and let his wrist drop. She shifted his head, searching for marks on his neck, then checked his other wrist. "Hence him being here and not emergency. I'm not seeing any visible bite marks. Why is he languishing?"

"He, ah, bit the attacking vampire," I said, and Dr. Ophees turned, interested. "Kisten shifted to his undead state with no downtime," I explained. "He knew he couldn't overpower his attacker, so he intentionally bit him to save me."

Dr. Ophees's expression remained rigidly professional. "You were there."

It wasn't a question, and I nodded, jaw clenched. "He mixed their blood to take that bastard down with him. He died to keep me and someone else safe." *And it still hurts.*

She eyed him. "So where's the attacking vampire?"

"He fled," I said to explain why Art hadn't shown up in her morgue, because that's what it was. "I expect he'll be dead in three days. Don't look for him. He's gone."

My lip twitched as I stifled a surge of anger. Art had hidden himself in the tunnels with his scion. Both died horribly, as Art had drained his scion in a desperate attempt to stave off death. It didn't seem like enough.

"I'm sorry." Dr. Ophees set Kisten's hand atop his chest. "The amount of virus he received from his attacker was slight, but it was enough. He's fading. Sunrise, perhaps, when his aura runs out. Maybe longer."

"You want to see the spell?" I ground out. "Or would you rather browse the racks for the next forty minutes?"

Dr. Ophees lifted her gaze to take in the ugly room and sighed. "Sure," she said flatly, her back to Kisten as she pulled out one of the rolling chairs and sat before the table. "Impress me."

She obviously thought this was a waste of time, and maybe it was. The spell would create smut. I knew Dr. Ophees wouldn't go for that, so I'd take it, using the collective to handle the exchange if she would give, say, ten percent of every aura she gathered to Kisten. If I registered the curse with a fee-for-use, I wouldn't even have to monitor it.

Motions rough, I unpacked the box, my anger easing when I used the ion-repelling scarf I had borrowed from Sylvia to prep the area and Dr. Ophees began to take an interest, either at the high-end spell-prep precaution or the tinkling of the bells or, most likely, the sudden scent of burnt amber. Regardless, she was paying attention, and I decided to go all the way and shimmied into the robe. I *was* working with auras . . . sort of.

"You want some help?" Elyse asked, her gaze going to her robe jammed into that round hat.

"No, but thanks." Head down, I retied the sleeves up past my elbows. "I know the original curse, and I saw the pentagram she used. I should be able to figure it out."

Elyse shifted to stand between me and the doctor. "Ah . . . I thought . . . you don't . . ."

"Just sit down," I griped, stifling a flash of worry. "Let me know if I get close to violating the coven's precious double standard," I added bitterly, and Elyse frowned, giving the second chair a tug to roll it halfway across the room before she dropped into it, a scowl on her face and her arms over her chest.

Do the charm, register it as a fee-for-use curse, link the payment to Kisten. Easy said, easy done.

Right . . .

"Okay." My eyes went to the unlit candle as I thought out loud. "The original curse is illicit not simply because it's taking someone else's aura and leaving them vulnerable but because it requires a hard linkage by blood, bone, hair, and three passions indicated by the first three auratic shells of the, ah, donor. Earth, stone, and water are handled by the hair, bone, and blood, and the last three aspects of fire, air, and ether are more spiritual. A six-themed curse or spell is complicated but necessary when dealing with stealing someone's aura."

Dr. Ophees's lips parted in surprise. "You have taught before?"

"Not often, and not well, but I have a good instructor," I said. "He rarely tells me everything unless I chatter my way through a lesson, so it's kind of habit." I hesitated, thinking of Al. He was out to abduct me at the moment, and I missed him. "We don't need the precision of a six-themed curse, since the donor and recipient linkages are more or less voluntary here and can be worked right into the spell." I lit the candle with a thought and set it aside. "A standard pentagram using the cave as a connection point will be enough."

"You've never done this."

I glanced up at Dr. Ophees, deciding to ignore that. "The parent curse utilizes a phrase to invoke aura movement," I said. "I will keep that intact, seeing as the phraseology dictates where the aura goes. Once the link is made between the two pentagrams, the aura shift could go either way. A morally corrupt curse can be made into one that is less so if it leans to helping another voluntarily." I turned to Elyse. "Good?"

Elyse shifted her chair back and forth, appearing bored. "Good."

Dr. Ophees gave Elyse a sidelong look as if wondering why I cared what she thought. "There is no voluntary here," Dr. Ophees said. "It's a sack of blood and a jar."

I bobbed my head, intent on cleaning both scrying mirrors of free ions. "I'm simply pointing out that in the original curse, apart from the less savory ingredients, intent plays a role in determining if it's illicit or not." Again I turned to Elyse. "Right?"

"Pretty much." Elyse crossed one leg over the other, foot bobbing. "It's still going to create smut, especially if you need hair, bone, and nail samples from the original blood donors to link the donation pentagram to the transfer pentagram."

I set the mirrors down and arranged them just so. "I'm going to pare that part down. Connect them another way."

"My God," Dr. Ophees whispered. "You're making this up as you go along."

My brow furrowed as I met her horrified gaze. "If it doesn't work, all you lose is your two-hour lunch break. I'll buy you a bowl of Skyline chili you can take back to your desk."

"You gave me the impression you had a working spell!" she exclaimed. "How much smut is this going to leave on my aura?"

"None," I snapped. "I'll take the smut, but ten percent of every aura you gather will go into the demon collective for *my* use. Or is your ego going to get in the way of me giving you a shovel to dig yourself out of the basement?"

"No smut makes it very legal," Elyse said when Dr. Ophees hesitated, the thought to walk out almost visible on her.

"Yeah, remember you said that," I muttered. The candle had warmed enough that there was melted wax, and I began to spill it into an even pentagram on the first mirror.

"Ten percent goes to you?" Dr. Ophees's attention flicked to Kisten and back again.

A drop of wax threatened to drip onto my first finished pentagram, and I caught it, feeling the hot liquid burn for a telling second. "Consider it a royalty. You want me to stop?"

"No." Her gaze went to Kisten, and then she gestured. "Go on."

Yeah, I'd give ten percent to get out of that basement, too, I thought dryly as I scribed the second pentagram, finishing it with an ease and perfection that I would have envied two years ago. I blew the candle out, watching the smoke curl as I wondered if making a permanent connection between the two mirrors instead of the pentagrams might streamline the process. The mirrors couldn't be used for anything else, but the link would be ironclad. That, though, was for another day, and I turned to Dr. Ophees. "Is there a way to take a sample from a blood bag for testing? I need a drop in the jar."

"To link it to the pentagram," she said, and I bobbed my head. "Sure. There's a port. You can decant what you want with a syringe." She hesitated. "You didn't ask me to bring one."

"I have one." *Thank you, Ivy,* I thought as I shuffled in my bag, glad that she had put it in there so I could fill my splat balls. The rasp of the protective paper seemed loud, and Dr. Ophees checked her phone as I settled the bag of blood in the cave of the first pentagram and fiddled with it to figure out how the port worked. *Easy-peasy.* Quick from practice filling splat balls, I pulled a cc out, then unfocused my attention to see if the aura was still present.

A haze of brown and green swirled like stardust against the darker blood. It was fresh, perhaps only a few hours out of a body. "If you don't want to use the syringe, a yew stylus will work," I said, mostly to pull Dr. Ophees's attention from her phone.

I set the waiting jar in the cave of the second pentagram with a loud thump. Breath held, I decanted a drop halfway between the wall of the jar and the middle. *"Juncta in uno,"* I whispered, using the words to place-set the blood and join the jar to the pentagram. *Yeah, joining the two mirrors would make this faster.*

"What's that?" Dr. Ophees scooted forward, probably thinking I was trying to hide something from her.

"Joined in one," I said, translating the Latin. "Make a spiral of six dots for the aura to follow."

She nodded, expression empty. Six dots linked it to the original curse, but I thought it important, and I set the last five with the same word. Each utterance in my mind brought a stronger connection to the ley lines, and I ran a hand over my hair when I was done, feeling it spark from mystics.

"Kind of loose, isn't it?" Elyse asked, and I blinked to bring my thoughts back from the Goddess. Invoking her presence seemed like overkill. The insane deity and her mystics didn't recognize me anymore, but why take chances?

"It's fine." I didn't like spiral magic, but auras did.

Dr. Ophees inched even closer. "Sympathetic magic is forgiving as long as your mind is not."

That was a nice way to put it, and I started, almost dropping the syringe, when Kisten took a slow breath. *This has to work,* I thought as I glanced at him. Sunrise. I might not even be here at sunrise if Trent caught us.

"You should feel a growing connection to the ley lines with each drop," I said, and Dr. Ophees frowned.

"Obviously," she said, her gaze on my staticky hair. "What did you use to join the blood to its associated pentagram?"

"Ah, same word as with the other," I said, touching the bag in question with an unsaid *Juncta in uno.* "Okay. Pentagrams are scribed. Jar is linked to receiving pentagram, blood is linked to the giving." I looked at Elyse. "Anything yet that would kick this into illicit?"

Elyse bobbed her foot. "Not as long as the blood was freely donated."

Again Dr. Ophees frowned at the clearly younger woman as if wondering why I was asking her.

My pulse quickened. I had modified curses before, but not in front of anyone as ego-ridden as Dr. Ophees, and I'd once spelled in front of the entire body of demons. "Then let's see if it works with the original invocation phrase." Because if it didn't connect to the demon collective properly, I was going to have to show my work and do it the long way. *Yuck . . .*

Power fizzed from my toes to my fingertips as I strengthened my hold on the lines, and I stifled a pleasant shudder. "You want to write this down?" I said, stalling, and Dr. Ophees made a rude laugh.

"Go," she said, attention on her phone again. Clearly she thought this a waste of time.

Why did you even come down here? I thought as I steadied my grip on the lines, feeling them hum through me like a second sun. Exhaling, I settled a protection circle about the two pentagrams, glancing at Dr. Ophees to see what she thought about the hint of smut decorating my aura's gold and red. *Please work, please . . .*

"*Du ut des,*" I intoned, and a slip of air left me when a trill of connection tripped down my spine. It had connected to the collective. It was going to work.

"I give so you may give," Dr. Ophees said as if surprised. "Huh."

"Whoa!" Elyse's chair rattled as she stood. "It's working."

My annoyance that she had doubted me vanished as an odd pulling sensation tripped through me. Again I opened my second sight, relieved at the hint of a brown and green aura within the bag of blood swirling in a diminishing spiral.

"Don't touch it," I warned when Elyse moved to take a closer look. Brow furrowed in annoyance, she crouched to put the jar at eye level.

"This is not my first spell," she griped. But I could see why she was fascinated. A soft upwelling of glow was filling the jar. I could feel the aura funneling through me, tasting of the memories of the man it had come from. He liked cats, and bitter chocolate, and the smell of pine trees, and the touch of wind at sunrise. His emotions swirled, connecting me to the All, making me a larger part of the universe.

Is this what a vampire feels? I wondered as the last of it trickled through me and was gone. Loss remained in its wake, a lack that I'd never known I had. This, I realized, was what kept the undead alive. The emotions were stolen but no less sweet, and my throat closed as I touched Kisten. If he woke, he wouldn't remember what it felt like to love, to exist, to be a part of the whole. That's why he hungered, and what he hungered for: the connection to the world, our collective past experiences, our joy. That's what he took with blood. The lack of memory and emotion was the payment for life never ending.

It had been a poor exchange on the vampires' part, in my opinion.

"So you what? Open the jar and pour the aura on the, ah, patient?"

Dr. Ophees's voice jerked my thoughts back to the present, and I rubbed my fingertips together, needing the sensation. The older woman was frowning at me. She knew something unexpected had happened. Either she would do the spell right and find out for herself, or she wouldn't. She might understand what had passed through me better than I could.

"Sort of." I picked up the jar, feeling it tingle against me. *You will not die of starvation, Kisten.* I took a steadying breath. *Rhombus.*

"Ah, Stef?" Dr. Ophees cautioned as a circle formed around me and Kisten.

I licked my lips, nervous. "You're right. I've never done this before. I don't want the aura to escape if I don't get the binding part right the first time."

"I can't believe I agreed to this," the woman muttered. "I don't even know whose blood that is."

But I did. Sort of. He had been kind, and loving, and I opened the jar with no fear. Besides, auras had no power. They were the expression of the soul, cast like shadows to act as the connective fluid between mind and body, linking them to each other and the soul both. Auras were simply conduits. It was the soul that could act, not this sparkling memory of existence that tricked the undead into thinking they were still alive.

My stomach knotted as I poured the aura onto Kisten, and for a moment, elation filled me as it settled into the thin patches of his waning aura . . .

. . . and then with a sparkling haze of discontent, began to dissipate, thinning as it expanded and drifted away as if seeking its owner.

"Crap on toast," I whispered. It wasn't sticking, and panicking, I invoked a second circle to catch it. The bright haze sparkled as it hit the edge of my circle, and I condensed the globe down until it was no bigger than a basketball.

"It didn't stick," Elyse said, stating the obvious.

"You should have told me you hadn't done this before," Dr. Ophees said as she stood beside my circle. "I might have had an idea to adhere it to him."

I couldn't take my eyes from Kisten. "I'm all ears," I said, feeling overdressed in my spelling robe.

"Perhaps . . ."

I followed her gaze to the syringe on the table. There was a little blood left in it, and I bobbed my head, hands shaking when I decanted a drop onto my finger.

"*Utraque unum*," I whispered as I touched it to Kisten's lips, sure Dr. Ophees heard me when she didn't say anything. *Both into one.*

"That should do it," Dr. Ophees said, and I broke the circle holding the aura. It was a simple spell, and slowly, like bees into a hive following their queen, the aura settled onto him, coating him in a veil that would fool his mind into thinking his soul was still there. The aura would do nothing to help him fight Art's virus—but he would not starve to his second death in front of me or alone in some forgotten tunnel, and with that demon stasis curse, he wouldn't decay in front of me after he died from Art's virus, either.

A ragged gasp for air startled me, but it was only Kisten taking another breath. He had not woken. He wouldn't.

"Dude." Elyse came closer and poked at him. "It worked."

"Don't," I said, pulling her hand away when it threatened to pull his borrowed aura from him.

"Sloppy, but it's holding." Dr. Ophees's gaze was unfocused. "Ten percent? It is acceptable. I lose thirty percent of my patients from simple starvation as their body repairs itself. A few more days of aura will make a huge difference."

Oh, yeah. I renewed my grip on the lines. *Evulgo, Jariathjackjunisjumoke,* I thought, laying a hand on Kisten's chest as I opened a more certain link to the demon collective. *I take the smut for the use of this fee-for-use curse, in return for ten percent of the aura gathered, to be stored under my name and given to this vampire at need.* I shivered as I felt the curse slip into the public domain. I was being noticed. I had to get out of here. *Ut omnes unum sint,* I added to seal it, then dropped the collective from my thoughts before the rising buzz of inquiries could zero in on me.

The curse was registered. As long as Dr. Ophees used it reasonably often, Kisten wouldn't starve.

"I give him three additional days." Dr. Ophees squinted at me as if looking for the smut I'd just taken on. It was about the same as lighting a candle. I'd made out like a bandit. "He will still die," she added as she saw my smirk. "Two versions of the vamp virus can't exist in one body."

My eye twitched. "I know. But with your sponsorship, the spell will clear FCSA and maybe save someone else." I lifted my hand from Kisten's chest. "You still have fifteen minutes left of your lunch hour. You want me to write it down?"

Oblivious to my sarcasm, she went to the table, inspecting the waxed scrying mirrors before carefully putting them in the box. "No, I've got it. I'll scrape the pentagrams when I get back to my office."

She didn't care about Kisten. She didn't care about the vampires she could save. All she wanted was to get out of that basement, and an ugly feeling knotted about my chest. "You're welcome," I said, ignored but for Elyse watching with wide eyes, silent as she shifted her attention between me and the doctor. "Why don't you escort her upstairs?" I asked Elyse, wanting to be alone.

Elyse pushed away from the bookcase, her brow furrowed. "Sure. I'll walk you up."

Dr. Ophees tucked the box of supplies under her arm and strode out without another word, her head down over her phone as she texted someone.

I watched her go, sure she was going to spend the rest of the day—hell, the rest of her life—perfecting it. She'd be saving the undead by the end of the week, get her upgraded lab by the end of the month. I'd given the ego-driven woman more than a spell. It was an escape from her personal hell and a shot at redemption, payment for the elixir to soothe the pain of Kisten's passing.

And as I gave Kisten a kiss on his forehead and dragged Elyse's chair closer so I could sit beside him and hold his hand, I decided it had been worth it.

CHAPTER

23

IT FELT ODD DRIVING UP THE LONG, FIVE-MILE DRIVEWAY TO TRENT'S estate. The flickering of the low sun through the mature forest was familiar, but the nervousness plaguing me was not. At least not for a long time. Elyse wasn't much better, her eyes on the sky and her fingers fiddling with her hair whenever we met anyone. I don't think she liked its straw-blond spelled state, but because I'd used the transposition stone to disguise her, she looked the same to me.

That any oncoming car might hold Trent was a real worry despite the both of us having borrowed the images of two random people on the street. We both now appeared vaguely like elves: slim, angular facial structure, straight blond hair. It was a thin disguise, but because I'd used a demon curse, it would hold up to a cursory elf or witch spell checker. It could only be severed by me or the harsh, unaided scrutiny born of knowing it was false—the certainty of one's will. And seeing as there was no reason to doubt who we were, it would hold.

I promised Trent I'd never break into his home again, I mused, fingers tightening on the steering wheel. That I hadn't actually made that promise yet somehow made it worse, not better.

"We should have taken the Cadillac," Elyse muttered. "Rentals can be tracked."

"And you think a stolen Caddy can't? They won't track a rental until they know it's missing, and it was in the detail area. Besides, their first thought will be screwed-up paperwork, not theft." It was Kisten who had taught me how to borrow cars that wouldn't be missed, and my chest hurt. I'd just left him there. What if I never got back?

The young woman brought her gaze from the sky and scowled at me. Her concern, though irritating, was well-founded. I'd taken the time to scrape the rental barcodes off, but if they ran the plate at the front gate, we might have trouble.

"Bullying our way in," she said. "If there's a way in through the stables, why aren't we doing that?"

"Three reasons." I grimaced, not caring about her ego issues. "The stables are busy right now with foals and have more security than Trent's front office. We can't go in over the pastures until after dark, and I don't know how long they hold Trent at the I.S. after I arrest him. Besides, the pastures are monitored. Anything bigger than a badger shows up on their heat scanners. But mostly it's because I will be breaking in through the stables in a few months, and I don't want them to know they're vulnerable and plug the hole."

Elyse pulled the visor down to look at herself in the vanity mirror, head tilted to gauge her new, model cheekbones. "I still say this is risky."

"It is. But if we pick up the right glamours and IDs we need at the gate, we can walk in with an escort. It's the weekend and the labs will be empty."

She flipped the visor up with a snap. "If you say so."

Whatever. And still, a thrill trickled through me as I drove the bland black car into the small visitor lot this side of the gate and parked. I wished that Jenks was with me, not some sullen, ego-ridden, deadly skilled coven member. *Why am I doing this again?* Oh, yeah. If I went home without her, they would assume I'd killed her. But that was just an excuse; getting her home was the right thing to do, even if it made my life impossible. Besides, I was starting to like her. *Damn it, Rachel, you have to stop making friends with your adversaries.*

Trent's gatehouse had the feel of a military installation. The expansive building straddling both sides of the wall had a small kitchen, break room, holding cell, and full communication array. There was even a small meeting room for news releases. There could be as many as six people manning the gate or as few as two. Seeing as Trent was spending the evening off-site, I was betting the latter, and I sat for a moment in my car and watched the man at the desk through the thick green glass. We'd been noticed, but I knew the procedure. With no appointment, we'd have to do a face-to-face with security, which was why I didn't bother trying to get a car through the gate.

"Ready?" I tugged my glamoured bag onto my lap. "Try to stay out of my way. I don't want you damaging your synapses before they finish healing."

"I'm fine," she grumbled.

"The guardhouse has layers of complexity," I tried to explain, but she wasn't listening. "You do the wrong magic, and you trigger them."

"I am not your apprentice," she muttered, and my fake smile became stilted.

"You got that right." I took a deep breath as I got out and squinted at the low sun. Jenks could have put the cameras pointing at us on a loop, done a quick recon as to how many people were inside and who they were, maybe check the logbook for who was expected today—which was probably no one, seeing as Trent was getting married in a few hours. Someone would eventually check the security footage, but for now we were just two women from the I.S. who had been sent out in error.

A smirk found me as I waved to the man watching us. *Not.*

The whine of a cicada echoed in the rising warmth of the day, but it was the chortling rattle of a crow that drew my eye to the woods that stretched beyond the wall. My suspicion tightened. *Elyse's familiar, Slick?* An entire mile of road ran past the gatehouse to get to the compound, but here it was an old, planned forest that had grown up around and through Kalamack Senior's technological fence—and if I hadn't ridden through the grounds with Trent, I never would have known it existed. That was kind of the point.

I stifled a jump at the soft thump of Elyse's door, and I waited for her in front of the car. "That's not your crow, is it?" I said, and her attention shifted to the woods.

"No. I still say I should be the I.S. runner and you the intern," she muttered.

"Not happening." I pushed off the car, heading for the small door and gatehouse lobby. She was way too casual in her I.S. sweats and ever-after-stained shoes, even if everyone else saw gray flats, black slacks, and the blah black summer sweater her doppelganger had been wearing. My image donor had been wearing something similar, and I was hoping that it was close enough to Trent's security black that we'd blend in.

"No offense, Elyse," I said as we found the landscaped walkway. "But your entire attitude screams newbie. And as my intern, you should be happy to get the door for me."

Grimacing, Elyse took a long step to get ahead and yank the thick glass door open. "Thank God that ugly bag of yours glamoured up."

I tugged my shoulder bag higher, appreciating the two years of wear it lacked. I'd have to take her word that it looked like the leather satchel my doppelganger had been toting. "It's not ugly, and I need everything in it." Head high, I walked in as if I owned the place. I didn't recognize the man at the desk in his security uniform with a spell pistol on his hip. Oddly enough, his very anonymity gave me a feeling of confidence. Quen wouldn't keep anyone at the front gate after they'd been taken down—and take him down I would, spell pistol or not.

"Good afternoon." I stifled a shudder as the door snicked shut and the air-conditioning iced through me. "Is Quen Hansen available?" I knew Trent's number one security would be busy, either finalizing everything at the Basilica or, more likely, doing whatever best men do before the wedding. Dropping his name would give me some cred, though. I had a fake I.S. ID, but the magnetic code was a strip of foil from a heat-and-serve oatmeal box.

The guard glanced at my spelled bag, suspicion showing when I set it on the high counter between us. His name tag said MADISON, and I fidgeted. "No, ma'am," he said in a slow drawl. "Perhaps I can help you?"

"Denise Monty," I said cheerfully, using my dad's first name as my last again. "We got an anonymous tip about a possible break-in during Kalamack's wedding, and they sent me out here to give you the heads-up."

Madison glanced at his computer screen. "A call would have sufficed. ID, please?"

"I did call." I put the flat of my arms on the top of the counter. "That's why I'm here. I was asked to come out with our information."

Madison reached for his keyboard. "When was this? Who did you talk to?"

The second man was still nowhere to be seen. It was taking too long. Elyse had begun to fidget, and smiling, I leaned over the high counter as if to try to see his screen. "*Stabils*, sweetheart," I whispered.

"Hey!" Madison's eyes widened as the curse hit him. I felt a tug on the line as he tried to fight it, and then he was falling, his control gone. "Bob!" he shouted, red-faced as he slid to the desk and then the floor. "Hit the alarm! Hit the alarm!"

Crap on toast, here we go! I vaulted over the counter, cursing Al's desire to hear his victim's pleas for mercy; it was his spell I was using. I quickly grabbed the spell pistol from Madison's hip and shot him with it, sure it would be both effective and legal—and, more importantly, not trigger the gatehouse's more nebulous security measures.

The man's eyes rolled up as he became unconscious. Sleepy-time potion, but anything more invited lawsuits.

And then my head snapped up at a scuff. A small man stood at the archway leading deeper into the building. "Hi, Bob."

Teeth clenched, Bob pulled his splat pistol.

"*Captus!*" Elyse shouted, and I cringed as a building-wide spell invoked with the feeling of spiders crawling through my aura. *Twist it back to the Turn, she can do magic?*

Bob hit the floor as a soft buzz from a hidden speaker began sounding.

"Elyse!" I cried out, annoyed as the alarm was joined by a request from the com for information. Bob, though, was down, his motions muffled as a purple and red haze coated him. He struggled, a choking gasp of air sounding dangerous. "Is he going to be okay?"

"Of course," she said, but I didn't like how he suddenly went silent. "How come your spell didn't trigger the building's security?"

"Because it's not a spell, it's a curse," I said, annoyed. My magic had slid right under the radar, but that's what a good curse did. My back to her, I faced the screen and tapped my way through the building's security system as a terse "Gatehouse? Please respond" became more insistent.

"Why didn't you tell me there was an alarm associated with magic?" she said, brow furrowed as she tried to rationalize her mistake.

"I did. Why did you lead me to believe your synapses were still too raw to spell?" I snapped, and she flushed.

Yeah, you made two mistakes, Madam Coven Leader. Grimacing, I wove through the system. The voice on the radio lost its concern as my actions showed up on their end, and I began to relax. Elyse, though . . .

"We are done. We gotta go," she said, the first worry wrinkle showing.

"Give me a sec," I said as I typed in the silence code and the alarm went still. "Can you be quiet for a moment and not touch anything?"

I glanced at Bob to make sure he was still breathing. Madison was out cold. Elyse nodded, and I thumbed open the communication.

"We're good, estate," I said, voice pitched in a comfortable, annoyed drawl. "We have two potential gate crashers in custody. Sorry about the delay. I'll keep them in holding here for Quen."

I took my thumb off the button, and the speaker crackled to life. "Do you need any assistance?" the voice asked.

Relieved, I looked at Elyse. *Gotta go, my ass . . .* "No, but can you spare someone to help Bob secure the gate? I want to do a quick walk-through of the lab facilities. We think that's where they were headed."

The speaker crackled again. "We'll have someone there immediately to relieve you."

"Rachel . . ." Elyse whispered as the connection ended, and I followed her gaze up the road to see two cars coming from the estate.

My pulse hammered. They weren't the expected security golf carts but Trent's seldom-used limos, one for him, one for Ellasbeth, full of the wedding party, no doubt. I lurched to hit the button to raise the gate. "Where's my bag? My bag!" I held my hand out as Elyse yanked it from the counter and vaulted over it to duck down below the level of the desk with Bob and Madison.

Fingers fumbling, I found the transposition stone and peered at Madison through it. *"A priori,"* I intoned, feeling the energy spill from the demon collective to me. *"A posteriori,"* I added, and the tingling increased. *"Omnia mutantur."* I whispered the words through the stone and walked into the haze of the waiting charm. Ice shivered over me as my image shifted, and Elyse chuckled.

"That's a good look for you," she said as I flipped the low trash bin over and stood on it to put myself at a more correct height.

"You'd make a good partner if you weren't so me, me, me," I said, grip white-knuckled on the stone as the first of the cars passed through. Quen's head came up as if sensing my alarm. The dark man was sharp in his tux, and I bobbed my head in respect when our eyes met. He would have been told about the attempted incursion, but if Madison was at the desk, he'd assume everything was fine.

Trent was beside him, and my breath sort of caught. As usual, he was preoccupied, with his head down over his phone. His hair was slicked back and his tie was perfect. There was nothing like an elf in a tux, and I felt a pull of attraction.

I hardly noticed the second car full of white silk and lace as Ellasbeth and her bridesmaids followed, and my hands shook when I hit the button to lower the bar and lock the gate. *You'd better be there to stop him, Rachel.*

Giving Elyse a gesture to be quiet, I thumbed the radio open again. "Mr. Kalamack has left the facility. We are at code green with two fish in the freezer."

"Code green," the voice echoed. "Confirm."

I stifled my sigh of relief. I hadn't been sure if the code words were in use at this time. "I'm heading up," I added into the mic. "Bob will be here."

"Hey!" Elyse whispered, angry, and I waved at her to be quiet.

"You're coming," I mouthed, though I was tempted to leave her behind, then louder to the estate security, "Ah, could you have someone meet me to take me through the labs?"

The speaker cracked again. "I'll see who I can find. We're at minimal staff. Out."

"Out," I echoed, then thumbed the connection closed. Shoulders slumping, I allowed myself three seconds to gather my thoughts. We were halfway there.

"I thought you were leaving me behind." Elyse straightened from her hunch over Madison and handed me his ID.

Surprised, I fastened it to my lapel. "The gate is not supposed to be left unattended, but it's easier to get forgiveness than permission. If we take a cart and meet them halfway, they'll be in a hurry to get someone up here and won't ask questions."

"Win-win. You okay? You look . . ." She shifted her shoulders like she had a spider on her back.

"I'm fine," I said, but I wasn't. Seeing Trent had shaken me almost as much as seeing Kisten. In a few hours, I was going to piss Trent off more than anyone had ever done in his life. At the time, I'd been pretty proud of myself, but thinking back on it, it had probably been the closest I'd ever been to death. I just hadn't known it.

"Let's get you looking like Bob," I said as I took the transposition stone in hand, and she nodded, shuddering when I did the spell.

I only had Elyse's satisfied "mmmm" as she eyed herself in the one-way mirror to tell me that it worked. We had a few minutes before someone arrived to relieve me, and the need to get the real Bob and Madison in the back lockup and out of sight was pressing.

"Big guy first," I said as I grabbed Madison under his shoulders, and we half dragged, half carried the man to the small short-term holding room. The placard on the door said MEDIA ROOM THREE, but that was for the inspectors. It was a cell.

"The door locks, right?" Elyse said as we laboriously lugged Madison into a comfortable chair, the woman totally missing that it and the coffee table were bolted to the floor and that the floor-to-ceiling partition hid a tiny sink and toilet.

"It locks," I said, and we hustled back to get Bob. Three minutes later, he was propped up against the wall, his ID now on Elyse's collar. The thought to glamour them flickered as I shut and sealed the door, but was immediately dismissed. The only people to lift an image from were me and Elyse. And besides, Quen might waste hours trying to break a spell that didn't exist if he thought the "intruders" had made themselves look like his security.

"Your bag lost its disguise," Elyse said when we returned to the control room. I hadn't broken the spell. It must have been rubbed out when I took Madison's image.

"That would have been awkward," I whispered as I pulled my bag close. "Hand me that satchel, will you?"

Elyse tossed me the oversize carryall with the Kalamack logo on it, and I stuffed my shoulder bag into it. The woman had taken not one but two spell pistols from the weapons caddy, looking like she knew what to do with them as she checked the hoppers and wedged one at the small of her back and the other in a borrowed holster.

Damn it, Jenks, I miss you, I mused as I grabbed a key to one of the golf carts. There was a second, smaller parking lot on the estate side of the wall, only this one held electric carts to make the one-mile drive manageable.

The sun was just as warm, the breeze just as pleasant, but it felt different as I pushed out the door and into Trent's estate, safer, even as we were under more threat should we be discovered. I'd spent too many weekends here to feel anything but pleasure as I matched the key to the number on the cart.

"Car would be faster," Elyse said as she jogged to catch up.

"Madison would use the cart," I said. "We need to be well within the labs before this goes sideways."

"They wouldn't wake up at all if—"

I turned to her, disappointed. "If I had what? Killed them?"

Elyse frowned. She still looked like Elyse to me, a little young, a lot overconfident in her I.S. sweats and dusty shoes. Like Vivian, she could probably spell me into the ground. What she lacked was the ability to weigh cause and effect, the knowledge that she'd have to own the outcome of her actions and act accordingly. But then again, she was coven. Maybe she didn't have to.

"Knocked them out with something stronger," she finally said, but it was clear they weren't her first choice of words. Annoyed, I slid behind the wheel of the cart and fitted the key.

"Light footprint, Elyse," I said as I got the cart in motion and headed up the main road at a brisk twenty miles an hour, woods on one side, pastures on the other. "When we leave here, I want nothing to link to you or me that might change something. Right now, we're simply two enthusiastic reporters trying for a story on Trent's wedding."

"Ahh . . . right," she said, her attention fixed on the black car coming toward us.

I immediately pulled to the middle of the road and came to a halt—as if I had all the time in the world. "It's okay," I said, recognizing the blah-black sedan. "It's your relief."

Tires a soft hush, the car came to a halt, the window already whining down. "You left the gatehouse unmanned?" the woman behind the wheel accused, and I shrugged.

"I wanted backup and Kalamack is already through. I knew you were on the way. Hey, leave the two spelled and in holding until Quen returns. He's going to want to talk to them himself." I visibly shuddered. "Remember the last time he caught someone on the grounds?" I said, and the woman winced. "They're glamoured," I said to explain why two of Trent's finest were locked up in a conference room. "I wouldn't mess with it. Quen will want to see them before it's broken."

"Ah, yeah." Her gaze was on the nearby gatehouse. "Dr. Scrim will meet you at the elevators. Take you around. You're just doing a quick check, right?"

"An hour at the most," I said, and she puffed her air out in relief.

"Good. Kalamack isn't expected on-site until almost four a.m. I do *not* want to be at the gate when they return."

But that four-a.m. arrival was likely going to be pushed up to midnight after I trashed Trent's plans, and I waved to her as she put her window up and headed for the gatehouse. Trent would not be dancing with his new wife come midnight but be getting bailed out of jail by Quen. Ellasbeth would be on a plane heading home, pissed that her wedding day was ruined. If we weren't gone by then . . .

I put the cart back into motion, and Elyse exhaled. "This is criminally easy," she whispered.

"Easy?" I barked. "No, this is me spending the last two years learning Trent's system from the inside out, the right phrases, when to banter, when to not, the SOP for intruders, not to mention the code to cut off the alarm and that the media room is really a cell." A twinge of guilt took me, and my grip tightened on the plastic wheel. "This isn't easy at all, and that you think so means you don't know shit, Elyse. Open your eyes. Maybe you'll learn something and we will survive long enough to get home."

Her lips pressed together, but she said nothing, scanning the pastures with the mares and foals as we passed the stables. As promised, the parking lot there was busy. Everyone would be gone in a month, but a feeling of vindication found me when Elyse grimaced, realizing I'd been right again.

And yet I still felt guilty for abusing Trent's trust as we pulled into a large empty lot in front of a two-story building within easy walking distance of Trent's residence. "That's probably our escort," I said as I brought the cart to a stop right at the stairs. "Dr. Scrim, was it?"

"Yeah-h," Elyse drawled as she studied the man fidgeting at the door. His lab coat was pale blue, and his hair was cut close. He waved as we got out, and I felt a surge of nerdy kinship.

"Don't spell him," I said as I hoisted the satchel holding my shoulder bag. "We need him to find the magnetic resonator if it's not already running. And remember, I'm Madison and you're Bob. You called me Rachel in front of Newt."

Elyse's attention turned to a congress of noisy crows as we took the shallow stairs. "Sorry." She hesitated. "I can't afford to get caught."

"Me either. We'll be fine," I said as I nodded to the waiting man.

But in truth, I was worried. Trent's estate was like a lobster trap. Getting in was one thing. Getting out was another.

"Hey, hi," the young man said as he ducked his head and extended his fist to Elyse, then me. "I'm Scrim. Security said you wanted a walk-through?"

"Madison," I said, stifling my sigh of relief that we didn't already know each other as we bumped knuckles. "Just a quick check on the lower levels. We detained two people trying to gain entry with a false story. I'm thinking they're after wedding gossip, but with Quen out, I want to be sure Mr. Kalamack's more sensitive endeavors are not at risk."

"No problem. I can take you down." Utterly oblivious to possible danger, Scrim led us into a small, empty lobby. The air was stifling after the pleasant breeze outside, but they probably didn't run the air-conditioning on the weekend. "Wow, a break-in." The man casually hit the call button for the elevator. "Those usually don't happen until after dark. I don't even think the dogs are loose in the day."

Oh, God. The dogs, I thought, stifling a shudder. "I'm sure they were hoping to catch us sleeping, with Kalamack off the grounds."

"You're lucky I was here," he said, then lurched into the elevator when it opened. "I came in to check on the shrimp. I'm out in an hour."

"We should be gone by then," I said as I followed him in.

"Shrimp?" Elyse asked, and Scrim hit the button for the lowest level.

"Mr. Kalamack runs his toxicology studies on freshwater shrimp," he said as the elevator began to descend. "They're very sensitive and have a reasonably fast generational period. Anything special you want to check?"

We were almost too low to reach the ley lines, but I could feel Elyse was pulling on one, her potential energy prickling over my skin. Suddenly I realized her gaze was fixed on Scrim with a predatory gleam.

"No!" I shouted, and the man jumped. Elyse's attention flicked to me, and I scowled at her as Scrim nervously laughed. "Sorry," I ad-libbed as the elevator descended and we lost the ley line entirely. "I just had this conversation with Bob on the way up from the gate. Let's start on the lowest level and work our way up. You have access to everything, right?"

Scrim shrugged as the elevator dinged and the doors opened. "Yep."

"Great. That's why we need you," I said, talking to Elyse as we followed him out.

He laughed, but it sounded nervous this time, and I gave Elyse a look to behave herself. I recognized the hallway. The expected camera at the ceiling was missing, and I wondered if it had been put in because of this little stunt. "So is it just you?" I asked.

Scrim bobbed his head. "I haven't seen anyone all day. Research and development got a three-day weekend. Unfortunately I'm essential, but it's only a half day."

"Security never rests," Elyse said, and Scrim shrugged good-naturedly.

"Hey, someone told me about a magnetized resonate, resonator . . . or something down here," I said. "Said it could pull your watch right off your wrist."

Scrim perked up. "The magnetic resonator? Yeah. We got one. It's on this floor, actually."

Elyse batted her eyes at him, probably forgetting she looked like Bob. "Can we see it?"

"Ah, sure." He hesitated, probably thinking more about "Bob" flirting with him than anything else. "This way," he said, turning down an empty hall. "I'm kind of glad you're here, actually. This place gives me the creeps when everyone is gone."

"It's bigger than I expected," Elyse said softly. "There's what? Eight floors?"

Scrim grinned. "That we know about. There's a couple of buttons in the elevator that don't work when I push 'em. You've never been down here?"

Elyse lifted a shoulder, but I was not surprised. Maybe she had been thinking that Trent was piddling around in a one-person lab. It had taken a Fortune-500-class business to keep his species going until we recovered a drop of ancient, pre-curse elven blood and patterned a cure. That one act had ended—or would end, rather—a lot of misery, not just for the elves' children but for those Trent blackmailed for the money to keep the scientific advances going. Funny, I couldn't recall what I got in return for helping him. I'd done it because it was the right thing to do. *Or is that just how I remember it?*

"It's through here," Scrim said, bringing my wandering thoughts to a point, and we came to a halt at a thick glass wall that looked in on a large apparatus. "Seems okay," he added as he gazed in at the quiet keyboards and dark screens.

It wasn't running, and I reached for a ley line, not able to find it. *Crap on toast, how am I going to do this?* "I want to go in," I said, and Scrim snorted.

"I don't have clearance," he said, his gaze darting to the card reader next to the door. "You want to see the animal labs?"

"I think you do," I said, hand moving fast as I snatched the ID card from his waist and ran it. The beep shocked through me, and I reached for the handle, feeling as if a stopwatch had just clicked on. I was sure the door was wired into some kind of security. They wouldn't bother Quen for it apart from a quick update possibly—but someone would come and investigate even if they knew Madison and Bob were down here checking things out. Especially, maybe.

"Hey," Scrim protested as I pulled the door open, and I gave him his card back.

"I want to see it take the watch off my hand." Elyse pushed past me, and we were in.

Scrim caught the door, holding it open as he lingered in the hall. "Ah. I don't think we should go in."

"Relax." Elyse pressed close over the dark keyboard, then hit a button to make the screen light up. "Three-day weekend, right? Let's have some fun." She turned to me, suddenly worried. "You know how to switch this on?" she whispered.

I eased to a halt beside her, lower lip between my teeth. "How hard can it be?" I mean, there weren't that many buttons, and one of them was green. *Green means go, right?*

"Hey, um, you shouldn't mess with that," Scrim said, ignored as he came in and let the door close.

Elyse frowned at me. "I thought you said you'd done this before."

"It was already running the last time. I've never been in this room."

"Ah, excuse me," Scrim said faintly, the man pale as he realized something wasn't right. "I need to check on something," he added, voice high as he inched to the door. "I'll be right back."

"Bob, he's yours," I said, and Elyse practically crowed.

We were too deep for a line, but as Scrim made a mad dash for the hall, she pulled a wad of energy as if from nowhere and threw it at him with an exuberant *"Captus!"*

I jumped at the loud pop, remembering being at the wrong end of her spells before.

"That wasn't from your chi," I accused when Scrim collapsed as if his strings had been cut. "How . . ." And then I got it, squinting in annoyance at her smug expression. "One of those crows out there is your familiar, isn't it. Damn it, *Bob*. You are making it very hard to trust you."

"Trust?" the young-seeming woman said, chin high. "I am the coven. You are—"

"The one getting you home!" I exclaimed as I knelt to check on Scrim. *Breathing, check.* "And you are making my job harder than it needs to be." I stood up, frustrated. "This is not a contest over who knows the most magic, and if you keep withholding from me, we might be stuck here." I grabbed Scrim's shoulders and dragged him out of sight of the hall window. "He's okay, right?"

"He's fine," she said, clearly annoyed. "I do not kill people."

"Yeah, you only incarcerate them and feed them magic-killing amino acids." Uneasy, I left him there to go back to the screen. It wanted a password, and I typed in the nonsense word written on the side of the keyboard. "We're in," I said as several windows opened and a prompt asked me what cycle I wanted to run.

"He'll be out for a few hours." Elyse stared down the empty hallway. "Wake up on his own with a headache. I didn't hurt him." She hesitated. "Can you turn it on?"

"I think so." Lip between my teeth, I told it to run the last program and tapped the enter key—only to get an error prompt. "Mmmm. Hit that green button."

Elyse went to the machine, her steps silent in her ever-after-red sneakers.

"This one?" she said, punching it—and then we both jumped as an odd sensation rippled over my aura.

"Pixy piss, I think that's it," I said when a faint whine blossomed in my ear. On the screen, data began scrolling past, the machine asking for information I had no clue about. But when I reached for the ley line, it was there.

"It moved!" Elyse exclaimed as if she only now believed I'd been telling the truth. "It's working! The line is there. It's like right there."

Excitement tingled down to my toes. "Let's move." I grabbed my bag and headed for the hallway. "We have to be in and gone before someone gets curious enough to try to unspell Bob or Madison and figures out they aren't."

Elyse bolted into motion, pushing past me and into the hallway.

"Yeah, now you're in a hurry," I added as I followed, wishing again that Jenks was with me. The pixy would have put the camera at the ceiling on a loop, but I'd have to break it—which would tell them exactly where we were.

"Which way?" Elyse halted at a junction, fidgeting as she looked one way, then the other.

"It's behind a set of wooden double doors." Exhaling, I sent my senses searching for a hint of ley line power.

Elyse's eyes widened. "You don't know where it is, do you."

"I do! Just give me a sec to orient myself." The memory of fleeing before Trent's hounds intruded, making it hard to think. I could not be caught. It would destroy the next two years, and I loved Trent desperately. Breath held, I followed the sensation of the ley line, sensing where it dipped and then rose anew. "This way," I said, quickening my pace. "Follow the line, and we find the vault."

I broke into a jog, Elyse tight behind me. "There," I said as I recognized a corner. "Go right."

"It's a dead end." Elyse slid to a halt after making the turn, and I slowed, confused at the small alcove set off the short hallway. There was a couch against the back wall, and several chairs around the low table, making an informal meeting area. There was no locked door, no key panel, but the ley line had been pulled down to run through it. We were at the right place.

"Is it?" I asked as I unfocused my attention, shuddering when the walls and ceilings of reality went opaque and the multistoried, high-ceilinged demon mall flickered into existence just outside my blind spot. I could almost hear the Carpenters done instrumental. Under my second sight, my old demon marks practically glowed an evil, smutty black. Elyse's aura, I couldn't help but notice, was almost too clean. *Is she sloughing her smut off on someone?*

Just behind the wall with the red couch was Trent's dad's vault, accessible only through a ley line. You had to pass into the ever-after to go through the wall, then will yourself back into reality. It was only four steps, but two of them were in the ever-after.

"Stay here," I said as I moved to the couch. "Keep watch. I'll be as quick as I can."

"Rachel, it's the demons' underground! I can see it!"

"How did you think I was getting in there?" I said, annoyed. "You go into the ever-after to get through the wall, then come out in the vault. I thought you understood."

White-faced, she stepped up onto the couch and then into the line, vanishing.

"Son of a fairy-farting whore!" I shouted, but no one was there to hear but me. She was there. In Trent's vault instead of watching my back.

Frustrated, I stepped onto the couch and into the ley line. Energy played about my hands and middle, mystics snarling my hair when I shifted my aura to match the line, become a part of it—and I felt myself spill into nothing as I stepped into the ever-after.

CHAPTER

24

THE STEP FROM THE COUCH INTO THE EVER-AFTER WAS A LONG, sudden drop. I came down hard, the reek of burnt amber a choking assault as it filled my nose, my lungs, my very pores. If the surface was bad, this was almost intolerable. A sticky heat and a loud thump of music slammed into me, the myriad conversations continuing as if someone stepping out of nothing into a demon coffeehouse was commonplace. But when in the ever-after, it sort of was.

I didn't see Elyse, but the door to the coffeehouse was before me and I grabbed it, wondering if my Kalamack Industries uniform glamour was any good here. The transposition curse was demon based, sure, but that didn't mean they couldn't see through it.

But the scent of burnt amber was finally slipping into the background, and I opened the door and stepped in.

As I had already seen while using my second sight, the shop was busy. Everyone was talking, and I held the satchel with my bag closer as I scanned the familiars standing in line, their diverse outfits making it feel like a studio commissary. I wasn't as out of place as I had first thought. More familiars served as baristas, efficiently moving the line as they used magic to prep the drinks and light fare. Their banter with their regular customers seemed cheerful despite their enforced servitude. Elyse wasn't here, and my shoulders slumped. *Crap on toast, you've got to be kidding me.* She must have gone all the way into the vault.

"Hey, sport," a low voice said, and I spun to see two demons sitting at a high table, one in a wide-lapel, bold-color seventies leisure suit, the other in a pair of running sweats and enough jewelry to please even Constance—both staring at me in interest. "Your aura is too bright to have been here long. Who let you out so soon, little man?"

Boz and Clemt, I thought, knowing every demon by their common name after having fended off their interests more than once. For as long as I had known him, Boz was stuck in the disco era. Clemt had recently abandoned his penchant for penal-colony Australia for the eighties rap scene. The two were somewhat ostracized for their modern tastes, hence them palling around in the Coffee Vault, but I'd always appreciated their attempts to fit in.

At least I know my disguise is holding. Even so, it was never good to be interesting to a demon, even one you knew, and I turned to the last person in line. "Hey, was there a, ah, guy just here?" I asked him. "Blond hair, dressed like me, scared looking."

"I said, who owns you?" Clemt demanded, gold chains jingling, and the familiar ahead of me shook his head and pressed forward, divorcing himself from any possible trouble.

Boz smacked Clemt's arm for his attention. "I think he's from the Kalamack estate," he said. "I swear he came through the line."

"Yeah?" Clemt's interest sharpened.

"Seriously?" I said as I decided how I wanted to play this. Elyse was nowhere. I didn't want to leave her if I was wrong and she'd run out into the mall. *Damn it, Elyse . . .*

"Yeah," Boz said, echoing Clemt. "That shiny little elf shit pulled the line down again. See?" He gestured at me with his cracked ceramic coffee mug. "Trying to get into the vault and lost your way, little elf? He's a thief, I bet. Think he's worth the effort?"

Clemt grunted in interest. "He's not afraid, so either he's really good or really dumb."

The demon slid from his high chair, his intent obvious, and I took a step back into the ley line, my hair snarling in the unfocused magic. "Let's go with dumb," I said.

The demon reached for me, but it was too late, and I vanished, willing myself into reality. This time the move was seamless, and I blinked, trying to see in the utter darkness of the Kalamack vault. The reek of burnt amber lifted from me, and I felt the air, trying to find a wall or rack. Eyes open or shut, it all looked the same.

"*Visio deli!*" a high-pitched voice rang out, and I ducked, squinting as a brilliant light exploded into existence—headed right for me. If it hit, I'd be temporarily blind.

"*Rhombus!*" I countered, cowering as the glowing orb smashed into my protection circle. "Elyse, it's me! It's me! Demons can't cross on their own. They have to be summoned. Damn it back to the Turn! What are you doing here? You were supposed to keep our exit open!"

There was no second attack, and I peered past the glowing forces twining about themselves, snapping and popping. *Lenio cinis,* I thought, finding Elyse when my globe of light blossomed into existence. She was half hiding behind a rack of books, both scared and determined. Boz and Clemt were undoubtedly watching the entire thing with their second sight, laughing their asses off if I knew demons.

"Rachel?" Elyse peered suspiciously at me, and I made a "well?" gesture as our energies canceled each other out and I let my circle drop. "Where you go, I go!"

I had lost any idea of what might be happening in the hall, and I ran a hand over my snarled hair, wishing Jenks were here to tame it. "Elyse, you are the worst partner I have ever had to work with. How the hell are we supposed to know what's happening on the other side of the wall? If they switch the resonator off, we're stuck here. That's why I brought you!"

"Then you go watch. I'll find the amulet," she said, making her own light, brilliant and eye-squinting. Clearly her synapses were fine. *Two days, my pixy puff ass.*

"Out," I said, pointing at the wall. "Do what you're here for."

"Through the ever-after? While you get what you need and leave me? Not a chance." Elyse continued to study a shelf of ancient elven books. "There are demons there. I barely got away the first time."

And now, getting back would be harder. Worse, other than knocking her on the head and moving her across the wall myself, I couldn't force her.

"Oh, my God!" she exclaimed as she reached for a book. "Where did he get that?"

"Don't touch it!" I shouted, and she jerked away. "They're covered with security spells."

"These are all illegal," she said, clearly miffed,

"Well, that's why they're in his vault, and the only reason they are banned is because they make people uncomfortable." I bypassed the rack of elven porn that had lured me in here the first time, going right to the unlocked drawers built into the wall. "Knowledge isn't right or wrong. How or if you use it is." I glanced at her, frowning when she reached out again. "I said don't touch. You want to tell Trent's security where we are?"

Grimacing, she drew her hand away. "I thought we had the last copy of that." She stared at it, her want obvious. "Ours is missing pages."

I slid open the drawer, making a soft "mmmm" at the ancient-looking metal circlet amulets in their little custom-foam compartments, most complete with their invocation pin. "Everything on that shelf is wired. If you're nice, maybe I can get Trent to show you his library when we get home." But I doubted it. The coven had proven themselves to be grabby paws.

"The charm we need is probably in here," I said, then whispered, "*Abundans cautela non nocet,*" to check for safeguards. A haze of gold and black settled over the drawer, but nothing glowed a warning, and I deemed them free of any magical entanglements. They were all defunct. The only reason they were down here was because the room was temperature and humidity controlled. That, and the engraved circlets were ancient.

"As soon as I find the one we need, we are out of here," I said as I picked up the first to read the invocation inscription. The metal felt entirely dead, cold in my fingers as I squinted at the faded writing. *Nope.* It wasn't the one I wanted, but it was still an amazing piece of art, the twisted circle of metal still retaining the original invoking pin. It made it more valuable, kind of like the toy still in the box. Value because we give it value. It was useless.

Good thing I'd spun useless into gold before.

The next was the same, and the third. I glanced at Elyse, satisfied when I found her at a stack of paintings, flicking through them as if she was at an art fair and looking for something to hang over her couch.

But when I moved to the second row, an odd sensation tripped over my aura as I rubbed the old silver clean and read the invocation. *Thank you, Trent.* Elated, I curved my fingers about it, searching for a flicker of magic, but it was just dead metal. *I could have sworn I felt something . . .*

"Uh, Rachel?" Elyse said, and then I jumped when the overhead lights flicked on. In the distance, a faint hooting sounded through the walls.

Crap on toast, I had triggered the very alarm I had warned Elyse about.

"Time to go," I said, stuffing the charm into my pocket as I pushed her to the ley line. It was still here. They couldn't shut it down until they came through the line themselves.

"Where?" she said, white-faced. "Rachel, we can't bull our way through Kalamack's security."

We had two minutes, tops. I could not be caught. Both Trent and Quen would assume I was the Rachel who arrested him, and he was so angry at me right now. He would not think. He would kill me. Change me into a fox and run me down in the night.

Never again. We were going out through the ever-after.

Scared, I grabbed my transposition stone. *Finis,* I thought, shuddering as I felt our glamours dissolve. Madison's image wouldn't help me anymore. I had to be myself in the ever-after if I was to survive.

"What are you doing?" Elyse said, eyes wide as I shook my shoulder bag out of the Kalamack Industries satchel to get our robes and hats. Familiars. We had to look like familiars.

"Put it on," I said, motions sure as I threw her robe at her and she caught it. "We can't go out through reality."

"You want to go through the ever-after?!"

I shimmied into my robe, frantic as I jammed the hat on my head and tied my sleeves to make pockets. Embarrassment kept my eyes down, embarrassment that I had tripped one of Trent's safeguards—right after warning Elyse. Madison's splat gun went in one of the robe's pockets, my cherry-red one in the other. After a moment of hesitation, I moved my last forget potion to a jeans pocket . . . just in case.

Elyse stood there, her robe in hand, a horrified expression on her face. "Why aren't you getting dressed?" I asked.

And then we both jumped at the sudden thud at the bare wall. Plaster chipped and fell.

They were trying to break in. *Why?* I thought as the muffled sound of splintering drywall grew louder. Trent's security knew how to move through the ley lines.

And then I figured it out. Everyone in Trent's security knew how to move through the ley lines. They *knew* demons were waiting to snag them if they tried. *Son of a fairy-farting whore . . .*

"Elyse, we have to go," I said as the cracking of the wallboard became louder. "The ever-after is the only way out. We'll get to the surface and walk to a ley line." And still she stood there, staring at me. "Put on your robe!"

Her chin trembled in what I thought was anger. "You planned this. This entire charade was to sell me to Newt for that damned mirror with no witnesses. There's no way to rekindle a used ley line charm, and I believed you! You're going to sell me to Newt!" Head shaking, she retreated as the wall splintered.

"Elyse . . ." I protested.

"I'll take my chances with Kalamack," she added bitterly. "I'm not the one who arrested him at his wedding. I'm the little girl you kidnapped from camp as a hostage." She turned to the widening cracks. "Help me! Please! She's going to sell me to the demons!"

"You little . . ." Furious, I lunged for her. She yelped, backpedaling to crash into Trent's elf porn. We went down, me atop her. A thought flickered through me of Boz and Clemt, either laughing their asses off or taking bets as to who was going to win.

Elyse howled, clearly pissed as she tried to shove me off her.

"Put on the robe! I am not trying to sell you!" I shouted, then jumped as energy zinged through me. It was Elyse, flooding me with raw power, straight from the line we had fallen into.

I didn't have time for this, and I pulled the fizzing energy in, forcing it into established patterns worn painless from use. Her power hummed, tasting of salt and lilac as it filled my chi. I added to it, jaw clenching when I shoved it right back.

Elyse screamed in pain, and then she went slack. I'd knocked her out.

"Get away from the woman!" someone demanded, and my attention jerked to the ragged hole in the wall. It wasn't wide enough for them to see me yet, and when it was, they'd start slinging spells.

"If I wanted to sell you, I would have done it already," I said, pissed to the ends of the earth as I shoved myself up and off her. The display case was shattered, statues rolling and glass tinkling as I grabbed her robe and hat, giving them a little shake before stuffing them into my shoulder bag. Had she learned nothing from the last time we argued?

"Ow . . ." came a whisper, and I stomped over to Elyse. Motions rough, I took the splat gun from her holster, then rolled her over with my foot to reach the one at the small of her back.

"Can you walk?" I yanked her up, struggling to manage her weight. "If you're lucky, I singed your synapses so you can't do anything that will get you killed."

"Rachel . . ." she slurred, a hand going to her head. "You will rot in Alcatraz for this."

"Yeah, well, I have to get you home first." She couldn't stand, and my stomach muscles clenched as I caught my shoulder under hers and took her weight. Behind me, chunks of plaster hit the floor as they widened the hole. "I won't let you be taken," I said as she blinked at me. "And if someone does take you, I will get you free. I promise. But we have to get out of here. They won't dare follow us into the ever-after or they would have jumped in here already."

"Wait . . ." she rasped, alarm widening her eyes. "Rachel, no!"

"Do me a favor and don't do any magic," I whispered. And with me in my spelling robes and her in her I.S. sweats, I shifted both our auras to match the line and we were gone.

CHAPTER

25

IN LESS THAN A HEARTBEAT, WE WERE THERE, THE ACIDIC BITE OF burnt amber scorching my lungs until it retreated to a background annoyance. Elyse was deadweight, and I let her slide to the spotless floor of the coffeehouse, filling my chi with energy as I looked up to see that not only Boz and Clemt but everyone in the shop was watching with rapt attention.

"Got it," I said, and the entire place erupted into noise, gold coins representing favors exchanging hands. They'd all been watching, and I shoved my alarm down deep. The next thirty seconds would either make my life harder or impossible, and I ignored Clemt as he shifted his bulk closer.

Elyse was at my feet, and I tugged her up as the conversations began shifting away from us, the noise continuing unabated. Boz had noticed my transposition stone, and I tucked it behind my robe, then shifted my shoulder bag higher. Elyse began coughing, bent double as she tried to adapt.

"You're a thief." Clemt narrowed his goat-slitted eyes suspiciously.

"And a *girl*," Boz said, leering. "You have some stones on you, Red. Tell you what. You give me that book and amulet that you stole, and Clemt and I will let you walk out of here. I've had my eye on that book ever since that Kalamack shit put it there."

Book? I turned to Elyse, furious. "You took one of his books?" I exclaimed, and her unrepentant gaze flicked to me as she finally got a full breath of air. "*You* triggered the alarm. I thought it was me!"

"It shouldn't be in an elf's possession," she said as if that made it right.

"Agreed." Clemt held out his hand, and I backed up a step with Elyse.

"Put your hand down before I put something you don't want in it," I said, hoping Elyse would stay quiet. I doubted very much that I had singed her, but if she did anything stupid, we'd both be laid out on the floor.

Boz nudged Clemt's elbow. "I think that's the witch Gally spent his futures on. Red hair. Clean aura." He ran his gaze over my robe, correctly tied. "He went broke snagging you. No doubt he's got you stealing from Kalamack instead of stirring spells."

If they thought we belonged to someone, they wouldn't touch us, and chin high, I showed him my wrist, the demon mark standing out like a dark beacon. "No doubt," I echoed. "You want the charm and the book, you talk to Al, ah, Gally. Excuse us."

I linked my arm in Elyse's, striding importantly to the pickup counter as if I'd placed an order. There were two drinks sitting there, and I grabbed them and handed one to Elyse. "Don't drink it," I whispered as I angled her to the door, then louder, "Put it on Gally's tab!"

"He's back?" Boz said, and then we were outside. The air was slightly less stifling, but I could feel them watching as I marched Elyse across the commons toward the chattering fountain. It mimicked the one in Cincinnati's Fountain Square. The Goddess knew why.

"You okay?" I said, knees a little wobbly. Damn. Trent's people had torn the wall down to get us. *Hence the new oak doors in the future,* I thought.

Elyse stumbled on a raised paver, gasping as she caught herself. "They let us walk out," she whispered. "Why? How do you breathe? Is it always this hot?"

"Yes, they did, and yes, it's always this hot." I slowed, seeing it as she was, for the first time. "They live underground where there's nothing in reality to cause a distortion, but the air exchange isn't that good, seeing as what's on the surface is pretty bad to begin with. No one bothers with a spell to clean the air other than in their apartments."

The scent of burnt amber was choking, and I blinked the tears away, trying to keep my breath shallow. It was easy to pick the demons out from the familiars even though they were often dressed the same, and though the workers were mostly familiars, the occasional demon sat behind a register working off a debt. No one was afraid, and no one was trying to escape. It wasn't that they didn't want to. There simply was no way out other than a demon line jumping them elsewhere. After a few hundred years, the fear sort of wore off.

"Why aren't they trying to abduct us?" Elyse half hung on my arm, her wide eyes taking everything in.

"The same reason Clemt and Boz let us walk out. Everyone not a demon belongs to someone," I said. "Body and soul."

"Why don't they just leave? Claw their way to the surface and escape?"

I slowed our pace even more to try to match the indolent saunter of a demon. "Because they've lost their soul to a demon. Once that is gone, you are theirs. Don't ever wager your soul." I stifled a shudder. I'd learned that little nugget of knowledge by accident. It was how I escaped Al, or would, rather. Agreeing to voluntarily become his familiar let me retain my soul. And because I had, I could say no, refuse to cross the ley lines to the ever-after. He couldn't force me, and from there we found common ground.

Her head dropped. "I think I'm going to be sick."

"Don't you dare." My grip on her arm tightened. "Look. Those are jump pads around the fountain. From there we can get to Newt's apartments." Elyse pulled from me, and I stopped. She'd gone white.

"Why? You don't need the mirror," she said, retreating a step. "You're fine. I won't put you in Alcatraz. I trust you. Vivian did. That's enough for me. We can go home right from here. How do you get out of here? Is there a stairway?"

A stairway? Is she serious? I leaned into her space until her jaw clenched. "Simple as that, you trust me, eh?" Just as long as her butt was in danger, maybe. "I am not here to jump through your hoops to gain my freedom. I am here for Brad. I need that mirror for him, not you, and since there's no way on this green earth that you will walk out of here alone, you're sticking with me."

"So you can sell me to Newt for that damned mirror?" she said hotly, and I glanced behind her at the coffee shop, worried.

"Hey! I told you to stay in the hall, remember? Coming was your idea, and now that you're here, you're going to ride it out. Newt will remember us." *I hope.* "We'll jump to her apartments, trade her the book you stole for the mirror and a way to the surface, and be gone."

"I'm not giving her the book!" Elyse exclaimed, a hand going to her shirt to tell me where it was. At least I knew I hadn't triggered the alarm. A smile quirked my lips at the thought of Quen staring at the broken wall when he got home, and then it faded. There was no feeling of triumph in besting his security. None at all.

"Well, she's not going to want a used-up stasis charm," I muttered, worried as I shifted my bag higher up my shoulder. I needed more than a riddle, and the book was convenient. If Trent was here now, he'd say sell it.

Elyse paced beside me, shaky and pale. "There has to be a tunnel out of here."

"There isn't." I continued to the jump pads, glancing once over my shoulder to see Boz and Clemt watching us from the outside tables. "Relax, she's not going to want your soul. That's an overly inflated price set by pissed-off demons who don't like to be summoned into a circle. Jumps aren't that expensive unless they have you over a barrel. Besides, I'm going to put it on Newt's tab. For all Pan knows, we were sent out for coffee. Here, hold this for a sec."

"Pan? You mean that demon?" Elyse stared at the bored demon in his red robes bellowing dramatically, sparkling energy spilling from him in great, unnecessary waves as he popped package-laden familiars to their owners. "You know him?"

"I know everyone." But they didn't know me, and I handed my coffee to Elyse, frizzed my hair out, and put the hat back on my head. Attitude in place, I took the coffee in hand, sneaking another glance at Boz and Clemt. Attitude would get me out of this, and lots of it. "Be quiet and sullen," I prompted. "Can you do that?"

No one did sullen like Elyse. It was the quiet part I had doubts about.

My pace quickened as we neared the fountain. Demons could jump from anywhere to anywhere, but having designated in-out spots helped prevent accidents. Familiars, of course, couldn't jump at all. Hence no one worrying about them escaping to the surface.

All of which meant that demons had to do the actual jumping for them. Pan had more than a flair for the dramatic. He also had a light touch and liked to take things that didn't belong to him, which was probably why he was out here doing community service. That, and he was bored out of his mind. They all were.

"Pan!" I called, knowing he wouldn't recognize me. I was a faceless familiar. "Get caught selling a bad curse?"

The demon turned, laughed, then looked closer, his flamboyant energy curls fading with a soft hiss as he set a pair of glasses spelled to see through charms on his nose. "Hey, hey, hey. We got us two new slabs of meat, except you aren't new, are you, despite your lack of smut. So, Snow White, who's been hiding you from the rest of us and for how long?"

Smiling with a comfortable familiarity, I twined a finger in a curl of his visible aura, not letting his energy mix cleanly with mine but keeping them separate, like oil and water. It was a practiced move, and one I hoped would give me the street cred I needed to pull this off. "Maybe the question should be *why*," I said as I let his energy swamp mine in a tingling wash. "I'm Newt's latest indulgence. You mind?" I lifted the coffee in explanation and stepped up onto the jump pad.

Elyse pushed up onto it with me, white-faced.

Pan's goat-slitted eyes narrowed. "Since when?"

"Since Gally did something uncommonly stupid." I gave Elyse a nudge to get off. "One at a time."

Elyse shook her head, arms wrapped around her middle as she stared at the coffeehouse.

Crap on toast . . . It was Boz and Clemt, both headed this way. "Fine. You first." I stepped down, and the woman froze in indecision. "I'll be right behind you. Get off the circle when you arrive so I don't land on you."

"Ah, Rach—" she started.

My skin tingled as Pan shifted her aura to match the line, bellowing an utterly needless *"Vade!"* There was no spell here, just simple physics, and yet as Pan's wildly swinging arm ended its sweep in a fisted hand, she was gone, jumped to Newt's apartments by Pan.

Get off the jump pad, I thought as I stepped into her place and handed Pan my coffee. "Tell them we went to see Dali, will you?" I said, giving a nod to Boz and Clemt.

Pan took it, his lips quirked in disbelief. "For a coffee? Oh, Snow White, you gotta do better than that."

I tapped the top knowingly. "Think of it as a placeholder. Next time I'm in reality, I'll bring you a real one."

Thinking I was joking, he laughed. "Deal. You get that much for making me laugh," he said. "I haven't laughed in twenty-seven days, eight hours, forty-nine minutes—"

And then he dramatically flung a hand and I was gone with his shouted *"Vade!"* nothing more than a thought echoing in mine as Pan shifted my aura to pop me out at Newt's apartments.

Blinking, I took a breath as I found myself standing on a flat gray disk set within a gray tiled floor. The ceilings were high and the walls were draped with white gauze. Soft, indulgent cushions covered the multitude of chairs and couches, and a low, green slate table the size of Kisten's pool table nestled between them. There were no windows, but a curtained spell frame showed an image of a flat pond circled by big trees. One entire wall was nothing but shelves and lighted nooks holding knickknacks from various ages. Nearby was a spell bar with vials of potions arranged like pill bottles. It looked spacious and beautiful, but the air still stank of burnt amber and I could sense the hard rock behind everything.

"Elyse?" My skin prickled, and I breathed deep. *Is someone baking cookies?*

"Circle!" Elyse shrieked, and I rolled, my shoulder bag slamming into my gut as I fell.

"*Rhombus!*" I exclaimed, and my circle rose up, crackling as a black haze hit it, skating over its entirety to try to find a way in. Only now did I see Elyse in the corner, flat out and under what was probably a *stabils* curse, as she could talk but not move.

"Who are you! Get out of my rooms!" Newt shrilled at us both. The demon had apparently forgotten who we were. *Crap on toast. Why can't I catch a break?*

"Newt!" Immediately I stood up and broke my circle as if unafraid. But I was, and I kept a light thought within the ley lines, finding strength in the faint tickle of power. "Hey, ah, we brought you a coffee," I said, wincing when I saw it spilled on the floor. "Ah, we can get another one if you want."

With a twitch of her robe, Newt halted between Elyse and myself. Her chin was high, and it was obvious she was embarrassed, possibly thinking that she'd forgotten something important. Again. "Coffee?" she said, eyeing the brown puddle. "No."

"Okay." My pulse hammered and I forced my hands to unclench. "Where's, ah, Minias?"

"Hiding." Newt almost spat the word. "I think I know you. Is your name Futility?"

She was talking. We had a chance, and I eased my grip on the lines. "Elyse, you okay?"

"I spilled the coffee," she said, unmoving on the floor, and I began to inch toward her.

Newt cocked her head. "Or perhaps it's Ignorance."

"Ignorance will work," I said sourly. "You can call me Iggy."

Newt made a small sound. "Iggy, did I kill Minias?" she asked, arms going over her middle to drum her fingers atop her arm. "Bartholomew's balls, I hate bringing up a new familiar. You don't have enough smut to be of any use." She smiled, her black eyes fixed on mine as I moved around the edges of the room. "Yet."

"Minias is fine. I'm not a familiar. I have my soul, and so does Elyse. You and I were making a deal and were interrupted so I tracked you down so we could finish. Minias dosed you with a forget spell." Yes, it was a lie, but only one of timing. Minias spelled her at will.

"So I surmised." Scowling, Newt dropped into the couch where she could see both of us, almost disappearing in the indulgent cushions. "It may be time to retire him. Who owns you? That's Gally's mark. I can smell it from here." She hesitated. "And mine. On your foot. Perhaps I shouldn't have tried to kill you."

My gaze flicked to my boots and back. "I don't belong to anyone until I have three strikes," I said, suddenly worried.

"Three is traditional, but there are exceptions." Energy drifting about her fingers like a fog, Newt sat up, interested. "Are you good at potions? If I buy Al's mark, I will have two. He's got himself in some trouble. Selling his option might be his only way out." Her focus went distant as she played with the energy, making it spark. "He's in reality. In the sun. How is it, do you think, that he has found a way past the curse that keeps us here? I'm the only one who knows how to do that."

I froze as Newt pushed up out of the couch and strode to her wall of knickknacks, ribbons of black hazing behind her.

"Ah, give it a few more weeks. Don't want to be rash," I said with a little laugh.

Newt had her back to me, watching my reflection in a flat pewter plate. "I remember you now. You were at the Basilica. You wanted something, little demon summoner." Her gaze went to Elyse. "For her."

"I am not for sale!" Elyse shouted, red-faced and totally helpless.

"Half right." I inched forward to get between her and Elyse. "Elyse is not available. We had already come to an agreement before you left. I gave you a vision of the future, and you promised to give me an Atlantean mirror and two line jumps." Yes, it was another lie, but how else were we going to get out of here? Dosing her into forgetting wouldn't help, and I only had the one potion left.

"Line jumps that were never in the deal, and a vision you gave me of the future that I no longer remember." Newt laughed, but there was too much hopelessness in it to be a pleasing sound. "No line jumps. Besides, I may not have three marks on you, but you're in my living room. You're not leaving it."

I had reached Elyse. With the barest hint of line energy prickling through me, I touched her and broke the *stabils* curse. She sat up, almost sobbing in relief, her forehead on her knees as she shook. Across the room, Newt cleared her throat, clearly surprised.

"You okay?" I whispered as the last of the spell tingled through me and back into the ground. Elyse nodded—her head still on her knees—and I took the spilled coffee and crossed the room to Newt. "There's a swallow left," I said as I held out the half-full cup.

Newt silently considered me, probably thrown by how easily I'd broken the *stabils* curse. It wasn't hard to do, but it spoke of me having dealt with demons before. Still, she wasn't taking the cup, and I finally set it down.

"You were at the bar. You told me to run." Her black eyes narrowed to slits. "And I did. Why?"

Nervous, I backed up to the table and sat on the edge of a chair as if I was her equal. I wasn't. "The coven found us. We had to go."

"Us girls have to stick together," she whispered, and I stifled a wince. If she remembered that I had dosed her, we were up shit creek. "I forgot what I was doing there," she added. "Minias wants me to make a tulpa of it. He says if I immerse myself in it, I will remember. It might work." She watched me like a lioness at a waterhole, her aura edging into the visible spectrum as she pulled heavily on the ley lines. "Or you could tell me."

For a price, I thought, a flicker of hope rising through me despite her show of strength.

"Tulpa?" Elyse said cautiously as if to prove she wasn't scared.

"A memory made real so everyone can enjoy it." Silent, I pushed the coffee toward Newt as an offering to parlay. Not long from now, I'd make a tulpa to prove that I was a demon. It had stunned them, not just that I'd succeeded but that I'd given them a vision of the sun . . . and wide horizons . . . and purity. All things they ached for.

Newt rubbed her forehead, the prickling of her aura against my skin vanishing as she went from an active threat to merely a possible one. I knew how fast that could change, though, and didn't trust it. "If nothing else, tulpas fill the bank account," she muttered. "Why anyone will want to partake in a strip club is beyond me when they could bathe in the sun of preindustrial Africa. I think Minias is after something."

"He is." I shrugged out of my shoulder bag, careful to keep it closed. "About our deal. I give you a vision of the future and you give me an Atlantean mirror. And because I've had to track you down to finish it, I'm adding on two line jumps to the Basilica. I can get to reality from there on my own."

"That's where I first saw you." Newt's gaze fixed on Elyse, and the woman froze. "The Basilica. I was going to filch your familiar."

"I'm not her familiar," Elyse said from the corner, her face pale but determined.

"No?" Newt snickered. "You act like it."

"I do not wear her smut!" Elyse exclaimed, and Newt's smile went knowing.

"She's not mine to sell," I said. "Besides, look at her. She's right. What little smut she has is her own."

"Well, if she's not yours to sell, you won't mind me taking her."

I waved a hand at Elyse to stay put. "She's my friend, and I do."

Newt took the nearly empty coffee in hand. "That's hard for you, not me," she said, then tipped it high, draining the last swallow.

"Not happening, Newt," I said, feeling as if we were running out of time. "Now, about the mirror? Reasonably, what do you want for it and two jumps home? I have a book—"

Newt stood, and I tensed, the ley line sparking through me as I tightened my grip. "You are home," the demon said as she went to her spell bar, robe brushing the floor in a soft hush. "I've always enjoyed coven members waiting on me, but you, Iggy, I will crack slowly. Something good inside there."

She was getting erratic again, and I stood, motioning Elyse to get behind me. The need to fill myself with the strength of a ley line ached, but if I did, Newt would, too, and the demon was far more adept than I was. "Not happening," I said softly, gut hurting. "How about a book from the Kalamack estate? Apparently it's a complete volume. No missing pages."

"That belongs to the coven," Elyse hissed, and I gritted my teeth.

Newt turned, a bottle of something in her hand as she glanced at my shoulder bag. "I want to know how Gally escaped the ever-after. I'm the only one allowed to do that. How is it he's in reality when the sun is up? Can you tell me that? No? Then you're mine."

"Yes!" I exclaimed, almost shouting the word. "I can. I know! I saw it!"

Newt paused and put the cap back on, little sparks of energy falling like pixy dust. "You *saw* it?"

"Lived it, you might say."

Elyse put a hand on my shoulder from behind. "Don't," she whispered. "You can't."

Newt frowned. "You. Junior coven member. Shut it." Confidence absolute, Newt sat down, her arms draped across the back of the couch as she faced us. "You know," she added, gesturing for me to join her. "How could you possibly know? Entertain me with your stories. If I like them, I might keep you alive a little longer."

Speak truth only to the dead. That's what Al had said, and I felt a quiver race through me. Ah, well. Minias would probably make her forget. "I know because I was there. I can tell you how he did it. I can tell you why he did it. And I can tell you when it's going to fall apart and he's tossed back into the ever-after like a fish too small to be bothered with." I took a slow breath, my pulse fast. "And I can tell you what you were trying to find in my church and why Minias dosed you into forgetting. All of this in one simple act."

Newt's hand trembled, and I wondered if I'd gone too far. "That's where I know you," she said, her expression blanking, and I stifled a shudder. "That church. I blasphemed it to get to you. But you are not you. You were . . . unripe. Now you're bursting with potential."

Unripe? I suppose I was, two years ago. "The mirror and two jumps to reality," I prompted, and she twitched her robe in agitation. "Promise it,"

I added. "The mirror and two jumps to reality. I want to go to the Basilica. Both of us when I ask. Not when you feel like it."

Her black eyes narrowed on me. "Providing you tell me the truth, Iggy, and not a story."

I nodded, and Elyse inched closer. "You can't," she protested.

"She's going to remember it eventually," I muttered, and Newt beamed beatifically. "I need a knife," I said, knowing I didn't have one in my shoulder bag.

"What for?" Newt eyed me suspiciously.

"To show you the why, the how, and the when concerning Al's actions," I said, and the demon took one from her sleeve and flung it at me.

It hit the cushion beside my leg with a soft thump and I jerked, hesitating briefly at the bite of cold on my fingers before I tugged it free. "Thanks," I said, then used it to pierce my thumb. Red welled up, and I smeared it on the knife, standing so as to carefully hand it to her over the slate table.

"What? Am I supposed to be impressed?" she said, and I resettled myself, knees watery.

"Al— I mean, Gally was," I said.

She slowly tasted it, then lifted her eyes. "You are not a witch," she said, then flipped the knife in her grip to rend. "I killed all my sisters!"

I twitched, forcing myself to stay put, to not yank the line into me, and to sit quietly, hands in my lap. "I'm not your sister," I said. "I'm the way back, born a witch with the right amino acids to kindle demon magic and join the collective. Kalamack Senior repaired the damaged portions of my genome so the elven curse laid on you so long ago wouldn't kill me."

The flicker of unharnessed magic vanished from Newt's hands. "You are witch born?" she said, voice harsh. "And now the spawn of a Kalamack owns you!" she finished, furious.

"Trent does not own me!" I shouted, warming as I made a fist to hide the ring he had given me. "I'm currently arresting him at his own wedding. Does that sound like he owns me? My dad paid that debt with his life. I do what I want!"

"As do I." Newt hesitated, black gaze shifting between me and Elyse. "You are here and there both. You are yourself and yet different."

Ripe and unripe. I nodded. "This is how Al escaped and how he will be forced to return shortly after sunset tonight. I wasn't the only infant Kalamack Senior fixed. Gally's newest familiar, Stanley Saladan, was repaired as well in the hopes that in a few months from now one of us would fulfill Kalamack Senior's wish and steal a pre-curse elven DNA sample from the Basilica to cure the elves."

Newt sneered, shifting to sit almost sideways on the couch. "Over my dead body."

I shrugged. "Oh, you seemed happy enough with it." Elbow on my knee, I leaned forward. "I am going to bring back the elves, and because of it, I have the strength to save the demons. Put them in reality's sun where they belong." I hesitated. "Promise. It's already done."

Newt considered that, her black eyes giving nothing away. Behind her, a bottle began to crack, a thin spiderweb of fractures spreading over its surface.

"I need the mirror and two jumps to reality. Right now." I held my bag close, fingers trembling. "In that order. I've held up my end of the deal."

She stared at us. I could feel Elyse behind me, jerking when Newt leaned over the table and exhaled a warm mist.

"There's your mirror," she said, and I winced, remembering her doing the same at the bar. Mist and fog. She was giving me a riddle. "How is Gally getting around the curse that pins us here?"

Maybe if I spelled it out, she would do the same. "He's possessing Stanley Saladan, the link lasting past the sunrise because Stanley is genetically a demon. It wouldn't work with anyone else. *Except me.* But I will circle Al's frustrated, angry ass tonight and send him back to you."

Newt smirked. "Might be difficult if you're in my larder."

I shrugged. "It's already done." And it was, or it would be. Tonight would be the first city powers meeting that I called. Al would try to choke the death out of Piscary. I would circle him to save the undead vampire, banishing Al and finding out too late that I was trying to gain protection from the very undead vampire who had sent Kisten to die. *A lie learned too late.*

My throat closed at the memory. I had thought Kisten was gone. Jenks and Ivy, too. Despondent and seeing no way out, I would take the focus into myself to keep Piscary and Trent from getting it. The Hail Mary spell would all but drive me insane until it was removed. Jaw clenched, I shoved the remembered heartache away.

Newt was looking at me when my eyes opened from their slow, strength-gathering blink. "You moved through time using a curse developed to gauge abnormalities in the ley lines. Brilliant. How is it you are smart enough to do that and still be so blind about an Atlantean mirror?"

I licked my lips, angry at how badly things had spiraled out of control. "Don't trust Minias. I'll give you that for free."

With a little huff, the demon shook her hand and a sparkling of energy filled it. "That I already know. I remember you now. I remember every-thing. The deal is off."

"What? Hey!" I jumped, startled when Newt flung out a hand and a black haze sifted through my aura like cold snow. *"Rhombus!"* I exclaimed, but nothing happened. The line was gone. It just wasn't there. That fast, I was helpless before her.

I was an idiot, playing with gods, trusting that I knew what I was doing.

"No!" Elyse shrieked, that same black haze sticking to her as she stum-bled back, terrified as she hit the wall, helpless.

"You can't call off a deal after you get what you want!" I exclaimed, and Newt stood before us both, a ribbon of black playing through her fingers like a little snake, the tail of which wound around both Elyse and me.

"We both got what we wanted," she said. "You are just too stupid to see it. You, coven witch, I will entertain first."

"Newt, don't do this!" I cried out, and then I gasped as Newt shoved me into a line, and from there, a little tiny hole.

CHAPTER

26

I SCRAMBLED FOR BALANCE AS I SLID ACROSS A POLISHED FLOOR IN the absolute dark, jerking when I hit something that fell with a harsh clatter. Effectively blind, I reached for a ley line, elated when I realized she had lifted her block.

"*Lenio cinis,*" I whispered as I wondered why, and faintly glowing light blossomed off the floor of the cell. And it was a cell: low ceiling, flat floor, no windows or doors, only fifteen feet across, maybe. The walls themselves were curved, making it look as if I was sitting inside a hollow doughnut, the ceiling of which was just over my head.

My shoulder bag had not made the trip, and I had a moment of frantic panic as I patted my pockets to make sure I still had my dad's broken stirring rod. It was still there, and I exhaled in relief. Everything else could be replaced, and I slowly sat where I was and rubbed my elbow. It was obviously Newt's oubliette, the "little forgotten space" where she stuffed people until she remembered them—if she remembered them. And from the pile of purple and green silk still sheltering the bones and hair that I'd fallen into, I clearly wasn't the first.

"Hey, hi," I whispered, not as horrified as I should be at the skeleton curled up at the base of a wall. "Sorry about running into you, Fred," I said, naming my cellmate.

My expression pinched as I realized this was probably the oubliette that Nick would die in. Maybe I'd still be here when Nick showed up. I could throttle the neck of my onetime boyfriend myself.

But no. Al had discovered Nick's body. He would have told me if I had been there beside him. I think. Maybe not. Just two spell-robed mummies in the desert.

Frustrated, I eased myself into a more comfortable position, smacking the dust off my bejeweled jeans as I stole little glimpses of my cellmate. My breathing was the only sound. It was warm, almost stuffy, but a hint of burnt amber and dust led me to think there was an air vent somewhere.

"I am so sorry, Elyse," I whispered, imagining what was going on in Newt's chambers right about now. The proud woman wouldn't submit, and Newt would run a ley line through her as punishment, trying to quash the woman's will and strengthen her carrying capacity at the same time. It hurt. Al had done the same thing to me until I had learned how to spindle line energy in my head and throw it right back at him. Ah, good times.

I'd told her I could keep her safe, and my pride and overconfidence had bitten both of us on our collective asses. Even if I could return myself and Elyse to reality, she'd never trust me. None of the coven would. And if I kept making such stellar mistakes, perhaps they shouldn't.

"Knock it off, Rachel," I said as I gathered myself and stood. I was in a box. I'd been in a box before. If air was coming in, there was a way out— robed skeleton aside.

The ceiling was only a few feet over my head, and I reached up to touch it to make sure it was real. The stone was warm under my fingertips. Perhaps I was closer to the surface than I had first thought. I had access to a line. I wasn't helpless. The air was coming from somewhere. "Hang on, Elyse. I'm coming."

Slowly I began to pull the ley line energy into me, gathering it, spindling it into a wad. Scintillating, it pooled in my chi, and I raised my hands over my head, forcing the energy into my palms until they glowed an unreal gold and red, ribbons of smutty black tracing through them. I was going to bust out of here right now. Newt could make a new oubliette for Nick.

"*Celero dilatare!*" I shouted, forcing a small bubble of air to expand.

It hit the ceiling and rebounded, smacking into me with the force of a train.

I hit the stone wall, arms and legs askew. Groaning, I slid to the floor, a hand clenched to my shoulder. My light had gone out, and I willed it back into existence. "Ow," I whispered as I sat up, that pile of bones and silk clattering with my movement. It had been pushed into the wall with me, and I felt a twinge of guilt. Whoever it had been, they probably hadn't deserved being left here to die of dehydration.

"Sorry," I said, an inane feeling of companionship welling up as I scooted away. My head hurt, and I held it as I willed the room to stop spinning. Regret tightened my chest, and I dropped my forehead to my knees. Elyse was right. It had been stupid thinking I could waltz into the ever-after and make a deal with Newt. Trent might have killed me for trying to steal from him, but he would've given me a sporting chance. Newt was erratic and unpredictable. She moved on instinct, and I had stomped all over hers. I'd been so intent on proving to Elyse that I knew what I was doing, I proved to her I didn't—even if she hadn't been making the situation any easier.

But regardless of my pride being ground to a paste under Newt's heel, I had to get out of here. Kisten was languishing under the library. I couldn't save him, but I had hoped I could say good-bye, maybe, when he left. Now, even that was gone, and I blinked the sudden tears away.

"Way to go, Rachel," I whispered, throat tight. I had dropped myself in the past thinking that, with everything I'd learned, I would be okay, but it hadn't been enough. I needed my friends. I was never going to get out of here. I was going to die in this cruddy little hole in the ground, and Nick was going to find my bones next to Fred.

"I'm sorry, Elyse," I whispered, knowing there was no return for her, either. I'd never see Ivy or Jenks again, never see Trent, touch his face, feel his strength, his gentleness, his love.

I sniffed back the tears as I spun the ring he'd given me, indulging in my pity party. It wasn't as if I had anything else to do. I had risked everything for what? Because I was scared of the coven? Because I couldn't leave Cincy to its fate? Because of my pride?

And then I sighed, the pain about my chest easing. No. I'd risked everything because I had used a dark curse and hurt someone. I'd come here not to evade the coven's snare but to find a freaking Atlantean mirror and uncurse Brad. That it would free me from the coven was simple justice.

But it was still my pride that had gotten me stuck.

"Son of a moss wipe, pixy-pissed, troll-turd excuse of a demon!" I shouted, hearing my voice hit the smooth walls and floor.

Maybe if I made myself look like Fred, Newt might throw me out with the garbage, I thought. Newt had my bag and everything that was in it. Apart from being able to tap into a line, all I had was the transposition charm. That, and my wits.

Grimacing, I got to my feet. Maybe it was like an escape room where, if I could find a way out, I'd be worthy to be her familiar. I'd been down here a good ten minutes. The air wasn't getting stale. There had to be an exchange.

More careful now, I began to explore, skirting Fred's remains as I ran my hand over first the walls, then the ceiling, searching for the way out. Not a glimmer of magic or a hint of fresh air found me. The walls were perfect, almost as if I was in a bubble and the rock was only an illusion, like a holodeck on a sci-fi flick.

Like a glamour, I mused. Lips pressed, I fumbled for the transposition stone and peered through it. Inch by inch I went over the walls and floor and ceiling, pulling the air into my lungs with a pained slowness as I searched for a stronger scent of burnt amber until, with a jolt, I found it. There in the ceiling under my questing fingertips was a laced mesh of power glowing with a silken thread of black. It had to be covering something.

Eyes narrowed, I stared up at the ceiling. *"Adaperire,"* I cautiously whispered, yelping when even that mild of an open spell bounced back with a vicious fire, flicking over my aura and soaking in with a harsh warning. And yet it was proof that something was there to protect.

Stymied, I stood where I was, head craned and arms over my middle. I'd found the opening. I couldn't see it without the stone, but clearly something was there. It was magical in nature, meaning only magic could break it. I needed something subtle to pare the spell away. I needed a knife, but not just any knife, which I didn't have anyway. I needed a magic knife.

I lifted my brow at the first hints of an idea. I could tap a line. I had been accessing spells from the demon collective since we got here. I'd taken a summoning name this week if I had my timing right. Maybe I could get into the demons' vault? Not for a lethal charm but for something with the exquisite precision needed to cut through a powerful spell.

I sat down right where I was, a thread of excitement spilling through me. Eyes closing, I exhaled to quiet my thoughts . . . then sent them into the collective. My breath caught and I felt a moment of familiar vertigo as the multitude of conversations beat at me. They were all in my head, and I tried to muffle my confusion and sly hope amid the deals being struck, complaints being made, and gossip finding a foothold.

I say Gally has no proprietary claim on the spell that allowed him to break the summoning curse, came loudly into my mind. *Even if he would use it to pay his debt for letting that bitch of an elf Ceri escape knowing how to spindle line energy. The spell to give us reality again belongs to everyone.*

It was Dali, the self-appointed leader of the demons, second only behind the erratic power of Newt, and I hid my presence behind a cluster of thought revolving around Newt's recent disappearance, and perhaps it was time to trade Minias out for a more careful caretaker?

"*Reserare*, Jariathjackjunisjumoke," I whispered, shuddering when the word to enter meshed with my password and I felt my thoughts drop into the vault.

The conversations vanished with a shocking suddenness as my mind shrank down to just me. But it didn't stay that way, and soon the long-fallow memories of the demons who had died over the eons rose up from the shadows, their presence clinging to the spells they'd made, their essence angry and vindictive as they demanded I use the war curses they had twisted and stored here. I ignored them, my thoughts on one thing only:

Al's dagger. I hadn't accidentally given it to Dali yet. It had answered to me once before. Perhaps it would again.

Quaere, I whispered into my thoughts, framing my request with my belief of its obedience. *I summon you, Quaere, not to soak in my enemy's blood but to sever their snare that would see me languish into death. I summon you at the will of your maker, Algaliarept.*

Either it would come or it wouldn't, and I felt a smile find me as my hands in my lap began to thrum, an eager thirst tickling the edges of my awareness.

My eyes opened, my sight pulling me from the demons' war vault. In my hands was a small dagger, hazed with magic and prickling against my aura. Actually, it *was* magic, and with it I could kill demons and elves.

I was sure it would be disappointed when it found out all I wanted to do was escape.

"Thank you," I whispered, knowing the dagger had a quasi-intelligence. It didn't recognize time, didn't know that I shouldn't be aware of it until two years from now. All it knew was that I had called with the assurance that it should answer . . . and it did.

I stood with a renewed hope. Peering through the transposition curse, I angled the knife to the faintest haze of black, cringing as I boldly slashed through it.

Magic cramped my hand and arm, and I hunched with a muffled cry. The dagger, though, pulsed in satisfaction, and my head snapped up at the new scent of dust. The glamoured mesh was gone. A three-foot-wide shaft rose straight up through the rock. At the top, a patch of night sky showed, blacker than the walls lit by my light, and I stifled a quiver of angst. *Not too late . . .*

"Yes!" I exclaimed, deciding that if I could get into the smooth shaft, I could wedge-walk my way to the surface. I hesitated to make sure Newt wasn't coming to investigate, and then I jumped for the opening, fingertips brushing the inside before falling short.

There was no way.

Peeved, I looked over the cell, seeing only Fred. The thought to animate him to give me a boost came and went. I couldn't do that. Fred wasn't going to be much help. Using a charm to propel me up the shaft wasn't happening, either, lest I miscalculate and snap my neck. I needed something to stand on or someone to pull me out. Unfortunately, the only things up top were surface demons and the occasional gargoyle.

Gargoyle? I mused. I couldn't call Bis, but maybe Adagio would help.

Licking my lips, I stood right under the opening, staring up at the patch of red-tinted darkness high overhead. The sun was going down, and a cool wind blew in, bringing dust with it.

"Adagio!" I shouted, hands cupped.

Nothing.

"Adagio!" I called again, my hands going to my ears when the word bounced around the room, beating on me. *Crap on toast . . .*

Frustrated, I slumped against the curved wall and slid down to sit, staring at my dusty boots. The thought to try to contact Bis rose and fell. He hadn't been at the church at this time, didn't know me. My melancholy thickened as I recalled his shy smile when he tried anything new, his deadpan seriousness when pranking Jenks, and his utter devotion to me even as he gave me the space I thought I needed. He had trusted me when I said I'd make it home. I missed him, and he was the one whom I fell short with the most. And now he would be alone.

"I'm so sorry, Bis," I whispered. "I didn't mean to leave you." Depressed, I thumped my head against the wall and sniffed back a tear.

A soft scrape pulled my eyes open, and I stared at the ceiling. "Bis?" I whispered, a horrid mix of dismay and delight cramping my gut. He shouldn't see me. He shouldn't be here!

But it was a rougher voice, older and cracking like stones, that answered me with a slow, "Why do you pine for my kin?"

I sat up, neck craned. "Adagio?" He had heard me. Relief it wasn't Bis washed through me, shortly followed by heartache. "I need your help," I added as I got to my feet and peered up the hole to see nothing. He was blocking the view of the sky. "I know you have no reason to give it, and probably a few not to."

A flash of the night showed as he shifted his head—then was gone. "Why do you pine for my kin?" he asked again, and the dry scent of feathers and iron drifted down to remind me of Bis.

"Because one of them looks to me. But he doesn't know me yet and I don't dare call for him."

I shifted as a few pebbles sprinkled down, and then the brighter light of the night returned. "I can't help you," he said as he moved away.

"I know." I whispered it, more for me than him as I sank down, clear of the falling pebbles. "He lives in reality. Just a kid. Size of a big cat. He showed up on my church one day, and he never left. Even when he should. He stuck with me. Lost his life saving mine."

A soft rumble of confusion echoed in my prison, and his face filled the opening. "And yet you call for him? When he lost his life?"

I lifted a shoulder and let it fall. "Because I held it in trust until he got it back."

"Mmmm," he rumbled, the sound almost a force pressing down on me. "You say you are bonded. I know all the demons. I do not know you."

"I'm new," I said listlessly, thinking Al was right about my chances of making it to old age. But, man . . . I thought I'd make it further than this. "Just like Bis," I added. "Not being there for him is my biggest regret." I hesitated, wondering if Adagio had talked to Fred, too. "Hey, Adagio? What is it that you regret the most?"

More pebbles sifted down, and his billows-like breathing grew fainter. "I do not regret."

"Everyone has regrets," I insisted, and the gargoyle made a huffing rumble.

"I do not," he insisted. "I have a wish."

Wishes were cousins to regret, and I fiddled with the pebbles, trying to stack them up. "What do you wish for, Adagio?"

"That I knew how to give peace to the one I care for."

"Newt?" I smiled ruefully. "Yeah, she's a churning mess most of the time. It's hard being confused when everyone else seems to know what they are doing. I have a secret you can tell her. No one knows what they are doing. Some of us simply know how to fake it better." My pile of pebbles slid into nothing, and I started again. *Click, click, click* . . . "I think I saw her at peace only once. You were with her."

"I must go," Adagio said, and a slew of pebbles sprinkled in, destroying my new miniature tower. "It's not safe after dark, even for me."

"It was The Hunt," I added, not caring if he left but wanting to talk. "Jointly led by Newt and a Kalamack son, if you can believe it."

A rumbling chuckle of laughter drifted down. "I do not."

"Everyone was there, even Dali in those ugly torn robes he wears when he wants to remind everyone of their civic duty to hate elves." I stared at the black hole in the ceiling. "Bis was too small to carry me, so his dad did. We followed our quarry through both realities, through every ley line until we drove our quarry to ground. I've never seen anything like it, and I probably never will again. It was magnificent."

"This thing you say that hasn't happened yet," Adagio prompted, his disbelief obvious.

"It has for me." My voice went wispy as I used *Quaere* to cut the last of the sequins from my shirt and flick them one by one across my cell. "Bis fixed them all. Every single line. And then together they killed the idiot who set the lines' resonances against each other as easily as he had set the demons against themselves. Demons need each other, like the flower needs the sun. That's okay. I need my people, too."

Adagio was silent, but I knew he was up there, and I found I could still smile. My life might have been short, but it had been full. Trent would remain to remember The Hunt. It hadn't been for nothing.

"She was happy," I said softly. "Flying astride your shoulders, meting out justice. Saving those who looked to her from a pain she didn't want them to carry." I tilted my head to the ceiling. "That's why she takes my place as the Goddess. To save me from a pain she didn't want me to carry.

But she will be happy, Adagio. And later, she will find peace. She will be allowed to set down her promise to keep her kin from heartache. She will be free. I promise you. Soon, not in forever. You will get your wish."

I guess wishes *were* different from regrets.

Adagio made a long, rumbling sigh. A drift of red sand sifted down the shaft . . . then nothing. He was gone.

My shoulders slumped . . . and then I jumped when the air grew stuffy, and with a scrabbling rasp, a thick, lion-tufted tail flicked into my cell. I pushed to the wall, jaw dropping when the tail was followed by gnarled feet, wiggling hips, and finally a wing-wrapped body as the ceiling gave birth to a craggy old gargoyle.

He hit the ground hard, catching his balance easily. I stared as Adagio shifted from foot to foot, wings rasping as they settled and he filled the space that was left. Glancing up at the hole, he shuddered. Dust sifted from him and he looked at the knife in my hand.

"I don't know how to put it away," I said as I set it on the floor. He was down here with me, and I felt myself go pale. Dude. The guy was huge, his gray skin crisscrossed with lumpy white scars. Something had shifted, and I didn't know what.

"I listened to you at the Basilica. You rely on your friends because your friends rely on you. You understand demons better than they do themselves. What is your name?" he asked, his low voice rumbling like distant thunder against the curved walls to sound as if it was coming from right over my head.

I licked my lips. He wouldn't hurt me, but this was really odd. I knew he didn't care about me, but he was down here nevertheless. "Rachel Mariana Morgan," I whispered, his presence demanding I use all three.

The tip of Adagio's tail twitched, and I felt a pang of heartache when it curled about his feet like Bis's. "That name will be forgotten," he rumbled. "What is the name you will be remembered by?"

"My summoning name?" I blurted, sure that's not what he wanted.

Adagio grimaced, his red eyes squinting at me in annoyance. "That is your name that no one speaks. Who *are* you?"

I started to say no one, and then I hesitated. I was no one to him already. He didn't care about who I was, only what I was to Bis. "I am the world breaker's sword," I whispered, letting go of my ego and becoming smaller. "I belong to him. To Bis."

"Ahhh." Adagio's ear flicked. "That one I know. But that is a thing of the future, not the past. The ever-after abides. As foul and broken as it is."

I stiffened as he shuffled closer, closing one eye in a wincing squint when he breathed deeply over me.

"Or not," he mused, a hint of confusion in his gravelly voice. "You have already ridden the back of the universe, turning the shadow of memory to bone and dust and air."

He meant creating a new ever-after, and I smiled in remembrance. "Yeah, but Bis is the real artist." *And I am going to miss him.*

"*You* are the sword used to break the worlds?"

I squinted at him in apology. "Sorry if you were expecting more."

Wings clamped tight, Adagio looked confused. "The world breaker lives," he whispered, almost unheard. "He's among us even now."

"He is alone," I countered, and Adagio seemed to start, his wide-ranging thoughts coming back to the now. "Or he will be."

A low rumble rose from him, vibrating through me. "Wait," Adagio said, and then he stretched a long, muscular arm up, easily finding the opening and pulling himself up and into the shaft.

"Hey! Where are you going?" I called as he struggled, chunks of rock falling as he dragged himself upward. "Wait for what?"

But he was gone, and I stared at the ceiling, tense until, with the scrape of metal on stone, the grip of Adagio's beaten sword dangled just within my reach. I was going to get free.

But Nick wasn't. He was not anyone's sword, and as Adagio called down to find out if his sword reached, I used *Quaere* to scratch a note on the wall to Nick in the hopes that it would survive until he found it.

"Grasp the sword!" Adagio demanded.

"Just a sec!" I called, scribbling, *Ta-ta, Nick. Kiss, kiss, Rachel.*

Okay, maybe that had been unnecessary and snarky, but I felt better.

I felt even better yet when I grasped the ancient silver handle with both hands, holding *Quaere* between my teeth as Adagio pulled me up. I bowed my head, teeth clenched when my shoulders bumped and pebbles rained down. Something passed through my aura, and with a shocking suddenness, I was free and the gritty wind pushed on me.

Adagio held the sword high, and I let go to drop lightly to the ground. It was dark, but the sun couldn't be too far away, and the pinch of time dug at me.

"Thank you," I whispered, and Adagio leaned heavily upon his dented sword.

"I do this for the world breaker. When you hurt, he hurts. And he does not deserve to hurt."

"No, he does not." I reached out, his muscular arm warm under my hand as I looked into his red eyes, squinting at something familiar. "I only want to get home to him."

"Be more careful. He needs you."

I nodded, surprised when he ran a single gray-scarred finger across my jawline. A hint of the ley line lifted through me, and then his attention shifted over my shoulder.

"Gotta go," he said, suddenly panicked. His hand dropped and his wings flashed open. Pushing down once, he was in the air, leaving a swirl of gritty red dust.

When I could see again, he was nothing more than a fast-moving shadow heading west.

I managed a weak laugh as I stared up at the red-smeared sky past the black clouds. "Come out to the ever-after," I mocked, tired and sore as I beat the dust from my spelling robe. "We'll steal a few spells. Have a few laughs . . ."

"Adagio!" came a piercing scream, echoing against the heavy, dusty air.

I spun, face going cold. It was Newt.

CHAPTER

27

PANIC FROZE ME AS NEWT SHOUTED CURSES AT THE FLEEING SHAPE of Adagio, his craggy silhouette a darker slash against the sunset-gloomed red sky. The ley line was right there. All I had to do was back into it and will myself across. *Elyse,* I thought as Newt howled in anger, a sparking glow rising from her when she drew heavily on that very same line. My resolve strengthened. In the past, surviving had taken everything I had. I would not allow it to take everything my friends had, and damn it, even if Elyse wasn't my friend, she had trusted me.

I wouldn't abandon her. *If it's the last thing I do,* I thought, hoping it wasn't a prediction as I fingered *Quaere.*

Exhaling, I centered my thoughts into the same ley line Newt was drawing on. Energy roared in and Newt spun as she felt it, her dark eyes wide when she saw I was still here and hadn't fled. A quiver of angst rocked me; I was standing up to Newt.

"You. Stay," she intoned. "I'll deal with you in a moment."

I took a breath to answer her, gasping when the ley line suddenly grew slippery. It was the same curse she had used on me before, and I gathered it to me, completely oblivious to the second spell barreling at me. Too late I saw the arc of black and red, and her spell struck, knocking me to my knees as it crawled over me, seeking a way past my aura. My breath froze in my lungs, knees pained on the cold red soil. Tighter, her grip wound, black bands crushing as I scrambled to maintain my hold on the ley line to break her spell, but it was as if it was made of sand.

"*Ad coelum!*" Newt shouted, her back to me and her arms out as energy ripped from her into the sky, where it exploded into an aurora borealis of red and gold to rival the sun. Spinning madly, the spell whirled the dust into a sparkling tornado about Adagio to bring him down.

I struggled to get free, but the more energy I drew in to break her spell, the more her spell crushed my lungs—until I finally figured it out and let go of the line.

With a ping, her spell broke.

I looked up, gasping for air when Adagio hit the ground with an earth-shattering thump, his chin plowing a furrow as he scraped to a halt before Newt.

The whirlwind dissipated and I stood, shaking as my eyes went from the dusty, disheveled gargoyle to the handful of surface demons scattering. I hadn't even known they were there, their auras ragged as they ran for cover. They didn't go nearly far enough, and even as I watched, they began creeping back like coyotes searching for scraps.

"Adagio," I whispered. Newt stood before him, hands on her hips as she stared up at his massive strength—an ant before a monster.

"You freed her?" she shouted, furious, and the enormous being clamped his wings about himself as if embarrassed.

"She found her own way out," he muttered, voice rumbling like distant thunder as he stared into the middle distance and lied.

I followed his gaze to the nearby line. He was telling me to leave, but I couldn't. I wouldn't abandon Elyse. I had to outsmart Newt, and my grip on *Quaere* tightened as my attention flicked from her to a surface demon, scuttling from rock to rock—ever closer.

"That works," I whispered, then used the transposition stone to make one look like me. Quickly I overlaid the image of myself into one of them. It might give me the instant of distraction I needed, and as the remaining surface demons began to stalk the disguised one, I fell into a hunch and scuffed closer to Newt.

Adagio pinned his ears, not at Newt still yelling at him, but at me as I began to use *Quaere* to scrape a circle, wide and perfect, around them both. It was a stupid idea, but it was the only one I had. I couldn't hold Newt in a circle. But maybe one drawn by *Quaere* could.

Until she spun on her heel, robes furling as she turned.

"And you!" she shouted, and I froze, breath held as she blipped right over me, her attention going to the disguised surface demon. "*Implicare*," she intoned, and the surface demon howled as a black mist tangled about its feet and sent it down.

Crap on toast, she was moving, and I skittered out of her way, my circle only half drawn as she stopped before the thrashing surface demon. Adagio clearly knew who I was, the gargoyle carefully stepping out of the circle as I finished scraping it. Only trouble was, Newt wasn't in it, either.

"You slipped my snare," Newt said, clearly thinking she was talking to me as Adagio vanished, the large gargoyle using the ley line to make his getaway. "And my oubliette," Newt continued, four steps from backing into my trap. "Perhaps you have some worth after all."

The surface demon writhed, puffs of red dust rising where it scraped and pawed to escape—and Newt frowned, the first inklings that something might be off pinching her brow. I stood with my larger circle between us, shaking. Once she figured it out, I'd have a split second to invoke it and snare her. I wouldn't have even that if she didn't walk into the circle.

"Still silent? That's a nice change." Newt shifted uneasily. "Elyse Embers can't keep her mouth shut to save her life. Literally. Don't you worry, I will have her soul by sundown. She as good as gave it to me."

I licked my lips, hands shaking. "You will *not* have Elyse," I whispered.

Newt spun comically fast, a hand going to her flat-topped hat to keep it on. "You . . ." she stammered, black eyes shifting from the captured demon to me. And then her expression went virulent with anger, settling on the stone about my neck. Clearly she was seeing through the glamour. Al had said it wasn't foolproof.

"*Accipe hoc!*" she shouted, and the demon within her circle curled up, screeching as a haze spun it into a fist-size nothing and it vanished. "I will not be made a fool!" she shouted, and I quailed, backing up a step as she pulled on the line and my skin prickled. She was moving. Crap on toast, I had one shot at this.

"*Rhombus!*" I exclaimed as she crossed the scraped line, and Newt jerked to a halt, mouth open in utter shock when the circle invoked, carrying not just my aura but Al's, thanks to his knife having drawn it.

I flinched as Newt flung a surge of line energy at the circle—but it held. Al wasn't stronger than her. And the Goddess knew I wasn't. But Al had made *Quaere*, and I had used it to circle Newt. It would hold.

For a time.

"No one circles me!" Newt strode across the wide circle, halting when a black haze formed between us, the power of the circle condensing where she stood. "I will kill you a hundred times over for this!" Fist hazed with darkness, she struck the glittering barrier, only to be thrown back in a flutter of robes. Grunting, she planted a side kick on it, getting the same results. Frustrated, she howled at the sky . . . then threw her hat at me.

The hat, oddly enough, passed through, and Newt choked, almost choleric.

"What are you?!" the stymied demon shrieked, and I shifted uneasily.

"Lucky," I whispered, and Newt went utterly calm. It was worse than her ravings, and I stifled another shiver. "I'm sorry. I didn't want to circle you, but you won't listen. I am not a familiar and neither is Elyse. I already bought free passage for me and Elyse from you with a taste of my blood. Make good on that, and I'll let you go."

The barrier hummed between us as Newt's gaze dropped to *Quaere* in my frightened grip. "You are sorry?" Stymied, she retreated until the circle quit the annoying whine. "Gally's knife answers to you? Did you kill him?"

I shook my head. *My God. Had I actually circled her?* "No, but by my reckoning, I'm about ready to circle his ass and send him home, so let's make this quick. You have things to do. Like lock him up for uncommon stupidity so he leaves me alone."

Newt cocked her hip, her androgynous features sliding to the feminine. "More riddles," she muttered, then slowly pushed her fist into the barrier, pulling away when smoke began to rise from her knuckles. "Free passage, you say? Is that what we agreed upon?"

My lip twitched. "For both Elyse and myself. No reprisals."

Newt mockingly lifted a single eyebrow. "Wouldn't you rather have the mirror?"

"I want Elyse!" I shouted, my voice coming back hard from the surrounding rock and dirt. "And free passage. And her soul if you tricked her out of it!"

"That's three things." Newt hesitated, thinking. "Elyse Embers is not an option. So you get nothing. Further, if you won't be tamed, you will be killed."

My breath came fast as the demon again pushed a fist into the circle. Smut swirled from the surface to her point of contact, thinning the circle but for where she touched it. Oh, God, it wasn't going to hold, and I retreated, my gaze going to the blade in my grip as it began to warm, and heat . . . and burn.

I dropped it, yelping as my fingers flashed into pain.

Immediately my head snapped up. I had made a mistake.

Newt crowed in success as the circle dropped.

"No!" I exclaimed, scrambling for the ley line—just as the insane demon crashed into me.

"Thief!" Newt shouted as we went down, her atop me. "That curse is mine!" she exclaimed, and I gripped the glamour spell as she tried to pry it from my grip. "How did you prime it to you? Let go. It's mine!"

Raw energy poured into me as she dug at my fingers, and I gritted my teeth, my hold on the stone tightening when I funneled her raw torrent of burning energy into the earth. "No . . ." I ground out. I couldn't get rid of it fast enough. And then I gasped, back arching when Newt doubled the force. Pain raked my mind, became my entire world.

"This is mine!" Newt shouted again, black eyes wrathful as she pulled my closed fist to her. "How did you get it?!"

"Al!" I cried to make the pain go away, my voice echoing in the dark. "Al gave it to me. He helped me b-bind to it!" I stuttered, just wanting the pain to stop.

"How did you get out of my oubliette?" the crazed demon demanded. "Was it Adagio? Tell me, or I will burn you past all mending!"

My pulse hammered as I struggled not to answer. "Off!" I exclaimed, feeling my will splinter as the agony mounted. *"Ta na shay, sisto activitatem!"*

Newt howled, her hands springing from my neck as the Goddess's magic arched through her. I bucked her off, hand to my throat as I spun into a crouch and stood, shaking. Spent magic hung between us, sparking as it sifted into the ground.

"Elyse," I rasped, shocked by my ragged voice. "Give her up, or this starts again."

Newt's black eyes narrowed on me. "You won't survive a second time."

"Stop!" came a faint voice, and we both started. It was Elyse, the young woman running toward us, the robes Newt had dressed her in fluttering blackly in the moonlight. She had my shoulder bag over her arm, and I stiffened. Adagio was behind her, his wings clamped in misery as he waited for his punishment for jumping her here.

"Newt, she won! She won!" Elyse exclaimed, her color high as she slid to a halt between us, my shoulder bag slipping from her. "We made a bet."

A bet? I thought, then ducked, yanking on the ley line when Newt's energy sizzled past my head.

"Which you lost." Newt's gaze went from one to the other as if deciding whom to pin first. "Adagio, you will starve for this."

"You made a bet with the coven leader," the gargoyle rasped, looking embarrassed. "It stands. Let the world breaker's sword go. Elyse Embers got the best of you."

Elyse? I thought, taking in the frightened woman's shaky confidence even as she backed up into his protection, my bag clutched to her chest. *What did you give her, Elyse?* I wondered, worried that she'd done something that would haunt her forever.

"We made a bet," Elyse said again, to make Newt grimace. "Now hold to it. Rachel escaped your snare; she goes free. She came for me; I go free. It's done."

I scooped up *Quaere*, uneasy. I was between the ley line and Elyse. To make a move toward one might result in losing the other. "You made a bet?" I questioned, and Newt dropped her head and beat the dust from her robe, her bad mood worsening.

Nodding, Elyse carefully inched toward me. "I did." Her gaze shifted. "You might break your word with her, but I am a coven member, and you will hold to it with me!" she shouted at Newt.

The insane demon fumed, her robe hem shaking and her bare feet red from the dust that was all that was left of the ever-after paradise. "I call foul. You used an elven spell," she spat, though I knew for a fact that she alone among the demons still tinkered with elven magic. "You broke my oubliette!" she added, her steps forward faltering when Adagio rumbled like an elephant, warning her. "That rubs out anything that scrawny coven member might gain."

"*Rhombus!*" I shouted, but Newt brushed my undrawn circle aside as if it never existed, grasping my robe front and dragging me forward as Elyse shouted a protest.

"How did you get out!" Newt raved, and I struggled, my hand atop Elyse's as we both pried at her grip on me.

"*Quaere!*" I said, my hands tingling as I dug at her fingers. "I used *Quaere*. Let me go or I'll stick you with it!"

"Stop!" Elyse shouted, frustration coloring her angry stance. "Both of you. We made a bet, Newt. She got free and she came for me. Now go away! Now!"

I gasped as Newt's grip vanished. Shaking, the demon stared at us, wrathful and angry with little sparks of energy moving like rills over her. Behind Newt, Adagio was gesturing at the ley line as if wanting us to make a dash for it. One of us might make it. Beside me, Elyse stood, elated that she may well have gained our freedom. And wary. And sore. And beat up. Actually, she looked like I felt. *Newt gave her slippers?*

"She circled you when she could have run," Elyse said, actually shifting to stand in front of me as if in protection, though I was the one with the magic dagger spitting sparks. "She circled you with the intent to force you to let me go. We made a bet, and bets made under the full moon cannot be broken."

Newt's expression was sour. "It's not a full moon."

"It is where I come from," Elyse said, throwing the agitated demon another curve. "She gets her freedom if she finds a way out of her oubliette, and I get my freedom if she comes for me." Elyse focused on the demon. "Well, she didn't abandon me, Newt. She circled you. Demanded you free me. You lose."

I wanted my bag, but didn't dare reach for it. "The circle didn't hold. I never got her to free you," I said, and Elyse smirked.

"Yeah. I figured you might not best her, so the bet was to try, not succeed."

I felt myself quail when Newt turned those black eyes to me, glinting in the moonlight. "And if I didn't?" I asked.

Elyse shrugged. "You die in the oubliette and she gets my soul," she said, and then louder, "but that's not what happened, so leave! I beat you at your own game, demon."

Newt seemed to shake where she stood. And then, without a single word, she vanished, red dust swirling in to replace where she had been.

I exhaled as the dust settled, and my grip on *Quaere* finally eased. Dirt stained my fingers red as I studied it, shoulders slumping. Maybe someday I'd figure out how to put the thing away.

"My God," Elyse said as she came forward and handed me my bag. It was heavy, and I looked to see not only my book in there but the one she'd stolen from Trent, too. "Rachel, thank you. I never want to do that again. I can't believe you got us free."

The night was empty. All we had to do was walk to the line. Even Adagio had vanished. "I didn't make her hold to our deal. You did," I said as I slung my bag over my shoulder. It felt good there, and I finally began to think we might have done it. "How badly did she singe you?"

"She didn't."

I stared at Elyse, shocked. "How—" I started, and the young woman smirked.

"I said I'd be her willing slave if she wouldn't hurt me. But she'd have to win a bet first."

I closed my mouth, more than a little impressed. "Damn, girl. That was a good deal."

Elyse's smile faltered. "Thanks, but I don't think she would have agreed to it if she had thought she'd have to live up to it. You got out of the oubliette. No one has ever done that."

Go away, I thought at the dagger, shocked when it actually vanished. "Well, don't sell yourself short." I hiked my bag higher. "If you hadn't made that bet, she would have snared me as soon as she broke my circle." I squinted at the moon, placing myself. "You saved both of us. I thought I had this, and I didn't. Thank you."

Smirking, Elyse linked an arm in mine, shocking the peas out of me. "Biting off more than you can chew shouldn't be a reason for a lifetime of servitude."

"You say that now." I glanced over my shoulder before I started forward, squinting in the dark and the gritty wind. "You could have lost everything."

Her arm slipped from me. "Yeah, well, I thought it was a good bet. You said you wouldn't leave me, and you didn't." She dropped her head, focused on the slippers Newt had put her in, the red dust looking black in the dim light. "Hey, about the mirror . . ."

"I don't want to talk about it." Good feeling gone, I stomped to the ley line. I wasn't familiar with this one and had no idea where it was going to come out in reality. It didn't exist in the future, meaning it had been made by a demon long dead, the line lost when the ever-after collapsed and was never reinstated.

"Then let's talk about Vivian," she said, and my lips parted in surprise. "I know now why she trusted you."

Her cheeks were flushed, and mistrusting this, I eyed her. "Yeah?"

"Rachel, you are a good person."

My breath left me in a sigh. Crap on toast, I was tired. "Good never got anyone anywhere."

"When we get home, I won't be advocating that you be sent to Alcatraz."

"Yeah, you said that before," I muttered.

"The mirror wasn't the problem," she said, her young face and authentic demon robes making her seem naive. "Brad's curse wasn't the issue."

"Again, really bad timing on your part," I grumped as I stomped forward.

Elyse pulled me to a halt, mere steps from the ley line glowing in the dark, little trills of energy hissing about. "Will you listen? I'm going to make the argument to the coven that you cursed Brad by accident as you claim. God knows that you went to every length possible to secure his cure. You tried, Rachel, more than anyone has a right to expect."

My stomach hurt. I couldn't remember the last time I ate. "Okay. Great. But your threat of Alcatraz is not why I'm here. I need to uncurse Brad, and as much as I appreciate your trust, the rest of your club is convinced I'm demon slime."

"Perhaps, but it takes a unanimous vote to put someone into Alcatraz."

I laughed bitterly and started for the ley line. "Right. If you go to them with that, they will kick you out and replace you with someone who will vote the way they want." Mother pus bucket. Elyse trusted me, and I was still going to end up hiding in the ever-after. I knew it.

Elyse frowned as she followed. "They wouldn't dare."

"Don't be so sure." I stepped into the line, shivering at the sudden rush. I was ticked at her, at Newt, at the world. "I'm sorry about everything. I really thought I could outwit Newt."

"Rachel . . ." Elyse's eyes pinched in heartache as she stepped in beside me, shuddering when she found her place in the energy flow. "Brad's curse was an accident. You tried to make amends. Don't do it again. I'm not going to force you into anything."

"That simple, eh?" Hesitating, I immersed myself in the ley line and matched my aura to it. With a roaring rush, the energy stretching between our world and the ever-after ripped through me. Past the white noise, a chime rose, pure and heartrending. It was a reflection of the soul of whatever demon had made it, and this, more than anything else, was why I worked so damned hard to bring them back to reality. They *did* evil, but they were *not* evil. They were angry and had been for a very long time. So long that they thought that's all they were.

But I knew better.

My heart beat once, and I let go of the half-twist I'd put my aura in, stumbling as the ley line spat me out. The influx of energy vanished into memory, replaced by the shushing of distant traffic and the scent of wet cement. *Downtown,* I mused as I peered out of the alley, placing myself. The street was empty. It was too late for the light-challenged night walkers to be out, and too early for the human rush hour.

Too bad this line doesn't exist anymore, I thought, giving Elyse a sidelong glance as she stepped from the ribbonlike haze of energy. Exhaling loudly, she gazed up at the tall black buildings to either side of us. Immediately she took her hat off and reached to unfasten her robe. It was a good idea. We already smelled like demons. No need to look like them.

"Vivian tried to tell me, but I didn't believe her," Elyse said softly.

"Tell you what?" I asked. The head of the coven appeared as tired as I felt, her hair mussed and the slippers Newt had put her in now red with ever-after dust. And still, success gave her cheeks some color and her eyes a bright shine. She had escaped a demon without so much as a sensory burn. I knew the feeling of exhausted exhilaration; I just didn't care anymore.

"That for all the trouble you cause and are mixed up in, the world is better with you in it."

I laughed at that. "Okay. Now you're just sucking up. I'm not going to leave you here to take the long way home. Relax."

"I'm serious," she said as she shook out her robe and we both cringed, holding our breath at the billow of dust. "I had no idea that the elves had to modify their children's DNA to such an extent for them to simply survive.

Kalamack's labs alone . . ." She hesitated, thinking. "The scope of Kalamack's illegal genetic medicines is downright scary. No wonder he was trying to take over the world. He needed a country's economy to just keep them alive."

I reached for the hem of her robe and together we folded it. Trent had been a different person since I brought back a clean, pre-curse DNA sample to pattern a final cure upon. People changed when you took away their fear. "The elves are still trying to take over the world," I said as we made a neat package of her robe.

"Sure, but the desperation is gone." Elyse took the rolled-up robe and stuffed it into her hat. "The farther in the past their fears are, the less inclined they will be to make trouble. And then the demons . . ."

My motion to take off my robe fumbled. *The demons.*

"I still don't like that they can come to reality whenever they feel like it," Elyse said. "But you did get them to play by our rules. Sort of. This madness that's going on now . . ."

I shook out my robe and Elyse snagged the bottom hem. "That took a few times before it stuck," I said, remembering.

"Even I can tell that they aren't as angry. I mean, in the future. To be forced underground to avoid your war waste." Elyse's expression emptied as we folded my robe. "Don't tell anyone I said so, but you did a good thing there. They seem to be healing." She hesitated. "Any chance you can get the curse lifted that prevents witches from—"

"No." I took the stinky silk from her grip and rolled it up. The everafter was for the demons until they opened the doors themselves. "And don't kid yourself. You still can't trust them."

"Perhaps." Elyse watched me stuff our robes, hats, and sashes into my bag to take to Sylvia, a half smile on her, content, tired, and satisfied. Sylvia was going to walk away with a net gain of one robe, seeing as Elyse's original robe was still in my bag, all of them now reeking of demons. "But I can trust you. Maybe if I'd trusted Vivian more, we wouldn't be here now." Her gaze went to the empty street at the end of the alley. "I am so hungry, I could eat three Burger Daddies."

I had no clue what a Burger Daddy was, but I was totally on board. "I've been thinking. Leaving a drawer empty at the morgue might not be a good idea. I want to move Kisten into it when we move John out. Exchange their appearances so it looks like nothing has changed. We can drop the robes off at Other Earthlings on the way." I squinted at the end of the alley. "These things stink. Sylvia will be thrilled. If we're going to move Kisten, we should do that right after we shower. It's going to be sunrise soon."

I took a step forward, and Elyse was quick to meet me, step for step. "Rachel, you can't help him. The spell doesn't bring him back to life. All you'd have is a ghost."

My chest hurt, and anger flashed through me. "A vampire ghost can hold the city while I go into hiding. Keep Constance safe. I promised to keep her safe."

"I'm not pursuing that anymore. You don't—"

I jerked to a halt. "Look. You might think you're the leader of the coven, but a vote put you there. Another can take you out." She started to speak, and I held up a hand for her to wait. "They can and will replace you with someone who votes the way they want. I have no mirror to uncurse Brad. I will have to go into hiding. The least you can do is help me get my house in order before I leave. I risked both our lives to get that stinking stasis charm from Trent's to get you home. You said you'd help me get a replacement body. So help me get a body."

Yes, we had the charm, but it wasn't reinvoked yet. She still needed me.

Knowing it, she twisted her expression up in distaste. Five feet past the alley, cars whooshed and people hurried to their jobs in the predawn light. Her gaze flicked to my pocket where Trent's stolen amulet lay, then up to the stone pendant about my neck. "I said I'd help you and I will," she said, and I let out a breath I hadn't realized I was holding. "But I want to see how you rekindle that ley line charm."

"Sure. Why not?" I said, and together we stepped out into the world, red dust on the soles of our feet, and reeking of demons.

CHAPTER

28

"IS HE COVERED?" THE STREETS HAD GOTTEN BUSY IN THE PREDAWN glow. Anxious, I sat up straight, one hand on the wheel as I looked behind us to make sure we weren't being followed.

Elyse half turned to stretch into the narrow back seat of the maintenance truck we'd found in a weedy lot of a car dealership. Her hair was still damp from her shower, as was mine, but hers wouldn't dry frizzy, and I stifled a surge of envy. Changing vehicles had seemed like a good idea, and the blue flatbed smelled like boat gas and the lingering aroma of burnt amber from our clothes. The tags were two years out-of-date and the bed itself was rusted through in spots. The second-row seating was torn from the Turn knew what. Probably the dented, empty toolbox we'd found there.

Clearly the vehicle wasn't on anyone's radar. Which was why I had said nothing when Elyse had magically hot-wired the thing after I reset the plugs and knocked the dust from the air filter. Getting Kisten into one of the library's wheelchairs and then the elevator had been an adventure all on its own. He was now lengthwise on the rear bench seat, but the wheelchair was sliding around in the bed.

We were almost to the morgue, and my death grip on the wheel was only now beginning to ease. Worried the truck would crap out on us, I'd taken the longer way that took us past several emergency shelters. I had wanted Kisten no more than a ten-minute walk from six feet under.

"He's fine," she said, even as she tugged the brilliant blue tarp over him more securely. "The expressway would have gotten us here in like five minutes."

"I know."

We had forty minutes until sunrise, and it still felt as if we were pushing it. Tension ached through my shoulders and neck when I pulled into the morgue's lot and took one of the spots closest to the door. It was a rear entrance, and an eerie feeling of déjà vu trickled through me when I turned the key and the engine died with a choking cough. Two years divided this moment from when Ivy and I had brought in Brice, but it felt like less than a week for me.

Exhaling, I sat for a moment, hands on the wheel. So far, all I'd done was take Kisten for a little drive. Stealing a body, cremating it . . .

The things I do for Cincy, I thought, head down as I pulled my shoulder bag closer and shuffled past the robes stinking of burnt amber to find the defunct stasis curse and put it in my pocket beside my last forget potion. The bag stank; I could not take it downstairs, and I reluctantly stuffed it under the seat before getting out.

I snapped the chair open with a hard-won practice, the sound of the frame securing in place tingling through me with the memory of helplessness and vulnerability. I wasn't that person anymore. I wouldn't be that person ever again. And yet my jaw clenched in a remembered frustration as I pushed the chair to the truck's back door and locked the wheels.

Elyse had gotten out, her brow furrowed as she scanned the lot, gaze lingering on the camera above the entrance. "You're just going to walk in with him?"

I put Kisten's feet on the floor, groaning as I pulled him upright. *I'm sorry, Kisten.* "Pretty much," I said, then blew the hair from my eyes. "I could use some help."

Elyse nervously inched closer, her hesitant grip growing stronger when we took his weight and half slid, half carried him to fall into the waiting chair.

Hard part over, I thought, glad no one was back here. The black sky was brightening, and I quickly got his feet on the footrests and ran the strap around his waist.

"Could you get the door?" I asked, and Elyse shut first his, then my door before quickly jogging to the building. Elyse probably wasn't on the hot sheets for breaking out of I.S. holding anymore, but Scott might still be searching for her. And I, of course, was a known entity. Neither of us was in any sort of disguise, other than our general lack of usual style, and Elyse kept her head down to avoid the cameras.

Still crouched before Kisten, I put my forehead against his knees. I loved Trent, loved him to the ends of two realities. But I would do anything to see Kisten's smile one more time. He wasn't dead twice yet, fighting for his undead existence.

I stood, unlocked the chair, and began pushing it over the uneven pavement. Kisten's hands looked uncomfortable and unnatural on his lap, but Elyse was waiting at the door, so I ran Kisten up the ramp, the rhythmic bumps easing into a soft rumble as we found the tiled floor inside.

"Morgue is downstairs," I said as I angled her to the elevators. Which in hindsight was a stupid thing to say. I wasn't nervous. Or maybe I was, seeing as I was about to steal a body with the head of the coven.

"No door attendant?" Elyse said softly from my elbow. "That seems sloppy."

"Far end of the lobby," I said, nodding to the woman staring at us from behind an outdated computer. She reached for a phone, and I shook my head, one hand leaving the chair grips to make the gesture I'd seen Ivy give the night guard.

Sure enough, her face paled and her reach pulled back. I exhaled, relieved. She thought I was on the city's business. If I had my days right, Piscary had just bought the farm, a fact that wouldn't come out for a few days. I was currently in a magic-induced coma battling a Were curse. Again, something hidden from the press. It was a golden span where I could walk the city as a ghost, my alibi absolute.

"Shouldn't we . . ." Elyse said as she walked beside me.

She was staring at the stone around my neck and I shook my head.

"Believe it or not, I'll get farther as me. I was here a few days ago with the FIB looking at some Jane Wolfs."

Her eyebrows rose. "The ones your alpha killed."

Clearly she'd done her homework. "He didn't kill them." I scuffed to a halt before the shiny doors and hit the call button hard. The woman at the desk was watching us, that frown of hers making me wonder if she had recognized Kisten. "No one knew it was possible to turn a human into a Were. They committed suicide."

"Sure, who wouldn't," she muttered. "Can you imagine suddenly turning into a wolf when you weren't biologically designed to?"

The cheerful ding startled me. "It was an accident." Head down, I pushed Kisten in, then swung him around to face the front. Elyse had already hit the button for the morgue, and I stood there, arms over my chest, not happy at the reminder. I still felt bad about it. I was the one who had given David the focus to hold on to. But if I felt bad, David had been devastated.

"You might want to fill your chi," I said, glad that Newt hadn't so much as singed her. "It's too deep for a ley line."

"Slick is up top," she said, and I bobbed my head, pulling heavily on the line until the lift dropped too deep and I lost it. I was at a disadvantage. Kisten, though, was safe underground, and I clenched the chair harder to hide my trembling fingers.

Elyse glanced at me. "You okay? You look a little rough."

Her eyes were on my death grip, and I forced myself to relax. "I loved him once," I explained. "He deserves better than this." *God, Kisten. I am so sorry.*

The elevator dinged and the doors opened, cutting our conversation off. Her expression closed, Elyse strode out into the bland hallway, glancing both ways before following the blue arrow and the faint scent of pine disinfectant. "We could have left him at the library," she said, pace slowing to let me go first as we passed a gurney taking up half the hallway.

"I don't want to leave an empty drawer. And besides, the library is open. Someone might come down and find him. He'll be safer here."

KIM HARRISON

KIM HARRISON

"Fair enough." Elyse made fists of her hands and then shook her fingers out. "How do you want to play this?"

Did she just ask for my opinion? "Ah, you have access to a line, but Iceman knows me. We go in. Confirm there's a John Doe Vamp here. Then knock Iceman out."

"Can do." Her hands flexed in anticipation as we wove our way past abandoned gurneys and wheelchairs to a set of battered double doors. The sign over them proudly proclaimed, CINCINNATI MORGUE, AN EQUAL OPPORTUNITY SERVICE SINCE 1966.

Be right back, love, I thought as I left Kisten parked in the hall. Jaw tight, I stiff-armed the door open and walked in, Elyse trailing behind. I had no building ID. Not even a fifty to bribe him. *Piece of cake.*

"Yo, Iceman!" I said boldly, scaring the college-age kid behind the metal desk.

"Holy shit, Rachel!" the blond man said as he yanked his feet from the desk and sat up. His handheld game nearly hit the scratched-tile floor, and he exhaled, blowing his bangs from his eyes when he caught it. "You almost gave me a heart attack." His gaze went to my lack of a building ID, then to Elyse. "Ah, you know I can't let you in there without an official presence."

Behind me, Elyse took a breath to be "official."

"That's okay." I bumped her shoulder, immediately rocking away from her. The woman was practically sparking with line energy. "I'm here to get some info for Glenn."

Iceman's dented rolling chair squeaked as he leaned back. "Why didn't he call?"

I shrugged, looking over the small outer lobby/check-in area with the cluttered desk taking up one side, rows of ancient cabinets the other, and enough space in between to handle maybe five gurneys if everyone was friendly. The fourth wall was another set of those swinging double doors leading to the morgue itself. "Because the I.S. doesn't like the FIB checking up on their misfilings, so I was never here, okay?"

Grinning, Iceman laced his hands over his middle and reclined in his chair. His body language said it all. We weren't getting the drawer key. Not without the right bribes anyway—which we didn't have. "What do you need?"

Elyse beamed at him, playing the helpful assistant. "He wants to know if any John Doe Vamps came in since the Jane Doe Wolfs," she said, her high voice sounding out of place down here. "He's thinking there might be a cross-species connection."

"Oh!" Iceman sat up and pulled his chair to the desk. "Just Johnny."

My heart gave a pound. Dr. Ophees's failed charge. "Johnny? How can he have a name if he's a John Doe Vamp?"

"Because he's going to be here for a while and we're all friendly." Iceman smiled at Elyse, and the young woman's expression went stiff.

"You sure he's twice dead?" she asked. "Maybe he's an undead sneaking out for snacks."

Iceman laughed. "Pretty sure," he drawled, then hesitated, sniffing suspiciously. "Ophees brought him in after sunup, so even if he *had* been an undead, he's twice dead now. I doubt he has anything to do with the current Jane Wolfs. Johnny came in with no body trauma, clean apart from his blood." The man sniffed again. "As in he didn't have any. No blood, no aura, no chance. Do you smell something burning?"

I glanced at Elyse, glad now I'd left my bag in the truck. We'd done the best we could to clean up, but the scent of burnt amber sort of stuck to a person. "Keep it quiet," I cautioned as I felt her pull in even more ley line energy through her familiar.

"Oh, I can be subtle," she said as she sashayed to the desk.

Iceman blinked, the man clearly oblivious as she smiled and put her palms on the desk. A whispered something passed her lips, and then she blew a haze of aura-tainted magic at him.

The guy didn't have a chance. His eyes rolled to the back of his head, and he slumped where he sat, hands hanging slack.

"Whoo!" she exclaimed, beaming. "That felt good! He'll wake up in about twenty minutes thinking he dozed off. He won't even remember us."

Which meant it wasn't just a sleepy-time charm but one affecting memory as well.

"I know what you're thinking." Elyse tugging at Iceman until she had his head resting on his arm lying across the desk. "It doesn't erase what happened. It simply prevents recollections from moving into long-term memory."

"Same difference," I muttered, tired of the double standard. Like I would *ever* work for them. If I was going to bend the law, I'd pay for it like everyone else. Was paying for it. *Wake up, Rachel. Take the easy way out for once.*

Elyse flushed, her pride taking a hit. "What, you want me to wake him up?" she said as I went to get Kisten from the hall.

"No," I said lightly. She was ransacking the desk when I came back in, and I cleared my throat. "Morgue key is on the Bite-Me-Betty doll."

"You're joking." Expression dubious, she looked at the naked doll hanging from a nail in the wall, finally using two fingers to retrieve it.

I backed Kisten through the swinging doors so I wouldn't have to knock them open with his footrest, and Elyse followed me in, slowing as she studied the two walls of drawers, each four rows high stretching the length of the long room. At the far end, a comfortable arrangement of chairs and a coffee table sat for anxious relatives waiting for their dead to arise. The morgue was for self-repair and the truly dead only, vampires on one side, humans and the rest on the other, though I had been assured every drawer had an interior release mechanism.

"They usually keep the unclaimed at the end," I said, glancing at the names on the drawers and wincing at the three onetime Jane Wolfs now sporting their real names. It seemed odd that I'd been here just a few days ago, though it had been two years.

"I've never seen a waiting room in a morgue." Arms over her middle, Elyse lingered by the doors to keep watch on the outer lobby.

"Key?" I asked, and she tossed it to me, the naked plastic doll landing hard in my hand. Leaving Kisten parked, I began searching. "The morgue has been here a long time," I said softly. There was a reason Cincinnati had once been known for its grave robbing, and it had nothing to do with providing the schools up north with cadavers. Our Inderland population had always been high.

"Where's the furnace?" she asked, and I glanced up at her uncomfortable tone.

"Through there," I said, and her attention followed mine to the heavy metal door tucked almost out of sight at the end of the long room. My foreboding swelled when she went to pull on the handle and it clunked against the lock. "The door code is 45202," I said, and I heard her sigh as she began to punch numbers. "Found Johnny," I added as I reached the last drawer.

The rhythmic beeps of the door lock were loud as I unlocked Johnny's drawer and pulled it open. Johnny was older, brow creased and crows' feet about his eyes. It seemed likely that once he lost his youth, his master had gotten tired of him and decided to move on. He'd been drained too far and then killed a second time, circumventing the promise to become an undead. Perhaps it had been a blessing. He might not have had the social structure to maintain his undead existence.

"I'm sorry," I said, thinking vampire mores sucked.

"Good God. It's really old. Are you sure it still works?" echoed out from the furnace room, and my jaw clenched.

"Yes!" It worked, leaving no digital record, no image capture. *Thank you,* I thought as I took in the young man's torn neck and bloodless pallor. *Thank you for helping me save the man I once loved.* "You think you could give me a hand here?"

"Sure." Leaving the door open, she sauntered out. "Mmmm," she added, brow furrowed as she took up his death chart. "Ophees was right. He's scheduled for four weeks of storage to allow for identification before being disposed of. The I.S. has zero information on him. Looks like he's a D2. Drained and dumped."

Irritation sparked. "You could have a little compassion," I said, and her gaze shot to mine. "Sure, his master treated him like a chunk of meat, but someone loved him."

Elyse scowled, clearly annoyed. "You want to stop? This was your idea."

"No," I said immediately. "He is one of the lost. But living vamps stick together in the face of the abuse they put up with, and I know to the bottom of my soul that Johnny would go along with this if only to make things better for his surviving kin." I fought the urge to smooth out a forehead wrinkle. "And this will make things better."

Elyse was silent. "So . . . Johnny in the wheelchair, and Kisten in the drawer? I'll get Kisten."

Depressed, I tucked Johnny's modesty sheet around him as Elyse trundled Kisten closer. I wasn't sure whom to move first, but Elyse went right for Johnny's shoulders, waiting until I took his feet and together we lifted him up and out to set him gently on the floor. *I am so sorry . . .*

"You want to unstrap him?" Elyse suggested, and I fumbled for Kisten's waist belt.

I am putting Kisten into a morgue drawer . . .

The reality of that hit me hard, and my hands shook as I grasped his feet, struggling to lift his weight.

Kisten took a breath as his body came to rest, and I almost lost it.

"Ah, Rachel?"

"I'm fine," I said, jaw clenched. He was in a morgue drawer, and my heart was breaking. "Let's get Johnny in the chair."

I sort of blanked out the next few minutes. Fortunately we didn't have to change their clothes as the glamour charm would do that for us, but I did take Kisten's shoes off so I could put Johnny's toe tag on him. Even so, a rigorous inspection would see through the deception. Good thing that wasn't in anyone's playbook down here. As I did the charm twice to exchange their images, I couldn't help but wonder if Elyse was helping me with the intent to bring me to trial for everything we were doing once she got home. The leader of the coven of moral and ethical standards could not be known for stealing trucks, moving bodies, or knocking out city workers.

But if I believed that, I was screwed twice to the wall.

"Well?" I said, gut tight as she strapped Johnny into the chair and arranged his bare feet on the footrests. I thought about putting Kisten's shoes on him, then stuffed the flat boat shoes into my shoulder bag instead. He still looked the same to me, but Elyse bobbed her head, her obvious satisfaction convincing me the switch had been made.

"It would fool me," she said, her gaze fixed on Kisten. "Damn, I can't tell, and I know it's fake."

My hand was on the drawer, but I couldn't seem to shut it. He looked like Johnny, the deception furthered by the toe tag now dangling from his foot. As a John Doe Vamp, he'd be safe here. *I will be back for you, Kisten.* Throat tight, I closed the drawer, tensing at the loud snap.

"Great. Let's get him to the boat," Elyse said, her mood clearly good as we ticked one more thing off my list before I took her home. "Kisten's aura looks great, by the way."

"Swell." Head down, I pushed Johnny into the lobby. Iceman was still out cold when I hung the doll on the nail behind the desk. The numbers on the wall clock had gone red, meaning the sun was up. Johnny wouldn't care. He was already dead twice.

Elyse got the door for me. Her silence remained intact as we found the elevator and she hit the button for the upper lobby. "This feels too easy," she said, and I unclenched my jaw.

I'm so sorry, I thought again as I glanced down at Johnny. *Thank you.* "Piscary has a history of leaving corpses," I said aloud as I watched the numbers count up. "The entire city is on edge with Al running around, breaking things to get me to come to him. No one cares about one dead vampire."

Elyse fidgeted, starting when the elevator dinged and the door opened. "I don't blame you for staying clear of Al. In this time, I mean," she said as she strode out. "You've got two demon marks, after all."

I glanced at my wrist, wheelchair bumping as I followed her. "He wants me to testify on his behalf, and I'm rightly afraid that it will end up with me as his familiar."

The lobby had gotten busy in the twenty minutes we'd been down there, and Elyse moved quickly to the door, ignoring everyone as if taking a corpse-white body out into the sun was an everyday occurrence. "But that's what happened, isn't it?" she asked. "You became his familiar?"

"Not exactly." Not surprisingly, the very thing that had freed Al from the accusation of uncommon stupidity had bound me even closer to him. He'd been forced to take me as his student, not his familiar. It was a claim that was still being played out even though my position as a witch-born demon was indisputable.

Elyse held the door for me, and I bumped over the sill, head coming up at the dawn-clean feel of cool air. My smile vanished.

"Son of a bitch," Elyse whispered, her gaze tracking mine to the truck. A huge crow stood on the tailgate, head bobbing and wings flashing open as it saw us. But it was the tall figure getting out of the adjacent rental car that had pulled us both to a stop.

Scott.

Crap on toast. My bag. If Scott has my phone . . . "I thought you told your crow to leave us alone," I said, disgusted as Scott pushed his hair from his eyes and squinted at us. His suit was a mess and he seemed tired. His phone was in his hand, and I could almost hear someone on it. It didn't see my bag anywhere and I hoped it was still under the truck's seat.

"Get Johnny in the truck," she muttered, feet shifting to find a secure stance. "I'll distract Scott. Don't wait for me. This is going to be fast."

I took a breath as I counted the steps to the truck. *You think?*

"Elyse?" the man said in wonder as he looked at his phone as if in betrayal. "How—"

I twitched, feeling it when she yanked on the nearest ley line. "Light footprint!" I cried out, but she was winding up hard. Her hair wild and her eyes alight, Elyse gestured a spell into existence, her aura flashing into the visible spectrum as Scott stared from her to his phone.

"Teneo!" she exclaimed, the single word of Latin exploding from her as an aura-tainted ball of energy hissed through the air to slam against Scott's hastily erected protection circle. Snapping and popping, little arcs of power skated over the man's circle, slowly dissipating.

Head down and skin tingling, I pushed Johnny down the ramp.

His jaw set, Scott stepped through his bubble of protection, oblivious to me. "Who the hell are you?" he exclaimed.

"*Crescit eundo!*" Elyse shouted, my pace bobbling when the pavement in front of Scott blew up as if a bomb had hit it.

Scott stumbled, safe under his protection circle as rock and asphalt rained down. Shielding Johnny the best I could, I ran for the truck.

Scott found his height, his face red in anger. "By the authority of the coven of—"

"*Crescit eundo!*" she exclaimed again, and I winced, skin tingling as the boom echoed between the buildings.

"Son of a—" Scott rolled, aura sparking as he came to a halt beside the dumpster. I wasn't too happy, either, as chunks of rock and pavement fell thumping around us. Elyse was clearly enjoying herself, her expression alight with the joy of rubbing out past slights. Faces were showing at a few windows. We had to get out of here. Now.

"Hurry up, witch!" she said, and Scott's gaze jerked to me. His brow furrowed as he realized she hadn't been trying to hit him, but only to distract him.

"Stop!" he shouted at me, then yelped, his half-formed curse falling back in on itself when the ground exploded again at his feet.

I was at the truck. Heart pounding, I locked the wheels. I itched to turn and fight. Elyse was yelling something, but I didn't dare look as I fumbled the door open. Crows were cawing, more than one diving down to distract Scott as I worked the lap belt free.

In a sparking-haired glory, Elyse stood just outside the building, her hands moving in sweeping gestures as she gathered power. Line energy dripped from her fingers, glowed from her limbs, her obvious passion of working magic making her almost unreal. I stifled a gasp when one of Scott's charms hit a crow . . . But it was only an illusion, and the black shadow exploded into a shower of sparks that hissed against the broken pavement. *There's only one crow . . .*

"Get in there," I muttered as I yanked Johnny's deadweight into the back of the truck.

"Hurry up!" Elyse shouted as she hustled down the stairs. Scott was picking off her illusions, but for each one he took out, two replaced it.

I scrambled in over Johnny and pulled him the rest of the way. Struggling, I lurched back out, shoved his legs in, and slammed the door. Behind me another spell-based boom rocked between the buildings, the tang of spent energy like tinfoil on my teeth.

This was as backward a run as I had ever been on. Jenks would laugh his lily-white ass off. Ivy would cringe at the lack of planning. Trent would . . .

I grimaced. Trent would do something drastic, like bring down a wall or wrap Scott in a twining, Goddess-born snake of destruction. And as I stood beside the driver's door, my fingers tingling with the strength of the line, I thought that fortunately for Scott, I wasn't Trent.

"*Quod periit, periit!*" I shouted, slipping my spell behind Scott's defenses when he dropped them to destroy another of Elyse's illusions. It was a joke curse, but Elyse was pinned down and we needed to get out of here.

Scott yelped as the spell struck him, the man freezing as he scrambled to figure out what he needed to counter. I yanked open the truck door, jumped in, and started it in an exploding thrum of old Detroit muscle. I shouldn't have worried about the truck. It was solid.

I put the truck in drive, arm reaching to make sure my bag was where I'd left it. It was. "Let's go!" I shouted through the open window to Elyse.

She bolted forward, looking back when Scott shrieked in terror as his hair cascaded from him in a dark wash. Eyes round, he stared at me, his arms hanging as if afraid to move.

Elyse vaulted into the truck bed and pounded the side. "Drive!"

Asphalt chips popped and flew as I hit the gas, tires slipping until they found good pavement. Sirens wailed in the distance, and I hunched low in the seat as I wove through the destruction. Chunks of asphalt lay everywhere, in the road, on dented roofs.

But as I glanced into the rearview mirror, I realized Scott was wreathed in a green glow—staring at us. My expression emptied.

"I've got this!" Elyse shouted as she knelt in the truck bed.

"No, no, no, no!" I shouted, then winced when she screamed something and the truck seemed to shiver. Power exploded from her palms, and

I yelped, hands clenched on the wheel when the truck was shoved forward. Through the mirror, I watched the buildings crack as a huge ball of force slammed into them, windows breaking and entire walls dented inward to show a perfect arc of a circle.

We bounced out onto the street. Behind us, Scott slowly got up, a hand to his head.

"I don't remember that happening two years ago!" I shouted over the wind. A sick feeling had settled in my gut to spin in mad circles.

Elyse dragged herself to the little window between us, one hand on the side of the truck, one hand supporting a cawing, excited crow. "Maybe they blame it on your demon," she said as she wedged herself by the window and tried to soothe the bird.

Maybe . . .

"Hey, ah, it's only twenty-five through here," she said, so I took my foot off the gas to slow down. Though to be honest, people weaving in and out like it was the Indy 500 was pretty normal for Cincy.

"Sorry." I flicked my gaze from her to the road and back again. She was tired but elated. Kind of like me when I had survived something stupid. *And this is better than Trent how?*

The sirens were two streets off, but they were also two streets too close, and I fumbled for Newt's charm. *A priori,* I thought, looking through the stone at a passing pickup truck, shiny in the early morning light. *A posterior,* I thought, scanning what I could of the truck we were in. Blowing through the hole, I felt ley line energy tingle through me as I finished the curse with a shaky *Omnia mutantur.*

Relief was heady when a haze of energy tingled over the truck and lifted my hair. The engine hiccuped, then roared on as we merged onto the expressway. I glanced behind us, breathing again at the absence of blue and gold lights.

That was close. Too close. *Ivy, I will never laugh at your plans again.*

"Who's a good crow? You are!" Elyse crooned as she soothed the bird. "And here I thought you had shacked up with a lady crow while I was at camp. You were here, helping me."

I took a breath to protest, then let it out. Maybe she *had* been here. How was I supposed to ever know? "Hey, um. I appreciate that Slick helped us back there, but can you make him leave?" I asked, having to nearly shout it.

Her fingers stroking her bird slowed. A heady fondness found her face as she used her feet to wedge herself in place and pet the crow into a blissful state. "I doubt it."

My grip on the wheel tightened. "Can you at least not pull on a line through him?"

Elyse shrugged, her attention going everywhere but to me. "As long as we stay aboveground. You think we could pull over so I can come up front? I don't think they're following us."

"I can do you one better." I flicked the turn signal on and took the next exit. "Burger Daddy. My treat." I didn't have much money left, but I probably had enough.

Elyse glanced at the body slumped between us, half on the floor. "What about him?"

I could hear her better now that we had slowed, and the air shook in my lungs as I took a moment to pull my bag onto the seat when I halted at a stop sign. "He'll be okay. He's already dead, and if I don't eat something soon, I'm going to join him."

She laughed as I eased forward, my eyes on the gaudy sign two blocks up with an unusual fierceness. All that was left was reinstating that ancient ley line charm.

Damn. I think we had done it.

CHAPTER

29

UNFORTUNATELY BURGER DADDY HAD BEEN CLOSED DUE TO AL having busted a main water line two days ago. Waffle House, though, was open, working under a limited menu. Elyse's bird and I were at a corner table, the original pattern in the Formica long since rubbed into a haze of bleach and time. The sun was well up, and traffic was surprisingly busy, seeing as only a few nights ago Al had been terrorizing Cincy's citizens. A sense of anticipation, of a long-held breath, seemed to hang over the city now that the demon had been exiled in the ever-after and Piscary had been announced as twice dead, leaving a power vacuum that Rynn Cormel was slated to fill. *How bad,* I wondered, *could it be if Waffle House was still open?*

Our borrowed, glamoured truck was outside. Johnny was in the back seat, covered in a tarp. Even if he was spotted, it was unlikely that anyone would say anything. Not in the Hollows.

Elyse had gone to the eat-at bar to order for us since they were low on staff, the last of our dwindling funds in her hand. My shoulders slumped as I sighed, and the crow beside me cocked his head, his sharp attention on the stone around my neck. "Mine," I said, and the crow chortled, bobbing in place like a mad thing. He clearly knew what "mine" meant, and he clearly wanted it anyway.

Waffle House, I mused as I glanced over the all-but-unoccupied restaurant. It had been packed when we had gotten here, but now there was only the old couple in the corner nursing their single coffees and the guy swabbing the floor.

Wincing, I pulled my bag closer to hide it, my eyes watering at the faint but persistent scent of burnt amber. "Hey, Slick," I said, and the bird shifted his attention from Elyse to me. "Can birds smell?"

Again the crow chortled, bobbing his head dramatically.

"Sorry," I added, and he side-walked to the other end of the table.

And yet a smile found me as I followed the bird's attention to Elyse flirting with the man behind the counter. Though cheerful, the strain was beginning to show as the adrenaline of besting first Newt, then Scott wore off, leaving space for the aches and fatigue. *Welcome to my world, babe.*

Slumping, I stretched my legs out under the table, feeling the bruise developing where Adagio had pulled me out of the ground. Or maybe it was from jumping into the truck, or dragging Johnny into it. My elbow, too, hurt. I hadn't a clue when I'd banged it.

Slick fluttered his wings in excitement as Elyse came over with a tray holding two bottled waters and two baskets. It smelled like warm bread, not pancakes and hash browns, and I sat up, curious. Burgers and chicken?

"Limited menu," she explained as she set the tray down and collapsed in the chair across from me, her hand immediately going to fondle the crow's neck. "I got a hamburger and a chicken sandwich. Take what you want. I'll eat what you don't."

I claimed a bottled water and cracked the top. "Ah, I'll take the burger unless your crow has a problem eating chicken."

"Slick?" she said, blinking to turn her into a high schooler. "Good God, no. Crows eat baby birds all the time." She grabbed a basket and cooed at the bird now at her elbow. "Don't you, my little savage?"

The crow politely took the offered sliver of steaming chicken as I chugged my water. I'd forgotten how thirsty the old ever-after could leave a person. "Ah, thanks," I said, lifting my burger in explanation. "How much do we have left?"

"All of it." She fed the bird another sliver. "I sterilized a vat of water for them in exchange. They have coffee now for the rest of the day."

"Oh! Great." I took a bite, my shoulders slumping. "Good thinking..."
The burger might be thin and the tomato slice skimpy, but I was starving
and it tasted like heaven. Mouth full, I watched the bird accept a third
sliver of chicken, holding it in his foot as he delicately nibbled the edges.
"Scott will follow him right to us," I added. "You might not be chipped, but
your bird is."

"Yeah, I know." Elyse sighed, wiped her hand clean, and then took the
bird's head and forced him to look at her. "Slick, go play hide-and-seek
with Scott."

The crow bobbed up and down, then launched into the air, a cry of
annoyance rising when he flew into the kitchen and presumably out an
open door.

The flash of satisfaction on Elyse's face was almost embarrassing, and
I shoved the thin slice of tomato back atop the burger before I took another
bite. Waffle House was one of the few multispecies restaurants to serve
tomatoes. But Waffle House didn't give a flying flip what anyone thought.
"Hey, after we get Johnny on the boat, I want to take the truck back."

Elyse went still. "Why?"

"Because it's not ours?" I said, thinking it was a child's question.

"We got it running," Elyse said between bites of her sandwich. "No one
wanted it."

My breath went in and out. "Just because we got it running doesn't
make it ours."

Elyse's brow furrowed. "How about sleep?" she said, clearly annoyed.
"You got sleep scheduled in there anywhere?"

I pushed away from the table, water bottle in hand. "I'll take care of
the truck if you want to crash in the library."

"No, I'm good."

I bet. I stared out the tall windows, watching humans and other day-
loving citizens filter into the streets. There'd been too many sirens the last
few days. Too many fires, too many threats. Al, though, was back in the
ever-after.

"What I really want is to see you rekindle that charm," she said. "If we hadn't nearly lost our souls in the ever-after to get it, I'd say you were making it up."

I stared at Elyse, her mouth full as she chewed almost belligerently. "I'm not making it up."

Swallowing, Elyse leaned in closer though there was no one around who could hear. "If it could be done, the coven would know how to do it."

A smile quirked half my mouth. "Maybe the coven did, and everyone who knew died before they could show you." Which wasn't true—it was a demon skill—but the reminder that the coven had probably lost a lot of skills from untimely attrition might bring her pride down a notch.

"Okay." Elyse set the last few bites of her sandwich down and wiped her fingers on a thin, almost useless napkin. "Show me."

"Now?"

Elyse mockingly gestured at the all-but-empty restaurant.

She wasn't wrong, and I drew the defunct charm from my pocket. Elbow on the table, I cradled the ancient amulet in my fingertips. Elyse inched closer, shifting to hide the table from casual view. Yeah, I'd be interested in the impossible thing that might get me home safely, too.

"As I was told, you're basically refilling the remnant shadow of energy that the original spell left in the metal," I said, and Elyse nodded, focused on it with an eerie intensity. "You couldn't do this with a wooden amulet. The surface decays and the pattern is lost. But you have to be delicate. Energy taken straight from the line will break it. You have to use the energy from your aura, and you can't do it all at once. You have to layer it shell by shell."

"Shell by shell?" Elyse questioned, making me wonder if she had the background for this. "You mean you separate your aura into its shells?"

"Exactly," I affirmed. Amulet in one hand, I used the other to physically draw my aura off my fingertips, pushing it up past my elbow. The naked flesh ached, sort of like having the flu, and I wondered if I should have put myself in a protection circle. An aura was a person's first line of defense, and I had just bared myself to whatever psychic ill might be stuck to the underside of the table. But it was a Waffle House, and I figured I'd be okay.

"Ah, did you just . . ." Elyse started, and I nodded.

"You'll get more out of this if you use your second sight." And with that, I shifted my entire aura to a clear red.

I knew she was watching when Elyse exhaled with a soft sound. "Oh, wow."

Holding everything as it was, I glanced up at her. "You know how to separate your aura into its shells?" I asked, and she bobbed her head, her attention riveted to the amulet perched in my fingertips. The old metal felt colder, and I stifled a shudder as I allowed a thin trace of my all-red aura to spill down my arm and puddle in my hand just under the metal circle. It wasn't touching it yet, but I could feel the metal wanting to join with it. Which was a relief. If I had a light enough touch, I could rekindle it. Until just that moment, I hadn't been sure.

"Yes, I've done that," Elyse said, attention fixed to the amulet. "Not what you're doing," she quickly added. "But I've used auras in a few spells. Yeah."

Annoyance flickered through me. A few spells, she said. Probably ones that were illegal for the rest of us. "Okay. Well, every artifact holds a memory of the maker's aura," I said, feeling like Al as my words found an instructive patter. "If you can ease that energy back into it, a layer at a time, it might rekindle. Red is the first color, and you follow the chakras on up."

Breath held, I allowed the aura in the cup of my hand to rise, bathing the amulet perched on my fingertips. The thin trace enveloped the old metal, the single wavelength of energy setting it to ring a beautiful, very much subliminal chime. My breath eased out. Pierce had taught me this. And then he had died trying to kill Ku'Sox. The guilt was old and not warranted. I had told him not to. The pain that Ceri, Ray's mother, had died along with him . . . That was harder to let go.

"It takes a fine touch," I said as I shifted the red puddling in my palm to orange. "Too little won't invoke the charm." A second tone joined the first as almost all the red in the amulet shifted to orange, leaving only a thin trace of the original color remaining.

"Too much, and it will break." I shifted my aura to yellow, frowning when the new tone rang with a discordant harshness. I had only applied three shells and the amulet was full. I had begun with too much red and would have to start over.

Frustrated, I pushed all the energy off my hand and set the amulet down.

Elyse stared at it on the faded Formica table, wisely not reaching for it. "Why did you stop? You want me to do it?"

"No!" I barked, then softer, "No. I was just getting a feel for how much energy it will take to reinvoke it. I started with too much, and those three shells had reached its carrying capacity. Any more, and it would have broken completely."

Elyse cocked her head, studying it. "How many shells does it take?"

"Six or seven, depending on the finesse of who made it."

Her brow furrowed. "If you don't want to tell me, fine."

"Elyse, it's an art, not a science," I protested, and her frown deepened as she fiddled with her drink. "Whoever made this had a very light touch. I had assumed it was a demon, seeing as it's a demon charm, but now I think it was an elf." I picked it up, studying the invocation words engraved on the outer rim. "An enslaved elf," I added, setting it down again. "This needs more concentration than I can probably find at a Waffle House."

Across the street, a black shape flew straight down the road, Scott in hot pursuit.

"But I can try," I added. *Good bird.*

"I'm not some kind of wannabe dilettante," Elyse said, clearly insulted. "I have practiced dividing my aura into its separate components since I was ten. I am not a kid."

My eye twitched. "Have you ever done this?" I said, angry. "Anything at all like this? You tell me you're not a kid. Well, you certainly aren't acting like an adult."

Elyse's lips parted. "Did I not drive off a high member of the council without him realizing who either of us were?"

"You caused severe structural damage to two buildings and a parking lot. You couldn't wait to use your big guns to impress me."

"I was trying to cow Scott!" she barked. "How does that make me a child?"

I leaned in close, annoyed. "It's not what you did that's the problem. I'm saying only a child would think that what you did was okay." Because she clearly thought it was.

"Well, what would you have done?"

I picked up the amulet, worried she might make a go for it. "Other than what I did? Circle him, maybe? Knock him out with a kick? Make him temporarily blind? Give him bad luck? You, in your infinite wisdom, decided to damage two buildings and a parking lot. Fine. It's a choice. But only a child doesn't acknowledge that you stomped all over everyone who works or lives in those buildings, then went on with your life as if their pain and monetary interests don't matter."

Elyse stared at me. "You think I should have let him catch us? It's just a couple of buildings and a parking lot!"

I rubbed my chin, exasperated. "You are not listening," I said, feeling like a demon as I pitched my voice low. "You are so privileged that you can't comprehend the chaos you leave in your wake. Most people who do crap like this are reminded with jail time or fines or restitution. *The Turn knows I am.* But not the coven, no," I added bitterly, and maybe a little enviously. "Under the auspices of protecting us, you are allowed to create havoc with no consequences. None."

A little chuckle eased from her, and her anger vanished. "Oh, my God. You're jealous."

Maybe I was, but that wasn't the point. "Listen. To. Me," I said, every word a hammer. "You use spells and charms that others can't. And then call yourself more skilled? I don't think so. You have put everyone at the bottom of a hill while you stand at the top and say you're better. Try working with what we have before labeling yourself an elite."

Elyse's air of self-righteousness faltered, then returned.

"You know what?" I said, tired of it. "Fine. Try it." I held the charm out to her on the palm of my hand. "Knock yourself out. If you break it, I'm not waiting for you. You take the long way home with Kisten."

"No." She lifted her chin defiantly. "I want to see if you can really do it."

I closed my fingers about the amulet and drew it close. "Good choice, but if I thought for an instant that you have the skill to duplicate this, I wouldn't let you even watch. The coven didn't lose this ability. They never had it, and they never will." Anger flickered over her as I pushed the aura from my hand again, and a warning of achy pinpricks flooded my arm. "You don't have a delicate enough touch. It's a demon thing," I added, just to piss her off.

Ignoring her huff of disbelief, I shifted my aura to red again, sending the lightest trace down my arm, so light it felt like a butterfly kiss. Exhaling, I allowed it to find my palm, rising to envelop the waiting charm, sending the old metal vibrating with a chime so faint it was almost not there. *This*, I thought, *might work*, and I shifted my aura to orange.

A second chime joined the first, only a rare sliver of red lingering against the sunset-colored haze in my hand. Already I knew it was better, and my head ached from the pressure of holding the full flood of my aura back.

Yellow was next, clear like sunlight as it washed through the light haze. The orange vanished under the living glow as a third tone melded to the others. A faint itch of building power crawled down my spine, aching for me to free it.

I quickly shifted my aura to a healthy green, startled when the resonating metal pulled it in more than the others, worrying me that I might not have left enough space. The tone became richer, deeper. Pinpricks stabbed at my hand, and I tensed, my heart aching with someone else's longing to see living fields. It was the maker of the amulet, and my brow furrowed as the definition between me and whoever had twisted the amulet began to blur. There were no cracks in the amulet, no threat of the harsh, discordant tone that I'd heard before, each sliver of aura slipping in as if it belonged.

Blue, I thought, desperate to have this done, and pinpricks painfully stung my arm. My aura resonance shifted, cramping my fingers as another tone melded with the rest, aching through me with the feel of angel wings beating upon the air. It was a good ache, a thunderous ache. I blinked, trying to focus as the amulet found a darker hue.

I was almost done, and I struggled to see past the muffling haze. I felt myself breathe, power cramping my lungs as I shifted my aura to ultraviolet. Elyse gasped. It was as if living smut had snaked down my arm, pooling under the glowing amulet but refusing to blend. Softly, surely, a whisper of it reached up to the metal as an identical haze stretched down.

And with a ping, the two threads met and the amulet rekindled. The separate shells of aura wrapped separately around the amulet had blended. It had needed only that one last color as a catalyst.

I gasped, fingers spasming open as a pulse of energy cramped up my arm like lightning.

"No!" I cried when the amulet slipped from my numb fingers and fell.

Elyse flung out a hand, catching it as her eyes met mine. "Rice crackers," she swore mildly, wonder filling her expression. "You fixed it!" She stared down at it in disbelief. "This is amazing. The lost magic we could find again."

I couldn't smile, couldn't meet her relieved expression. The heartache of the elf who had originally created it was still echoing in me, his anger, betrayal, revenge, and longing slowly blurring into one emotion of despair.

"Sure," I rasped, fingers trembling as I reached for my water bottle. "Knock yourself out. But if you don't do it right and try to seal it with too little or too much energy, it will break. You can't rekindle a charm once broken." I took a swallow, draining it dry. "Like I said, I wouldn't have shown you if I thought you could do it."

Elyse lifted her chin. "I might surprise you."

I was tired, relieved, slightly angry, and feeling a lot like Al trying to explain something to me. "Yep, I would be. Don't lose it."

Her fingers closed possessively over the charm, and a flash of annoyance crossed me. All of a sudden, I couldn't handle her attitude anymore, and I stood. After she had saved us both from Newt, I had somehow expected more from her . . . and I wasn't seeing it. She had busted two buildings and a parking lot when a simple hold spell would have sufficed.

Worse, she thought it was her God-given right to do so and walk away. Like a demon.

My eye twitched as I put my bag over my shoulder and looked down at her. "Let's go. I want to get rid of the robes and we need to get Johnny on the boat. I have a few hours before they find him, and I'd like to spend them sleeping before we have to cremate him instead of Kisten."

Elyse stared at me, clearly startled when I snatched up our baskets and paper napkins, wadding everything up into one mass as I took it to the trash and shoved it in. Arms swinging, I headed out to the truck, sure she would follow.

She might be holding the amulet, but I was still her ticket home.

CHAPTER

30

I PUT A HAND TO MY MOUTH TO STIFLE A YAWN, THE OTHER ON THE dash as Elyse slowed to make the tight turn onto the dirt road that led to the dock where Kisten's boat was. Old swamp trees arched overhead, and the low sun made flashing bars instead of a dappled shade. Two to-go coffees sat in the center console, but mine was decaf and would do nothing to get me through the next hour of placing Johnny, cleaning the boat of our presence, returning the truck, and then maybe getting a few hours of sleep.

My bag was a great deal lighter without the robes, sashes, and hats—now stuffed into Sylvia's night drop box with a note of thanks—but I could *still* smell burnt amber, and I cracked the window a little more.

Elyse looked as tired as I felt, the drive out here and the silence that had accompanied it leaving her with very little stimulation with which to stay awake. Getting Johnny on Kisten's boat wasn't going to be easy, physically or emotionally. Right about now, Ford was helping me relive Kisten's death. Shortly thereafter, we were going to come out here and find him. That it was really Johnny I'd be crying over didn't help. Knowing Kisten was safe in a morgue drawer did.

The likelihood of Kisten waking up was less than slim. He was battling Art's virus. The best I could hope for was getting his body home intact so I could use Elyse's curse to bring back his ghost. Every. Single. Night.

My shoulders slumped even more.

Elyse wove through the potholes, her sluggish motions holding a hint of wariness as she wheeled the truck around and parked facing the boat. Eyes on the rearview mirror, she cut the engine.

"I could sleep for two days straight," she said as she undid her belt . . . and then sat there.

I studied her, reading her fatigue, her relief that after cremating Johnny, we'd be on our way home. "Ah, hey. I'm sorry I said you lacked finesse. I'm sure you have what you need to rekindle a ley line charm."

Her attention flicked to me. "Apology accepted," she said, and then her gaze went to the tarp-wrapped body. "Still want to do this?"

I stifled a little huff. "It's a little late to be worried about the laws we're breaking."

Elyse smirked, but her attention was on the mirror again. "Please. That's not what concerns me."

"Well, it worries me." Uncomfortable, I gathered our trash and stuffed it into a bag. Yes, I had repleted his aura from a faceless donor who liked cats, and if Dr. Ophees used the curse I'd given her enough, he wouldn't starve from aura depletion, but he was still going to die twice somewhere along the way home. If not for the ley line stasis charm I'd rekindled, I'd arrive with a badly decomposed body with which to raise his ghost. *Is this worth it, Rachel?*

Suddenly concerned, I squinted at Elyse. "You're not going to forget your promise to show me the curse to raise Kisten's ghost, are you?"

Gaze on the road behind us, she shook her head. "It's yours. I can't believe you really want to use it, though. I mean, Ivy is your friend. She's remade her life and you are going to make her deal with this again? Every night? She can't be his scion and Nina's both. Who is going to feed him? You?"

"No," I said quickly. "He'd be a ghost. He won't need anything." At least I didn't think he would.

Elyse's gaze flicked from the rearview mirror to me. "You'd have to stir the spell every night. It's a lot of effort for a questionable result. Who are you really doing this for? Kisten? He's fine with being twice dead if it means you and Ivy are okay."

Maybe, but I wasn't *fine* with it. Kisten had just begun to find himself, and Piscary had killed him to solidify his grip on the city. "I'm doing this for Cincinnati," I said, well aware that I might be dumping Ivy back in the morass of heartache we'd worked ourselves out of once. "If you get sacked and I have to go into hiding, Kisten can keep Constance in line and the DC vampires out. I vowed to keep Constance safe. This would do it. Ghost or no." I sighed. "Kisten was very popular, and he was Piscary's chosen scion before he died."

Elyse's brow furrowed. "I told you," she muttered, "I'm not pursuing that anymore."

A bitter scoff escaped me. "And I told you that one voice out of six will not keep my ass out of Alcatraz. Without that mirror, I go into hiding come June."

I reached to open the door, hesitating when Elyse didn't move. She was still staring out the rear window via the mirror. "What is it?" I said, turning to look as well.

"Nothing." She opened her door and got out.

That's what she said, but I wasn't sure I trusted it. "Then why are you so edgy?"

Elyse slammed the door shut. "I've got a dead vampire disguised as Piscary's scion in my back seat, that's why." Her brow furrowed as she scanned the open scrub. "Maybe I just miss Slick."

That I understood, and I got out of the truck. I might not have a familiar, but I had a veritable village of people who made up for it—and I couldn't wait to see them again: to listen to Jenks bitch about something or other, see Ivy's eye roll at my lack of planning, sense Al's increasingly thinly veiled pride, feel Trent's arms about me.

I glanced at the ring he'd given me, the little ruby glittering dully. My hand fisted. Leaving the trash in the truck, I opened the rear door, grabbed Johnny's shoulders, and pulled.

"Elyse?" I called, and she came back from her study of the road we'd come in on, slipping between Johnny's feet and grabbing his knees. "Got him?" I asked, and she nodded, pushing me into a shuffling, awkward motion.

My sight alternated between the boat, Johnny, and my feet, and I frowned when I realized I was walking on my own prints. "We're making a lot of in and out traffic," I said, arms aching.

Elyse huffed, her face red with strain in the morning light. "I have a cleansing spell."

Of course you do, I thought sourly as we reached the dock and I hiked Johnny's weight into a more secure hold. Such a spell would make it tons easier to work around the law. "You ready? I've got a big step here."

She nodded and I made a lurching stride that was more faith than anything else. My foot landed on the oiled teak, and I exhaled as the boat lightly shifted, waves lapping. I inched down along the seat, unable to step down into the cockpit until Elyse took the long step over the water and onto the boat as well.

"Whoa, whoa, whoa!" she exclaimed, and suddenly I was floundering, having taken all of Johnny's weight.

The heavy man slipped from me, and both of us swore as the corpse hit the floor of the cockpit. Embarrassed, I jumped into the recessed seating area and bent almost double to scoop my arms under Johnny's shoulders.

That's when the black ball of magic hissed over my head, little trills of energy prickling through my aura as it hit the water and bubbled into an ugly froth.

"Down!" I lurched to grab Elyse as she half slid into the lowered cockpit with me. We were under attack by someone who fought not dirty but smart. A pro. Whoever it was had waited until we were over the water. I couldn't tap a line. Elyse might, through Slick, but I only had what was in my chi. Maybe one good pop.

"You see anyone?" I questioned as we peeked over the seating to scan the low scrub and tall weeds.

Elyse's jaw was tight. "I knew someone had followed us."

"I'll throw a spell. Cover for you. Get off the boat." I put a hand on her, jumping in surprise when a flood of ley line energy filled my chi from her. *Two good pops.* "You can't make a protection circle over—Elyse!"

She had stood, my fingers slipping from her as she marshaled the line energy into a spell and tossed it straight up. The purple sphere arched into the fragile blue of the sky with a hiss, trailing golden sparkles until it burst like a signal flare to leave a golden haze glinting in the sun.

"Stay down!" I yanked her back, wondering why she had wasted a charm to light the area. I didn't see our attacker, but that golden haze wasn't doing anything that the sun wasn't already.

"Give it a second." Elyse crouched beside me, her eyes alight. "Whoever he is, he's subtle."

"Scott?" I guessed, but I didn't see Slick, and if he had followed the bird here, the crow would be on her shoulder, cawing in delight.

"There," she said, pointing.

Confused, I followed her pointing finger to the golden haze condensing behind a huge, scraggly bush. *Oh . . .* It hadn't been a light. It had been to suss out the attacker. Kind of like how Vivian had used drifting flower seeds to find an illicit magic user at the farmers' market.

"It's attracted to magic use," Elyse said as she shifted her weight, clearly uncomfortable as she crouched beside me. "He's got a light touch. It's not Scott. Scott is a bull in a china shop."

"Wait."

But she had stood again, her hair staticky as she swung her arms in a gloriously exuberant motion to pull in energy through Slick. The woman did like to spell.

"Light touch, light touch!" I shouted, reaching for her. It was going to be something big. I could tell. "This is a crime scene!"

She wasn't listening, and energy darted from her to our unseen attacker with an exuberant "*A minoread maius!*"

The boom of a counterspell exploded upward, pushing the leaves of the trees, rattling them in the sudden wind. Like a hurricane, they swirled upward, shredding into confetti before drifting downward.

"You are tearing the area up!" I complained as Elyse scrambled from the boat to the landing. "There was no evidence of an attack out here. Knock it off!"

But she ignored me, striding confidently into the parking lot, her aura almost visible as she pulled on the line, eager to engage. Way too eager. She was going to kill someone.

"I said stop!" I lurched off the boat, and when she formed another spell within her hands, something in me snapped.

"*Dictum factum!*" I shouted, pissed as my spell hit her. It was a demon spell Al had used on me until I began listening to him. It was basically a babysitter charm that forced the recipient to do what I had said. In this case, to stop.

Elyse choked as her gathered energy fell back into her. Wide-eyed, she turned to me, an angry, hot betrayal in her gaze.

"I'm sorry," I said as she tried to make a spell and reddened when it failed. "You aren't listening—"

Her attention flicked over my shoulder ... and then fire and ice hit me, crawled down my spine and stole my will. I fell to one knee, breath held as I coolly analyzed the spell and found it to be elven before balling it up and asking the Goddess to take it when I shoved it into the ground.

Teeth clenched at the ache it had left, I got to my feet and promptly lost every thought.

"Quen!"

The black-clad elf stole forward on soft shoes, as dangerous and slippery as the night that birthed him. Green and gold energy wreathed his hands, dripped from them. His expression, though, held only the barest hint of anger. "A step too far, Morgan. This gives me no joy."

Oh. Shit. Quen was the only person this side of the lines who scared me. Not for his illicit magic but because he had no qualms about using it to defend those he loved. Kind of like me.

"Quen, wait." I retreated as he came forward, flushing when I remembered joyfully humiliating Trent in front of Cincinnati's oldest families. Yeah, I'd been an idiot. "I handled it badly. You're right. But you have to listen—"

His lip twitched. It was the only warning I got as suddenly the very earth I stood on erupted, going soft beneath my feet to swallow me up.

"*Teneo!*" I exclaimed as I floundered, sending a mass of black coils about my feet to writhe through Quen's spell and give my feet purchase. Awkward and scared, I staggered out of the spells, hand raised for patience. "We need to talk."

"*Voulden*," Quen intoned, and I batted it aside before it knocked me down from the inside out.

"He didn't want to get married!" I shouted. "He told me himself!"

Quen stopped, the green ball of hurt hissing in his hand making his knuckles white. At the edge of the trees, Elyse stood, tense and trying to find a way past that babysitter spell I'd put on her. She looked as pissed as Quen ought to but didn't.

"Then why send me to kill you?" he asked.

The thought to put myself in a circle rose and fell. It would only make me seem vulnerable. Which I was. "Because he can't admit it yet," I said.

Quen's lip twitched. "You stink like demons. Both of you."

I stiffened as the energy in his hand swelled and a high-pitched squeal erupted from it. Elyse dropped, hands over her ears, clearly in pain.

"Wait! Wait!" I shouted, tears pricking as I stood my ground. "I know Trent's mad, but I am his Mal Sa'han. Or I will be. See?" I held my hand out, fingers trembling as I showed him his mother's ring. "He gave me his mother's ring to trade to Newt for a stupid mirror. Would he do that if he was mad at me? If he wanted me dead?"

"Where did you get that? I thought it was lost."

"Probably his mother's old lab behind the fireplace," I said. Quen had gone ashen, and I pulled my hand back when he reached out. Satisfaction found me, warmed my hope when Quen's next words caught in his throat. "Yeah, I figured you knew about that," I added.

The older elf's focus sharpened on me. "How do you know about his mother's studio? No one but Jonathan and I know about it."

I exhaled, slow and long as I found my full height. "Good. You can keep a secret. I need you to keep one now, or we all lose. *All* of us."

Elyse took a quick breath of air. "Shut up, Rachel. We can figure this out."

She meant the forget spell. It was in my pocket, sure, but if I made

Quen forget me here, he'd focus his attention on my current self at the church.

I had to tell Quen. Either he would believe me, or one of us was going to die.

"That was you in the vault." Quen glanced behind me. "Both of you."

I nodded, wincing. "I'm so sorry about that. Quen. Please." My throat thickened. "I love him. Not now, but in the future. And he loves me. Desperately, he says. Desperately."

Quen's head shifted back and forth. "You think a lie will convince me to let you live?"

"I'm not supposed to be here!" I shouted. "Or Elyse."

Elyse glowered at me, unable to act. "Shut up, Rachel."

"But we are," I continued. "And we're trying to get home."

The energy in Quen's hands began to diminish, the eye-hurting ache about his fingers easing. "Which is where?"

"Which is when," I corrected him, and Elyse groaned. "Two years from now, I modify a demon spell to get here. I need something from the ever-after before it falls. You can't tell him. You can't tell me." Al had said speak truth only to the dead. I now knew what he had meant, but if I didn't tell Quen, one of us would *be* dead.

The energy in his hand flickered and all but went out, leaving a thin haze of potential death dabbling about his fingers. "He told me to kill you. I agree with his decision. It's long overdue."

I shook my head. "Decisions made from pride are seldom good, and you know it. If you don't believe me about moving through time, go to the church and see for yourself. I'm probably coming out of a demon-induced coma just about now, caused by Minias pulling the focus out of me." I grimaced. "You can tell Trent he can stuff it for trying to take it. It belongs to the Weres."

Quen huffed in amusement, but his gaze was sharp. "You say you love him," he mocked. "And that's why you moved Felps out of the sun until he died twice."

"Kisten is still undead," I said. "That's not him on the boat. It's a John Doe Vamp from the morgue."

That set him back a little, and his weight shifted to his other foot. "You used a demon spell—"

"Modified," I interrupted.

"A modified demon spell to save your vampire boyfriend's undead life, and you expect me to believe that you're in love with Trent? And he's in love with you? Two years in the future."

It sounded like a fast romance when he said it like that, but damn, we had been through a lot in that time.

Elyse wrapped her arms around her middle. "How come when I want to break the timeline, it's a problem, and when you do it, it's okay?"

A misplaced anger flickered. "Because I was here when it happened and you weren't!" I gathered my courage and turned to Quen. "Kisten dies twice. I can't stop that. But the coven has a spell to raise his ghost, and I need someone to handle vampire affairs while I hide out in the ever-after." *With Trent and Al. Yeah. He'd believe that.*

Quen glanced at Elyse, and she twiddled her fingers at him as if to say, *Hi. Yep, I'm coven.* "Why do *you* need someone to handle the vampire affairs?" His brow furrowed. "Who is Piscary's replacement? Ivy Tamwood? Are you helping Tamwood?"

"I'm stopping Kisten from being cremated. That's it," I said, not wanting to get into why I was shepherding Cincy's vampire population. He'd never believe it. "I can't let you kill me, and you can't tell Trent why you didn't. He will thank you in two years. I promise."

But the haze was beginning to thicken about his fingers again. "There's nothing I can say that will satisfy him if I don't come back with your head."

Boy, did I understand that. "Tell him . . . Tell him that as we fought, you realized that I am his dad's magnum opus, not Stanley Saladan," I said, suddenly breathless. "Tell him that Lee puts his own family first and always will but that I can be tricked into anything, even into the ever-after." Elyse cleared her throat, but I thought the statement innocent enough.

"Together we can get the pre-curse elven DNA as our fathers could not. And after that, he can kill me. Tell him he has to wait. He's good at that."

Quen's expression creased. "How do you know about your fathers working together?"

"My mom," I said. "Though Trent confirms it when he tells me Takata is my birth father."

Quen's doubt began to shift to incredulity. "You know who your genetic father is?"

"I will," I said cryptically. "Don't tell me. Trent does when he's angry and wants to hurt me. He needs it. Can you do that? Can you keep your mouth shut? I need this to happen, Quen. Trent needs this to happen, and if you tell him what's to come, it won't." And if it didn't, he would never . . . I would never . . . Oh, God.

Quen's lip twitched again, and I panicked. He wasn't going to believe me.

"Please!" I held up my hand to stop him, Trent's ring glinting in the morning light between us. "I'm sorry, but we fall in love. No one wanted it, most of all us. You don't want it, Trent doesn't want it," I practically moaned. "The demons don't want it, but it happens. And it makes Trent better, whole. Quen, he becomes the person he wants to be, not the person his dad made him to keep your people alive."

Quen stared at my hand, his lips parting as an unknown heartache crossed him.

"He changes," I gushed, wondering what had shifted. "Once he no longer has to struggle to keep his people alive, he changes. He adores the girls. He's so good with them, it makes my heart ache. He makes peace with Ellasbeth. He strives to make peace with . . . his enemies," I said, knowing that to tell him Trent voluntarily parked his tent next to a demon's RV would be too much. "He finds love in so many ways. Please. Don't tell him the future or you might change it, and I can't bear the thought. I can't lose him. I wouldn't have told you, but I won't let you kill me, and I can't kill you; he would have to go through it all alone, and he needs you."

Elyse stared at me as if I had just ripped the time continuum apart and crapped in it, and maybe I had. But I couldn't kill Quen, and I couldn't let him kill me.

And then Quen rocked back a step, his head bowing. "Take good care of it," he said, his attention flicking to my hand. "It saved your life."

My hand closed into a fist. "What?"

"That ring." Saying nothing more, Quen turned and walked away.

"Quen?" I called, but he didn't stop. Four steps into the brush, and he was gone.

"I knew someone had followed us," Elyse muttered.

I licked my lips, not sure anymore what Trent had given me. Suddenly I was more afraid than I'd been before.

"I can't believe you told him," Elyse said. "Hey, you want to break your hold spell? We have to get Johnny in place and get out of here." She squinted at the bare branches cutting the perfect blue of the sky. "It won't take a lot to clean the area. I doubt they will do much of an investigation anyway. Seeing as he's a blood gift."

I severed the curse, and Elyse took a relieved breath. "No, they don't," I whispered, eyes still on the last place I'd seen Quen. He had known about me coming here for the last two years and had never said anything. Thank God I hadn't told him about Ceri.

Head down, I followed Elyse onto the boat, no longer sure what I would find when I got home.

If I got home.

CHAPTER

31

THE COFFEEHOUSE WAS RIGHT ACROSS THE STREET FROM THE morgue downtown, which meant it was noisy with people meeting up for lunch or on their phones and laptops playing office—though there were fewer now than when Elyse and I had stumbled in, both of us bedraggled and tired after not nearly enough sleep. Yawning yet again, I sat with my back to the wall at a table tucked into a corner and my phone plugged into a socket. I had an extremely large cup of coffee in my hand, and it still didn't feel like enough to wake me up. A bag of miniature pastries was open between me and Elyse's empty chair, and after glancing at the door to the bathroom, I ate the last one. *You snooze, you lose, babe.*

The shop was nice, with high ceilings and big windows that looked out onto the street, but it wasn't Junior's and I felt out of place, nervous as I pulled my stinky bag and everything I'd brought with me on this magic carpet ride closer: my never-used splat gun, Al's broken necklace to mark our exit from the curse, the curse book and all my modifications that got us here.

Elyse had her stasis ley line charm in her pocket. It seemed prudent for her to have it, and it gave the woman a needed feeling of control.

My gaze shifted from my charging phone to the barista at the far side of the shop, and I made a stupid wave when she stared at me. Clearly annoyed, the dark-haired woman returned to her work. She'd been eyeing us since we'd stumbled in like two bandits off the desert. I figured she thought we were homeless, which we kind of were, but we had paid for our food so she couldn't kick us out—even if Elyse had been in the bathroom for the last twenty minutes using their sink to try to rub off both a trip to the ever-after and a night spent in the library basement. *And I still stink like burnt amber,* I thought as I plucked my shirt and winced at the puff of air.

Focus distant, I sipped at my coffee, startled when my phone hummed. I glanced at it out of habit, breath catching. It was my mom.

Tuesday, I mused, looking at the time. I was probably bawling my grief out in my room as my heart broke to make room for Trent, the girls, hell, maybe even Ellasbutt. I loved Kisten, but I couldn't go back to what I had been.

The phone, though, just kept buzzing. My other self was probably too engulfed in grief to pick up, and my mom would keep calling. I missed her, and knowing it was a bad idea, I hit the accept icon. "Hi, Mom."

"Rachel? Oh, honey." Her voice was living comfort, and my chest tightened. "I heard about Kisten. Are you doing okay?"

My throat closed. It was one of her good days when I didn't have to be the smart one. "It hurts," I whispered, feeling her loss twine with Kisten's. She was right there, a few minutes away by bus, not on the other side of the continent. And yet I could do nothing but grip my phone and press it harder against my ear.

"I'm on my way," she said hurriedly. "You're at the church, yes?"

I blinked fast, trying to remember. "I think so."

"Oh, sweetheart. Give me five minutes. I can't make it better, but I can help you bear it. You'll be okay until I get there?"

She knew what I was going through, had walked it alone when my dad had died. "Mom?" *My God. She is the bravest woman I know.* "I love you, Mom. I don't tell you that enough." Because in my grief, I would forget to say it as she rocked me, whispering things to make me feel connected, to convince me that I might be whole again someday.

"I love you, too. Five minutes."

The phone clicked off and I closed my eyes, squeezing them tight so the tears wouldn't start. She was the best mom, having the bravery to let me make my own mistakes and the courage to be there with a Band-Aid instead of a lecture.

My eyes opened, pulled by the rasping whirl of the blender. "Yeah, that was a mistake," I said as I yanked the cord from the wall and put the phone in my shoulder bag. The door to the bathroom squeaked as Elyse came out, the young woman clearly in a better mood than when she'd gone in there. Her hair had dried flat and her shirt was spotted, but she met my forced smile cheerfully as she sat down and reached for the pastries.

"Man, I'd kill for a toothbrush." The paper bag rustled, and then a frown crossed her face when she found it empty.

I stood and tugged my shoulder bag closer. "Ready? I think I saw the morgue van go by while you were in there." My bag was heavy with both the book she'd stolen from Trent and mine, the faint scent of burnt amber coming from the one I'd brought stronger now for having been in the ever-after again. "I'm going to take the image of the barista, and then we can go."

Elyse glanced at the woman still watching us from behind the counter. "Really? Yesterday you wanted to be yourself."

"Yesterday I was stealing a body. This time I'm cremating one."

She chuckled. "Fair enough."

Crap on toast, she was in a good mood. All I felt was a growing sense of impending destruction. We were going home, but without the mirror, it wouldn't be the happy-happy, joy-joy moment that she thought it was going to be. They would kick her out if she told them to drop their plans to make me their unwilling muscle.

I fumbled for the stone about my neck as I sent a stray thought out to the nearest ley line. Sure enough, my no-spell, no-product hair frizzed, making a veritable halo as energy ran a delicious thread through me. "*A priori,*" I whispered as I glanced at the woman. "*A posterior,*" I added as I then looked at myself reflected in the shiny stainless steel wall. "*Omnia mutantur.*" I whispered the words through the hole, aiming them at my middle.

A shudder rippled over me, and the world seemed to fade for a moment as the glamour took hold. "Good?" I asked, and Elyse stepped between me and the woman behind the counter.

"You should have waited until we were outside," she said as she shoved me to the door. "Go. I'll be right there."

It felt good to be moving, and I went to stand among the street-grimed tables and tattered umbrellas. Motion made things better. Motion always made things better. Maybe that's why I always seemed to be going somewhere. But moving meant changing, and that usually hurt.

Tired, I faced the sun and let it warm me until I heard the door open and felt Elyse sidle up beside me.

"Light just changed. Let's go," she said, and I took a long step to keep up with her as she headed for the street.

"What's with all the coffee?" I asked, seeing as she had four cups in one of those single-use trays. "We can't take it down there. I was told the scent might wake someone up early."

Elyse smirked and handed it to me as we crossed the street. "You look like the barista from the coffeehouse. You're making a delivery."

"You stole someone's coffee—no, you stole four people's coffee to further a glamour?" I resisted the urge to glance behind us.

"I didn't steal them. I bought them." The woman seemed embarrassed. "If you weren't going to lift her image, I was going to ask you to lift it for me."

She bought them? A chuckle escaped me. "Be careful, Elyse. You might be developing a conscience."

"Shut up," she muttered, and my grin widened.

"Don't listen to me. It was smart." I paused. "If I'm the barista, who are you?"

"I'm a coincidence wrapped in a mistake and rolled in luck sprinkles."

"Got that right." We took the building stairs fast. I hadn't seen Slick, but I figured her familiar was around. Bold as brass, we walked in the front door. No one even looked at us. It was late afternoon, and the tall-ceilinged lobby had a moderate amount of activity, both in and out.

"Stairs," I said, looking at the fire door, and Elyse nodded, scanning the lobby as she held the door for me . . . and then we were in the echoing stairwell, the door slamming shut behind us.

I took a breath, my skin tingling as I pulled armfuls of energy off the line and spindled them in my chi.

"You okay?"

I glanced at Elyse, wondering how we had gone from antagonists to partners in a mere three days. I liked her, and there was nothing but misery waiting for her back home. She thought she could make a decision and the rest would follow . . . but I knew better. "Ah, I took a call from my mom," I finally said, and her expression scrunched up in sympathy.

"Ouch. How did that go?"

She didn't know it, but she needed the mirror as much as I did now, because breaking Brad's curse was the only way she was going to keep me out of Alcatraz and her leading the coven. Trusting me was going to ruin her career. "Mmmm, about what you would expect," I said lightly, and she chuckled, almost bouncing as she went to get the door at the landing, slamming her weight into the heavy metal to shift it.

The hallway was its usual cool emptiness, and the scent of the coffee seemed to become stronger. "You want to play this same as before?"

Elyse bobbed her head. "I've got ley line. I'll go first. Save your ergs."

"Right. Try not to break anything."

She put a hand on the door, her smile mischievous. "Unreasonable expectations seldom make for a happy life."

Eyes closing in a strength-gathering blink, I gestured for her to have at it. She seemed eager enough, and after seeing her in action, I had no qualms about her doing the heavy lifting. Me, though? My gut was in knots. I was going to cremate a perfect stranger, take any closure his family might have away from them. It bothered me.

Rachel, you need to think a plan through before you commit.

Elyse, though, was boldly pushing through the swinging doors, ready to do whatever I said if it would get her home. My God. The woman had gone to the ever-after, made a bet with a demon, slept in a library basement, and stolen a body. Why she trusted me now, I didn't know.

Tense, I listened to her feet scuff on the disinfected tile . . . and then nothing.

I started when the door shifted and she poked her head out. "There's no one in here. Or the morgue area," she said.

"Huh." I followed her in, slowing as I studied the waiting gurney with its locked wheels and carefully folded modesty blanket. Senses searching, I set the coffee on the disorganized desk and felt the chair. It was warm, and a frown furrowed my brow.

"The back is empty, too?" I whispered, hoping we hadn't gotten Iceman in trouble.

"Key," Elyse said, and I took the naked doll from the hook on the wall.

"I don't like the feel of this," I said as I yanked the top drawer open, shuffling about until I found the oversize key to open the furnace. Elyse was waiting by the second set of double doors, and together we pushed through them. The sound of fans and the scent of disinfectant grew stronger as we looked the space over. "I've never seen the morgue without an attendant. There are undead here undergoing self-repair. What if one of them wakes up?"

Elyse swung her arms as she strode between the rows of drawers, an almost cavalier attitude flowing from her. "You said Kisten was cremated before you could identify him. Clearing the room would facilitate that, wouldn't it?" She turned at the end of the long room. "We're good. I don't sense anyone."

"Yeah, but I have been working under the assumption that we were responsible for it." A sigh slipped from me. She was the one who could connect to a ley line, and after a last glance at the empty reception area, I let the door swing shut behind me. "Let's get this done," I said as she flounced to the door to the furnace and punched in the code.

"We're good. It's clear," she said as she peeked inside.

Good, she said, but it felt anything but. Uneasy, I moved down the truly dead side of things, searching for Kisten's name. A pang of anticipation hit me when I found K. FELPS, and I set my bag on the floor to wrangle the key-draped doll forward to unlock his drawer. *Someone ought to put some clothes on this thing,* I thought as the Bite-Me-Betty doll hung upside down, the key fastened to her foot in the drawer lock.

I pulled it open with a rasping rattle. As expected, it was Johnny draped in a modesty sheet, a little worse for wear from his night out at room temperatures and his ride in the back of a truck, but just the fact that he was in the drawer marked FELPS meant that the glamour was holding. I hadn't liked leaving him on the boat. But almost as fast as it had come, my relief shifted to guilt. His family would never know what happened to him.

"Elyse, can you get me that gurney?" I called, and the young woman came out from the furnace room.

"Sure."

I winced at the metallic clang of the gurney, but the outer lobby remained quiet as she locked the wheels and we shifted Johnny onto it with a precision born from necessity. The toe tag with Kisten's name on it fluttered, and I stared at it, a lump forming in my throat.

"You want me to . . ." Elyse's words tapered off and I followed her gaze to the open door.

"Yeah. Wheel him in." I dug into my pocket and handed her the oversize key. "This opens the furnace itself. If you take care of him, I'll get Kisten in a chair."

"You got it."

I pushed the empty morgue drawer shut, leaving it unlocked and stuffing the drawer tag with Kisten's name into my pocket to help confuse anyone who might come looking for Kisten's ashes.

"Hey, Rachel!" Elyse's voice was faint. "How do you move them from the gurney and onto the rack? You just roll him over onto it? They don't process them face down, do they?"

"Be there in a sec." Her nonchalance was not inspiring, and I went to the drawer I'd left Kisten in, unlocking it and pulling it open with a soft rattle.

"Hi," I whispered as I saw Kisten's placid expression. His face was white, but you could tell he was still there, peaceful under his modesty sheet. My gut clenched. He wouldn't make it home, but his body would, and with that demon ley line stasis charm, he would look just this beautiful. No one would care if a John Doe Vamp vanished, and I took the drawer tag and stuffed it into my pocket along with Kisten's.

And then my head snapped up, every thought vanishing when the double doors pushed open with a little squeak and Scott stepped in, the light shining on his bald head and a purple haze of power filling his hands.

"Drop the line and step away from the corpse," he intoned. "I won't ask twice."

"God bless it," Elyse swore as she appeared at the door to the furnace. "How many times do I have to flush this turd?"

My eyes never left Scott as I reached for Kisten, skin prickling when Elyse yanked on the line through her familiar.

"You are both being detained for questioning by the coven of moral—"

"*Teneo!*" Elyse shouted, and I yanked Kisten from the drawer, slipping as his heavy weight pulled free. We hit the floor, most of him atop me.

Scott ducked, a short-lived protection circle snapping into place around him. It absorbed Elyse's spell, and then it was gone. Brow furrowed, the man pulled himself to his full height, Latin spilling from him to make the very air shimmer.

This was so not good for the sleeping undead, and I tugged Kisten's legs free from the drawer, almost losing it when he took a breath.

"Go!" Elyse stood, a weird mix of deadly skill and slovenly dress in her institutional sweats and demon slippers as she shot tiny little balls of pure energy at Scott. "Get him in the back! We have what we need. We do the spell here. Don't you dare leave without me."

Scott shifted from one side of the room to the other, avoiding the fiery balls from hell until one tagged his shoulder and he realized they held no magic and weren't a real threat. "Who are you?" he shouted as he began to gather her energy like thrown apples to use for himself.

"*Teneo!*" she shouted gleefully, and Scott yelped, his reach for her next energy nugget faltering as he dove out of the way. The coven's go-to hold spell hit the drawers and sputtered, working its way inside to invoke on whoever was in there.

She was doing my job again. Teeth clenched, I dragged Kisten to the furnace room, his toe tag making a ridiculous hiss as it scraped along. My skin tingled from the spent energy filling the room, the little rills of power racing from my fingertips to my chi demanding I do something or simply explode from it.

Johnny's gurney was taking up most of the room, and I propped Kisten up in a corner and tugged his sheet to cover him. "Stay here," I whispered, jumping when a thunderous boom shook the dust from the ceiling. *So much for harassment charms and passive deterrents . . .* She was going to wake someone up if she didn't cut that shit out.

"Sorry, Johnny." Gut clenched, I rolled the long-dead body from the gurney to the rack. The door to the furnace was heavy as I pushed it shut, but I hesitated at the last moment, taking a hair from him so he could be identified later before I locked it and pocketed the key. I had to thank his family. Tell them Johnny helped save another. It might help when his body went missing.

Out in the main room, Elyse shouted a curse . . . and Scott gagged, an ugly, dry-heaves cough sounding as he struggled to breathe.

"Don't kill him, Elyse," I whispered, and then the reek of decay washed over me, pungent and thick. My eyes teared, and I held a hand to my face, trying not to pull in the stench. *Sweet ever-loving pixy piss . . .*

"One-spell wonder, huh?" Elyse shouted as Scott gagged. "Choke on it, old man!"

I could hardly see as I pushed the buttons and got the furnace going. The burners came on with a soul-shaking thump, and I turned, shoving the gurney out into the room to make space. "Let's go!" I fumbled in my pocket for my chalk and drew a huge circle, taking up almost the entirety of the floor space—big enough for three.

"Almost home, Kisten," I whispered as I made sure he was safely in it. Al would frown at me, Jenks would laugh his ass off. Ivy would . . .

Elyse's shriek of pain cut through my thoughts like a cold slap.

I looked up, chalk in hand. "Elyse . . ."

"Who the hell are you!" Scott shouted at her, and I lurched to the door.

Anger flared. Scott had her down, his hand fisted about her shirt under her chin. "Get off her," I threatened, and he almost laughed, judging me weaker.

I had two good pops, maybe three if I chose my spell well, and my pulse quickened as Scott did foolishly nothing. "*Visio deli!*" I shouted, flinging a tiny amount of ley line at him.

Eyes wide, Scott flung himself from Elyse, thinking if it hit him, he'd be blind. In truth, there wasn't enough energy in the spell to cloud his vision. But he didn't know that.

"*Implicare!*" I paced forward like a vengeful spirit, the remnants of Elyse's stink spell furling about my feet.

Face white, he skittered away from the black curls snaking about where he had been, coils that would tighten about him and choke the words from his throat—if I had put the energy behind them. They were so weak, they hardly had any form.

I had reached Elyse, and I stood over her as she held a hand to her neck. Her eyes were wet, her anger a quick flash as she broke the spell Scott had put on her.

"*Parvus pendetur fur, magnus abire videtur,*" I intoned, feeling the dark curse crawl over me like spiders as I threw first a tiny pop of nothing at him to make him shy to the left, right into the real charm waiting for him—the one that I had saved all my energy for. It was illicit magic from the demons' vault, the curse designed to twist his next spell against him. If he did nothing, he'd be fine. But I doubted that's how the next five minutes were going to play out. Whatever he dished out, he'd get himself.

Scott gasped as he felt the curse take him, and he froze, energy gathered to combat whatever it was. But nothing happened. Nothing would until he acted. "Who are you?" he said, and I snapped my fingers for Elyse to take my hand. I didn't dare look away from him, and relief filled me when her cold fingers gripped mine and I hauled her to her feet.

"You cannot hide from the coven," Scott said, his confidence returning as two people burst in, their attitude more than their I.S. insignia telling me we were in trouble. That and the power sparking through their auras.

"I can't fight three alone," Elyse whispered, and my determination swelled.

"You don't have to." My hand was still in hers, and her breath caught as I pulled on a line through her and Slick, my hair cracking with the sudden influx.

"Fire in the hole!" Scott dove for the swinging doors.

But it was too late, and I shouted an exuberant *"Detrudo!"*

Scott escaped, but the two I.S. agents were shoved to the walls, arms flailing and spells sent awry.

"That was a demon curse!" Elyse said as I dragged her into the furnace room and slammed the door shut.

What did she expect? I was a demon.

My gut hurt. I let go of her to hold in the nausea. On the other side of the door, a rhythmic pounding began.

Elyse stood in the middle of my circle, shaking as she looked at Kisten, the roaring furnace, then the door. They had stopped hammering. That did not bode well. "Soon as they get the code, they'll be in here," she said, and I tugged Kisten to the circle's center.

"Then we go where they can't follow. You still have that stasis ley line charm?"

She felt her shoulder, wincing as she nodded. "Yes. But your bag . . ."

Crap on toast. It was out in the main room. "I have everything I need here. If they don't kick you out of the coven when we get home, you can give me my book back. 'Kay?"

"Rachel . . ."

"You're in the circle? Sit," I directed.

"Rachel, where's the broken stirring rod? Do you still have it? How are you going to know when we go far enough?"

She looked scared, even when I reached into my pocket and found the pieces. "We're good." *Please, God. Let this work,* I thought as the ceiling shook when the three witches tried something. "You're right. We aren't getting out of here." I held out my hand. "Give me the stasis charm." I couldn't look at Kisten. He wouldn't make it home as an undead, but I wouldn't have to watch him decompose in front of me when Art's virus finally killed him twice. *Thank you, Trent.*

White-faced, she took the charm from her pocket and handed it to me. "If he wakes up and bites me, I will have your head on a platter."

Oh, if only, I thought, fingers cold as I took it.

"You are brave, Rachel Morgan," Elyse said as she nervously resettled herself. "You are strong in spirit, and you are good. If this doesn't work and I die in front of you, it wasn't your fault. Don't let anyone tell you different." She took a slow breath. "I give you permission to pull on a ley line through me to perform a possibly illicit curse to get us home." Her brow furrowed. "Be careful. Slick means the world to me."

I took her hand when she extended it, tasting her fear and trust through the line as I linked to it through her. "I will see you when we get there," I said.

She opened her mouth to say something, and I pulled the pin. "*Recepe-ratam sol. Ta na shay,*" I whispered, and the ancient demon charm twisted by an elven slave invoked, spilling a reddish-green haze over her and Kisten like a blanket.

Elyse went still, her eyes open and her lips parted, her next words frozen in her mind. Worried, I tucked the circlet of charmed silver into my pocket, pin and all, praying that it worked as it was supposed to. She looked . . . not dead, but like a thing. Kisten, too, looked about the same, but unlike Elyse, he wouldn't wake up when I broke the curse at the end.

A muffled shouting had begun behind the door, and I stood between Kisten and Elyse, fingering the ends of the broken stirring rod. When it mended, we'd be home. *I hope.*

My breath shook on my exhale and I closed my eyes. I was going to have to join the demon collective to access the curse. Every other time I'd done it, I'd been noticed. The only saving grace was that both instances were in the future. I would have the element of surprise today.

One hand holding the broken rod, the other on Elyse's shoulder, I reached out a ribbon of awareness, tapping into the nearest ley line through her and Slick. The lines felt different in the past, more convoluted, more complex—more familiar. The soft hum of energy tingled to my extremities and rebounded, and with a careful thought, I slipped a sliver of myself into the demon collective.

Immediately my shoulders slumped as I soaked in the myriad background conversations. It was very much like being in a crowded restaurant, the anonymity of your conversation ensured only by the multitude of other discussions. And like a restaurant, if you strayed too far from accepted norms, you'd be noticed.

Using one of Newt's spells was like standing on the table and singing "*Non, je ne regrette rien.*" Using this one would be doing the same, but naked.

My eyes opened and I steadied myself as I checked one last time that both Kisten and Elyse were in the circle. The door panel was beeping, and adrenaline pulsed. They had the code. I had seconds.

Ab aeterno, I thought, and with a little jolt of connection, the circle and everything in it went indistinct, as if viewed through a fog. We were separated from reality, though still connected to our current time.

The Goddess take it, came a bitter, jaded thought as a ripple of awareness went through the collective. *Whose turn is it to check on Minias? She's spelling again.*

They thought I was Newt, and a splinter of fear tripped down my spine.

Regressus, I thought, to link the stasis spell to the curse that held my stored energy, the one that would keep me from starving to death on the way home. Sensing it, the slow alarm in the collective became razor-sharp. Outside my circle, a widening crack of light showed.

Who is using my curse! thundered through the collective, scattering the increasingly worried thoughts like dry leaves. *I did not put that in as fee-for-use. That's my private store!*

The door slammed open. Scott stood there with my bag in his hand, his bald head shining and two angry witches with him. "I'm sorry," I whispered, and all three seemed to freeze.

You again! Newt snarled, her thoughts reaching to crush mine.

Prospice! I shouted within my mind, invoking the curse to send everything in the circle forward in time. With a mental lurch, the collective was gone, the beginning of Scott's shout was gone, everything but what existed in the circle was gone, melted into a gray haze. Agony lanced through my head. Hunching, I slowed the energy influx until the pain was tolerable. My gaze fixed on the broken stirring rod as I held my breath.

Alien and uncomfortable, my stored energy rippled over me. Snippets of conversation flitted just under my awareness, whispering to leave traces of feeling: joy, boredom, frustration, ecstasy.

Elyse? I wondered, my grip on her shoulder tightening. The emotions were familiar, but the fleeting images joined to them were not.

I stared at the broken length of redwood, my synapses beginning to singe as bloodlust poured through me and vanished. An image of a child on a swing in the sun, blond hair and blue eyes. But it wasn't Kisten. Nor was it his joy that filled me. Thoughts burning, I looked at Elyse's empty expression. Kisten, too, was unmoving as the days turned to weeks, turned to months outside my circle. Emotions too fast to realize cascaded like ice through me with the roughshod clang of a bell rolling down a hill. It was overwhelming, and I groaned, my grip on Elyse spasming as I hunched over her and Kisten.

"Mend . . ." I groaned as the scent of burnt amber filled my world. It was my mind burning. I could not shut my eyes, gritty with stardust. I could not breathe, bands of time clamped around my chest. I could not stop. I would make it home. I would make it home to Ivy and Jenks and Al. *And Trent . . .*

The rod refused to mend as a faint haze of auratic rainbows pulsed painfully through my leg pressing against Kisten's back. Kisten was glowing, a glimmer of what I would swear was aura pulsing like a heartbeat as more bloodlust, more heartache, more guilt, more joy flooded through me almost too quickly to be perceived.

That is not my energy, I suddenly realized. These were not my emotions, my life. They weren't one person's, but many. *The collective?* I thought, but it made no sense, even if my energy had been stored there.

And then the broken rod in my violently shaking hands magically became whole.

"*Stet!*" I exclaimed, the word escaping me in a rough croak of sound.

I sagged as the pain in my head vanished. I fell into Kisten, scrambling to find a ley line through Elyse. Utter silence filled the room, and it was chill. Numb, I tucked the mended stirring rod into a pocket, my gaze coming to rest on Elyse's slippered foot.

No noise came from beyond the closed door, and the furnace was cool. "Elyse . . ."

I fumbled for her shoulder, my tension easing as the energy slipped in through her, rough and painful over my singed synapses. "*Surrundus,*" I whispered.

"On the other side," she said, her clear words almost painful in the absolute silence. It was her unvoiced thought, the one that the spell had caught and suspended. And then her eyes met mine. "Did it work?"

"I think so." I blinked fast, refusing to cry. She was all right. We'd done it, and she was okay. I bobbed my head, and she pulled her gray sweatshirt from her chest and looked down.

"My tattoos are back!" she said, grinning, as she rushed to get to her feet. "Oh, my God. I never want to be eighteen again. Are you okay? That didn't hurt at all. How are your synapses?"

"Singed, but workable. I took it slow." Kisten was slumped at my feet. He looked the same, thank the Turn. We were home, but my elation was tempered with the knowledge that, without the mirror, nothing had really changed. It had been a big waste of time, one that was going to cost Elyse her career when she tried to convince them to cut me some slack. I couldn't stave off Ivy's grief, but maybe I could do something about Elyse's coming heartache.

"Elyse, about your promise to stand up for me."

Elyse's expression went empty. "Eden Park," she blurted, grabbing my hand and pulling me to the door. "We have to get to Eden Park! We have to stop them fighting."

"Elyse . . ." I glanced at Kisten, unwilling to just leave him there. Jeez, he still had Johnny's toe tag on him.

She flung open the door, and we hesitated for a moment, half expecting to see Scott and two I.S. witches. But it was only an empty room. "We have to call a car!" she shouted, tugging me into motion.

My hand slipped from her as she raced to the end and blew through the double doors.

"Holy shit!" Iceman bellowed faintly. "Who the hell are you? You're not an undead."

"Be right back," I said as I shifted Kisten to look more comfortable, arranging his hair and giving his cold forehead a soft kiss. "I have to stop the coven from destroying itself."

I stood, gathered myself, and strode out into the receiving room with a confidence I did not feel.

Iceman might let me borrow his car. Maybe.

CHAPTER
32

ICEMAN'S CAR WAS A BURNT-ORANGE DODGE CHARGER, IMMACU-lately clean and smelling faintly of morgue disinfectant: sunroof, heated seats, monster hemi, stick shift—no problem. It cornered like a Thoroughbred and was just as fast. Elyse had grabbed the chicken strap at my first quick start and hadn't let go as I wove through Cincy's streets, taking the fastest, but not necessarily shortest, route to Eden Park.

I wasn't sure when we had arrived exactly as the car clock was clearly not set right, but it was dark and the streets were moderately busy. I used the stick shift with an aggressive force, finding relief in the extra task. Motion, motion, motion. It was the only thing keeping me halfway sane at the moment. I couldn't believe I had left Kisten in the morgue—even if it was the best place for him.

Elyse fidgeted as she scanned the sky for Slick. Ten minutes ago, it had been late July. Now it was November, and I was cold, having left my jacket at Sylvia's two years ago.

A faint boom echoed between the buildings, and I looked up through the tinted windshield. A pale glow of magic had blossomed over Eden Park. My grip tightened on the steering wheel as Elyse studied the light slowly fading on the cloud bottoms.

"That was Yaz," she said in excitement. "I'd recognize her magic anywhere. Her spells always have that faint purple haze."

I nodded. One's aura invariably colored one's magic. It was how the

I.S. caught illicit magic users. I had brought us to the right day, the right time, but my worry grew no less as I made a tight right and entered the park, heading for the overlook. Trent was up there. And Ivy. Al, Jenks, Bis. Everyone I cared about was fighting to give me the chance to find that damned mirror so I could stay in reality—and I had returned with nothing. Less than nothing, seeing as Elyse was going to ruin her career to keep me out of Alcatraz.

A deep foreboding took root as she gripped the strap and leaned to peer out the window in anticipation, waiting for the next blast of magic. "Ah, Elyse, it might be better if you don't spring your decision to ignore me on them right away."

She lifted her gaze from the road. Her face was a little leaner, a little more careworn, but all I saw was the same enthusiastic young woman who, for all her wisdom and knowledge, didn't yet understand how fear rules most people, makes their decisions.

"I'm the lead member," she said confidently. "They'll listen."

But she'd been leading children and hotheaded teenagers, not peers whom she had spent a lifetime building trust with.

"Elyse . . ."

She stiffened, pointing into the park. "There they are. Merlin's beard, they're still at it."

"Whoa, wait!" I protested, pulling to the curb when she reached for the door, forcing me to halt as she got out.

And then my heart seemed to stop. Ivy was down, kneeling under Trent's protective bubble as she tried to shake off a spell. Al was with them, but neither of them could effectively fight from inside a circle. Magic hazed Trent's hands, and Al was grim, that cane of his held at the ready, the length of wood clearly an oversize wand holding a spell or two.

Scott, Orion, Yaz, and Adan stood at the four corners, the haze connecting them probably something to destroy Trent's circle. Scott might appear like a towheaded child under his curse, but power dripped and hissed from him, embers of energy pinging off Trent's bubble like sparks from a stirred fire as Orion, Yaz, and Adan supplemented his spell. If there had been five, they might have managed it, but as it was, Trent was holding his own thanks to Jenks and Bis dropping squawking, wing-flapping ducks on them.

Even as I watched, another hapless animal struck Yaz, and the young woman's arch of magic went wild, hitting an overhanging tree, where it exploded. Sparkles sifted down, burning when they touched Trent's bubble. But Trent's circle remained secure and the duck half flew, half ran away.

"New target!" Scott shouted, a new spell forming between his hands as he followed Bis's looping, erratic flight.

Oh, hell no . . . "Bis!" I flung the door open, watching Scott's charm arch through the air after Bis as the gargoyle spun wildly to avoid it. A thin trail of pixy dust from him said Jenks was with him.

Cold. It was too cold for Jenks out here. If Bis was hit, they might both die.

"Spells *off* the gargoyle!" Al shouted, a premade spell tearing through Trent's bubble.

The curse was headed right for Scott. Jaw clenched, the magic user blasted the curse to nothing, then rose, smug with satisfaction. In his effort to save Bis, Al had taken Trent's circle down.

"Stop!" Elyse demanded, and Bis did a somersault in the air, my breath catching as his red eyes found mine and widened. Trent spun, magic hazing his hands. Ivy, too, looked up, blinking to focus. Al seemed to catch his step, emotion blanking his expression as he pulled himself to a magnificent stance of confidence . . . and relief.

"She made it!" Bis shouted as the coven circling them seemed to hesitate. "She's back!"

"And she's got a bitching car!" Jenks exclaimed, the clothes-heavy pixy wiggling out of Bis's grip in a burst of blue dust.

"Stop! Everyone stop!" Elyse called again as she came around the front of the car, pace fast and looking innocuous in her gray institutional sweats. "We're all right!"

"Hey!" I exclaimed as a dark shadow dove at me, but it was only Slick, the crow cawing and flapping his wings as he landed on Elyse's shoulder, demanding attention and warning everyone off all at once.

Jenks struggled to hover before me, weighed down by layers of woven spider silk. "Tink loves a duck, where did you get the car?" he said as he landed on my hand. "You okay? You stink like burnt amber. Where's your bag? What did you do to your hair?"

"I'm okay," I said, wishing I was four inches tall or that Jenks was six feet in height. "Crap on toast, I missed you." I jumped when Bis's feet found my shoulder, his feet clamped as if he would never let go. "Both of you."

Ivy slowly got to her feet. Heartache swelled as I remembered Kisten, and feeling it, Bis's wings drooped. The coven members had knotted together, and the need to be with Trent, Al, and Ivy almost hurt. "Where's Laker?" I asked. My God, Trent looked every part the elven warlord, his straw-blond hair staticky with mystics and his aura flicking in and out of existence as his next spell flitted through his mind at the ready.

Jenks shifted to my shoulder, his wings cold as he plastered them to my neck to warm up. "The lunker left thirty seconds after things got gnarly. You've been gone for like fifteen minutes."

Whoa. I did good. "Fifteen minutes?" I started across the field with Elyse, the woman's attention utterly on soothing her familiar. Shoulder to shoulder, we must have made an unsettling sight, both of us ragged, tired, and inappropriately dressed for kicking ass. *Both of us easy with each other's company...*

Bis's grip tightened on me. "The longest fifteen minutes of my life," he said, glancing at Slick in mistrust when Elyse told the bird to leave him and Jenks alone.

"You owe me a jar of honey, old man," Jenks said proudly. "Where is it, Rache? Where's the mirror?"

My gut hurt, but I didn't shift my pace, didn't change my expression. Even at this distance, Al could read my mood and he slumped, knowing that I had not gotten it. I took a breath to tell Jenks I'd failed... hesitating when Elyse's expression flicked from annoyance to alarm.

"Down!" she shouted, and energy zinged over my skin as she yanked on the ley line. I dropped to my knees, trusting her as she flung out a hand with a dramatic *"Sisto!"*

Bis's feet clamped tighter, and Jenks rode it out on my shoulder as well. I peered up at Elyse as the coven spell fizzed in a shower of red and purple sparks.

"Knock it off! Stand down!" Elyse exclaimed in annoyance. "I'm fine, Scott. The entire thing was a mistake." She extended a hand to help me up and I took it. "It was my fault I got caught up in Rachel's spell. If not for her, I wouldn't have made it back."

"Back?" Scott shouted, his childlike voice high. "From where? She can jump the lines?"

Oh, if only, I thought. The anger on his face looked wrong on someone so young seeming. But as Orion, Yaz, and Adan clustered behind him, lending him their strength, Scott's aura flickered into existence. He was pulling on the line. Heavy.

"Mother pus bucket, he's going to do it again," Jenks whispered.

Fear tightened my gut—not for me but for those who would stand between me and the coven. Angry, I pulled on the line as well, and Trent's attention shot to me.

"Stop, all of you!" Elyse shouted.

"Detrudo!" I exclaimed, my hair flying as a huge wave of aura-laced air pushed from me, rocking the trees and shoving the twin ponds sloshing out of their confines and onto the grass. My lips parted, not at the coven members rolling ass-over-teacup across the park but at the new, obvious tracings of smut among the usual gold of my aura. Al alone stood tall, his cane held out to part the force around him as Trent knelt with Ivy. Bis's grip on me tightened and Jenks held on to my ear, his madly fluttering scarf tickling my neck.

I looked down at my hand, my thumb rubbing against my fingers as I gauged my new level of smut before my aura vanished. It was more than I had expected for the trip back, and I winced as the cold water sloshed back into the pond, dragging sticks and leaves and candy bar wrappers. *Sorry,*

Sharps. Still, it felt good to be home, where I could throw spells around and not worry about changing the past—only the future.

"Damn, girl," Elyse said as the leaves settled. "Why didn't you do that with Newt?"

I touched Bis's feet in apology. "Because she would have hit me harder," I said, and then louder, "Elyse is right. You all need to knock it off and listen!"

Scott picked himself up with the stoic pain of the sixty-year-old that he really was. "Save it for your trial," he said, his little-boy voice at odds with the anger in it. Behind him, Orion, Yaz, and Adan stood tall. "You are done, Morgan." Scott wiped the blood from his nose. "By order of the coven of moral and ethical—"

"Oh, for Medusa's apples," Elyse interrupted, her arms wrapped about herself from the cold. "Rachel was not fleeing. She went to get a mirror to break the curse."

Al harrumphed as he came to stand behind me with a pompous air. Not a hint of magic wreathed his hands, but I knew Trent, at least, had a thought in the lines. I could feel it.

"And did she?" Scott asked as if already knowing the answer.

Elyse scuffed to a halt, the two of us making the tip of the triangle as we all faced off. "She did better than a mirror," she said, and Bis's wings slumped. Jenks, too, made a small sound of worry. I hadn't gotten the mirror, and now everyone knew. "She saved my ass, Scott."

"And Elyse saved mine," I added, touching Bis's foot in reassurance.

"Huh." Al glanced at Trent for a telling moment. "You saved a coven member's life, itchy witch?"

"It happens," I said, and the demon guffawed as he cautiously eyed Elyse beside me, his opinion clearly wait-and-see.

Scott shook his head, his hands confidently on his hips. "Nothing has changed."

"Everything has changed." Elyse looked away from Al's goat-slitted eyes. "Let go of the line, Scott. I just spent three days with Rachel. We are dropping our case on her."

"Tink's teacups, Rache. What did you do?" Jenks asked.

Orion stiffened. Yaz, too, obviously disagreed, but Adan seemed relieved. Scott, of course, shook his head.

"That man is going to be the death of us all," Elyse said darkly. "Okay. I'm going to talk to my guys. You talk to your guys. Maybe we can all go home tonight. I am so sick of sweats, I could scream."

"Right there with you," I said, and her expression brightened. Besides, if they were talking to Elyse, I could talk to Trent and Ivy, and I desperately needed to.

"Good luck." She touched my elbow and walked away—far too confident. She was headed for a fall.

Al was hunched when I turned to him. "I know how you work, Rachel, but you can't make friends with the coven," he muttered as Trent helped Ivy limp closer. She'd taken a beating in the fifteen minutes I was gone, and my guilt doubled as I remembered leaving Kisten slumped on the morgue floor.

Bis shifted to Al's shoulder when I reached for Trent, but Jenks refused to leave, swearing as Trent yanked me into a hug.

"You're okay," I whispered, glancing over his shoulder to the nearby ley line. It wasn't safe for him to be here. But even that thought vanished when his arms went around me, holding me to him with a fervent relief. His grip shook as he caught his emotions, and his eyes were wet when I pulled away to give him a quick kiss.

"If you hadn't come back . . ." he whispered, and I nodded, not surprised when he shrugged out of his coat and draped it over my shoulders, surrounding me in his warmth and the electrifying scent of spent magic. Never again. I would not move through this world alone. I would face my trials with him, and he would face his with me.

"Tink's tampons, Rache," Jenks grumped as he made the quick, scarf-fluttering flight to Bis. "You were gone fifteen minutes."

I stifled back any hint of tears and let Trent go. "Try three days," I said, then spun to give Ivy a hug. Her arms were cold, and her grip was fleeting for all the unsaid questions in it. "We, ah, landed two years ago, not five."

Her expression went still as she thought about that. "Two . . ."

"That explains a few things," Al muttered. "Let me guess. The span of days I spent in Stanley Saladin's body? Perhaps Newt was not as crazy as we believed."

I felt my face warm. "Elyse interfered with the spell. I had to stop early." I fumbled in my pocket for the spent stasis charm and handed it to Trent. "Ah, this is yours. Thanks for letting me borrow it. I think the coven might have one of your books, too."

Trent took it, a proud smile quirking his lips as he recognized it. "That was you? My God. Quen was furious. That was when I put the door in. What good is a vault if your security is too afraid to use the door when someone else breaks in?" He fingered the charm. "Not that I blame them. Demons would have snagged them halfway there."

"Yeah, um, I only took it because I knew you'd want me to," I said, and he grinned, fingering the defunct circle of metal. "It was the only way to get Elyse back safely." My gaze went to Ivy, not sure how I should break the news to her. She'd dealt with Kisten's death, but now he was here and she would have to do it again.

From the coven, Scott exclaimed, "And you trusted her?"

"She didn't spell me," Elyse tried to explain, and everyone sort of zeroed in on her. "She saved my life. Got me out of the ever-after twice."

But Scott was putting it all together, and his stare at me was cold. "That was you," he said, and then spun to Elyse. "And you. It wasn't a look-alike. It was you."

She was going to get kicked out of the coven. I knew it.

"No, listen. It was Elyse!" Scott said, shutting down everyone's questions. "Two years ago, right here in Cincy. Remember when I was called in—"

"That was when you cursed yourself," Orion interrupted, and Al stiffened, knowing I had lost my book, not just tucked it somewhere to take the long way home.

"You did that to *yourself*?" I said, and Scott flushed, angry and embarrassed. "You tried to follow us, didn't you." And then I went still. Crap on toast. He'd tried it right after I'd set that magic-knotting curse on him. No wonder his body was moving through time with the sun. *Is this my responsibility or his?*

Jenks's wings rasped as he resettled himself on Bis's shoulder. "Dumbass."

"None of this is Rachel's fault," Elyse said, but it only made everything worse. "I interfered with her spell. She found a way to get me home. At great cost to herself, I might add."

"Ah, guys?" Jenks said, peering over his scarf to the townhomes across the way. Bis drew himself tall upon Al's shoulder to follow Jenks's gaze, but I couldn't look away from Ivy rushing headlong into heartache.

"I can smell him on you," Ivy whispered, her face going white as she fingered my hair.

My throat tightened into a lump. "I'm so sorry," I whispered as I took her hands in mine. "I didn't look for him. He found me. By accident. At a stupid bar. He was going to run." I couldn't look at her. "I didn't tell him anything, but he could see I was different, and he thought the world was better without him in it so he went back to his boat. He went back because of me. He was going to run, and changed his mind because of me."

Adan was whispering something to Yaz, the two of them watching whatever Jenks and Bis were staring at. Al, too, the demon taking his glasses off before turning to me in shock.

"Ivy, I'm so sorry," I said as I squeezed her fingers, but she wouldn't look at me.

"Oh, my God," she whispered, eyes tearing as she stared over my shoulder, shaking.

"He went back to the boat to save your life," I said. "And mine. I couldn't change it."

"Kisten," she breathed, her expression empty as if she hadn't even heard me.

"Please," I said when she pulled from me. "I didn't want to tell you like this, but I know how you bottle everything . . . up." I stopped talking. She wasn't listening to me. No one was.

I turned, expecting the worst, surprised to see only two figures coming across the grass. One was in a lab coat, his hands in his pockets. He moved with a stilted quickness, holding himself a little apart from the other. The man beside him was taller, dressed in a simple but timeless outfit, his jeans tight and his shirt open at the collar. His pace was confident, his head up as he walked barefoot over—

Barefoot? Oh, my God. It's Kisten.

"Tink's tampons, it's Felps!" Jenks shrilled, his voice muffled behind his scarf.

Ivy swayed, balance gone.

"How . . ." Elyse said, her jaw dropping. "How did he survive the trip?"

"You brought him with you?" Scott exclaimed. "You risked the timeline to rescue your *boyfriend*?"

"No." I blinked fast as my vision swam. "He was undead, suffering from biting Art. I put him in a stasis charm so I wouldn't have to watch him . . . uh . . . I don't know how he survived." Because there he was, a hint of deviltry in his gait as Iceman touched his elbow and veered off to check on his car.

Al sighed. "I can't wait to hear this," he said as he thumped his cane thrice on the ground and a tattered book with the spine falling apart appeared in his hand.

"Me either," Trent muttered, worry crinkling his brow.

"I don't understand," I said, gobsmacked. "I used a demon stasis charm so Elyse wouldn't die on the trip back, but that wouldn't help him survive Art's virus." And yet there he was, smiling as he tossed his head to get the hair from his eyes.

"Perhaps two years is enough time for one virus to overcome the other," Al said as he put his glasses on so he could look over them at the book. "My question is how did a stasis spell keep him from auratic starvation?" Engrossed, he turned a page. "Demon based or not, that's not how that spell works."

"He's got an aura," Jenks said. "It's not his, but he's got an aura."

"I don't understand," I said as I remembered the fleeting feel of thousands of selves when I traveled back. But even that thought failed me when Kisten cheerfully waved and we all moved to make room for him.

"Kisten?" Ivy warbled, and then I jumped when she flung herself at him, burying her face in his shoulder as she gave him a fierce hug, holding him in a white-knuckled grip. "You're here!" she exclaimed. "How? You were twice dead."

His arms were around Ivy, but his gaze was on me. "I don't know," he said, voice melodious as his attention dropped to her. "I would have gotten here sooner, but I had to find some clothes and it took a while to get a cab."

My God. I had left him on the floor of the morgue. "Where are you getting your aura?" I whispered, and then I felt the world shift as I put it together. The fee-for-use had sustained him. Dr. Ophees had indeed been using the curse I'd given her, the ten percent of the auras she gathered stored in the collective and funneled to Kisten in the same way I'd taken back my own energy—for two years. Somehow he had fought off Art's virus.

Kisten was alive, or undead, rather. And he was here. Right now.

Shocked, I looked at Al. The demon stared at me, gaze flicking to Kisten before he snapped the book in his hand closed, knowing I had the answer even if he didn't.

"Where did he get the aura?" Trent asked as if Kisten wasn't standing in front of him.

Jenks's dusted a cold blue. "It's not his. It's got too much yellow in it."

Clearly concerned, Trent dropped back as the coven clustered together, each of them trying to get their opinion heard. Al alone stared at me, that book of his tucked under his arm as he waited for my explanation. It was Kisten, but it was not. He had always been graceful, but now his every motion held the smooth, unhurried refinement of the undead, an unsettling innocence. It pulled at me . . . until I saw Trent's worry, his outright fear that he would lose me . . . and any bloodlust I might have felt vanished to the last tingle.

My breath shook as I exhaled, and I felt for Trent's fingers, seeing the light in Kisten's eyes dim when Trent grasped my hand tight and pulled it to his chest. This, I knew, was love, and I felt my throat close for what I was leaving behind; what I had with Trent summed far greater.

"Ah, I could use some context," Kisten said as Ivy stared at him, touching his arm, his face, his brow as if he was going to evaporate.

"Me too," Al said dryly.

Kisten put his head against Ivy's for a moment. "I woke up on the morgue floor," he said softly, and I winced in guilt. "In the furnace room. Naked and with a John Doe Vamp toe tag. Scared Iceman." Bare feet shifting on the cold ground, he drew a manila tag from his pocket, the scuff it'd gained from my dragging him across the floor standing out against the otherwise clean paper as he showed it to me. "I know I'm undead, but how? I should be twice dead. I bit Art. Where did the aura come from? I don't remember biting . . . Did I . . . bite someone?"

"Ah, about that," I said, and everyone turned to me, coven and friend alike. Elyse winced and gestured for me to have at it. Maybe she thought it would help my case. "Um, I taught Dr. Ophees the spell to pull an aura from donated blood. She wouldn't use it if it left smut on her aura, so I put a ten percent royalty use fee on it, storing my share of the take in the collective." I stifled a shiver as the remembered feeling of other people's auras tripped down my spine. "It went right to you. You've been getting a portion of every aura she collected."

"That's where your aura got smutty," Al said, and I nodded.

"For two years?" Trent said, and I gave his fingers a squeeze, glad he wasn't looking at me in disgust as the coven members were.

"I didn't want you to starve as Art's virus killed you," I said, and Kisten's smile softened as he put the toe tag back in his pocket.

"If he's here, who is on Ivy's closet shelf?" Jenks asked, and Ivy blinked fast, still not believing it.

"We never had any conformation that the ashes were Kisten's." I touched my pocket, hoping Johnny's hair was still there. "Elyse and I put a John Doe Vamp in Kisten's drawer. That's probably whose ashes Ivy has."

"You're an undead," Ivy whispered, and Kisten focused his entire self on her.

"Yeah, sorry, love," he said, hitting his fake British accent hard. "I know you wanted to go first." He smiled to show his long teeth. They were new, unstained by anyone's blood, and I stifled a shudder that might have its roots in ecstasy. "Where's Piscary?" he asked, a flicker of anger marring his beauty, and Jenks snorted.

"Two years dead," the pixy said from Bis's shoulder, as proud as if he'd done the deed himself, and Kisten looked at Ivy for confirmation—but she was still lost in trying to figure this out. "We got some crazy nutjob named Constance running the city. Rachel is her brains, and Ivy and Pike are her muscle."

Kisten spun back to me and I added, "Constance is a figurehead. Everyone is helping." I didn't like that the coven was hearing this. My throat closed, and I touched Trent's fingers again. Cincy was safe, even if I had to leave it. "I can't leave Cincy to Constance. She's not ready to solo yet. Ah, Kisten—"

"No one is putting Rachel in Alcatraz," Al interrupted, and Scott pushed forward, clearly peeved that he had to look up at everyone.

"The farce is over," he said, the jaded sixty-year-old man shining through his ten-year-old visage. "You don't have the mirror, and you won't by June. Come quietly, or you will drag those you care about into the same cesspit."

Jenks outright laughed, and the coven member flushed as Orion, Adan, and Yaz drew closer to Scott. "What part of Rachel doesn't go to jail don't you get, moss wipe?"

"She's wanted for illicit magic," Scott said, undeterred. "She can't untwist that curse. She goes to jail. Time is up."

"Time is not *up*," Al said haughtily. "Nor is it down. Time is relative."

"Rachel doesn't need to *do* anything," Elyse insisted. "I spent the last three days with her trying to get that damned Atlantean mirror. Survived a bet with a demon. Stole from an elf."

Trent's fingers tightened in mine. "You really need to stop doing that," he whispered, and a delighted shiver rippled over my skin.

"But you make it so easy," I whispered back. *Oh, man. Quen. I have to talk to Quen.*

"The coven's position should be hands-off from here on out," Elyse continued. "We will leave her alone as Vivian told me to do. Not in Alcatraz. Not leashed to the coven. Rachel doesn't need a leash. She needs a license to spell." She took a slow breath. "I intend to give it to her."

"Oh, my God," Yaz whispered, one hand clutched around an amulet. "She cursed Elyse. Morgan bewitched her."

"Rache did not bewitch anyone!" Jenks exclaimed, and Al's grip on his cane tightened.

"Ley line. Let's go," Trent whispered, a hand at the small of my back.

A chill raced from his touch to light my entire existence. Kisten jerked as if on a string, and I shook my head, both at Trent wanting me to leave and at Kisten for reacting to my surge of emotion. He was an undead. I couldn't . . . I just couldn't. I had loved him, but now . . .

He wasn't a ghost. Thank the Turn that that curse of Ophees would keep him in auras. He would only have to take in blood because he wanted to, not because he had to.

Elyse stood firm between me and the rest of her coven. "Scott, if there is one thing that I learned in the last three days, it's that it's better to have Rachel as a friend than an enemy. She might be able to untwist your curse. You ever think of that?"

Al tapped his cane three times on the earth, the thumps revibrating to make a distant car's alarm go off. "But not when exiled to the ever-after, and certainly not from Alcatraz," he said with a devilish smile as he peered over his glasses. "Surely we can come to some agreement, *honorable* coven members."

For a moment the coven held themselves still, exchanging knowing looks as they were faced with something they dearly wanted . . . and trying to decide if they could get it without paying the cost. Trent's jaw clenched as he tightened his grip on the ley line, energy tinging over my skin like silk. Kisten took note of their silence. Ivy was still too shaken, but she perked up when Bis shifted to her shoulder and whispered in her ear. Jenks, of course, was ready.

"They aren't going for it," I whispered to Trent, his fingers in mine making a delicious path of promise in me. *Damned vampire pheromones . . .*

"Then we will convince them." Trent's other hand lay lightly against my back, and our energies rubbed together and became as one.

"Enough!" Elyse shouted. "Scott, Rachel is off-limits until we have a chance to talk this out. I am the lead member, and we will follow protocol!"

"You are only lead member because we voted you in," Scott said, and my heart sank as Elyse saw her position crumble. "And we can vote you out."

There it was, and I winced, seeing Elyse pale as she realized I'd been right.

The coven was moving, the four of them beginning a mumbled Latin as they dropped back, their fingers weaving in unison. Elyse stared at them, shocked by the betrayal, but I wasn't surprised. They would kick Elyse out to get what they wanted. Desperate, I looked at Al's stoic anger as he dramatically gestured to the nearby line. Bis took to the air, Jenks with him, and still I shook my head, even as I understood why he wanted me to leave. He had known the coven would lie, cheat, and steal to enslave me, just as the elves had lied, cheated, and stolen to enslave the demons.

"Elyse Embers?" Magic wreathed Scott's hands, supplemented by the others: Orion confident, Yaz determined, Adan too scared to disagree. "It is the opinion of the majority of the membership that you have been compromised and are hereby—"

"Good God, Scott!" Elyse shouted over him. "Will you—"

As one, the coven members threw a net. Elyse yelped, invoking a protection circle as she tossed Slick into the sky.

"Enough!" Kisten exclaimed, pulling from Ivy with the quickness of the undead to backhand Scott and send him flying into Orion, knocking them both down. The net flickered and went out, spent.

"Kisten! Gentle!" I pushed forward, jerking to a stop when Ivy grabbed my arm. He was newly undead. He didn't know his strength. "They're just afraid!"

That he understood, and Kisten pulled himself to a stiff-armed, scary-ass halt. Like a thrown switch, he had become a true undead, and a chill dropped down my spine as the full force of his existence rippled over me, allure and threat twined together in a delicious promise of ecstasy.

Feeling his draw as well, Ivy yanked away from me, her eyes pupil black.

Scott looked up from the ground, his apparent ten-year-old self safe under his circle as the full allure and power of the undead hit him. My neck tingled, and I held my breath, hating that Trent and all the coven could see the connection that still lay between us. Bis's ears were flat, Jenks cradled in his hands as the pixy was too heavy to fly well. Ivy was alight, her hands clasped so she wouldn't touch me. She knew. Though newly risen, Kisten was a powerful undead. Constance would be safe. It was the rest of us I should be worried about.

"Okay, let's all take a step back," Elyse said, all but ignored.

"I know you now," Kisten intoned, and Scott and the rest got to their feet, the protection circle humming over their heads. "You will leave Rachel alone, or I will find you."

"You have no strength here, vampire," Scott snarled. *"Semper frigido!"*

"No!" I shouted when his spell tore through his circle, gathering its strength as it headed for Kisten. I'd seen this before. It would tear him apart, shatter him like broken ice.

"Kisten!" Ivy exclaimed, and I pulled on the line, feeling it sing through me.

"Rhombus!" I shook as I dropped a circle around not Scott but Kisten.

The vampire jerked to a halt, his first look of betrayal at me crushing.

And then I groaned as Scott's curse hit my circle, and my blood seemed to fragment.

I fell to a knee, gasping when Trent lurched to catch me. His hands were like hot daggers, and I shook as I tried to put myself back together before I fell apart. With a sodden crack, I took Scott's curse, making it mine. Relieved, I sagged as the magic vanished into the ground with little curls of color.

"Scott, knock it off!" Elyse shouted, her voice sounding as if it was a million miles away. "We need to talk this out, and we can't do that with you slinging spells."

I lifted my head, thankful for Trent's support as I got to my feet. The coven was staring at me in surprise, but it was Kisten my gaze went to. I had taken Scott's curse, but my bubble was a flat orange and red, the telltale aura that made it beautiful frozen in place, like a single snapshot of an aurora borealis.

"You froze her circle?" Concern pinched Al's brow. "And you call that legal?" He turned to me. "Release it."

But I didn't think I could just yet. It wasn't warm enough, and I shook with cold when Bis landed upon my shoulder, a gentle heat emanating from him. Kisten stood within my circle and used his finger as if he was leaving words on a misted mirror to write, *Leave Rachel alone, or I will find you.*

"Are you okay?" Bis said, his heat finally beginning to reach my core. Still, I could do nothing except stare at the words, fading when the skin of my circle began to shimmer as my soul warmed and my aura became fluid again, rubbing out Kisten's words like the heat of the sun.

"Rachel?" Bis questioned as the background chatter became louder. My expression emptied as the circle became malleable and Kisten's words vanished. The words, I realized, had vanished. Just as they had when Newt breathed upon the table.

I dropped my circle, shuddering when the still-cold energy raced through me back to a ley line. Numb, I turned to Elyse, the woman focused utterly on trying to talk to her peers. I had found the mirror. It wasn't glass or metal or anything shiny at all. An Atlantean mirror were words that were made with the intent to be transient—powerful but fleeting—like the Atlanteans themselves.

"I found the mirror," I whispered, and Bis's wings flashed open. "I found the mirror!" I shouted it this time, and the heated arguments faltered.

"Where is it?" The glow about Elyse's hands flickered as she faced off before Scott.

I shook my head, not willing to tell them the secret. "I found it," I said, and Al peered at me from over his blue-tinted glasses. "I mean, I know what it is now. I figured it out." My pulse quickened as I looked at Kisten. "I can uncurse Brad."

My hand in Trent's was trembling again, but it was in relief. I could uncurse Brad and get the rest of the coven off my case. Maybe save Elyse's career.

Scott's ten-year-old face screwed up in disbelief. "You expect us to believe that you found it this very moment?"

"Newt gave me a riddle," I said, glancing at Elyse. "Ask her. She'll verify it. I didn't understand it until now."

Elyse blinked, and then her lips parted in understanding. She'd been there when Newt had breathed on the table and sketched a pentagram, claiming she'd done her part to fulfill our deal. Dark eyes wide, Elyse jerked free of Orion's grip. "She has the mirror. If she can uncurse Brad, she has fulfilled our original bargain and is free of any taint of illicit magic." Her eyes narrowed in threat. "Or are we going to renege on that as well?"

Scott might as well have been eating slugs, his expression was that sour. "That was the deal," he said, and the others shifted uneasily. "But you will agree to undergo a thorough debriefing with the intent to detox any—"

"I am not bewitched!" Elyse protested, and Scott's gaze hardened.

"No, I think you were bedemoned. A little Stockholm syndrome, maybe."

"Hey!" both Elyse and I shouted, making things worse somehow.

The tension began to rise again, and Al stepped in between us, cane whirling in a not-so-subtle threat at odds with his pleasant expression. "Perhaps we can agree to take a break until Rachel demonstrates the mirror's effectiveness or not? You gave her until June. It's November."

My gaze flicked to the park's entrance, adrenaline clearing my focus as I noticed the blue and gold lights spinning up the drive. Iceman was gone, and I tightened my grip on Trent's fingers. "You should go."

Trent took a slow breath. Hands cupping my face, he gave me a lingering, warming kiss that went straight to my toes. "Keep her safe on this side of the lines, Felps," he said as he dropped back, his gaze fixed to me. "Or I'll find you."

It was nearly the same thing that Kisten had written on the frozen wall of my circle, and by Trent's hard expression, I knew he had put the same threat behind it. One in reality, one in the ever-after. How was I going to balance this? Because it needed to be balanced.

Kisten nodded, holding himself deathly still. "I know you love her. I know she loves you. I gave my life to protect that. I won't encroach upon this love. It is alive, and I know mine is dead . . . even if it is all I have."

"Kisten . . ." I breathed, my heartache shifting from having lost him to death to having lost him to time. I would not call what we once had wrong or simple or naive. It had been true.

And yet my gaze left him to follow Trent as he walked away, feeling him take a part of me with him.

Al harrumphed as he watched Trent pace to the ley line and vanish.

"That was fun." Jenks landed heavily upon my shoulder. "You think they will hold to their promise?"

"They will, or they will suffer," Al said, loud enough for the coven to hear.

"I need some coffee. Decaf," I whispered as I turned to see my car right where I had left it three days and three minutes ago. I had the mirror. I had Trent in the ever-after and Kisten in reality and Al in my backyard. Jenks was on one shoulder, and Bis flew above, doing exuberant barrel rolls with Slick until they both landed on my car's top with a thud and scrape to make Ivy wince.

But as I tugged Trent's coat closer about me and glanced at Elyse arguing with her peers, it didn't feel like a win.

EPILOGUE

THE PHEROMONES WERE UNDERSTANDABLY INTENSE AS I STRODE into Piscary's right before sunrise. There was no waiting line this time of day, night, whatever . . . But with three undead vampires below perfuming the air with their presence, it had been busy. The air exchanger hadn't yet caught up, and I doubted it had even been turned on. Most vamps enjoyed the subliminal pheromones given off by the undead, used them like a passive drug to heighten their nightly activities.

The jukebox was playing something both sultry and grungy, and the drinks in hand held their last swallows. A few tables were still occupied by those in the know, and my shoulders eased when their soft conversations hesitated at my entrance, then resumed after a respectful moment of silence and the lift of a glass. Even though I'd been back for several weeks, it still felt *very* good to be home.

And Piscary's, despite all the drama that had taken place here, did feel like home. From the six varieties of ketchup openly on the table to the tiny tomato lights over the bar to the picture of a rat and mink standing on the gas tank of an X-wing 2000, whiskers pushed back by the wind, Ivy driving.

And one urn of ash we can't identify, I thought as I glanced at the surprisingly small blue and gold jar. It was Johnny, and Ivy had put it in a place of honor over the bar beside the Mixed Public License. Not that Piscary's needed an MPL other than to serve alcohol. Offering tomatoes kept the humans out all on its own. John Doe Vamp or not, he had helped save Kisten's undead life, and that needed to be acknowledged. A lock of his hair might point me to his relatives, but I wasn't ready to dig up that grave quite yet.

"Hey, Rachel." Ivy's low, sexy voice was obvious over the piped-in music, and I shifted my path, eager to talk to her.

"Busy night?" I asked as I got closer to the bar, looking for a place to wedge myself in. Unlike the tables, the bar was full. A sidelong glance, a sultry smile with half-lidded eyes, and someone moved to give me space.

Ivy leaned in, her attention on the door as two sexy thangs behind her in lace and leather continued to take the last-drink orders between cleaning up. "About usual. Hey, was Trent supposed to help you tonight?"

I shook my head, a small smile quirking my lips. "No. Why?"

Her gaze went past me to the tables. "That bounty hunter, Laker, showed up a few hours ago. He's got some chops, trusting the MPL will keep him safe."

I turned, smirking as I locked eyes with the clearly uncomfortable man nursing a chipped cup of coffee. "Tell him to go home. Trent is safely in the ever-after."

"That's what I thought, but I let him stay. He's more entertaining than the paid band." Ivy's faint smile vanished. "I closed the upstairs. Pike is up there with Brad. And the coven," she added sourly.

The plastic bag with my spelling supplies rattled as I grabbed the shot of tomato juice she slid across the bar to me. "All of them?" I tossed the spicy drink back, downing it. *Breakfast of champions or nightcap. You decide.*

Her expressive eyebrows bunched. "Just one. The sixty-year-old kid."

"Scott." I said the word flat and tasteless. "Is Kisten around?" I hadn't seen him apart from in passing since we'd been home. After the first few put-offs, I had decided he was avoiding me. Giving me and Trent space, I suppose. Probably a good idea until Trent felt secure, but he could at least talk to me.

"Downstairs." Ivy's gaze went behind me when someone laughed a little too loud. "He took Constance out tonight to interview a new scion, one who might survive her, and he wanted to stick around in case he's needed. He's trying to teach her how to take a softer touch, maybe pretend to love them until she believes it herself."

I snuck a glance at Ivy as I fiddled with my empty glass. Constance hadn't initially been happy about sharing the spotlight with Piscary's heir, but the less she had to do, the less I had to do. "Is it helping?"

Ivy swabbed the ring of tomato juice from the bar. "It might. He's very close to the living yet. Sometimes I think him spending two years without any bloodlust cushioned him even if he wasn't conscious. Allowed him to retain an understanding most don't have."

I nodded, not sure if she was seeing it correctly or if it was just one of the lies that the living told themselves when faced with the soulless, empty slate their lovers had become. Ivy and Nina were solid, and she and Kisten hadn't shared blood those last few years. But Ivy loved him nevertheless. Her sight might be clouded. *Why won't you talk to me, Kisten?*

But I couldn't admit to Ivy that he wasn't even returning my texts, and I pushed from the bar, plastic bag rattling. "Okay. I'll be upstairs. I'll shout if I need you."

Her hand on mine stopped me cold. "You'll be great," she said, going up on one foot to lean over the bar and give me a kiss on the cheek, filling my world with the scent of happy vampire. She was happy. Kisten might be an undead, but she was happy. It had been worth every last burned synapse, every moment of pain.

I was smiling when she eased away, and I gave her hand a squeeze before it slipped from mine. "Great," she'd said, but I had my doubts. The coven didn't play fair. Neither did demons, but they, at least, didn't play dirty.

"Be down in twenty," I said as I turned to the stairs. It was getting close to dawn, and Brad's curse worked best in the hour before and after the sun broke the horizon.

But as I put a foot on the wide stairs, something shivered through me, a ribbon of desire from a hint of recollection, a wafting of scent on the brimstone-and-vampire-scented air.

I hesitated, tasting the emotion-charged air as it soaked into me with the warmth of a puddle-warm memory.

"Rachel . . ."

The whisper pulled me around as a quiver rippled over my skin. Black eyes found mine, freezing me where I stood even as a heated warmth soaked into me. Kisten waited at the swinging doors to the kitchen, his hand gripping the old wood as he half hid behind it, not wanting to be seen. His gaze fixed to mine, the faintest rim of brown showing as he held himself at a quiet stillness—waiting for my reaction. I took a slow breath, and it seemed as if the world melted away, leaving only the two of us. A small part of me wondered if maybe this was why he had been putting me off. He knew I loved Trent, and he was . . . irresistible.

I turned, my foot slipping from the first step.

And then a wash of alarm coursed through me, scouring every last hint of desire from me. It was too close to sunrise for him to be aboveground.

I came forward, my libido gone and plastic bag rattling as I put a hand on his biceps and pushed him into the kitchen. The staff looked up from their cleaning, then went back to work, ignoring us with a practiced oblivion as I hustled him unprotestingly to the small alcove that held the stairs and elevator. My grip on him was featherlight, but little zings of sensation prickled through me. It had been two years, but my body remembered. Ached for it. *I don't want this.*

But I couldn't let him go.

"You need to be belowground," I said as the door to the stairs shut behind us.

"I need to talk to you."

His voice melted into me, and I took my hands off him to rub the tingles away. He had always been attractive—that was how Piscary had bred him. Death had made him sex incarnate, and I shifted to keep the door behind me. "*Now* you want to talk? This close to sunrise? I've been trying to see you all week."

He winced, looking entirely alive, and a spike of something struck me. "It wasn't you. It was me. I had a lot to think about."

His voice was soft, but it filled my world, and I shoved the emotions away. They weren't mine to enjoy anymore. "You need to go downstairs," I said. "Come on. We can talk there."

"No."

I rocked to a halt at his single word. It was getting easier to ignore his pull. But maybe that was because he was refusing to do what was good for him. "No?" I echoed, and he shifted from foot to foot. But his very uncomfortableness made him all the more charming. Damn, it was as if he was still alive—only better.

Kisten looked at my hands but didn't take them. "I don't want you going downstairs. Ever. Not if I'm there."

That took me aback, and I hesitated. "I've been in Piscary's old apartments before," I said, trying to figure out where his concern was coming from. "I can handle myself. Nina—"

"It's not you I'm worried about," he interrupted. "Or Nina, or Constance."

If he wasn't worried about them, or me . . .

Fear was a quick flash. Kisten felt it, and I stiffened as his pupils widened. He was worried about himself. That's why he had been avoiding me. Not to give Trent and me some space. *Oh . . . shit.*

I took a breath. Held it. Let it go. Took a step back. He was worried about himself, and here I was, pushing his buttons. "I'm sorry," I whispered, my gaze on the white ceiling as I forced myself to relax.

Kisten glanced at the huge clock on the wall across from the elevator. The threat of the approaching sun seemed to calm him, and his eyes returned to their usual brown. "I wanted to talk to you," he said, his gaze flicking to my hands. "Say thank you for not letting the sun burn me. Keeping me safe. Not letting me starve."

I licked my lips. It was Kisten. He'd never hurt me. Would he? *I can't touch you ever again.* "You're welcome. I'm . . . sorry. It was a day for you."

"And two years for you." He smiled, his lips closed, and my heart seemed to break. "I'm trying to get my car back. Do you know who bought it?"

The world was out of balance, and I felt unreal. "No, sorry. I have your pool table, though. It's cracked again. Needs a new felt." Wincing, I met his gaze, once again a sedate, calm brown. "I used it for a spelling table."

He chuckled, and I relaxed. "Keep it," he said, smile fading as he realized the distance between us would never change. "I'll come over some night and play pool." He grinned, becoming my Kisten again. "Once you get it refelted."

"Deal." He wasn't touching me. I didn't think he would ever again. And it hurt even as I silently thanked him. "I didn't mean to fall in love. I thought you were gone."

"I was. I am." He looked at my hand as if wanting to take it. "This is better for you. I only want you to be happy." His gaze lifted to mine. "Tell Kalamack that if he makes a mistake, I will be there. Always."

I remembered how it felt when his hand held mine, and an odd feeling trickled through me. "That's kind of what I'm worried about," I half joked, and he chuckled.

"Me too," he said, then sighed as if actually needing the breath. "I said it in the bar, and I'll say it again so you believe me this time. I limit you. Kalamack doesn't. This is a good thing. Don't worry about me. I'm still getting auras from that spell. I don't need a scion, but I'm finding what I think is peace in caring for Pike, and he in caring for me. He has had a difficult life and deserves as much joy as he can find." His attention flicked to the clock. "I have to go," he added, taking a step back.

I nodded, sensation spilling to my extremities as he turned his back to me.

His steps were silent on the stairs. "I mean it, Rachel," he said over his shoulder as he descended. "Do not come down here. There are too many memories to confuse me, and I'm still trying to parse out the flavor between instinct and love. Don't make me ruin what you can be, what you already are."

"You could never do that," I whispered, knowing he could hear me with his new, undead senses. But we both knew it was a lie, and I lingered until I heard the door at the bottom shut before I turned to leave. Head down, I made my way through the kitchen, the space now humid with hot water and soap as the counters and grills were cleaned for tomorrow.

My mind whirled with everything I had forgotten to tell him: how I'd felt seeing him in that cruddy little strip club, that I ached for leaving him even as I had brought him home, that I was glad he was here. That I was sorry for having fallen in love again.

But clearly Kisten already knew.

Vampires sucked.

The main floor had a few patrons left as I passed through to the stairs, but the feeling was decidedly one of closing up. Head down, I went up the stairs, the *thump-thump-thump* of the bass becoming softer with each step until it was hardly noticed, a subliminal heartbeat of the world. The coven had been dogging me for months. It was all going to end tonight at the top of a vamp bar.

"Hey, Pike. Hi, Brad." Still trying to shake off thoughts of Kisten, I took in the upper room with its black-painted windows covered in thick drapes and its informal seating. Pike was at the rear behind the tiny bar, and I went to talk to the elegant, scarred man before we got started. He was caring for Kisten? In hindsight, I shouldn't be surprised. Both of them had been betrayed by those whom they had trusted, who should have loved them, whom they had loved.

"Scott," I said flatly as I passed him, thinking he looked uneasy in his ten-year-old visage, his primary-colored sneakers dangling as he sat at a low, round drink table. Brad was next to him, the older living vampire hunched over his handheld game, utterly absorbed. The witch took a breath to say something, but I just kept walking, ignoring him with a surly annoyance.

Pike smirked as I set my plastic bag on the smooth bar top. "Hi, Rachel. Almost dawn. What can I do to help?"

I pulled in the fuddling fumes rising up from the basement. They were better than a shot of tequila, and I glanced at Scott, wondering why he was here and what was in the tightly rolled paper bag at his feet. "Ah, I could use a bottle of ice water," I said, and Pike turned to the tiny fridge. "You good with this?" I added. "Brad is going to be pissed when he regains every-thing. What if he makes a go for you? I can handle the coven. I doubt Kisten will let any harm come to you, either."

Pike's eyes flashed black, then cleared, his sun-brown face creasing in a smile as he stood before me with a misted bottle of water. Now that I knew it was there, I could see traces of Kisten lingering about him like a second shadow: his scent, his calm, his touch. "Don't worry about it," he said softly. "I want my brother back, the consequences be damned."

"Your call." I took the cold bottle as he extended it. "Give me a few minutes to prep. It's a fast curse." Fast because I had been doing it for months as I tried to find a substitute for a mist-fogged mirror, not knowing what it actually was.

"Sure." He glanced at the bottle. "You want a glass with that?"

"Um, no." Turning, I studied the quiet space. The table was as good a place as any, even if Scott looked as if he was about to throw a tantrum. "Ah. I'm glad you and Kisten are hitting it off."

"You can't have him."

It was a fast utterance, and I could almost see his thoughts plinking through him like diamonds shining in the moonlight. A hint of threat, of possessiveness, flickered in his suddenly black eyes, and I shook my head, satisfied that a bond had been formed. They would die for each other. How had it happened so fast? "I cannot," I agreed, making it a promise. "Ready?"

He came out from behind the bar, his motion edging into a vampire quickness. My fingers were cold, and I made a fist, shaking my hand free of it as I sat down to put Brad and Scott across from me. Pike stood at my back, making me feel safe despite the stairway behind me.

"Where's Elyse?" I said, plastic rattling as I began to unpack.

Scott laced his hands over his middle to look like a mini-me villain. "It was thought that we should have an unbiased opinion as to whether you break the curse or not," he said, voice high.

I set an unmarked scrying mirror down beside a plate, the soft scrape grating. The two would nestle together nicely. "I'm not going to teach you how to break the curse."

"I *have* seen the instructions," Scott said dryly, but I was more interested in that paper bag at his feet.

"Technique is more important than a to-do list." He must want something, and I wadded the plastic bag up and checked my phone for the time. "You can watch. That's it."

Scott stared. "No blood? No wax? What kind of a curse is this?"

"A good one." A common misconception was that complexity made a curse strong. Will made a curse strong, and that's all this curse was—will and mist on a mirror. *And a dollop of raw power,* I thought as I reached my awareness out to a ley line and pulled the living energy in.

At my nod, Pike shifted to sit by his brother. "Hey, Brad. Can I talk to you for a sec?"

"Busy," the cursed man said, brow furrowed as he put his arches on the edge of the table.

The chilled water chattered as I poured it onto the plate. Water spilled, overflowing when I set the pristine scrying mirror atop it. "Give me fifteen seconds, then make him look up," I whispered.

"What the Turn?" Scott said, and I glared at him to shut the hell up.

For eight seconds, I held my breath, warming it in my lungs before bending low over the chilled scrying mirror and breathing on it. Like magic, the glyphs that I'd scribed there at sunset appeared, the oils from my touch keeping the glass from beading up.

The spiderweb I'd used to adhere the curse to the glass was long gone, but the intent remained, and I glanced at Pike, worry furrowing my brow.

"Yo, Brad, look at what the witch wrote. It will make you laugh."

With the innocence of a child, Brad glanced up from his game, going utterly still as his eyes locked on the mirror. A shiver ran through me, and my hold on the line strengthened. My eyes closed, and I fell into the demon collective. The countercurse was there. I only needed to access it. And the mirror was the key.

"*Sic semper erat, et sic semper erit,*" I whispered, eyes opening. *Thus it has been, and thus it will always be.*

A shudder rippled over Brad as the mirror cleared, the words gone, and with it, his curse.

The man took a rasping breath as his feet slipped from the table and he stared at the floor.

"Did it work?" Pike put a hand on his brother's shoulder. "Brad. Are you okay? Brad!"

Brad stared at his shaking hands, slowly curling his fingers in as if he'd never seen them before. When he looked up, his eyes were pupil black. "Is it real?" he said. "This feels real."

"It worked!" Pike yanked Brad into a back-slapping hug, right there on the couch. "You're okay. Brad, you're okay. Look at me. You're okay!"

He *was* okay, and I blinked fast as Brad's pupils slowly shrank and he numbly gazed over the room. "I remember," the older man said, and then his expression caved. "Oh, my God," he moaned, pushing Pike away as he dropped his head into his hands, overcome. "The fog. It was eating me. Every thought I had. I couldn't hold them."

"I'm sorry, Brad," I whispered, and he lifted his head.

"It came in like the tide every morning. It was you." He stared at me. "You brought it in!"

Brad gathered himself to stand, and Pike put a hand on his shoulder. "And she pushed it out. Brad, she pushed it out for good. You're back."

The distressed man sank down into the couch, his haunted gaze going from me to Scott.

"She pushed the fog out," Pike said again firmly. "She risked her life and the well-being of Cincy to dissolve it. It's gone."

Brad licked his lips, slumped and exhausted. "I know that. I was there, listening. I remember everything now. Everything you did. Everything you tried."

His head snapped up, and I jerked, startled when he reached over the table, pulling me into an awkward hug. I froze, then relaxed as he began to cry, huge racking sobs. "I remember," he said around his gasps for air. "I remember everything. Thank you. Thank you."

"Okay, big man," Pike said, and I patted Brad's shoulder when he let go, clearly embarrassed as he sniffed and wiped his face.

"I'm sorry," I said as Brad sat before me at a complete loss. "I didn't know what it was when I invoked it."

His wet eyes met mine. "I know." Brad took a shuddering breath. "I remember." He turned to Pike, a new wonder lighting his expression. "You kept me safe. You were more kind than I deserve. Oh, God. Pike. I tried to kill you. For money. Because that's what the family wanted."

Grinning, Pike stood and pulled him into another back-slapping hug. "It's okay. You want a beer?"

Brad blinked at us, looking a little thin, a little worn. But his eyes were alive. "I want everything!" he shouted, and I found I could smile. "I want to do everything! I want to remember everything!"

"Well, let's go!" Pike said, mirroring his joy. "I've always wanted a big brother, and now I have one."

Pike draped an arm over Brad's shoulder to lead the unsteady man to the stairs. At the top, he glanced over his shoulder. "Thank you," he said, lips moving soundlessly, and I put a hand to my mouth so I wouldn't cry. It was done.

"Brad!" someone shouted as they descended, and I blinked away the tears as the waitstaff began singing, *"We're glad you're back. You left too soon. Come sit at the bar. We'll all make room."* It was the death day song, and it seemed oddly appropriate as he had returned from a living death. They all knew him, had cared for him. Loved him. He was loved.

"He could still press charges," Scott said, clearly annoyed.

My smile vanished. *You are a troll's ass. No, you are the zit on a troll's ass.* Lips twisted wryly, I plucked the mirror from the plate and shook the water off. "So . . . I want to hear the words," I said as I dried it on an almost useless cocktail napkin.

The ten-year-old before me took a slow, steadying breath. "You have been found exempt of the penalty of illicit magic. That you performed it will remain on your record."

It was about what I had expected, and I leaned deeper into the cushion and took a sip of water from that cold bottle. "And my vacation at Alcatraz?"

"Is off the table as long as you keep your nose clean," he said in his high voice, and I stilled my bobbing foot.

"Not likely, but okay." My gaze dropped to the paper bag at his feet. "You still haven't told me where Elyse is." Scott had made no move to leave. He wanted something. Perhaps he thought he could trick me into doing something illegal? *Not happening, you little pissant.*

"She's fine," he said, rubbing his baby-smooth chin as if it had stubble. "That was really fast. I take it you prepped most of it earlier?"

"At dawn." I drummed my fingers on my knee. "You demoted Elyse? That's hardly fair, considering all she did was have an opinion the rest of you don't like."

"We disagree all the time. The difference is that this time we are disagreeing about you." Scott pulled the paper bag closer, his tawny head down as he opened it. "And we didn't demote her. She voluntarily removed herself after losing her lead position."

No wonder she hadn't answered any of my texts. "You fired her?" I pushed up from the cushions. "Who's the lead member? You?"

"She voluntarily removed herself," he said again, not answering my other question.

He wouldn't meet my eyes. My gut was tight, and I forced myself to relax. "Voluntarily," I muttered. "I'll believe that when I hear it from her."

"She broke our trust." His little-boy arms tense, he struggled until he dropped a heavy book on the table. It was mine. The one I had left in the morgue when he had attacked us. I knew it. Recognized it. *And he's not leaving here with it.*

"I didn't spell Elyse," I said again. "She saw for herself the hell of the ever-after and the anger that escaping it eased in the demons. She witnessed firsthand the pain that every single elf alive had to endure just to survive, and that helping Trent find a cure erased that fear and pain. She learned to trust me in the ever-after, and that trust saved both our lives. That's not brainwashing. That's educating. Scott, don't kick her out," I pleaded, inching forward to sit on the edge of the couch. "The coven is her life. What is she going to do? Go back to Seattle?" She could teach, maybe. But not as a failed coven member.

"It was her choice." A flicker of worry furrowed his young brow, and he set a hand on the book, pulling away when it shot a prickling haze at him.

Arms over my chest, I reclined deeper into the cushions. "What do you want?"

"My life back."

Head shaking, I sipped my bottled water. "You ruin Elyse's future, and you expect me to break your curse?" But in truth, it was a good time. The sun had just risen and the moon was about to set, the two balancing the world between them. "Sure. I can do that," I said, gaze flicking to him. "But I want Elyse reinstated as the coven's lead and for you all to apologize to her."

Scott smiled, the conniving expression utterly wrong on his baby face. "Not happening."

And yet he had brought my book. "Elyse—" I started.

"Elyse wouldn't return to the coven now even if we offered it to her," he said. "You untwist my curse, you get your book. That's it."

Arms over my middle, I bobbed my foot. It was my book. I shouldn't have to bargain for it even if I had left it behind. "What if it takes a curse to free you? I want assurances that there will be no repercussions."

Scott confidently shook his head. "There will be no repercussions using an illicit curse to break another on a coven member."

I eyed him suspiciously. "Which you are?" I asked, having dealt with demons before.

"Yes. Potential standing lead."

Of course you are. "Your position contingent, I expect, on me untwisting the curse?" I added, and a flicker of annoyance crossed him. "It must be embarrassing having a ten-year-old tell you what you can and can't do."

Red-faced, he waited, already knowing the outcome. I hated being a foregone conclusion, and brow furrowed, I reached out and drew my book across the table. Little rills of power snaked up from the friction, and the ley line pressure sparkled when I took it in hand and flipped it open, the pages humming as it rested on my lap. *Hi, sweetheart. I missed you, too.*

"You'll do it?" Scott said breathlessly. "Now?"

I glanced at the growing light past the black-painted windows. "Yeah, why not? Ah, can you confirm that trying to follow us was the first magic you did after we vanished?"

Scott frowned in annoyance. "I have no idea," he said, and then his expression cleared. "You know what? It is. I mean, was." His perfect, smooth face furrowed in anger, and he turned to the north as if able to see through walls. "At the morgue," he whispered as things fell into place. "That third spell you hit me with. I thought it fizzled. Nothing happened."

I shrugged, head down over the pages as he made an angry huff. "What did you spell me with?" he demanded. "You said, *'Parvus pendetur fur, magnus abire videtur.'* The petty thief is hanged, the big thief gets away. What is that? What did you do to me?"

I laid a light thought into the demon collective, relishing the feeling of connection. Sure, they didn't like me, but I belonged. "I didn't do anything. You did it to yourself. They are just words."

Scott's suspicion tightened about him. "Tell me."

It wasn't as if he could do the spell just by knowing the invocation phrase. He'd have to have access to the vault. "It twists your next spell against you," I said, feeling like a demon. "So the big thief gets hanged, too." I rested my fingers on the book, feeling the spell under it wanting to be used. *Not now, little one. Later maybe.* "A modern translation might be 'Go big or go home,'" I added. "Okay, you need to say the words. My slate is clean if I do this. No repercussions."

"Clean slate," he echoed sourly, and I frowned. Not at him but at the faint scent of . . . cinnamon and wine?

It had to be Trent, and my thoughts darted to Laker parked downstairs, the wizard suffering the sight of tomatoes in his drive to find Trent. Which meant Trent might be here, even if I didn't see him. Some might take offense that their boyfriend was checking up on them, but it only made me feel loved.

"Hold on to your gonads," I said sarcastically, looking for Trent even as I pulled heavier on the ley line. "If she's in a mood, I might only make things worse, but it's your nickel." Actually, now that I thought about it, that Trent was here might be a good thing—especially if I messed up. The Goddess loved to leave mischief in her wake.

"What?" he barked, sitting up. "She who?"

"Your full name?" I asked, suddenly nervous. "I don't want it to affect me."

"Um, Scott Silvus Sandearo," he said, and I nodded. If he was lying, we would both suffer. One did not call upon the Goddess and leave her a loophole to do mischief.

Rhombus, I thought, settling us both in a circle. "Little pinch," I said as my pulse quickened. He had tried to twist the curse to go through time. It had gone sideways, thanks to the last spell I'd put on him. Repeating the curse as if returning through time wouldn't work. I'd have to call on the Goddess to untangle him. Putting us in a space apart from reality seemed appropriate, and I drew heavier on the line. *Ab aeterno,* I thought, relieved when the thumping from downstairs cut off mid-beat.

"Wait. The curse tangled while I was twisting it," Scott said, gaze fixed on the black smut skating across the circle enclosing us. "You can't just wish it away."

"That's exactly what I'm going to do," I said, and he went white. "I bet the Goddess is laughing her ass off."

"The Goddess? Morgan, no!" He stood, his ten-year-old self looking scared.

Deal with it, I thought as I felt my hair lift when the mystics found us.

I could almost see them if I concentrated, and I let them play in my finger-tips, lighting my aura into a brilliant gold and red, my new coating of smut giving it a nice patina. Both real and unreal, the mystics passed through the book in my arms as if it was water, darting in and out, learning the spells, reminding the Goddess of when she had written them. *Dangerous fire, Rachel.*

I closed my hand into a fist, hoping I wasn't overstepping my bond with her.

"*Ta na shay,*" I whispered, and Scott stared, frozen where he stood as I called on the elven Goddess. "*Ta na shay, Scott. Pacta sunt servanda, Silvus. Regressus, Sandearo. Stet.*"

Scott gasped, unmoving as the mystics darted from me, enveloping him in a burst of silver that danced at his extremities until they soaked in. His lips parted, and his eyes found mine. Gulping, he tried to breathe.

My confidence faltered. "Scott?" I stood, head inches from brushing the top of my bubble.

And then I fell into myself as if pulled out of time itself. For a moment, I floundered. It was like being in a line. Or being a line. Or nothing like a ley line at all.

Mystics wreathed me, became me, wrapped me in a glow to keep me from flying apart as the Goddess focused one eye upon me. "S-stop," I stuttered, overwhelmed as the ley lines hummed in me, all of them, all at once. Their energies tangled as the now, the present, and the future be-came one and a shape rose.

It was the Goddess, and I watched in awe as the interweaving energies settled into an image of Newt. She had come to personally see to the curse. Swell.

"Oh, it's you," I said stupidly, blinking fast to clear the stardust from my eyes. I wasn't in Piscary's anymore. I was . . . somewhere else.

You, the Goddess said, and I felt her lift my chin. *You are more than mass with will. I know you. You give me this image, this vision of being. I remember it.*

I felt myself nod, though I doubted I had a head at the moment. "I need your help. Can you fix this?" I coughed, the mystics I had taken in with my words lighting through my lungs. "He twisted a curse to go through time and it went awry because of me."

I saw what happened, she thought, her fingers tracing the glow of a ley line, plucking it. *My eyes were there.*

"Can you—"

She let go of my chin, and I jumped at the reverberating twang echoing like whispers of forgotten conversations. "Obviously," she said aloud, and I blinked as I felt her sifting my thoughts, playing with a memory of Ivy, then Trent, then Jenks. Bis, she lingered over, mystics pulling through me to find every last moment I'd been with him, streaming like fire.

"Will you?" I gasped, pained by the sudden rush of emotions, even if they were all mine.

Her fingers within my thoughts vanished, and I sagged. "Will you?" she echoed.

I could have just taken the book. I didn't owe Scott anything, and yet here I was. "What do you want?" I whispered, scared.

The Goddess Newt sent a swirl of mystics carrying a memory of laughter to play about my hair. "It's not what I want. It's what you want," she said in typical delphic fashion. "When all is at an end and everything you love is gone. When all you have are memories, I will come. That is when you will close the loop. Promise it."

I had no idea what she meant, but it sounded like a long time from now, and if I broke Scott's curse, I could hold it over the coven and force them to leave me alone. That's all I wanted. The future would take care of itself. "Will it hurt?" I asked, and a warm hand lifted my chin.

"In every way that one can be hurt," she said. "But you will relish every sting. I guarantee it." Her touch slipped from me, mystics swirling wildly as she laughed. "You agree to close the loop if I untangle your thoughtless application?"

Thoughtless application? I wondered. "I do." Otherwise, why would I have called her?

She bent close, flooding me with the biting scent of stars. "As we will it," she said, and then I jumped, hunching over the book in my arms, cowering when the mystics burst from Scott in a silent, glowing wave to break my circle and vanish.

She was gone, and I was back in reality.

What have I done? I thought as the *thump-thump-thump* from downstairs resumed. But a very naked, very sixty-year-old man lay on the floor, slumped against the couch. As I had thought, his clothes had been magic based, not real at all. An ugly stubble covered his face, and seeing me staring, he reached for a pillow to cover himself.

It had worked. But what had it cost? *Close the loop?*

"You okay?" I said, and he fumbled for my scrying mirror, still out on the table.

A soft cry of relief escaped him as he saw his hands and then his reflection. "Is it permanent?" he said, voice cracking. "It won't break with the sun?"

What did I give the Goddess for this piece of shit? "It will hold." I exhaled, thinking the scent of moonlit nights and dancing had grown stronger. *Trent,* I thought. Had he seen? Had I sacrificed our future or ensured it?

Scott levered himself back up onto the chair, pillow in place as he stared at his reflection. "Take your hands *off* my mirror," I demanded, and his attention flicked to me. Silent, he gave it to me, and I tucked it under my book. I could smell cinnamon and wine, and I flicked a glance at the bar. Mystics had gathered over something, their glow fading as my brush with the Goddess moved deeper into the past. "Get out. Stay out," I added.

"Uh, can I borrow—"

"Now," I demanded, and he stood, pillow held tight. "Leave."

He hesitated for a moment as if wondering at my mood. Then, head high and pillow before him, he walked to the stairs, bare feet slapping the old wood. Awkward and stiff, he managed the stairs in an odd, almost sideways gait. There was no reaction from the waitstaff. But then again, the sun was up and I think everyone had joined Brad outside as he remembered the sky.

"You're welcome, you stupid fart-cake," I muttered, and from the bar came a familiar chuckle. Relief, then worry passed through me. It was Trent. It could have been Quen, and that was a conversation I wasn't ready for.

"How long are you going to wait until you break that glamour?" I said, and then Trent was there, his white-blond hair half hidden under a black stocking cap. Whatever I'd given the Goddess, it was done. No sense crying over lost mystics. Not when Trent was making his way to me, his skin-tight leggings and shirt making him into a vision of elven yumminess. I set my book and mirror down, wanting a full-armed hug.

Grinning, Trent came closer, his feet silent in black thief slippers. "You didn't see me?" he asked, and then my arms tucked under his, and I pulled him close, a relief heady as I breathed him in, relishing the scent of the wind and magic that clung to him.

"No, but I knew you were there." His ear was next to my lips, and it took all I had not to nibble on it. "I think it's sweet. Your checking up on me." *Oh, hell, why not?* I thought, and nibbled anyway.

He grunted in surprise, my teeth scraping as he pulled away with a devilish anticipation in his eyes. "You invoked the Goddess," he said, his hand running through my hair to pull mystics from it.

My smile faded and I shrugged, uneasy. Invoked, then chatted with. "I had no idea what he did to get into that state. It seemed prudent."

"It worked." He hesitated. "You seem to have a unique understanding with her."

"Don't ever let me do that again," I said, very sure I didn't want to get into it with him. *When all is at an end and everything you love is gone . . .*

"Deal," he said, and I leaned forward to give him a long, luxurious-feeling kiss. His lips on mine were light, little jolts of line energy sparking as our internal balances tried to equalize.

Smiling, I pulled back, loving him. "Laker is downstairs."

Trent nodded, clearly not bothered. "I knew he followed me. I never expected him to come in. I can slip him easily enough. Even in the sun."

I drew my plastic bag from the table and put all my stuff in it. I still hadn't bought a new shoulder bag. "Good. Let's go get something to eat.

Waffle House is open. Have you thanked Quen yet? For not killing me? We should do something nice for him. Take him a waffle, maybe."

Trent grinned, his arm looping in mine. "Last year, actually. I can't believe he knew. All this time. That elf can keep a secret like the grave."

"I've got no more secrets to keep." I paused at the top of the stairs and flicked off the lights. The ruby ring he'd given me glinted in the half-light right beside my pearl one, and downstairs, the music finally quit. *No more secrets. It's too hard to survive them.* "Trent, are you sure you don't know what this ring does? Quen was ready to kill me until he saw it."

"Mmmm." Trent eased to a halt three steps down, pulling me to a stop. It was a dangerous place to be, halfway to somewhere, but with Trent it felt more than safe. It felt right. "No idea. Maybe he gave it to her? You want me to ask him?" He held my hand in his so he could see it. "She had such small fingers."

The chatter between the waitstaff was pleasant, and I sat down on the stairs. Reaching up, I drew Trent down, feeling like a kid avoiding cleanup duty. "No. It doesn't matter," I said as Trent settled beside me with a happy sigh.

"It would be nice to know what it does, though." He ran a hand over his chin. "I know he loved her. He wasn't supposed to, but he did, and I think she loved him back. My dad was a cold fish."

I could see a sliver of the bar from where we sat, and I didn't move when Ivy shifted in and out of my view, oblivious to us as she prepped for tomorrow.

"I can get it resized. If you want. It's not really a pinky ring."

Something in his voice caught my attention. *He's looking at my ring finger,* I realized, and my breath caught. "Hey, is that the vamp phero-mones talking?" I said, uneasy. "That sounded suspiciously like a pro-posal."

"No, it's me," he said, and my expression emptied. "And maybe it is a proposal." He eyed me as I stared, my heart hammering. "Is that okay?"

I tensed, scared. *When all you have are memories, I will come. That is when you will close the loop . . .*

"I'm not saying we need to set a date and start interviewing caterers," Trent blurted, both my hands now in his as we sat on the steps between one life and another. "I know you need your independence, and a lawful link to me will only cause you trouble. It's a statement. For both sides of the ley lines." His gaze deepened in emotion, his grip on me tighter. "I cannot. I will not choose anyone else, and no one will choose another for me. It's you, Rachel, that I love. It's you who I want to spend my life with. I hope you feel the same. Let me resize this ring."

He lifted my hand and kissed my knuckle, sending a shiver through me. And as Pike's solid steps sounded on the floorboards, his cheerful voice calling out to Ivy and her contented answer, I nodded, breathless and alight.

"I'd like that. Yes."